DREAMING
IN A TIME
OF DRAGONS

Written and Illustrated by

G. Claire

Trimble Hollow Press

Dreaming in a Time of Dragons is a work of fiction.

Names, places, characters, and incidents are a product of the author's imagination or used fictitiously. Any resemblance to actual persons, living or dead, events, or locales is purely coincidental.

Title: Dreaming in a Time of Dragons / G. Claire

Summary: Eva finds her royal birthright could cost her life. She must decide what to do to save herself and the future of her kingdom. In doing so, she faces a danger far beyond the most frightening tale she knows.

ISBN: 978-1-63848-741-8 (paperback) – ISBN: 978-1-63848-638-1 (hardback)

Thematic Elements: 1. Young women—Fiction. 2. Identity—Fiction.
3. Good and evil—Fiction. 4. Healers—Fiction. 5. Prophecies—Fiction.
6. Magic—Fiction.

Published by
Trimble Hollow Press

T
pH

Acworth, Georgia

Dedicated
to my

Beloved

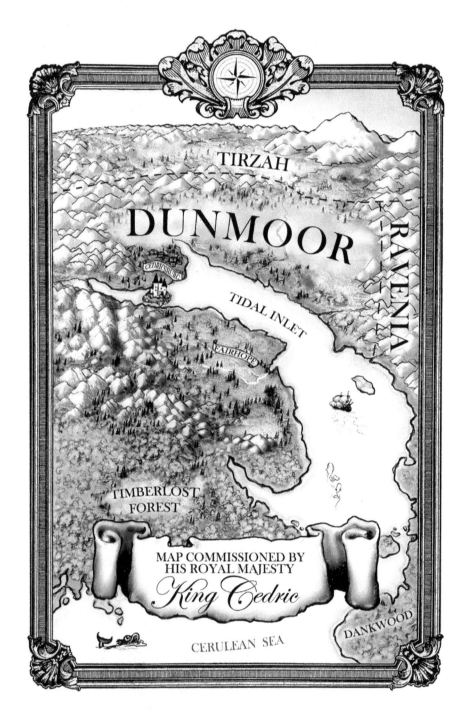

Our birth is but a sleep and a forgetting...

Wm. Wordsworth

The wind hushed . .

Prologue

Queen Lenore's child was born that strange summer night the north wind howled down from the mountains. Shrieking, it ripped through haystacks, lashed inlet waves, and pounded Dunmoor Castle's ancient stone walls.

An enormous creature rode the winds, his secret deep inside his ridged breast. Finding the turret above the lit castle window, he coiled his bulk around it and listened.

Lenore trembled, still and pale under satin sheets.

Isola, her new chambermaid, waited nearby, frowning and plucking at white cloths, now stained deep red. "Likely won't see the light of day," she said under her breath.

Lenore's eyelids fluttered. "A boy?" she whispered.

"You have a beautiful, healthy girl, Your Majesty!"

The Queen raised herself on her pillows and lifted trembling arms to hold her baby. "A girl," she gasped, pain knifing through her body. "My life slips away, little one. Who will love you?"

Mattie laid her nurse's cloth over her shoulder and bent to draw the fretful child from Lenore's arms. "You've lost much blood, Your Majesty. Please, rest yourself."

"No, wait." The Queen tightened her hold. "Before I go." She brushed cracked lips against Evangeline's cheek and whispered in her ear. Even the wind hushed to listen.

So, when all was said that must be spoken and done that could be done, the queen lay silent and still in the ancient mahogany bed. Mattie lifted the wailing princess from Lenore's lifeless arms, prying tiny fingers from her mother's gown.

Unseen by any but her child, Lenore's spirit shook loose from her body and paused above the nurse holding Evangeline. Bending, she kissed her daughter's cheek once more, then, caught the hand of the waiting angel. Turning her face upward, she was gone in a twinkling.

"You've come in on an ill wind and no mistake," Mattie spoke softly to the crying princess. "Who will love you, indeed?" Candlelight glistened both their tears. The old nurse rocked the child gently in her soft ample bosom, crooning the queen's song over her.

Isola pulled the embroidered sheet over Lenore's face, glanced around the room, and slipped into the dark hallway. She stumbled, and a small empty vial fell out of its hiding place in her sleeve and *clinked* on the stone floor. Two chambermaids stepped into the hallway behind her. Isola grimaced and left it where it lay. Scurrying around the corner to the outer courtyard, she disappeared without a trace.

An immense unnatural shadow slithered from the turret ledge. It soared northward over sleeping villages, fleeing a faint thread of light behind the eastern mountains.

King Cedric paced in the adjoining room, unaware, awaiting news of his son's birth. "Edwin. A name fit to rule. After all these years . . . a son," he muttered to himself in the dim candlelight.

Dawn stretched rosy fingers across the inlet, pinking grey castle walls. The midwife tiptoed in, trembling, and dropped into a tight curtsy. "My King," she murmured. Cedric turned to see the blood-spattered woman waiting in the doorway.

His jaw tightened. "Well, speak up, woman!"

The midwife stammered out her news. The King listened, waved her off, and stared out the window to the mountains of Dunmoor—his mountains.

Being a practical man, he would name the daughter for Edwin, the expected son and, of course, honor Lenore's last wish with the child's middle name—Edwina Evangeline she would be. He owed his queen that much. His vision blurred.

Mattie slipped through the door. "Begging your pardon, Your Majesty. Would you like to hold your new daughter?" she whispered

"Daughter? Oh yes, yes—later."

Thus the dark days began.

hey said she was strange, like the wind she was born into. No amount of training, straightening, or fluffing seemed to make much difference. The young Princess *would* sneeze and laugh entirely too loudly, burst into tears for no particular reason, and run off at odd times; her tiny shoes clattering down the stone hallways of Dunmoor Castle. Even with her hair properly braided and her waist cinched tight under satin and silk, something about her always seemed caged—and barely tamed at that.

Years passed and Edwina Evangeline learned how to manage herself, mostly. She kept her sad things buried in small boxes so very deep inside; her terrible questions almost never leaked through the cracks. Eva accepted her life. She stopped hiding and tried to find small comfort in her daily routines . . . until one day she just couldn't.

In the summer of her twelfth year the princess pretended to sleep in the royal carriage. Rumbling through Dunmoor's drab villages and fields, this gilded spectacle with matching white horses attracted much attention, hatred, jealousy—grudging admiration for the splendor rolling through their midst.

Inside the carriage cab, there were no thoughts of splendor from the three passengers.

Eva sat slumped, head lolling against the red padded interior of the royal carriage. Eyes shut; her hands rested limply in her lap. Her stomach squeezed into a knot. As usual.

Trying not to frown, she imagined running away. Maybe she'd disguise herself and join the village folk she'd watched from her high bedroom window. Across the sea inlet they sang on full moon nights around bonfires . . . they and their children circling together. *Singing. Holding hands.* Evangeline stifled a sigh.

Lurching over the rutted dirt road, Eva's tutor, Mrs. Fledge, had given up finishing her history lesson. She snapped her book shut and pulled her hood down on her grizzled head.

Shhh . . . we can't be sure she's asleep," the woman warned Modrun in a hoarse whisper.

The guard leaned across the cab. "Oh, she's sleepin' alright. I'd lay money on it." His whisper was a low rumble, barely heard over carriage clatter.

Eva hid a smile and snored softly.

Mrs. Fledge leaned forward, tense. "And how does he think the people of Dunmoor keep body and soul together? If it wasn't for my position." Her whisper was a controlled hiss. "But you know something, don't you. I see it on your face."

"That I do," came his reply. "Been twelve years. The lizard—" He stopped, looked out the window, and wiped a meaty hand across his face.

"Well . . ." Her lips pressed tighter.

Modrun shifted his gaze to meet hers. "Twelve years . . . and now *this!*"

Mouth twitching, the woman hunched forward.

They glanced at Eva leaning close, heads almost touching.

"It were Brumby's daughter, Hilde," his words puffed through his thick black mustache. "Hunted by the monster, the lizard—"

"And who's this Brumby?"

"Friend back home. Only Hilde's left. Pox took the rest."

The woman clutched her chest, crushing her white starched ruffles

"Hilde were runnin' home just after sunset, looked up an' there he were . . . divin' down on her." His voice dropped low, "the winged demon."

Eva's knees pressed together under her skirt. Her tutor gasped, fingers flying to her lips.

"Was . . . was she snatched?" The woman's words barely left her mouth.

"She weren't too far from the woods, The Way be praised. Made it there in the nick. But now—"

The carriage slammed into a rut. They all bounced to the floor, arms and legs flailing. Eva ignored Modrun's offered hand, scrambled up and pressed her back into her seat, a cornered creature.

Settling onto her seat, Mrs. Fledge smiled grimly and exclaimed, "Good! You're awake. Just in time." She opened her history book.

Eva exhaled loudly and looked out the window, grey sky glinting through her dark, coppery wisps of hair. She wondered how many people had actually suffocated inside a carriage, then there was the girl, the *Hunted One. Hilde. How old was she?* Eva imagined her screams. Her brow furrowed.

Fledge's voice invaded.

Gesturing wildly, she told of revolts, overturned kingdoms, entire royal families beheaded, (*beheaded!*) and new kings enthroned—people rejoicing. Then crushed again.

The princess glared at Modrun. He looked pointedly out the window. *Why does he never look me in the eye? He knows what he'll do one day—hand me over. Betray me. That's what. They all would . . . well, not Archie and Bea. Probably.*

Eva shouted over the carriage rattling, "How much longer?"

"Not far now, Princess." She heard the false cheer in his voice and chewed the inside of her lip; picturing the bloody revolt and Modrun marching her to the executioner's chopping block. There, standing in the cheering crowd would be Fledge smirking her told-you-so smile.

A bead of sweat trickled down Eva's itching back. The bone stays in her corset pressed the breath out of her. She bit her lip to keep from screaming.

Just beyond a stand of beech trees, gaunt, ragged men cursed and shook rakes at the carriage—at her—the daughter of King Cedric! The carriage sped on. They flashed by her window—a quick nightmare.

Princess Evangeline shrank back into her corner, heart pounding in her ears. *They hate me too. Nothing I can do!* Her nail-bit fingers twisted together.

More scenes of Hilde screaming—running for her life from the dragon— circled without permission in Eva's mind. "But, there are worse things," she said loudly and shivered in the hot, stuffy air.

Mrs. Fledge raised an eyebrow and finished the history lesson.

Modrun leaned back and sighed, "Poor devils," then caught himself. The princess watched a deep red flush creep up his neck. "That *is* to say; those devils is gettin' bolder all the time. Time to put their nonsense to an end." He shook his fist in hollow support of the King.

His words were for her benefit. The daughter of King Cedric knew this. Staring at the solid gold buckles of her green satin slippers—a flood of shame flushed her cheeks.

How many families could be fed by selling these buckles? And how bad does beheading hurt . . . and for how long? The dragon wouldn't dare come to the castle, would he?

Her lunch rose in her throat. "*Gaaaah*—why is this my life?" Her voice was a strangled shout. Mrs. Fledge reached over to lay a hand on her shoulder. Eva flinched away. "Don't *touch* me! *Ever!!*" Swallowing hard, the princess cupped her small pale hand over her mouth. Desperate to do something, *anything*, she slung her foot, hard. Her slipper flipped across the cab and cracked the window behind Modrun's head.

The guard and Mrs. Fledge sat poker-straight, eyebrows high. Side-eyeing her, they said nothing. She was having *'one of those fits.'* Her two keepers shared a look, glanced at her in mock indulgence, and frowned out the window.

Passing Cedricsburg, they crested the final hill. The spires of Dunmoor's castle speared dull grey clouds clustered low.

Eva squeezed her eyes shut, wishing herself somewhere, anywhere. *Else.*

The golden carriage with its cargo of misery thudded over another bone-jarring rut; then wallowed and rumbled across the drawbridge.

The princess squeezed her hands together in her lap. And, thoughts of Valentino with his funny crooked smile rose like bright butterflies, and beat back the dark mist inside.

Eva's eyebrows unknotted. Her fingers untwisted. She inhaled as deeply as her corset would allow. *Tomorrow*, she thought, allowing herself a smile. *I'll tell him then.*

The night was far spent.

The creature easily found the ledge around the steep turret above Eva's bedroom, having been there before, many times. Folding enormous ribbed wings against his sinewy body, His iridescent scales glinted purple, then green in the starlight. They scraped slate shingles, flinging them crashing to the walkway below.

A small version of the dragon landed on his bulging shoulder and clung there, sides heaving, back bowed. He leaned toward the jagged opening of the creature's ear. "I see you are firm in your decision, Master," the lizard hissed.

"And why should I *not* be, Maggot?" His voice was a deep, dangerous purr. "I've waited twelve years. A few more will make my acquisition of the princess much more, shall we say—useful."

Maggot squirmed. "But, Your Highness, surely—" he sputtered, and was immediately and violently shrugged off the bristling shoulder. His wings caught the wind and he flapped out of reach of raking claws, then, far from the castle.

Wrapping his spiked tail around him, much like a cat, the huge lizard inclined his armored head closer to Evangeline's window. Intent. Listening.

The crescent moon dipped below the horizon.

Eva slept, lost in a dream.

In a golden morning she and Prince Valentino, her Val, stood under a fragrant rose bower; their faces lit by sunbeams. Sharing bites of a raspberry tart, they laughed easily for no particular reason.

Reaching up, he picked a white rose, his head silhouetted in the circle of the sun. "For you," he said, smiling his beautiful, funny smile. Eva felt a thorn prick her finger. Looking down, her white dress was dotted with three drops of her blood. But no matter, she was with Val. Laughing; she looked up. Her voice caught in her throat.

He was gone.

Whirlwinds tore at her skirt, whipped her legs, and swept their roses away into nothingness! Trapped in another nightmare. Alone. The sun hot and high, the sky cloudless, she stood surrounded by a vast, dry field . . . trying to run, needing to find safety—but *horrible!* Her feet burned, buried in blistering sand. There was no moving them. Scorching blasts blew dirt and dead leaves into clouds full of angry voices swirling thicker and darker around her—their screams pounded her head, "Thieves! Murderers!"

Her dream shriek escaped her throat in a loud moan.

Hearing this, the creature shifted and lowered his head to peer into her window, his eyes, a hellish red. The end of his spiked tail twitched.

Finally pulling her feet free from the dreamscape, Eva fell hard. Her body jolted out of the nightmare. *Awake.* She gasped, kicking her twisted covers.

The dragon unfurled and hoisted his wings like sails, catching the wind. In an instant he lifted and was gone, his secret with him.

Eva touched the soft warmth of her coverlet. *Breathe.* Pressing her palms to her forehead, she tried to push the scene from her thoughts. "It was a dream. Get *Up!*"

She heard her voice as if it belonged to someone else. Sitting up, heart pounding, strands of hair stuck to her cheeks, her neck, plastered by beads of dream-panic sweat. She scraped her hair back with trembling fingers and waited. The horror. Surely it would go. But this time it remained, a fresh wound. She would never do what her father had done, and yet . . . Eva tried taking a deep breath, but her chest refused.

She sighed raggedly. Deciding not to risk any more sleep, she watched dawn color the sky and hugged her knees to her chin. The mullioned windowpanes kept the night chill out of her room and the warmth from her fireplace in. If she'd thought about it, she would have been grateful.

The sun crested the mountains, sparkling the water. It was high tide. Soon the inlet-moat, now deeper than a standing horse, would flow out to the grey-green sea and become a salt marsh. Eva remembered twenty armed men trying to sneak across the marsh on foot, sinking up to their doublets in mud. They'd been captured and executed as spies. *Beheaded.* Her own head prickled and a shudder traveled up her spine.

Tossing back satin covers, she leapt from her bed. Her toes touched the cold stone floor and curled. Ignoring this, she bounded to the window, flung it open, and looked down to the empty bridge.

It'd been six months since the last commonwealth meeting. *Maybe they'll come twice this year and stay a month like they did last year!* Valentino. Her face bloomed.

It was no good waiting for Mattie to dress her. Not today of all days. She snatched off her white nightgown and peered into her cavernous oak wardrobe. Shivering, Eva grabbed her blue dress because it laced up the front, not the back, and threw it over her head—*without* a corset. Silently congratulating herself for avoiding *that,* she twisted her hair into a quick braid, plaiting in a blue ribbon. The princess had a complexion that some might call creamy, the kind of skin that should avoid the sun during the middle of the day, according to Mattie. Eva felt this was unreasonable most days, so a growing flock of freckles decorated her nose, her cheeks and the tips of her ears. These bothered her only when Mattie bathed her face in lemon juice to try to fade them. It hadn't worked.

Eva slipped out her bedroom door, tiptoed down three flights of candlelit stairs to the kitchen—buzzing with preparation for the day's gathering. She stepped past a bloody side of venison draped over the chopping block and gagged then followed her nose into the bakery. *Fresh bread!* Before she could maneuver around the kitchen staff, a rosy-cheeked girl about her age stepped in front of her and dropped to a quick awkward curtsy. "Beggin your pardon, Your Highness." She blushed, making flour smudges glow on her face. "It's Brookin, Your Majesty. Truly an honor to meet you."

"And you." Eva nodded, smiled her thanks and turned to go.

"Been here about two weeks now, Your Grace," Brookin continued smiling shyly. "Been learning the ways o' bread since I could sit on a stool. Was taught in my village by the mum of my friend, Fulvick. He's just a friend—" She stopped herself and flushed again at her own boldness.

Evangeline's face lit up. Brookin talked like she'd imagined a friend would. Not like the courtiers and chambermaids with their simpering chatter to her face then furtive looks and sly winks behind her back. The princess ignored them, for the most part. But, the longing for a girl she could talk to . . . her heart felt this like her tongue was aware of her crooked front tooth. Now, here she was. *Maybe.*

Eva smiled into Brookin's eyes. "Yes. Please do go on. About your family and village, I mean."

"Your Highness, you've saved our lives. Pa died of the Pox and Mum came down with a fever—wastin' away, she is." She took a deep breath. "I've two younger brothers at home as well. They do what they can puttin' food on the table. We're very grateful for my position here." She beamed into Eva's face and tucked a straw-colored strand of hair up into her kerchief. "And, now I must return to my duties." She curtsied again. "If you'll excuse me?" She turned then and was caught up in the hive of kitchen activity.

Eva left the kitchen with a slice of crusty, buttered bread, and walked through the vast green marble entryway. Men's voices and pipe smoke drifted in from the hallway. *Father and Fagan!* She sprinted past twin curving staircases, down stone steps, and out into the gardens. Her shoes crunched gravel pathways as she ran past clipped hedges and ancient grey-stone buildings.

Archie waved his trowel in her direction. She smiled. The sight of the old gardener in his baggy brown pants banished clinging wisps of her nightmare. Eva ran around the rose bushes and disappeared into the labyrinth of clipped yew hedges.

She glanced at the sun now high above the trees. "They should be here by now—all the high muckety mucks, every last one," she panted in rhythm with her strides.

Valentino.

Worry creased her eyebrows. *He'd better remember. That's all.*

3

The dark, lavishly carved doors of the Great Meeting Hall were held open for Commonwealth members. Royal chamberlains, squires, and servants stood stiffly by and received the capes, canes, and gloves of nobility filing into the enormous, well-appointed room. A fire blazing in the massive stone hearth sent shadows dancing wildly on tapestry hung walls, as kings, princes, barons, counts, dukes, and archdukes passed in front of the flames and found their gold rimmed name-cards set on long, linen covered tables.

King Cedric looked around the room from his position at the head of the longest table and beamed with an expression that all would have called benevolent. All in the room, but one. This man had seen a darkness growing in Cedric's heart and spoke out against his cruel edicts.

King Cedric was aware of this. He privately cursed this King, intending to deal with him as one might deal with a fly. *Swiftly, and decisively,* he told himself. Cedric's invitation to the spring commonwealth meeting was well attended, and his chest swelled with pride. He knew why they thought they were there. In a word—Morach, the lizard.

However, his true agenda was cleverly cloaked in protocol. King Cedric, having a flair for the dramatic, would wait for the proper moment to reveal it. The trap was set. The prey was here.

Justin. His lip curled.

Eva leapt over a stream and found the hidden opening to the path—their path behind the quince bushes. Following the trail threading through mammoth evergreens and hemlocks, as they had every summer, she finally came to a clearing. Taking a deep breath, she muttered, "Calm down."

She found her tree, an enormous pine with roots bumping up here and there like knobby brown knees. Leaning against the rough trunk of this silent giant always made her feel more peaceful, *known* somehow. She closed her eyes. There in her thoughts—was Valentino with his funny grin—jacket rumpled, his nose peeling from sunburn. Somehow in this place, *their* place, everything finally connected.

It's been Val, just him, all these years. Her face flushed with warmth.

Their adventures—shining summer days together—rushed and roiled in her mind like the outgoing tide. "My best friend . . . If we lived to be a hundred, I'd never get tired of him. We're made to be together," she whispered aloud, hearing her voice quiver. "This time I'll tell him. I will." She drew in a sharp breath, imagining her words and the terrifying silence afterward. "Or I *could* ruin everything. What if he *doesn't?*" Her fingers twisted together.

After searching through the maze of hedges, Prince Valentino slapped his forehead. "What a buffoon," he laughed, and trotted toward the patch of forest.

He found their trail. Moving quietly through ancient evergreens, he paused a long moment, letting his eyes adjust to the deep shadows under the thick fragrant canopy. The trail twisted through giant evergreens, then opened into a clearing.

There she sat in a dazzle of shifting light, leaning against her pine. He smiled. This clearing had always been their secret, a place out of time. To find her here needed to happen. There was something he had to tell her. He cleared his throat.

"Took you long enough. I was about to send out a search party." She tossed him a half-grin.

"Well, you know . . ." His voice trailed off.

"Look, our village. Still here." She pointed across the clearing to tiny cottages made of sticks and straw with twig farmers tending fields of green moss.

He dropped down beside her. "How long ago did we build this? Two years?"

"Maybe. And, if I get to *live* after the—*you* know—I'll restore the kingdom so much better than this." Eva leaned forward. "I mean with orchards and schools and all, and not so much with the taxing," she said almost casually.

"Waaait a minute, wait . . . Back up. Get to *live?* After—what are you *talking* about?"

"You know, the revolt, the *beheadings*, the new regime. The one Fledge was talking about. She's so ready for it—*so* ready. They all are. I hear it in her voice. It's in Modrun's eyes. They hate us. And why shouldn't they?" Her words tumbled out. She sighed. "And I can't make them un-hate us. But, I'm not ready to die. Not yet," she finished in a small voice.

Val leaned forward. "Who cares if Fledge wants it or not—know this: Before anything like that could happen, I'd come for you." His jaw tightened. "I mean it."

Eva caught her breath and glanced at his eyes, bright. "So . . . you *would?*"

He sighed. "Course I would, what'd you think?"

"That works out well in fairy tales, but this is real life—just a reminder." Her words squeezed and broke.

"Hey *Eva*." He touched her shoulder.

"*What*," came muffled from behind her hands.

"I meant what I said." He sat back and waited.

Eva sniffed and wiped her eyes on her dress sleeves. "And, even if you could, how would you know . . . until it was too late, I mean."

"You'd be surprised what the good King Justin hears. People talk to my father. News like that would travel fast." He leaned closer. "I would hear. I would *come,*" he said flatly, as if that settled it.

Eva exhaled and smiled. "Well, good then . . . Thank, thank you."

He grinned. "How could I let that happen to Dunmoor's amazing future queen? But don't let it go to your head—*Ed!*" Two spots of heat flushed his cheeks.

She looked at her shoes then squinted up at him. "Actually, that might be the nicest thing anybody's ever said to me."

He smirked. "Good to know. It's 'Ed' then, from now on."

"Not the *'Ed'* part, you toad." She gave his shoulder a slap, sisterly.

The air between them suddenly felt awkward, crackly. Val looked at his boots and frowned.

"You might have heard," he began. "I'm to be educated at the monastery in Jarleth." Eva made herself look at the buttons on his blue jacket. "I'll be away for four years, maybe longer." He frowned over her head.

"No, no one tells me *anything*," she moaned. "Any chance you could learn stuff in Tirzah? You know, *tutors!* Why—?" She stopped, hearing her voice pleading.

"I did ask."

"And . . ."

"And, there is no cloister of learning in Tirzah like the one in Jarleth. It's known for excellence. So—"

"Right. You have to go." Eva heard the words leave her mouth and cringed. She tried looking happy for him and managed a grimace.

He broke a twig into tiny pieces. "Seems they teach music there too. So who knows, maybe I'll learn to play an instrument." His eyes shone.

"That would be . . ." Eva felt a wave rising inside her threatening to pound through her chest. Her thoughts crashed together and then calmed. So this was it. Her last chance.

"I, I . . ." she began.

"You—?" He glanced at the pine bark fallen in her hair.

"I have to just tell you—something." She paused, hearing her words squeeze and rise.

"Me too." He fidgeted with a white stone from his pocket. "But, go ahead." He glanced sideways and saw something sparkling the corner of her eye.

Just start. She exhaled. "I want you to know that you're my only true friend. I mean, Archie and Bea care about me, but that's different." *How do I tell him? He's . . . the One.* She saw it so clearly. They *must* be together. *It must happen.* She blinked and looked away.

He looked up from the stone. "I'm sure that will change later; you'll have more friends. You'll see. But, you can count me as your true friend, always. Forever. I mean it."

Eva snatched a quick breath. *He said, 'forever'!*

"Now that I'm thirteen years," he continued. "I have a say in my future . . . that is, who will, one day, be my bride. Father and I have this agreement." He cleared his throat. "Well, you and I have had our, uh, *stuff* and, well, you know. But there's no one I'd *rather*—!" He blurted, his face flushing hot scarlet. He fumbled the stone back into his pocket.

"Rather marry?" she whispered and bit her lip.

"Well, I *was* going to say—'Spend my life with.'" He shifted to his other foot.

"Yes." She clutched her stomach, butterflies rioting inside her ribs. Eva tried and failed to take a deep breath. "Yes, our lives. Of *course*, together." Her voice, soft and clear, rose from a hidden place inside . . . now open.

His face brightened. "Yes, well. Now that we have that settled, I have this for you." He drew the stone again from his breeches pocket. "Your hand—Princess *Evangeline*." Solemnly, he placed a white stone carved with EVA+VAL in her palm. "One day, when we marry, you'll have a ring for your finger instead of this rock." Val grinned and shook his head. "One day."

Lightning struck her insides. She leaned against the tree. "So, this is it, Valentino. I want to spend my life with you . . . side-by-side." Her head spun with the weight of her words.

"Yes, that's *it!* That's what I meant to say!" He beamed and lightly caught her hand. "So, there's one thing left, to seal our promise . . ." he began.

"Wait! I have something for you, too." Eva pulled a golden thimble from her dress pocket. "Keep this to remember—me." She placed it in his open palm. He smiled and tucked it in his vest pocket.

"When I'm away at school, it'll be with me. But, I won't need it to remember you. Not you." He pulled some bark off the tree, crumbling it between his fingers. "But, as I was saying," he brushed his fingers off on his jacket. "Our promise should be sealed with a, a ki—" He'd rehearsed it a hundred times, but hearing his words made his cheeks burn. He stepped back. "Actually, that is, if you want to."

Eva held up her lips to be kissed, giggled, and was about to call him a goose.

A shriek split the air and a mass of brown feathers crashed through the treetops and plummeted into the clearing. In a flash, Val ran under the creature and caught it. It quivered and flapped one wing, wailing a thin, reedy cry in his hands. The other wing moved awkwardly, strangely—pierced with an arrow.

"Someone's tried to kill Ciel," he whispered, his eyes wide.

"You *know* this bird?" She stood by Val's shoulder, incredulous.

Val's face was ashen. "Who would *do* such a thing?" He placed the shuddering creature gently on the ground. "She follows me, sometimes." He pulled his knife out of its sheath. Eva looked into the fierce golden raptor eyes and saw—trust.

"Here, hold this end. Don't let it move." He placed her hand on the red-banded arrow shaft.

Wordlessly, she held it steady under the impaled wing. Trembling feathers rested on her hand making her chin quiver. Somehow, she felt the pain of the pierced wing. A thought-shadow passed over her face making her eyes glisten.

"That's it Ciel, just hold still. We'll have this out in no time," Val murmured sawing through the wood. "Almost done." Just then the shaft broke, and he reached under the wing, gently sliding the arrow out. Ciel panted in silent agony, her wing bleeding out, soaking the straw beneath it. "We have to stop the bleeding. She'll die!" he whispered, panicked and snatched off his jacket to press onto the wound.

Eva gasped. The thought of this noble, ruined bird bleeding to death was more than she could bear. Her thoughts whirled. She held the bloody wing, felt the bird's bewildered suffering and terror; ached for her to live—to fly again. She leaned over Ciel's wing, her insides on fire, unable to stop a flood of tears. The wound was drenched and the clearing filled with her weeping.

Then a remarkable thing happened.

"*Eva!* Her wing—the bleeding—it's stopped!" He knelt beside her, his jacket crumpled on the ground.

Broad shafts of sunlight filtered through the pine boughs, glimmered the air, and lit the prince and princess where they knelt.

Eva heard Val's voice as though from a great distance. Peering into Ciel's amber eyes, Eva knew the wing would heal—she would fly!

"Eva . . . *Eva!*" Val touched her shoulder.

"I'm fine," she replied too quickly, then blinked hard as if waking from a dream. She felt Val's shoulder against hers.

He nodded silently toward
Ciel. The bird hopped up onto
her feet. Putting each feather in order;
she flexed her wing, and gazed, unblinking,
at her two rescuers. Then with a mighty flap,
she hopped up on a nearby branch as if nothing out
of the ordinary had happened.

"How did you—?"

"How did I what?" Eva stood, swaying slightly. She
steadied herself on the tree-trunk, her head prickling.

"You know. What you just did." He looked in her eyes.
"With the wing? With Ciel!"

King Cedric stood in the Grand Hall at the head of the table in front of the massive stone hearth, thinking what a magnificent spectacle he must present to the commonwealth council members. *They can admire me before I begin. It will make the casting out of this vermin so much sweeter.*

The chamberlain rang the bell, and the din in the room quieted until the only sound heard was the clink of silver spoons on silver chargers under the plates.

He smirked... *the element of surprise.*

"King Justin, rise!" It was not a request.

"Certainly." Justin stood with an air of someone placating a petulant child.

"It has come to my attention that you, King Justin, are attempting to spy on, overrun, and otherwise take my fair kingdom for yourself." He paused to let the weight of this accusation settle.

"Who would accuse me, *or* my men, of such a ridiculous thing? No, of course not."

"I thought you would say as much." King Cedric cleared his throat. "You are obviously unaware that reliable witnesses have come forward with a report to this effect."

"*Reliable* witnesses? And just how much did you have to *pay* these purveyors of truth?"

"I will ignore the insult to get to the business at hand." He walked around the table until he stood in front of King Justin, galled that he had to look *up* into his face. "Your knights have been seen in the northern border mountains of Dunmoor more than once, spying out the land for invasion—invasion by you and your army!"

King Justin didn't budge. "Let me assure you that if any of my knights or soldiers crossed the boundaries of your kingdom, they were in pursuit of our common enemy, Morach. You and your people should thank us for patrolling the borderlands. Your people there are safe." No one noticed Count Fagan shifting in his seat. "And, let's just set the record straight in front of these witnesses." He gestured around the room. "The side of the mountain range that faces Tirzah is Tirzan land. We may travel there. The land on the other side of the ridge is Dunmoor land. Need I remind you?" King Justin continued to look him squarely in the eyes until King Cedric looked away and coughed. He stepped back and recovered his composure, feeling the burn of all eyes on him.

King Justin continued to hold him in his gaze, his outrage scorching the air between them.

"You maintain that your guards are not spying. I say there has been suspicious activity on the Dunmoor side of the ridge." King Cedric cleared his throat again. "I will be lenient and press no charges against you or your men at this time; however, in the future, if you or your Tirzan guard are caught trespassing on Dunmoor soil," he said drawing himself up to his full height, "you and they will be immediately arrested as spies—and executed."

"This is outrageous," Justin said keeping his voice under control. "Who put you up to this?" He stopped himself then, seeing it was futile to protest.

The council room filled with murmurings. King Cedric strode back to his place at the head of the table. "According to tradition, we will put it to a vote," he announced. The councilmen rumbled in agreement. "All who stand with me?" A resounding "AYE" echoed in the grand meeting hall. "All opposed?" He said smugly.

"For the record—*NAY!*" King Justin's voice rang out. He remained standing. Then with a slight nod to the room, he strode out the door.

The meeting was adjourned.

King Cedric ordered the chamberlain to count the silverware.

"Princess Edwina! Prince Valentino!—*Ach!* Where are you?" Mattie puffed down the garden path, red faced, calling and muttering under her breath. "Quickly, you must come quickly!" Her voice rose shrilly, not unlike the royal geese.

Eva and Val ran from their secret place as soon as they heard her call. It would never do for this small shred of privacy to be discovered. They met her, breathless, on the hedge path.

"Ahhh!" Mattie bent over, hands on her knees, and wheezed loudly. Gathering herself with great effort, she spoke to Val. "Your Highness, you must meet your father in the courtyard. He's waiting for you now with your horses. Make *HASTE!"* These last words were hurled at their backs as they dashed up the curving castle steps.

Unseen by any, a dark figure, hidden in the shadow of the window, observed the whole scene with casual malice. He slipped his quiver of black, red-banded arrows into their case and adjusted the lace cuff on his sleeve. "All in due time," he muttered under his breath.

Eva sprinted up the worn, winding stone staircase to the watchtower. She saw Valentino and his father ride over the stone bridge. Val turned in his saddle to wave. Evangeline waved franticly from the high window, sobbing.

Not finding her, he turned and crossed over to the mainland.

My truest love. Her insides wrenched. Val's final whisper echoed in her ear: "I'll come for you. *Know* that." Val and his father, now tiny dots, soon disappeared from view behind Cedricsburg.

The Princess panted down the spiral stairway to the refuge of her bedroom, taking the stairs two at a time.

Until that day, Eva's imagined memory of being held in her mother's arms and hearing her voice was the most precious thing she owned. Now, the promise held in this white stone would be next to it. She tucked it under her mattress and cocooned herself in her coverlet. A swarm of fears buzzed around her head.

That night she didn't come down for dinner . . . or the next night.

5

Two days later, Eva sat at her writing desk absently rubbing her finger over its carved scrollwork. Afternoon light slanted through the arched window, sparkling her crystal inkwell. She sighed, dipped her quill and began.

Wednesday, September 4th

Val is gone. Or I should say—BANISHED from Dunmoor—UNJUSTLY!
Father is horrible!!!

    Why did this happen? Father must change his mind—immediately!
They are innocent!!

    Since we will rule Dunmoor and Tirzah as king and queen one day,
he and his father will be proven blameless. I'm certain of it.

    Father's life seems to be one long meeting.

    Signing off for today.

That week and then the next, no one had any answers for the princess. Her father stayed closed away. The guards discreetly stepped between her and the conference room door, as always.

Fall slipped into winter and winter melted into spring, as it does.

Eva sat staring out the window, not seeing the riot of color in the garden. Finishing her Latin, she wandered through dark hallways, and found herself in the garden. Roses and lilacs scented the ripe, salty smell of the sea and filled her lungs, tugging against her misery.

A falcon soared overhead in the clear blue sky then tipped down into a spiral. *Ciel? Did my tears really heal her wing? How does that even work?* She glanced around. *No one watching. Good.* Plucking three hairs from that tender place above her ear made tears come. Eva leaned over, letting them drip from the tip of her nose onto a broken red tulip. She waited. A snail crawled up the stem. Nothing. She exhaled loudly. "Never mind!"

Arlo, the barn cat, ran past her, his tail an exclamation mark. Following him around the hedge, she found Archie, bent over with a bucket full of leaves in his hand. He glanced up, radiating cheer.

"Weeding?" She suddenly felt lighter.

"Ahh, g'morning, Princess. Yes, that I am." Archie looked at his bucket as though it were full of naughty children. He pulled a kerchief from his jacket pocket with the slow fingers of age and wiped his wrinkled brow.

"So . . . the trash heap?" she asked.

"Throw 'em away? No, Princess . . . though these were a bird's doing, no doubt. Little seed droppers, they are." He waved his sun-browned arm at the sky, then clipped her a daisy and tipped his hat. Eva slipped the stem into her buttonhole and smiled wanly.

"You know, your mother talked of you often while we planned this garden. Standing right here on this very spot, in fact." He smiled broadly. "Planned it for you."

Eva listened to Archie the way a tulip drinks rain. "I've always loved this place." She took a deep breath and slipped her small hand into his broad calloused one. They walked on, their shoes crunching on the gravel.

"The missus's been asking after you." He sniffed the air. "Somethin' fresh out of her oven, I'll warrant." He chuckled; his brown eyes alight under bushy grey eyebrows.

Eva brightened. Then, imagined her life without Archie and his wife Bea. *Can't think about it—too awful.* "Yum," she said, glancing up in his dirt-smudged face.

"What is it, Princess?"

"I miss Valentino," she said simply, feeling safe saying the words.

They walked down the yew hedge path and he spoke. "Some things make missing people a bit easier."

"Like—?" She frowned, hearing her voice quiver.

"Like remembering good things about them—you know, happy times."

"No, sorry—tried it. Makes it worse."

"Maybe writing letters?" He offered.

"I've written him at least one every day since last September."

"—And?"

"*None* from him."

Archie looked down at the path, then into Eva's pale thin face. "Come see what I've done with the weeds?"

They turned down the path past clipped hedges and lush flowerbeds to a tiny, whitewashed cottage, hidden away . . . Archie and Bea's home. He swung open the white picket gate under an archway completely engulfed in yellow roses. Then ducking under gnarled branches of a plum tree, they entered Archie and Bea's kingdom.

Eva felt her shoulders relax. There was something in Archie's garden that few had seen, not because he kept it hidden, but because he and Bea seemed so old and ordinary that few bothered to visit.

Archie was a dove keeper. These birds were his messengers and lived in nesting boxes in the branches of an ancient apple tree, their dovecote. The boxes were held fast with living ropes of honeysuckle vines. Eva inhaled their thick, sweet scent and felt a bit lightheaded.

"Amazing." Eva steadied herself on the tree and gazed into his garden. Orange canna lilies with striped sword-like leaves rose above thick clouds of yellow and white daisies, alive with butterflies. Mounds of lavender lolled over, heavy with purple spikes. Archie's garden seemed to grow without interference, twining itself together, spilling and chortling over borders, so unlike the clipped castle garden.

He motioned her closer to the dove loft, and a soft *coo-coo-roo-ing* filled the air around them. Eva stepped under the shade of the tree and peered up into the boxes.

"These stay with me now, mostly. Olwen, moved to Cedricsburg, and keeps the rest with him there," Archie explained. "Loved the birds since he was a wee lad.

"Do you miss them?"

"The birds? Not a bit. I see them from time to time. They bring me and the missus news of the family." He filled their water bowls and stroked a light grey one on the head with his finger. "This one's Olwen's . . . trained to return since she was a tiny thing. Sending her back tonight with a message."

"How does that work?" She asked. "I mean how do they know where home *is* from so far away?"

"A bit of a mystery really," he said filling up the seed trough. "I do know this: the faithful homers have a reason to return . . . Their keepers are mighty good to 'em." He gave her a wink.

"Makes sense," she said. "May I?"

"Of course." Archie held his finger on the front of the nesting box, and a dove stepped onto it. "Your finger, Princess?" he said with playful pomp.

Holding her finger close to his, the bird hopped onto it with a quick flap. She felt his little bird strength grasp her finger and caught her breath, delighted. "When I'm grown, I must have some. I *love* this one."

Archie nodded. "Eiran's a handsome fella, he is. One of my most reliable." He unlatched the door. "Felt the same when I was your age," he said putting the bird back in. "And, just to let you know; many a life's been spared by a message sent on the leg of a dove."

"Why have I not been taught about this in my schooling?" She shook her head. "This is wonderful."

"Ah, yes it is, Princess." He picked up his bucket and turned toward the cottage.

Eva couldn't leave, not yet. "Could you tell me their names again?"

He chuckled and peered in the loft boxes. "Over there are three siblings, Aona, Riona, and Fiona. Up on the perch are two brothers, Seggie and Reggie. You met Eiran, and back on the nest is my night-flyer, Celeste." He latched the loft door.

"Night flyer?" Eva leaned forward to get a better look.

"She and her mother, both. They find their way home through fog or moonless night without fail—so far. Gifted, they are." He grinned. "Olwen keeps her mother on the mainland."

". . . Her name?"

"Clara." He picked up his pail. "Your own mother sent many a message on Clara's leg.

Archie's stomach growled. He laughed and turned toward the open cottage door. "Time to visit the missus."

Eva caught her breath. "Wait—my mother sent messages?" She half-whispered this to the back of his head, but he didn't hear.

"Ah, Princess, you poor dear. You must be famished, potterin' and palaverin' around in the garden with Archie." Bea gave Eva's hand a quick squeeze.

"No, not a bit . . ." Eva began, watching Bea spreading glistening chocolate icing on a tall chocolate cake still warm from the oven.

"Ah! There we go," Bea said beaming with pleasure.

"Yes, Princess, you don't want to miss the bumpy bingle-fruit filing in this one," Archie leaned back in his chair and chuckled. Eva giggled.

Bea sent him an indulgent smile and nodded to Eva. "Just so you know— it's raspberry," she whispered conspiratorially. "Now, come sit down, Dearie. Let me fix you a cup of tea and a bit of cake. And I imagine a dab of cream wouldn't be amiss, now would it? Wait right there. I won't be a minute." Without waiting for an answer, a hefty slice of cake was slipped onto a white plate and ceremoniously placed on the checkered tablecloth in front of her and crowned with a generous dollop of whipped cream. "This should put some meat on those bones of yours," she said with a twinkle.

Eva laughed and her eyes grew big. "Wonderful! Thank you." Her mouth watered.

"Got to keep your strength up." Archie said, sipping his tea loudly. "Feed the inner woman."

Bea giggled. If Archie's wife could be described in a word, it would be "comfort". From her rounded shape to the upturned creases around her clear cornflower-blue eyes, everything about her put Eva at ease. And the smell—the aroma that seemed to live in her kitchen; she closed her eyes blissfully. *Such a wonderful place . . . always something delicious, always someone smiling.* She thought of the bustling castle kitchen; the frantic shouting and pushing to get everything arranged perfectly and on time. "When I'm queen, this is the kind of kitchen I'll have," she announced. "And Bea, you can be the head cook!"

Bea's round cheeks pinked and she laughed good-naturedly. "Thank you kindly, Princess. We'll just see about that won't we?"

So, they drank cups of tea and ate and laughed until Eva's cheeks ached from smiling.

She noticed suddenly that the sun was low in the sky. "*Oh!* I have to go! There's a commonwealth dinner tonight. Father wants me to entertain Count Fagan . . . the big lump." She rolled her eyes, sighed loudly, and pushed her rough wooden chair back from the table. Archie and Bea exchanged a look. "Must turn back into a princess now," Eva flashed a half-grin and hesitated. "I hardly know—"

"No need for thanks; it's just mighty good to see you smiling again," Bea wrapped her up in a hug. "And you're always welcome. Know that." Eva knew.

Archie walked Eva to the garden gate and paused, frowning.

"What is it, Archie?"

I know you have to get ready, so—" He leaned on the gate, his lips pressed together, making his white mustache and beard bristle.

"I'm listening," she said, then, caught her breath. "Wait. Is this about the revolution?" Her hand unconsciously touched her throat.

Archie's eyebrows climbed up his forehead. "A revolt?" He looked at the darkening sky. "I almost wish it were. Then we could hide you away. But, no Princess; there's something you must know. It's time." He cleared his throat and looked in her face. "About twelve years ago, your father and Count Fagan started meeting; sometimes here, other times at his castle in Ravenia. Things started changing."

"What kind of things?"

"The word around the castle was the count had somehow bewitched your father. He seemed to have a strange power over him.

"Bewitched?" she laughed. "Archie, you know how those busy-bodies talk—especially in the kitchen. They love the scary stuff."

Archie waited for her to finish, his eyes dark and solemn. "Your father began traveling often and alone to places he never named. When he returned, he shut himself away, not speaking to anyone for weeks at a time."

"So, it wasn't just me he hated . . ."

"No, Princess, it's not you. Never you. He's not like the King we knew when your mother—"

"—Was still alive," she finished for him and looked down at the shadowed pathway.

"For twelve years, the people of Dunmoor have been taxed without mercy. The kingdom shrivels like a winter apple, you might say."

Eva thought of the angry, rake-wavers.

"In fact, Olwen knows many who've been reduced to eating roots and berries. They can't buy shoes, so they wrap their children's feet in rags in the dead of winter. My son helps them as he can, but with a wife and children of his own . . ." He looked at his shoes.

"Horrible!"

"That it is, Princess. I told you because you live on an island, away from it. It's time you knew. If you were my daughter, I'd also advise you to keep your eyes open at dinner tonight; there's mischief afoot. Be sure to stay near a crowd of people—and when you leave the Great Hall, go directly to your room. Lock yourself in." He looked into her eyes gravely.

Eva felt her stomach tighten. "Archie, I'm supposed to make conversation with this count. What do I say to such a, a—"

"Just ask him questions about himself, and you can't go wrong. That's the word Bea hears from Rhona." He exhaled loudly. "And keep your wits about you."

"Right. I can do that." Picturing herself sitting through an entire evening trying to entertain Fagan made her envy Brookin tucked safely away in the kitchen. "I hate the way he looks at me. Makes me want to vomi—" Her throat tightened and she looked into Archie's eyes, then, said with more confidence than she felt: "I'll be fine. Don't worry, *alright?* Probably this stuff about the count is just kitchen lip-flap anyway. They *do* love the scary stuff."

Archie patted her shoulder. "Would that it were . . . at any rate, we're here if you need us, Brave One. Bea and I love you like one of our own." He put his brown wrinkled hand on her's and looked into her face. "If you ever doubt why you were born, remember, it's no accident you are a princess at this time, and in this place."

Eva swallowed loudly. She squeezed his hand, not trusting herself to speak around the lump in her throat.

Turning toward the castle, the princess tripped on a rock. She jumped up and forced a laugh.

Trudging down the garden path, *Brave One*, echoed in her ears. She snorted. *More like— Awkward One.*

She glanced at the sky. It was getting dark faster than she expected.

6

The ladies-in-waiting mingled with dignitaries looking beautiful and uncomfortable in equal parts. Eva decided they decorated the room nicely, if you could ignore their mocking smiles behind lace fans.

Eva maneuvered through the warm candle-lit Great Hall to her place at the table. Her lips were composed in neither a smile nor a frown, but a refined expression that said, *"I am an impenetrable fortress."* She had learned that was the safest way to navigate the stormy seas of these occasions. Her face and eyes had the look of wary separateness. She was glad for the volume of fabric that made up her gown—imagining it as a type of armor against the world around her. Eva was well aware this world, these people, could topple her world at any moment.

Musicians played softly in the balcony overlooking the crowded room. Her eyes took in the tremendous stone hearth with fire blazing and familiar long tables covered in white linen, set with their finest gold-rimmed china.

Two courtiers stood near the musicians, furtively watching her and whispering behind fluttering fans. She knew she was gossiped about as odd, but didn't care. Not usually anyway.

This aside, Eva didn't think of herself as strange, just different, on the inside, and glad of it.

As the future queen of Dunmoor, she knew what she wanted to do. What she must do—but, not alone. *Valentino.* But how would it happen? Or could she *make* it happen? These were the questions that caused her to leave her warm bed at night and gaze out her window toward the distant Tirzan mountains.

Eva stepped around one of the brown leggy hounds. He wagged his tail, hoping for a morsel of food. "Patience, Nim," she whispered. Scratching him behind the ear, she greeted guests, making her way around the dining tables. They were laden with such abundance, they seemed to groan with the weight of it. In fact, the entire hall was filled to the very pinnacle of its arched, plastered ceiling with mouth-watering swirling aromas.

She passed by roasted pheasant and venison under domed silver covers, braised potatoes in cream sauce with parsley, spicy pumpkin pastries, and breads of every size and shape. "Enough food here to feed all of Cedricsburg," she muttered under her breath, then saw her seat, three places down the table from her father. *So he can keep an eye on me?* The thought brought no comfort.

So was Archie's story true or just idle kitchen gossip? This was a mystery she promised herself to find out. Eva pictured Brookin in the bakery—laughing, smudged with flour—sighed, and kept walking.

The count was standing beside her chair in a fashionable dark-green velvet waistcoat with a white silk cravat. Eva felt her stomach tighten and twist. She expected this. It happened every time he came to the castle.

Observing her progress through the room and nearness now to her chair, he bowed absurdly low from the waist with exaggerated fluttering hand flourishes that swished his lace cuffs, showcasing his glittering rings. Was there a touch of mockery in that bow? She was sure of it. "A pleasure to see you again, Princess," he purred.

"The pleasure is mine." Eva blushed slightly with her lie. "How was your trip, Count Fagan?" She inquired politely, making herself look up at his pale powdered face.

"Absolutely wretched, my dear—simply wretched. Didn't sleep a wink." He sniffed and tugged at the lace on his cuff. "The rutted roads of Dunmoor have become the stuff of legends; of course you know this. I could only recommend travel in your kingdom to the kind of person who would enjoy eating a bowl of pebbles before breakfast . . . a glutton for punishment, as they say."

He chuckled and glanced around to see if there was a larger audience for his wit. There wasn't.

Eva believed the not sleeping part. In fact, his red-rimmed eyes gave silent testimony to many such sleepless nights. She forced a smile and said, "I'm sorry to hear that." *So maybe leave and never come back?* Imagining actually speaking this thought made a laugh flutter in her throat. Eva swallowed it and bit the corner of her lower lip.

The king sat, and the rest of the room sat after him.

Fagan lowered his considerable bulk into his chair. "I must say," he remarked, tucking the starched white napkin in his collar. "Your father has spared no expense," he gestured toward the food and fine linens. "Ah, except my pickle fork. Someone has forgotten to set one at my place." He feigned dismay.

"Well, Count, please don't trouble yourself," Eva said. "Have mine. I won't be using it." She slid the tiny fork across the white linen cloth, being careful to avoid his fingers. But, before she could withdraw her hand to the safety of her lap, he reached over with studied casualness and patted her hand with his knobby manicured fingers. Invisibly, she drew inward like one of the snails in the garden. Arranging her face into what she hoped was a pleasant expression; Eva folded her hands safely under the tablecloth, thinking: *if he touches me again I'll spill my drink in his lap and make it look like an accident.* She glanced his direction and almost laughed out loud, but coughed into her napkin instead. *He looks like a big baby with a napkin bib, a black mustache and pointy beard!* She blotted her lips and arranged her face.

"Most kind," he said, pressing his thin lips into a smile; his face a mask of cultivated congeniality.

"Our kitchen staff is excellent," she said, falling in with his general tone of conversation. "Father has hired them from far and wide; some from places as far as Ketos and Sumarkland. In fact, that's where Rhona our head cook is from . . . Ketos, that is."

"You are probably not aware of this," he announced to her and the table at large. "The plague has become very popular in certain parts of Sumarkland. You could say people there are just *dying* to get it." His laugh came out as a kind of snarling snort. Clearly amused, he glanced around the table, but saw no one else laughing. They were suddenly busy with their own conversations. Eva quickly turned away, pretending she hadn't heard him.

He looked over his wine goblet at her and raised a quizzical eyebrow, obviously expecting a response.

She tried to look pleasant. "Actually, I am aware. It's a *very* sad time for them." It was the best she could do. Her stomach was beginning to heave in earnest. *Heartless swine* came to mind, but she bit it back.

"If you have any stellar points to make on your side of the conversation, now would be a good time to reveal them." He reached behind his neck and flicked his stringy black hair out of his collar.

What—? Were those scales on his neck? Surely not! She dismissed this as being ridiculous, a trick of the flickering candlelight.

"My Dear," he murmured leaning closer. "I have a wonderful surprise for you."

I'm definitely not your Dear; she leaned away only slightly. "You do?" she said aloud and took a sip of her drink to mask the smell of his breath. *What is that odd smell? And why do his eyebrows meet in the middle? They jump like a row of hairy black spiders when he talks.* She was momentarily fascinated by the spectacle.

"And, I've already spoken to your father and obtained his permission, so you don't have to be concerned," he continued, his lips turning up in an oily smile. Encouraged by her attention, he stroked his mustache, taking his time. "How would you like to ride with me in my personal gilded coach to Ravenia, *my* province, spend a few days and let me show you around? The whole trip would be well chaperoned of course." He paused, seeing the unconcealed panic on her face. "It would give me a chance to show you my gardens," he continued smoothly. "Knowing how you *do* enjoy gardens, I knew you would be excited to visit mine as well." He raised his eyebrow, smiling expectantly. "How can I help you understand; I am but a simple count." A tiny smirk played at the corner of his mouth. He dabbed it with the corner of his napkin.

Father how could you? Eva felt as though she'd been punched in the stomach. She stopped herself from retching, then a thought rose in her mind: *Fagan—you know I like gardens?* Suddenly she knew. *He's been watching me from the study window.* Eva felt like a stalked mouse. Saliva filled her mouth.

She swallowed hard and stammered. "I… I'm sure that would be a wonderful trip, Count Fagan—and I would enjoy a trip to Ravenia sometime," she said, blushing hotly with the lie. "It is tempting—very tempting, but I'm involved in an extended school project and can't leave the island until I'm done . . . Father doesn't know about it," she added hastily. "Not yet."

"Oh," he said, studying his rouged fingernails. "Extended is it? Just *how* extended are we talking about?"

Eva nodded her head solemnly and pursed her lips. "Very extended. *Looong* and involved. In fact, I couldn't tell you when I'll be finished. It's . . . it's about . . . about—carrier doves—their life habits and training." *That should do it,* she thought.

"Just imagine!" The count feigned interest. "A fascinating subject I'm sure." He leaned back, obviously bored. "Well, mustn't shirk your school responsibilities." He blotted his mouth with his napkin again, tidied the lace on his cuffs, and arranged an indulgent smile on his face. Only his eyes gleamed, cold. Dark. Malicious.

Eva felt her stomach heave again, but managed a tight smile. "Please excuse me, Count. I hope you enjoy your dinner—" The princess stood abruptly, crashing into the silver tray of walnut cheese balls held aloft by the server behind her. They tumbled to the floor and rolled under the table. "Please excuse me," was all she could think of to say. Inwardly, she screamed: *I need air! Let me out!*

She shot a glance down the table at her father. He wasn't looking. Engaged in sparkling conversation with Countess Constanza Flaunte (all rouged cheeks and fluttery green eyes), the king seemed unaware of anyone else. Eva couldn't ever remember him talking to *her* like that.

Father doesn't really mean to be unkind to me, she told herself. In Eva's mind, he was kingly, correct in voice and ceremony. Except when he wasn't. He would be praising Rhona for the banquet tonight. *But, Father feels as far away as the moon, whether he's here or a hundred miles away. He's always the man in the moon to me.*

The server stepped to one side and bowed low. Eva slipped through the archway—out of the din of voices, the clinking silverware on fine china, and whining dogs—away from the Count.

Stepping onto the candle-lit stairway, she saw no one. Gathering her voluminous green dress in trembling hands, she sprinted up to her bedroom. Shoving the door shut, she turned the brass key in the lock. It clicked solidly. Eva felt the knot in her stomach start to loosen.

"What a wierd night," she muttered. Walking over to her wardrobe Eva sighed at her reflection in its oval mirror and began unlacing the front of her dress. Suddenly it seemed ridiculous to imagine someone, anyone, with scales on his neck. A dragon-man. She laughed shortly. "Careful," she whispered. "They really *will* start saying you've gone off your . . ."

A small noise made her stop. *That's not the sound of my petticoats.* "Arlo, bad kitty. No *scratching.*" Even as the words left her mouth, she remembered Arlo was with Archie and Bea. Peering around her candlelit room, a movement caught her eye. The latch on her door moved slowly, scraping the wood as it lifted. *Someone's trying my door!* Thoughts blazed through her head. *Mattie? No she'd have a key. Same with Father. The servants would knock.* Archie's warning flamed up—a sudden bonfire in her mind. The hair on the back of her neck lifted; Eva tripped and fell into her velvet chair by the window, eyes wide.

Fagan?

The next morning, Princess Evangeline unlocked her door and went about her routine as though nothing had happened. *You probably imagined it,* she told herself, knowing full well she hadn't.

That afternoon, she had two hours to call her own. Soon enough, she would be confined to her embroidery class and forced to take up her needle and thread. Sitting still and making tiny stitches was harder some days than others. Today, she already knew—it would be agony.

Mattie and the servants were busy, so Eva stepped quietly down the hall to the stairs. In a few minutes, she was standing in front of her father's study trying the latch as she had countless times. This time it clicked open! She looked both ways . . . no one in the hall. Noiselessly, she pushed the heavy oaken door open just enough to slip through, then holding the latch, closed it silently.

Her father had been discussing matters of state downstairs with his advisors and Count Fagan. The count would stay on at Dunmoor again this year for a few extra days. This more-than-annoyed Eva. Talking with him last night at the banquet, had sickened her, a nameless dread prickling her skin the entire time. She shuddered. *And my door. What of that?*

She would understand later that sometimes tremendously important things register in flesh and bones long before minds can fully grasp what is happening. But for now, Fagan must be avoided whenever possible.

She tiptoed across the lush, green patterned Tamsian carpet in the lavishly appointed room. The walls, paneled with the same dark oak as the door, smelled of exotic pipe tobacco. The panels vaulted up, creating a ceiling that looked like six curved slices of oaken pie. The points of these met in the center where a carved mahogany rose graced the apex of their curve. On the walls hung the usual ornate gilt frames filled with obscure ancestors. She shivered involuntarily feeling their dead gaze. A fire had recently been laid in the hearth, which gave Eva a moment's panic. *Was someone just here or are they coming? Well, Father's busy downstairs. I have time.*

Stepping up to the bookshelves, she ran her fingers over the pebbly leather bindings, the massive volumes written on the history of Dunmoor and the world. *These must go back to the dawn of time*, she thought.

Eva had always been fascinated by her father's study. However, she had only gotten a quick peek at its walls of books when she was seven. Throughout the years, the door was kept locked—until today.

Eva's eyes glided over the history titles until she got to the end of the shelf where a purple velvet curtain hung that matched the one at the window. *Strange. Why would a curtain be here in the corner of the room?* She tugged and slid it easily across a tarnished bronze rod revealing a small alcove. The right wall had shelves to the ceiling filled with more books. The left side was paneled with the same dark wood. There was a small writing table and chair placed against the wall with a brass lamp on the corner. The pen and paper were slightly askew in the center. *Recently used? Very curious! Why would he come behind the curtain to read and write and not use his table and velvet chair by the hearth?*

She turned to look at the books, her eyes flitting across titles: *Flora and Fauna of Dunmoor, The Art and Lore of Bee-Keeping, How to Win Allies and Defeat Enemies,* and *Weapons and Articles of War in Post-Diluvian Earth. An odd mix*, she thought. *Those two must have been Mother's.* She opened the *Bee-Keeping* pages, breathing in a faint fragrance of flowers and honey . . . *maybe the scent of her hands?* She squeezed her eyes shut, imagining her mother in the garden. Eva exhaled, shelved the book, and promised to come back one day.

At the end of the shelf were three elaborately bound books: *Alchemy for Simpletons, Spells and Incantations,* and *How to Work Your Will in the Earth.* She felt the hair on her arms rise. *What is Father doing with these?* She was horrified and fascinated all at once, hardly believing her eyes. *Well, it wouldn't hurt to just look. After all they are only books, not the witches and warlocks themselves.* She chuckled to herself under her breath, "Silly goose."

With trembling hands, she pulled out the volume of spells and incantations, feeling the weight of generations of dark secrets held inside. To her horror, it slipped from her fingers and fell open onto the floor, filling the air with an ancient musty odor.

Eva sneezed three times then pinched her nose closed; suddenly terrified someone would hear. The open pages were inscribed with symbols and runes. She touched the black, red and gold inlaid border, feeling a strange tug as though an invisible hand were pulling her into the book. *Very odd*, she thought, then, shoved caution aside and read the open page:

"To effekt the changes you desire, make a liquid potion with these ingredients:
3 drops of dragon's blood
One dragon scale
Five black hairs from a maiden who neither smiles nor frowns
Bile from a black bull 3 years old
The web of an Orb spider, freshly spun, with no flye as yet . . ."

Men's voices echoed in the hallway.

I can't remember all these things! The list filled the page.

"I must have this," she whispered. Not knowing when she might find the door unlocked again, Eva tore the page from the book. The smell of sulphur wafted from the ripped edge. *Odd. I've smelled that before. Where was it?* She mentally filed the smell, together with the other strange things in the small room and stuffed the page into her dress pocket, hefted the book back into its place on the shelf and yanked the curtain closed. She quieted her breathing and peered through the narrow space between the curtain and the wall.

The door swung open. Her father and Count Fagan strolled into the room still talking.

"I thought yesterday's meeting went well," King Cedric said. He motioned for the wine steward to place the tray on the carved mahogany table by the window. "Yes, very well indeed." He dismissed the steward with a wave and relaxed into one of the velvet fireside chairs. "Did you think our plan—" He was stopped mid-sentence by the count gesturing and striding over to the massive oak doors. He swung them open and squinted down the hallway in each direction. Satisfied, he closed the doors. Eva saw him pour two goblets of red wine. "We can't be too careful these days," he remarked, and tipped his left arm toward one of the goblets.

"Thank you, Fagan," Cedric said, taking the offered glass. "Here's to our fruitful partnership, wealth restored, and safety across the lands!"

"Yes, your Majesty . . . to Dunmoor safe from hostile takeover, and from Morach, and with more riches than you can handle." Fagan's smile curled to a sneer as he drained his glass. He watched with interest as King Cedric drank his.

"Indeed, I haven't heard of Morach invading Dunmoor in years," the King mused.

"Yes," Fagan stepped over this comment. "We now have the groundwork laid for our plan." He sat in the chair across from the king, poking the fire. It sparked and blazed up. "It is widely known that all the House of King Justin of Tirzah are thieves and spies. They would like nothing better than to take every last bit of land for their own." He settled back in his chair propping his shiny black boots on the tufted ottoman between them. "And that would bring us to the next part."

"The next part . . .? Ah, I don't recall discussing another part."

"We haven't actually talked through it yet." Fagan shifted in his chair and smiled reassuringly. "I think it's time we spoke about this matter of your daughter . . . So far, the only rightful heir to the throne of Dunmoor."

"Yes, what about her?" the king frowned slightly.

"I would like to propose a little merger," Fagan said evenly, his eyes glittering like hard black stones.

Eva stifled a gasp, every muscle taut, thrumming. Glancing down, she was horrified to see the hem of her dress visible under the curtain edge and slowly pulled it back out of sight. Her heart pounded so loudly in her ears, she was terrified they might hear it outside the curtain.

Fagan paused, his glance flickering to the curtain edge. "Ah . . . yes. I have thoughts of some import to relate," he said smoothly, lifting an eyebrow. "But I can see this is not the time."

"... Not the time," the king parroted, his voice fading. "But ... an interesting proposal ... will talk more."

"Yes, we will. However, right now, the matter of rebuilding your kingdom wealth and not allowing it be taken over by *another* ruler is the matter of utmost importance." Fagan stood abruptly making his point.

"Quite so ..." intoned the king.

"When the son we have spoken of comes of age, we set the trap, he falls in, and we do away with him—permanently."

"Yes, yes ... permanently," the king agreed. "But, why is it he must be killed?" His eyelids fluttered then drooped. With great effort he opened them wide and pushed up straighter in his chair.

The count smiled dryly. He spoke to the king as if he were a slow-witted child. "He is the one who wants to take your kingdom from you, he and his father—remember?"

"But ..."

"No need to worry about it. I will handle the details. You just follow my lead. And let's just say I have an old, in fact, *ancient* grievance I need to settle. But no matter, it will be avenged. All in due time." Fagan saw King Cedric could no longer keep his eyes open or his head up. Tugging the lace on his cuffs, the count walked over to the window and looked out over the garden then glanced back at the purple corner curtain. "All in due time," he said under his breath.

Eva couldn't move. She hardly dared breathe.

And, who was this son the count spoke of? Surely not Valentino. Father and King Justin had a border dispute, but nothing worthy of death, certainly ... It must be someone else. But who?

After an agonizing hour, Count Fagan finally left the study. When his retreating footsteps faded, Eva crept from the alcove and put her ear to the door. Silence. She padded softly to her father's chair.

King Cedric still slumped by the fire—an empty wine glass on the table beside him. Smoke from his pipe encircled him. He seemed not to hear her footsteps. Heavy-lidded; he continued to stare blankly into the corner of the room.

Eva stood in front of him wondering what to do next. She cleared her throat. He seemed oblivious and blew a puff of smoke in her general direction. His glassy eyes narrowed and followed the smoke as it settled around her. She studied him. *How strange,* she thought. *Does he not see me?*

His once massive squared shoulders hunched forward as if protecting a wound to the heart. His face sagged under the weight of greed and disappointment. Even his ermine edged robe with its golden eagle clasp could not disguise the aching emptiness she felt from this man she called Father. Suddenly, her heart was pierced with grief for him. She wanted to do something to help him. *But what?* Another puff of smoke swirled around her head.

She coughed.

He looked up as if awakened from a dream and scowled at her, the intrusion.

"Who let you in?" He asked, hoarsely.

"Well, I let myself in, Father. The door was unlocked," she replied then hesitated, "I just . . ."

"Yes, yes—what is it." He said the words as if they tasted bitter to him. Then without waiting, he shook his head and squeezed his hands together as if cracking a walnut. "Your hands are like hers, and your mouth . . . just like hers."

"Are they, Father?" She held her breath. *Yes, and...*

He gathered himself. "Yes, yes, have a seat," he said impatiently, gesturing toward the green velvet wingback chair facing him by the fire. Propping his boots on the ottoman, he said, "Something I've been meaning to talk to you about..."

Eva sat up straighter in the chair. "Yes, Father?"

"It's about your appearance. You must always look your best, don't you see. When viewed by our common-folk and nobility alike . . . but, especially common-folk." Eva steeled herself for what was to come, staring at the furrow between his dark eyebrows to keep from rolling her eyes. He continued: "It gives them a lift to see us and how we live . . . a lift from their dreary lot in life." The King leaned forward. "And that means keeping your hair neat and braided, wearing clean dresses and also wearing a, a—" At this point he stopped and pointed with his pipe stem in the general direction of her midsection where a corset would have cinched in her waist, had she been wearing one.

Eva ignored the gesture. "But Father, *must* their lives be dreary and poor?" She smiled winningly. "Couldn't we help them? Even just a little?"

He leaned back into the plush softness of his chair and puffed his pipe, engulfing his head in smoke. "Balderdash and rubbish!" He grunted. "I should have known you would argue! Get this in your head—this is the way things are—always have been! It's time you learned to accept it." Eva coughed again, feeling herself shrinking inside her skin. No use talking to him about this, she decided, clasping her hands in her lap, she pressed her lips together in a semblance of a smile.

The King wasn't finished.

"And another thing," he said, "That was quite a scene you caused last night—should give people something to talk about for a while." His voice was a controlled growl. He drummed his fingers on the table beside him, waiting.

"Yes, and I am truly sorry, Father, for any embarrassment I caused you." *There, that sounded like I meant it.*

"Yes, I am sure, *Edwina*," he said her name like a dagger thrust.

"Truly." She ignored his scorn, feeling her cheeks redden with shame and something else she had no name for, not yet.

The room filled with prickly silence. She looked down, fidgeting with the lace on her sleeve.

Then he spoke. "Have I not provided you with every possible advantage and luxury — dresses of the finest silk; training in horseback riding, reading, embroidery; and tutoring in all subjects befitting a princess?" He looked out the window, avoiding her eyes. "And this is my thanks, humiliation for me and insults for my guests."

Eva controlled her voice. "Yes, Father, it has been made clear that I am to be made suitable that I might advantage you in my marriage. Would a marriage with Valentino of Tirzah not also be advantageous?"

"No, certainly not. The House of King Justin is full of thieves and spies. He would like nothing better than to take every last bit of land for his own," he snarled, flecks of spit flying out from under his graying mustache.

Eva heard the words of Fagan leaving her father's mouth. Remembering Archie's warning, Eva knew arguing was useless. She tried another approach. "Father, do you not care for me, even just a little . . . for *me?*"

"Ridiculous girl, of course I do. You are my daughter!" He turned to stare out the window. "And that would bring me to something we need to talk about." He stroked his beard, squinting his eyes. "It's about the count you were *entertaining* last night, Count Fagan." The afternoon light slanted, spearing the smoke-filled room. Eva stifled another cough. "The count has hinted at an offer of marriage. Not now, of course, but when you are of age."

"Father, *NO!*"

"Well, why ever not? Is one man not as good as another?"

She felt the room closing in. "No, Father, please not him! He's so, so—old! And I've heard things." *And seen things!*

King Cedric sighed loudly and looked at the ceiling. "Yes, you are so right. He will never see thirty again." His words dripped acidly. "And what *things* have you heard?"

"Just . . ." She chose her words carefully. "Talk of underhanded dealings. And, and that's not all!"

"You foolish girl," he growled. "What is that to you? You would live in riches and plenty; never wanting for a thing as long as you live. Surely you see that?"

—*As long as I live?* Then she said quietly, "I'd want for love."

"An overrated luxury." He cleared his throat. "And keep in mind, love can grow."

The thought of love growing with Count Fagan brought bile up in her throat. She gagged and swallowed. Changing the subject, she said, "You mean like it did with you and Mother?"

He closed his eyes briefly. "Yes, you are so like her. I saw that when you were very young. Even your voice reminds me of hers . . . a musical voice." Eva drank in the words. *He likes my voice.*

"However, your voice would be more pleasant if you'd hold your tongue and stop complaining for a minute." His brow furrowed.

Eva realized the good part was over. It was time to play her final card.

"Father."

He took his boots off the ottoman, finally looking in her eyes.

"It's about Count Fagan."

"What about him?" He tapped his pipe in the tray and adjusted his ermine-edged cape, preparing to leave.

"It's just that I think he might be some strange kind of reptile." She winced. Her statement hung in the air sounding ridiculous even to her.

"No, really? Oh, *horrors!*" He palmed his forehead and gritted his teeth. Eva bit her lip as he stood to leave. "The chancellor is waiting for me in the meeting room. You'll forgive me if I let that one pass." It was as if she were a child telling him about monsters under the bed. He leaned over and laid his hand heavily on her shoulder. She winced. "Nothing has been decided yet, but know this: Your marriage must be advantageous for all concerned. Period." She opened her mouth to protest. He held up a hand and stepped back toward to the doorway. "Now I think you have some dinner waiting for you downstairs. We will talk again when you're more reasonable."

"Yes Father," Eva said, and dipped in a shallow curtsy. Their meeting was over.

"There are other suitors interested. You'll meet them in times to come. You can thank me later." His curled mustache lifted slightly, briefly. Then turning, he walked out the door.

Eva stood stunned, not believing her ears. This possibility was unthinkable. *How could Father even consider signing my life over to this—horrible, vile—was that him at my door? Is he even human?*

8

That summer, Eva celebrated her thirteenth birthday.
True to his word, King Cedric arranged for royal suitors to visit the castle as future husbands for her. They seemed to come in droves; each one more *un*-suitable than the last.

Eva stepped into the high-domed cupola.

"Don't you have some deer to hunt or small animals to maim?" She eyed Prince Wilmot, known far and wide as an excellent huntsman. "You think to increase the boundaries of your kingdom by marrying me? Think again, *sir.*" Her open disdain was clear in her cool, narrow-eyed gaze.

Prince Wilmot had no immediate answer for this. He sat for a moment, gathering his wits. "Surely Princess . . ." he began, then imagined being married to her and thought better of it. "No, you are certainly right. My time would indeed be better spent on a hunt." He stood and clicked his silver spurred boot heels together and gave her a quick terse bow. "Farewell, Princess. I'll find my own way out." Eva curtsied in return. Wordlessly they turned and left the well-appointed drawing room through opposite doors.

The suitors who came to the castle to win and wed her left one by one as Eva thought of ways to insult, torment, and send them back to their own country. Finding it great sport, she made up a little song that courtiers and servants often heard her singing in the hallways:

One too fat
And another too thin;
The next too short,
And the last no chin.

What she never spoke aloud was this: Waiting on you, Val.

It was fall and Eva sat alone in the Grand Dining Hall . . . again.

Thirty-eight tonight. Short strides. She's in a hurry. Eva counted the server's echoing steps from the kitchen doorway to where she sat waiting at the end of the long, linen-covered, table. This game made her solitary meals a little more bearable. The princess lifted her eyes to the massive oak beams holding up the ceiling and slumped down in her chair, crushed by the room.

There on the white embroidered tablecloth, was placed a gold-rimmed plate holding venison, peas, and carrots. It sneered up at her. She pushed her food around on the plate. *I guess Father and his councilmen rode off to who-knows-where—as usual.* Her stomach churned acidly. *Always eating alone. If Val were here . . .* She shoved the thought violently from her mind, feeling the scrutiny of many eyes from the dark kitchen hallway. She could hear muffled giggles and titters and her name whispered—as usual. *As always!*

Eva chewed the inside of her lip and her eyes fell on the unicorn tapestry on the wall. It hung solitary and silent. Tonight, seeing the lonely white creature chained— imprisoned in the fence—made something claw the pit of her stomach. She stood, released her lip from its capture by her teeth and stumbled out of the room.

After that night, the princess made a game of annoying the servants. She gave commands such as; "Find out exactly how many leaves are on the cherry tree in the garden. I must know by noon!" And, "Arlo will be having lunch with me today, so he will need a tall chair, a small hat, and a bib." These orders vexed her personal maids and attendants alike. They soon questioned her sanity, privately of course.

This was not a good thing.

Eva did not care.

One afternoon Brookin found her in the hallway. "I know it must be hard for you, Your Highness," she said. "The loneliness, I mean. Please, come talk to me anytime."

"Thanks . . . thank you." Eva stammered and blinked hard.

Brookin's smile lit the hallway. They squeezed hands and went their separate ways, as royalty and servants do.

That night after dinner, Eva went to Vespers as she had done for years. The colors in the rose window above the chapel altar were fading with the setting sun. Archbishop Brogen murmured over the congregation. Eva murmured with him, reading from the prayer book. Her lips moved out of habit. Her thoughts were far away. Then, her eyes fell on the words: "I am the Way . . ." She caught her breath and whispered, "The Way? *My* way?"

The white robed man spoke a benediction and sketched the sign of the cross in the air. King Cedric walked down the aisle nodding to Eva as he passed, the rest of the congregation walked behind him. Clutching a silver crucifix to his chest, the Archbishop bowed in her direction and stepped into the hallway.

She found herself alone. Again.

Kneeling, she lifted her eyes to the gilded altar and whispered, "It's me. Evangeline. I'll get right to the point. I'm sure you couldn't possibly want me to marry this, this—*Fagan*—or anyone else but Valentino. I know you are busy, but surely you see what's happening to me!" The count's pale face and red-rimmed eyes suddenly loomed large in her mind. She mouthed silently, "Help me. Please! You know what I need. I'm sure of it." She waited. Candles flickered, glistening the tears on her face.

Any other night, Eva would have been up in the sanctuary of her room by now. But tonight, her insides were on fire. She faced the altar—expecting what, she wasn't sure. After waiting a few minutes, she felt silly. *How stupid.*

Expecting an answer. Eva wiped her nose on the sleeve of her purple satin dress. She gathered her prayer book and called herself a fool's fool. Stepping into the aisle to leave, she glanced at the altar one last time.

What she saw rooted her feet to the stone floor. The book slipped from her fingers and slapped the wooden pew. She didn't hear it.

As Eva watched, the ancient tapestry became transparent, and disappeared. The altar opened like a curtain, spilling a soft velvet night into the room, filled with tiny lights. Suddenly, she felt afraid. *What. Is. Happening!* She spun around. "Who's there?" The empty chapel echoed.

She turned again. The altar looked like it had every other night. No velvet night. No tiny lights. The tapestry hung in place. "Must have been my imagination," she muttered to herself. This thought relieved, disappointed, then, terrified her. *What is going on? Am I truly losing my mind, like they say?*

Her pulse pounded in her ears. Or was she being answered? A whispered thought insisted: *That was real.*

The princess picked up her prayer book and went upstairs to her bedroom, dazed. Mattie was waiting to dress her for bed. Eva dismissed her and her old nurse bowed out of the room.

Eva locked her door. Lying face-up on her bed, an ache rose from a deep solitary place. *I missed it . . . missed my answer.* This monumental thought stabbed her, turning her eyes away from the soft round face of the moon in her window. "I'm sorry," she whispered into the dark. "Please, give me another chance. I won't be afraid this time, I promise. Well I can't actually promise that, but I won't turn away." She turned her pillow over to the cool side. "Please. I have to know."

Eva waited, and waited into the night.

Then, she slept.

The night watch sounded off: "Twelve o'clock and all is well." Eva flinched awake. Miserable, she faced the window. The traveling moon could no longer be seen. Her hearth fire was now glowing embers.

Eva stared up into the dark vault of her ceiling and sighed.

A small faint light glowed high above her. "Strange." she whispered. "A light?" Eva folded her arms behind her head and gazed steadily at the light, now joined by two others. Were they real? She rubbed her eyes. *Still there.* A trill of excitement traveled through her body. Then she caught her breath. The three small glimmers multiplied a hundredfold, then became thousands and thousands—a field of living lights slowly swirling in shining clusters above her. She waited, hardly daring to blink.

Eva felt like a falcon with wings outstretched, waiting for an updraft. A breeze encircled her, lifting her from the bed. She was caught up, up—far above the highest turret.

No longer was she in her bedroom. The night sky had become a soft blue blanket sprinkled with stars. Strong arms wrapped her up in the Heavens, as a mother would swaddle her baby. Eva couldn't ever remember feeling so absolutely, so utterly loved . . . so safe.

She leaned back into the arms, against the chest, and closed her eyes, listening to the steady heartbeat of the One who held her. She allowed this measured rhythm to fill her own heart until it spilled over—a warm river of comfort surging through her with each pulse thrum. There was something so familiar about it, more than rhythm, a deep melody flowing, a song heard long ago. Was it her mother's song—or something more ancient still?

How long had she been there? She didn't know. It could have been seconds, minutes, days. Years.

Finally, a voice spoke: "I love you, child."

"Who are you?"

"Who have you been talking to all these years?"

"Oh . . . So, You *have* been listening?"

She felt the radiant warmth of a smile. "What do you think?"

"You know . . . what I think," she said simply.

"Yes, I do. But, I love hearing your voice." There was a pause. "Just so you'll know, some call me the True Voice and some the Way. I answer to both."

She considered that for a long moment before asking, "Will you help me?"

"Help is coming. I'm sending you a special friend. And as you know, I've given you a gift, in fact one of my very best. You will know what you must do to fully open the gift when the time comes . . . And to answer your question, it's not the *tears*. It's where the tears come from."

Wait! A friend is coming? "Oh, thank you for the *gift* . . . and, how will I know this friend?" she whispered, sensing her bedroom beginning to materialize around her—not wanting to return—not yet anyway.

"You will know. You'll recognize the signs." She was gathered in the great arms, then, slowly descended until she felt, once again, her soft feather bed under her back. "But wait, what if I *don't* know—the signs, I mean."

The voice seemed to shimmer inside her. "Don't worry, you will. And know this, even though you won't always see me, I am there with you, for all time. You invited me, remember?" The True Voice said.

Eva caught her breath in delight. Once again, an ocean wave of joy washed over her. She hardly dared believe this was happening.

"For always. And that's a promise," the True Voice echoed deeply.

But wait. "What *is* the gift?"

She felt the presence, but heard no answer.

Eva made a mistake that next morning . . . a big one, that would cost her dearly. She told Mattie about her experience in her bedroom, holding little back.

So, among the castle staff, and soon, across the countryside, Eva's loss of sanity was no longer hinted at, but now a '*known*' fact. She had become: The Dread Lunatic Princess who hears voices. Only Brookin, Archie, and Bea remained loyal, refusing to listen to twisted lurid tales.

Ignoring this, Eva's life went on as before, filled with lessons and training. However, she felt as though her world had shifted sideways. Her nightmares stopped. Everything looked different; felt different. Everything *was* different . . . brighter somehow.

She was sure of it.

He greeted her...

9

Mrs. Fledge was feeling under the weather the next Monday and couldn't teach. She sent word for the princess to read the next chapters in her history and Latin books, which Eva did.

"I have to stop thinking about Father and Count Fagan," she whispered to Arlo, who curled up in a spot of sun on the rug. "Something will show up… an answer… it has to." Not thinking of anything better to do, she stacked her books neatly on the floor by her writing desk. Then with the toe of her right foot, she nudged the top book until it teetered on the edge of the others. *One more touch and it will balance perfectly,* she held her breath. It wobbled for a few seconds then pitched over the side, knocking the others across the floor. Arlo opened one eye, glanced accusingly in her direction and stalked out of the room.

"You're right of course. I'm wasting time," she said and followed him down stairs. She saw the stable through the window and thought about her horse, Destry. *Good old Destry.*

Stopping by the kitchen, she found some carrots freshly pulled from the garden and laid them in a basket. "Where's Brookin?" She asked Rhona.

Rhona curtsied, smiled and pointed toward a white cloud of flour hanging in the air. "That'd be her there, showing the dough who's boss, Your Highness."

Whump! Wham! Another white cloud rose from a long table, and through it, she saw the shining face of Brookin. Eva stepped past rushing cooks, butchers, bakers, scullery maids, and servers—and made her way to the table. She wanted to invite Brookin to come to the barn with her. *No, that would be frowned upon.* So, for a few moments, she stood and envied the jovial jostling of the kitchen staff.

"G'morning to ya, Your Grace," Brookin said, her face rosy from the heat of the oven. In the sweltering small room by huge iron oven doors, Brookin grinned. "I pray all is well with you." She lifted the enormous lump of dough, slammed it on the kneading table, and folded it over onitself. "You'll see this dough again tonight, only it'll be a bit more appetizin'—loaves, breadsticks, and rosemary rollups." Her eyes twinkled, and she gave the lump another hefty punch.

Eva laughed. "And, why beat the poor thing like that? What's it ever done to you?"

Brookin snickered, breathing hard. "I have to pound the air bubbles out, or it'll rise all *cattywhumpus* like." She gathered the lump, slammed and folded it again. "Have a go?" she beamed with pleasure at Eva's fascination.

The princess hesitated only a moment, then rolled up her green satin sleeves and stepped around the table beside Brookin. Their eyes met. "Don't mind if I do," Eva smiled and grabbed the soft lump.

After only a minute of lifting, slamming, and folding the unwieldy lump of dough, Eva's shoulders ached. She glanced at Brookin's bare, muscular arms and felt a twinge of envy. "And back to you, O Mistress of the Mysterious Ways of Bread." Eva flourished her an exaggerated bow and stepped back from the table.

Brookin giggled and lifted the lump of dough ceremoniously and slammed it down with mock pomp. "A thousand thanks for the title, Your Highness."

"Ah, yes . . . and, please, call me Eva. When it's just us, I mean. Would you?" the princess asked, embarrassed by the quiver in her voice. She cleared her throat to hide it.

"Oh, Your Majesty, I mean Eva . . ." Brookin's eyes brimmed. "You honor me too much. I hardly know what to say." Her face flushed a deeper rose.

Eva pulled her sleeves back down and buttoned the lace cuffs. "This is just between us." She looked in Brookin's clear grey eyes. "I will do what I can to help you, whenever I can. And that's a promise."

"And, I will do the same . . . Eva. Not that I actually *would* have the opportunity—to afford help to a *princess*, that is. But I *would*." She looked down at the table shyly. "And . . . it doesn't matter what they say," she exhaled forcefully and smiled. "I believe you *know* what you saw. Some folk can't abide mystery, so they mock it."

Eva squeezed Brookin's dough-covered hand. Their eyes met wordlessly. The princess left the bakery smiling.

Eva grabbed her carrots and stepped out into a golden morning in the courtyard, blinking back brightness and tears. She had the enormous thought: *I have a friend.* "Brookin is my friend. Thank you," she whispered.

She hummed, walking around the pea vines in the kitchen garden and down the well-raked dirt path past the low-roofed chicken coop. She paused, looked for Alf, the stable groom, and stepped into the pungent smelling stable. Strolling around overflowing hayracks, she found Destry's stall. He greeted her with a low whinny.

"Hullo, old boy. Did you miss me, Destry?" She held out one of the carrots, and he chomped it down to a nub, then, ate the nub from her flat hand. She loved the feel of his soft whiskery muzzle and warm breath *huffing* on her palm. "Of course you did," she smiled. He shook his brown head as if in answer and grunted softly, eyeing the carrots in her basket.

When he'd finished all the carrots, she rubbed his satiny back and shoulders, running her fingers through his dark brown mane. "I know what you need," she said and began untangling and sectioning the long coarse hair into strands with practiced fingers. "You've missed this haven't you?" She smiled and leaned on the solid curve of his shoulder.

Eva, tucked away in the shadowy stall, braided quietly. It was a place out of time . . . a place of peace. Sunlight streamed through every crack in the stable roof, lighting the dust motes in the air. She thought once again of the night after vespers—of being wrapped up in the starry heavens. *Did I fall asleep? Was that a dream?* The only thing she could point to now, was the difference she felt on the inside. And how long would that last? No answers came.

The door creaked loudly and voices entered the quiet stable. It was Alf and two stable boys: Farin and his younger brother Merrol.

"Alright, you two been asking, so today's the day I'll be telling you—*both* o' you!" Alf announced, hooked two thumbs under his black suspenders and whistled low. Eva was going to greet them, then thought better of it and stepped further back into the shadows. *I'm eavesdropping,* she thought guiltily, but then salved her conscience: *Maybe I need to hear this.*

The boys sat on two short milking stools, leaning forward, bare toes burrowed under the straw. Alf began to speak, his voice deepening in tone and timbre to that of a storyteller:

"The legend of Morach has been passed from mouth to ear for decades. This is no children's bedtime story, so get ready. It's a tale told by King's guards around campfires and by villagers in front of a warm cozy hearth—with cups o' tea to make the wild darkness feel far removed."

"You *ready?*" He didn't need to ask. They were. "I'll tell it to you like it was told to me." They nodded silently, eyes wide. Merrol slipped his hand over and hooked pinkies with his brother.

"Long ago," Alf began. "A certain count and his province fell upon hard times. As a remedy, he taxed the people without mercy to fill his dwindling coffers. After years of trying to 'squeeze blood out of a beet' as they say, he realized it was futile. His people were dying on the vine. Something else must be done.

One day his advisor told him of a wizard so potent he could make the count's desire for wealth and power come to pass. The wizard was sent for, and seeing an opportunity, he decided to pay the count a visit.

"What do you want from me?" asked Zimrod, for that was the wizard's name.

The count explained he only wanted the usual: riches and power, and if long life could be added to the enchantment, that wouldn't be a bad thing either. Privately, he was surprised that the wizard looked so young.

Zimrod asked for the night to think it over. "In the morning," he said, "I'll tell you what I can do for you."

The count treated him royally. He was served a delicious dinner and given the best bedroom in the castle. *I hope he notices how well I'm treating him,* thought the count.

The next morning, in the count's private study, the wizard spoke first. 'Here's what I will do for you,' he said pulling a small glass cylinder from his black bag. The count was puzzled. He couldn't imagine what this lackluster thing had to do with his request. *Why, I could fit that in my pocket*, he thought. But, he wisely held his tongue. The wizard saw the doubt on his face and smiled. He had seen this look before.

"Contrary to what it appears, this glass vial contains nothing ordinary," he said. "The liquids inside will bring you your desires. It will happen every time you turn it over and shake it vigorously while you count to ten. Then set it on the table immediately." He looked at the count. "Do you understand what I just said?"

The count looked puzzled. "Not exactly sure what you *mean*." he paused. "Will bags of gold coins then appear in my room?" His eyes gleamed, imagining such a wonder.

"It could happen," said the wizard. "But, not in the way you think." They both looked at the vial. "As you use it, you will grow richer and more powerful than you can imagine in this moment."

The count reached for the little container.

"Not so fast," he said, stepping back from the count. "You would do well to listen to all I have to say. Then, decide to strike a bargain with me—or not." He said this seeing that the count was filled with greed, and would do or say anything to get what he wanted.

"All right, all right, yes—get on with it then," the count said, no longer concealing his impatience.

Zimrod smirked. "As I was saying, you will get what you want, and here is how it will be accomplished: First, nothing will happen until the bottom of the sun's circle touches the horizon. Second, these two liquids never want to combine." He held the vial up to the candle, 'As you can clearly see.'

The count saw two colored liquids, black and green. The transparent green liquid floated on top. "Just what *are* those?" He asked, feeling a bit squeamish; but he shoved that down, knowing he was viewing his future.

"The black liquid, as you might have guessed, is dragon's blood. The green is the juice from a plant that grows in only one place in the world. I am the only one who knows this, having *dispatched* my partner," the wizard said evenly.

"Dispatched? Ah, yes I see—of course."

"So, I can't fully answer your question, or I would be forced to kill you as well. I'm sure you understand. *Yes?*"

"Oh *yes*, certainly!" The count wanted to appear in league with this wizard. He straightened the lace on his cuffs and chuckled knowingly. But, beads of sweat appeared on his forehead and trickled into his beard, betraying his cheerful chat with the wizard.

"Back to the instructions... As soon as these liquids are combined by shaking, they will begin to separate," said Zimrod. "The black will start descending; the green will rise. At this moment, you will begin your descent into the form of a dragon—a powerful dragon soaring over lands," he added, seeing the count's dismay. "Taking what you wish and destroying what displeases you. You will have exactly two hours to accomplish your will as a dragon without conscience, before the liquids are fully separate once again. At that point, you will assume your human form."

This was an offer the count had not considered. Many things about it appealed to him. But he had questions. "And how about fire... will I breathe fire?"

A rasping cackle came from the wizard's mouth. The count thought it a strange ancient sound from one so young, but put it aside. "Fire?— Yesss," he hissed. "But only once during your transformation hours, so choose wisely how to use it!" He collected himself. "As long as the black droplets are still traveling down, you will remain a dragon. But remember—when the last black drop separates and comes to rest in its place, you will return to your human form, wherever you are. This will be so for many years," he paused, placing his hand on the vial. "Then there is the consideration of my payment..."

"Yes, yes," said the count, anxious to take the wondrous enchantment for himself. "You will be paid handsomely. I'll see to it!"

"I'm not interested in your gold," Zimrod said coming a step closer. "But first, there is something else you must know; every time you shake the vial to gain riches and work your will on the countryside, the nature of a dragon will grow inside you. However, you won't need to worry about this. It won't be seen by anyone until later—much later," the wizard assured him. "And as for *my* payment; I will receive a small portion of your life in exchange, as my wages, every time you fly as a dragon. It will be an amount so small you will likely not even notice; not for a long time anyway." The wizard smiled his knowing smile. He had seen this stupor come over many.

"So this dragon nature will be hidden away... and how will it show up later?'"

"It will be decades before anything will come through to your skin. And then it will just be a few scales, easily hidden by your jacket or covered by a little powder. I don't think you will find it a problem. Oh, and I almost forgot," Zimrod said smiling. "As your human life decreases, your life as a dragon will increase until one day you will no longer need the glass vial. You will *be* a dragon—Won't that be *wonderful?*"

The count thought a moment and decided this would indeed be splendid. People died, but dragons could live for a very long time, ages in fact.

"So that about wraps it up," the wizard said, tying his bag closed.

The count grasped his hand and shook it. "A gentleman's agreement," he said, eyeing the vial.

Zimrod cackled again. "We have an agreement, yes—but a *gentleman's?* We are above such things are we not?" He spoke as if to a child. "All I'll need from you now is a lock of your hair, if you would be so kind?" he handed the count a small knife.

This was quickly done, and the wizard poked the black hair into a pouch in his bag. "Well, I must be going," he said. "Don't bother to see me to the door. I know the way out." With that, he turned on his heel, but then turned back again. "Oh, and by the way," he said raising an eyebrow, "The only thing you will have to watch out for is two with hearts of gold; a prince and princess, they must be. These two could be the end of you."

The count was horrified. "What do you mean—?"

"You know, hearts that are truthful, kind, brave . . . unselfish, all that rot. Don't worry though I don't know of any, and I seriously doubt you will find such." He thought a moment. "No, none come to mind." He hoisted his bag onto his shoulder. "And, don't send for me again. I'll find *you* if I need to." And with that, he left.

The count was relieved. *I had no idea dealing with wizards could be so wearing. And about this heart of gold thing,* he thought. *I now have the strength of a dragon. I'll quickly snuff them out like a candle flame. No matter.*

He turned his thoughts to a more pleasant subject. *Tonight, I will see what this dragon can do.* He rubbed his hands together gleefully and sniffed. "The dragon must have a name," he muttered. "A fitting reptilian title—an ancient *antedeluvian* name to inspire fear and dread—*MORACH!*"

At the name, Alf leapt to his feet and shouted. The boys shrieked, fell off their stools, scrambled up, and bolted out the stable door. Alf chuckled and called after them. "Alright boys! It's only a story!" They were nowhere in sight. "I guess they had to go change their knickers," he chuckled, tucked in his shirt, and walked out the door.

Eva had fallen against a hayrack and was pulling her braid loose from a piece of wood. She was glad only Destry saw her leap when Alf shouted.

Even though she knew it was only a legend, deep inside something about it felt real. True. She pulled the last bit of straw from her hair. "And legends have to come from somewhere," she informed her horse. He nuzzled her for another carrot.

The back of the count's neck flashed through her thoughts. She laughed at herself. *Dragon-man!* A tremor traveled up her spine.

Remember

10

Eva wrote the legend down in her diary and went on with her life. Days rolled into weeks, weeks became months, and months became years. Except for all-too-brief times with Brookin, Archie, and Bea—Eva's days were strung together like dull tarnished beads hanging heavy around her neck.

She also noticed with increasing alarm; Count Fagan came more often, and her father grew ever more distant.

Loneliness clung to her, a constant, cruel companion. But somehow, writing in her diary helped.

Tuesday, August 4ʰ

Everyone is asleep, but me. Probably.

Yesterday I was sixteen years old . . . so what? How am I supposed to feel?

Valentino, what are you doing right now?

I finished my schoolwork—and deportment lessons from the ever-dreadful Duchess Constanza Flaunt. I'm not sure which is worse, her sickening perfume skunking up the room or her ridiculous son Fritz! Her blonde wig makes her look a foot taller than she truly is. I wonder if she's bald under there . . . Must see about that sometime.

I see how she looks at me when she thinks father doesn't see. She's a disgusting vulture. She wants me gone. In fact, I'm sure she would love to see me dead; then, she and Fritz could take over. I wonder what she thinks of Fagan. They both seem to want the same thing—the kingdom of Dunmoor—such as it is. Well, they can't have it. I AM THE RIGHTFUL HEIR. I have plans. Good ones.

Father seems determined to marry the countess. HORRORS—NO!

I wonder if he knows her son Fritz is eyeing his treasure room with a bit too much interest. I'll tell Father to keep an eye on him. He'll probably say I'm too suspicious for my own good. Probably.

Where are you tonight Valentino?

I know you are still alive. I feel it.

Are you out with the King's patrol? Are you safe?

It has been over four years. You said you would come back after four years. Are you dancing with another princess tonight? HOW COULD YOU?

And why haven't you written me?

My dearest love, I miss you so.

Eva understood the unspoken rules well. But, tonight at her writing desk, anger prickled the back of her head. Leaping to her feet, she wanted to kick and scream! Of all people in the castle, she surely had the least freedom. She was the most *managed*. She was sure Mattie and others reported to her father of her whereabouts. Her home, this castle, was her fashionable, lavishly decorated *prison*—and her father was the warden. Daggers of quiet desperation stabbed the base of her neck. She locked her diary. This time the key went around her neck on a golden chain. Eva paced to the window and stared down at the moonlit countryside.

No one must ever read this but me!

In the past month, Eva had walked into her bedroom at five unusual times. She'd found Mattie hurriedly tucking her sheets under the mattress where she kept her diary, every time. Not thinking much of it at first, Eva had gotten what she came for and left.

But I didn't always lock my diary then—so stupid. And often at night, she'd found it in a slightly different place than where she'd left it. *Maybe that's why Father's been acting even stranger than usual.* It hadn't occurred to her, until now. Mattie was *spying on her* and reporting more things than just her whereabouts; she was exposing things from her diary to her father and his council—her very *private thoughts!* Eva's face burned with shame and outrage . . . *But, Mattie was my nurse. She's looked after me since I was born! Why would she do such a thing?* Eva could almost feel Mattie's fingers on her scalp, tugging gently as she braded her hair. She pictured her nurse's broad face, grown so different now, anxious creases framing her aging eyes and mouth, and then she knew: *Father's paying her.* She sighed with furious grief.

Princess Evangeline reached inside the silken pocket of her nightgown and pulled out the white stone. Struck by moonlight, it shone in her pale palm, somehow comforting. For the thousandth time, her finger traced the crudely carved inscription: EVA+VAL. Then blowing out the candle, she padded over to her bed. Lifting the edge of her mattress, she kissed the stone and tucked it into its place for the night.

Need to find a better hiding place, she smiled acidly.

Her eyes blurred with helpless fury. *How can I bear this? How much longer?* She pulled her coverlet up to her chin and stared out the window.

Valentino, are you really still alive?

Her mind rejected this crushing question with no answer. "Please let him be alive," she whispered into the darkness. If I somehow knew he lived, that would be enough for me—well, almost enough." Rolling up in her covers, she pictured his face in the circle of the moon. Her jaw relaxed. The bitter tide ebbed away.

"Valentino, can you see the sky? The same moon shines on you and on me," she whispered into the dark. "Come back to me." Eva stared out the window until the moon had risen to the top of the arch. Her eyes closed. However, her words traveled out the window and leapt on the back of the wind to do their secret work that very night.

In the mountains of Tirzah, a prince lay on his bedroll and gazed at the full moon. Muffled snores rumbled around the dying campfire from the castle guard on his patrol.

"Do we see the same moon, you and I?" Valentino whispered.

Their whispers found each other in the night sky and whirled in a windy waltz.

After breakfast the next morning, Eva was summoned to the conference room for a meeting with her father. She braced herself against the heavy door and pushed.

"Ah yes, come in. Have a seat," he said motioning to the hearthside chair across from him.

She sat warily on the edge of the seat, letting the fire warm her feet.

"How is school going these days?"

"Very well, Father," she answered, knowing full well she wasn't here for a schoolwork report.

"That's excellent. Keep up the good work," he said and reached into his jacket pocket. He pulled out a small, blue satin drawstring bag and handed it to her. "It's time for you to have this. It was your mother's." Eva hesitated. He prompted her: "Go ahead, it's yours now. She wanted you to have it when you were sixteen."

Eva glanced at the face of the mystery she called Father. She pulled open the bag and looked in. There in its dark recesses glimmered a round object, she slipped it into the palm of her hand. It was a gold locket, delicately inscribed with leafy swirls and tiny rosettes.

"Father, it's . . . it's beautiful." she murmured, overwhelmed, and cautious.

"Well, it's all yours now." He smiled, seeing her delight. "Put it on," he said evenly. "I've tried to open it many times. No success. The hinge must be bent—can't think of any other reason for it. But it's a pretty enough bauble, closed as it is."

She slipped the golden chain over her head. The locket lay warmly on her skin, right below her collarbone.

"When you marry, your wealth will be shared with your husband, but this is yours alone. Yours to do with as you will . . . Maybe to hand down to *your* daughter one day." He leaned back in his chair and passed a hand over his eyes.

Eva leaned back in her chair as well, savoring this rare moment. Was that a tear in the corner of his eye? She noticed how tired he looked. "Thank you, Father—so much."

"You are most welcome. You actually have your mother to thank. This was her desire. One of the last things she said." He stopped, the words catching in his throat.

They both sat silently, staring into the fire for a few moments. King Cedric broke the silence. "I know she would have wanted you to marry well," he said quietly, almost to himself.

"Father, about this marriage thing," Eva began. "Valentino and I . . . could you and King Justin not patch things up . . . work out your differences?" she asked, using her friendliest, most reasonable voice.

"Silly child," he growled, flapped his hand impatiently and sat forward in his chair, "There is so much more to this than you know. And, I've heard reports that Valentino along with the crew aboard the the *Galina* were shipwrecked off the coast of Jakar. Of course, you can't trust every report you hear—"

He didn't finish. Gasping, Eva leaped from her seat and shouted: "No, it's not *TRUE! LIES!!*" She held her breath, letting eight long seconds slide past while storms and ships and floating bodies thrashed in her head. Everything stood still—everything, but the whooshing of her heart in her ears.

She bolted from the study and ran upstairs to her room. Her sobs hung in the dank air of the castle. Slamming her door and locking it; she fell across her bed, wailing into her arms until her breaths came in hiccups and snatches. Arlo padded across the coverlet and nudged her forehead with his wet nose, then laid his paw on her arm and waited.

After crying until she had no more voice to weep, she lifted her head and inhaled. Deep. Long. Ragged. She wiped her swollen eyes on her sheet. "Do we believe this, Arlo?" He purred. "Val and I . . . we're supposed to . . ." Eva pulled the golden locket over her head and held it in her hand. Light from her window struck it, making it gleam. "And I don't believe *you* won't open either," she muttered, her breath hiccupping with suppressed sobs.

Somehow this locket her mother wanted her to have must open. Surely it wouldn't be one more closed door. She examined it. The two round golden halves were separated by a deep side groove. She placed her fingernail in the seam and felt something. A tiny latch! She pushed gently and the locket sprang open, as if it had only been waiting for the right fingers.

She gasped. The two golden halves were displayed in her hand. On one side was a small painting of a smiling woman with dark hair, kind eyes and a crown. "Mother, you definitely gave me your hair," Eva mused, wiping her nose on her bedsheet. "And something about your mouth." She touched the face lightly with her fingertip and examined the other half of the locket. There was a word decorated by vines and flowers. Eva could just make it out: *DREAMS*. Circling it were more tiny words:

FIDUCIAM SOMNIA

FIDUCIAM IN VIA

Eva stared at it for a long minute wondering why her mother would send her a message in a foreign language. She suddenly recognized two of the words from her Latin book:

IN VIA— *"It means: THE WAY, Arlo!"* Eva's eyes lit up then she frowned. "The way. What *way?*" she said aloud. Feeling a rush of frustration mixed with hope dance on the top of her head, Eva walked down to her schoolroom as quickly as she could without attracting attention. She pulled the Latin textbook from the shelf and flipped through its pages, deciphering the rest of the message.

Finally it bloomed in her mind:

TRUST YOUR DREAMS

TRUST THE WAY

"It's a message. Somehow my mother knew. She sent me this," Eva muttered. "Valentino is alive. He has to be," she whispered to Arlo. "Now what?"

12

$\mathbb{T}$hat very night . . .

In the elegant dining hall in the castle of Tirzah, King Justin leaned over the table. Leaning earnestly toward him from the other side was his son.

"Valentino, you've exceeded my expectations in everything. Highest marks from your teachers at Jarleth *and* you've proven to be a trustworthy leader." He beamed at his son. "Well done."

"Father, I . . ." Val felt his throat tighten. "Thank you."

Reaching across the table, they grasped each other's forearms and rising from their chairs, soundly clapped one another's shoulders.

"And just to be clear, I will feel confident transferring the kingdom into your keeping," he said his voice growing thick. "When the time comes." He paused and looked his son in his dark eyes. "You and your *queen*, that is."

Knowing what they were about to deal with, they both sat again, leaning back in the plush, midnight blue chairs. The prince noticed his father's shoulders sloped as though they were weighted down.

"Yes, there is something I've been meaning to ask you, now that I'm home." Valentino shifted in his seat, finding the right words. He raked a hand through his black hair.

"You know I'll give you anything I can," King Justin said and rested his elbows on the table.

"I do know that Father." He exhaled forcefully. "It's about what I told you years ago. Remember that day we were banished from Dunmoor?"

"That wretched day."

"It's about Princess Evangeline."

"Yes, yes—and Ciel's wing, I remember."

"That's right, and our vows," the prince reminded him.

"Oh," the King said, his eyes clouding. "You were both so very young."

"That we were," Valentino leaned forward. "But in all my time spent with other princesses, royalty, and the like, I've not found one as true and good."

"That was a long time ago, Son. People change."

"Not her, Father. Not Evangeline. She has a heart of gold."

"It hurts me to tell you this, but you'll hear it eventually. Best we should talk about it."

Valentino leaned back and folded his arms over his chest. "What have you heard?"

"Reports have come, even to me, that she has grossly insulted suitors and gives outrageous commands to her servants."

"She's just lonely father."

"Yes, maybe. And living with that father of hers . . ." He cleared his throat. "And other reports have come."

"Like?"

The King met his eyes. "That she's mentally unbalanced. Some say—a lunatic, hearing voices; her mind taken by faerie beasts."

The prince looked as though he'd been slapped. "Surely not!" He gathered himself. "So, according to the ridiculous voice of popular opinion, she's an angry, outrageous lunatic." He laughed sharply. "Well that's gossip for you. I, for one, do not believe it."

"Good point. Word traveling through jealous hearts and flapping lips cannot be trusted," he said. "But, we must know how much truth is mixed with these lies. Your future queen must be of sound judgement and temperament to stand and rule beside you—above reproach."

"So, she has a bad reputation. That's not who she is. I know her! We grew up together, remember? She's so very kind and extremely smart —brilliant, in fact—and about the voices." He shrugged his shoulders. "I just don't know."

"Brilliant she may be, but without a heart that would put her desires aside for the good of the people—her intellect is worth nothing. I cannot, in good conscience allow someone like that to share the throne with you. Nor should you, *Prince* Valentino! The future of the kingdom and people of Tirzah depend on your choice of a bride." The King leaned back in his chair wearily. "Need I remind you—you were born a *prince* not a peasant."

"I'm sure what I've told you is true," said Valentino. "In fact I would stake my life on it—" He clenched his fist. "She just needs a chance to prove it."

"I want to honor your wish to keep your vow to the princess, however, we must know if her heart is still as pure and good as you say."

"True enough." They were both silent for a minute. "I love her, Father. We *belong* together." Valentino declared. "She told me about her plans to restore Dunmoor once she is queen. She can do it, just . . . married to the right person." Then, without really meaning to, Valentino slipped his hand down in his jacket pocket and touched a small golden thimble.

"That is a noble desire, Son." The King beamed, his dark eyebrows lifting. "If this is still and truly her heart, it would be my joy to send letters of intent to unite our kingdoms through your marriage. I think I know who was behind Cedric's ridiculous accusations anyway." He frowned briefly and shook his head. "So the only thing remaining . . . how to know what is true about Evangeline?"

"Father, what are you thinking?" They both leaned forward over the table.

King Justin stroked his dark, curly beard thoughtfully and mused, "What if you . . ."

13

he next morning, Eva discovered a secret.

It was her scheduled history time. Her teacher Mrs. Fledge was gone for the day. Mattie was in the kitchen helping Rhona. Eva was bored beyond belief with memorizing dates of foreign wars and sat staring out her bedroom window at the Trion Mountains. From these mountains, Eva knew she could see the mountain range bordering Tirzah.

"There has to be a way to get past the guards and to the top of those mountains—without being seen," she muttered, remembering the cursing rake wavers from her carriage-riding days.

Pacing about the room, chewing her thumb, she discarded one plan after another. Squatting on her heels in front of her hearth, she absently picked up the fire-iron and poked the coals. Sparks swirled up the chimney. Brandishing the metal iron like a sword, she jabbed the carved wooden hearth. *Take that!* Starting at the top and working down, she aimed for the center of each rosette, poking a black dot of soot on each one. The end of the iron struck the final flower in the lowest left panel.

Instead of a solid *thunk,* the poker tip disappeared into the flower; there was a click, a *whirr,* and the panel swung open. Eva fell back onto the carpet. Then fascinated, she peered into a dark opening large enough for a small person to squeeze through. *I've heard of such things!* She chewed the inside of her lip, and lit a candle from her hearth fire.

Taking a quick look down the hall, Eva closed her door, pocketed her flint and picked up the candle. She slipped into the secret passageway, carefully closing the panel behind her. Brushing through shrouds of cobwebs that could blanket a horse, she bumped into trunks, shelving and stacks of books from ancestors long dead. Musty smelling clouds of ancient dust made her eyes feel gritty. Then to her horror, she sneezed! Holding her nose she tiptoed over to what looked like another door in the wall. *No telling whose bedroom I'm behind. Maybe they'll think it's mice.* She stifled a giggle. *Sneezing mice!*

She saw a dark opening in the wall just beyond her. *Stairs!* Quietly stepping down what seemed to be hundreds of spiraling steps—Eva finally found herself in a large room, so high, the light from her sputtering candle only lit the rising cloud of dust around her, leaving the ceiling dark. *Anything could be up there . . . watching me.* Something small and dark scurried in the corner. Fear crept under her skin. "Stop it!" She whispered fiercely. "You've made it this far. Now *Go!*"

In the flickering light, she could see two doors, a tall one, and a low one. To her right, two crude wooden shelves were cluttered and piled with ancient books, glass bottles, a mirror with a broken frame, and a spy glass. A set of moose antlers balanced on top, strewn with cobwebs and the dust of ages. Under the shelf hung a large key ring heavy with keys. Eva lifted the ring off its hook and almost dropped it. She tried fitting the first twelve keys in the lock of the high door with no success. Sighing, she tried the thirteenth key, a long, rusty flat one. It slipped in and found the stiff springs. Shrinking back from the *scraanking* and scraping, she listened, her hand on the door latch. *This is the lowest part of the castle*, she thought. *So it's either the door to the outside or the dungeon.* But, which door was what? The stairs had twisted and turned to the point it was useless to guess.

Finally, she pushed her weight against the heavy oaken panel, and the door opened a crack. What came through that crack was a stench so foul, she heaved the door shut. *The dungeon!* She thought of the people confined in misery and filth down there while they awaited her father's good pleasure to call them up for a trial. "A trial," she groaned. "In a pig's eye."

Stepping to the right, she found the key to the shoulder-high door and pushed hard, bumping it open little by little until she could just fit through.

Eva stepped out into sparkling sunlight and birdsong, with a thick veil of cobwebs draped over her hair. Blowing out her candle, she stuffed it and the little tinderbox into her pocket. She then shoved the door almost shut. *For later*, she thought, stepping through tall weeds.

"Just enough time to get there and back before dinner," she said and untangled her hair.

Since she saw no guards, Eva casually walked around the front corner and behind the cover of the yew hedge toward the bridge to the mainland. It was day, so the drawbridge was down. Rounding the last corner, she nearly tripped over Archie on his knees weeding around the yew hedge. She gasped.

"Good day to you, Princess," he smiled. "Did I startle you."

"Startle? Not you Archie, never you. Only just surprised," she laughed lightly. "Going for a little walk now, no problem." Eva felt her face flush as she passed, brushing dirt and cobwebs from her skirt.

Archie watched her walk away. "Just a thought, Princess. You may want a guard to go with you. I hear Morach's moving about in these parts lately."

"Well, thank you Archie. I'll just be back shortly—And there's no need to mention this to anyone." This last comment was thrown back over her shoulder as she hurried down the raked path to the gate. "And give my best to *Bea!*"

Archie raised a worried eyebrow, stood up from his work and fanned his face with his hat, watching her.

Now Archie knows. Well, no matter. I'll be back by dinner tonight. As long as there's no trouble, who cares.

Making sure the front sentry was facing away—she quickly crossed the stone bridge over Tidal Inlet to the mainland. Eva skirted Cedricsburg and walked for what seemed like hours . . . much longer than it had looked from her window. *It's possible I won't be back in time for dinner*, she thought. *But, who cares? I sure don't.*

Finally, she found a narrow, twisting path leading up to the cliff she'd seen from her bedroom. Following it, she scrambled over fallen trees and crossed a rocky stream.

And, there it was.

She stepped out of the dense forest into a high, sunny meadow, shading her eyes from the sun. Its golden circle almost touched Tirzah's western mountain range.

Just a peek, then I'll go back, she promised herself. *It'll be fine.*

Wading through the tall grass, she looked out over the cliff. There they were, the southern borderlands. *Valentino's mountains.* She steadied herself on one of the boulders balanced on the edge of the cliff, and it shifted under her weight. She jumped back. *I could shove it right over this cliff!* She rocked it back and forth easily. *Better not. What's below?*

Squinting, she saw a knight on a grey horse enter the forest on the nearest hillside. He disappeared from view. *Could it be Valentino? Possibly. Will I even know him? It's been four years and five months.* She tossed a pebble over the cliff. It *pinged* far below. *How could Father be so, so . . .*

Shrugging in grief, Eva looked out over the valley. "Too many questions. Needing answers—*answers!*" She shouted. Her voice echoed back, mocking her.

The trees to her left suddenly exploded with a raucous din of crows, flapping and lifting, darkening the sky with deafening clamor. Diving and weaving back and forth, they moved as one frantic screaming black body into the southern sky.

Her heart pounding, Eva moved under cover of a stand of birch trees at the base of a hill. The crows, now in the distant sky, were swallowed by gathering clouds. The unnatural silence they left behind made the hair on her neck raise. *Was it my voice that spooked them . . . or something else?*

As if in answer, an enormous weight landed on the hill above her, its bulk smashing and splintering branches—crushing her question. She slid farther behind the trees as the immense creature scraped and settled on the boulders. Talons of fear pierced her shoulders, paralyzing her for a moment—but only for a moment.

Peering through bare branches, Eva saw the red eye of the sun melt across the mountains.

She remembered then. Sunset.

It was too late.

Mattie bustled into Eva's bedroom to see what was keeping her from her dinner. "Must be in the schoolroom," she muttered walking downstairs. The room was empty.

Then kitchen and castle staff looked high and low with no small commotion. Finally, after the entire island had been scoured and the castle thoroughly investigated, they asked Archie. He said she'd gone for a walk.

The servants approached the throne room, and Mattie broke the news to King Cedric.

"What!!" he exploded. "Why do I pay you all *exorbitant salaries?* This will change! *You,"* he said pointing to old Mattie. "You will gather your belongings and be gone by sundown tomorrow. And be glad to leave with your life!" The servants gasped. Mattie covered her face with her apron. Her shoulders shook. The kitchen maids glanced at each other in horror. What would she do now? What would her family do? Then, each one thought of their own families.

"Get out of my sight, the lot of you!" he shouted. In less than ten seconds the room was vacant except for the King. "Guards!" He bellowed. Four armed men stepped into the presence of the fuming king: Modrun, Peredor, and Glynne, his best trackers. "Leave now. Find her before dark." He turned to the fourth soldier. "Banon, you keep watch from the tower. Inform me immediately with any news."

"Yes, Sire!" they said in unison, thumping their fists over their hearts. Then turning on their heels, they marched out of the room. King Cedric strode back to the privacy of his study.

Why didn't I have her more closely watched? He berated himself angrily. Glenda the new courtier came to mind. *She would have been on top of this! I would have been informed the minute Edwina left the castle.* He thought of the meeting scheduled for domestic affairs in two days. The muscle in his jaw clenched. *Fagan will be here. Time enough for Edwina to be made presentable. I'll appoint Glenda as her new lady-in-waiting. She'll see to it.*

The king thought of Mattie with only a small twinge of conscience. She had gotten plenty of extra money over the past three years for gathering 'sensitive information' about the princess. *If she handled it well, she should be a rich woman by now.* He frowned and gazed out the window of his study. How she handled her life was none of his concern, he decided, and put her out of his mind.

The sun dipped below the horizon.

Morach.

Peering up through the branches to the top of the hill, Eva saw fading light glint on dusky green scales. Feverishly, she tried to remember how long he would be in his dragon form. The legend—what was it, one hour, two, or three? And if she could see *his* scales, could see *her* through the branches. She squeezed under a shallow rock ledge. *But, when he flies down to the meadow— what then? I'll be trapped under this ledge in full view—his next meal!* She trembled uncontrollably. Terrified. Plans rushed through her mind, elbowing each other out of the way.

Eva heard her teeth chattering and breathed, "No!" She clenched her fist and shed fear like a dirty stocking. *You're not a cornered rabbit!* Her breathing was shallow, quick. *This is a reptile. A big lizard! Now think!!*

She waited. But after what *seemed* like years, listening to sounds of grunting, squealing, and crunching on hapless animals, lunch rose in her throat. She swallowed forcefully. *A fire would be a diversion—and, I could use a smoke screen to get across the meadow and into the woods.* Eva felt the comforting bulge of her flint and candle still in her pocket. *If I can just get into the woods, I can make it home . . . I'm sure I can.*

Noiselessly she scooped up dry leaves at her feet and piled them against a dead-looking tree trunk. Then during a particularly loud bone-shattering crunch from above, she struck the flint. Sparks ignited the dry tinder, lighting the base of the dead tree. Soon, tongues of fire skittered up the trunk. It became a huge blazing torch.

The crunching stopped. *Did he fly away?* Eva couldn't see. She couldn't wait to find out. Flames leapt from tree to tree. The roaring crackle of this wildfire made it impossible to hear what else was going on. Her smoke-stung eyes poured tears. Her lungs convulsed in a fit of coughing, Limbs flamed, crashed, and splintered beside her, fell behind her, and spewed sparks on her dress.

Her mind, white with horror rose up; something deep and primal taking over. Eva grabbed her smoking skirts and ran. Bolting from her hiding place, she sprinted out into the open meadow, counting on the smoke screen—but not on the dragon flying high above it.

She pushed her legs faster, harder, teeth jarring, feet pounding. She heard her own voice, a nightmarish, wheezing scream.

Darkness overtook her, his shadow a living thing. Morach's *shriek* shattering the air— *"K-e-i-i-i-k-k-k!"*

Engulfed, throbbing with the blast, Eva screamed again. Her mind burned white-hot with one thought—her writhing body pierced and snatched into the sky by the creature's claws. She glanced over her shoulder and—*horrible*—her satin shoe caught on a root. Gasping, sobbing, she sprawled headlong onto the ground, her cheek feeling every rock. Talons *whooshed* by, tearing her shoulder and the side of her face. She tasted blood and dirt. Felt no pain. Not yet. Hands gouged, bloody, Eva heaved up to her knees, fell, dragged herself up again—and dashed for the woods *and safety.*

Morach wheeled overhead. Then, plummeting down, he closed the distance between them. Eva heard the whistling drone of enormous wings. Steeled herself for searing pain—*any moment.* Why wouldn't her legs stop trembling and run *faster!*

As if in a dream, she heard the rhythmic thud of horse hooves pounding the ground to her left. She ran on, not believing her ears. Then looking back over her shoulder, she saw a sword flash bright in the dwindling light. Something like a small tree trunk slammed across her back, pinning her to the brambly ground. An unearthly screech filled the clearing. Wings savagely beat the smoke-filled air. The dragon circled once, twice, then, flew out over the cliff, blood pouring into the valley below from the stump behind him.

In a moment, her breath was pressed from her lungs by the immense, writhing weight of Morach's severed tail. Panic-pain knifed through her. With her remaining strength, she tried pushing up on one elbow—tried throwing off this *thing* pouring dark blood the length of her body; gouging her back. Crushing her slowly. Through a dark veil of tears and blood Eva saw—*what*—a *scale* on the ground beside her? *The scale of a dragon?* She stretched out her free hand. Touched it.

The world went away.

The next thing Eva was aware of was the feeling of warm pressure on her lips and air in her lungs. Again, air filled her chest, or was *blown* into it, expanding it as much as her dress would allow. More warmth. *Lips.* Her eyes fluttered open. The knight immediately flipped his visor down, shielding his face from view. She opened her mouth to speak and coughed a rasping croak. With that, a tide of pain engulfed her and she moaned, squeezing her eyes shut against it.

Something cool splashed on her forehead. Was it rain? More came, sizzling on the still-twitching tail beside her. She vaguely heard drops *pinging* on the helmet of the knight as he lifted her from the ground.

Am I dreaming? Her hazy mind tried to grasp the questions as they floated by. *Did a knight truly just save my life?* Eva heard his deep sinewy voice as if from a great distance.

"You're safe now, Princess. You can relax."

Before slipping back into darkness, she felt two strong arms lift her over a horse's saddle.

How much later, she didn't know, Eva became aware of the sound of men's voices. The saddle pressed hard into her ribs, but that would have to wait. It was safer to keep her eyes shut. Stay limp. *You're unconscious remember?* Eva listened.

The first voice said, "I can see by your colors, you ride with the Tirzan guard. What's your business on Dunmoor soil, *Knight?*" She heard the *zhhiiing* of his sword being pulled from its scabbard and recognized Modrun's voice.

Eva clenched her teeth. A male voice beside her head said, "You see well, my friend. Do you also see who is under my cloak?" He said this gesturing toward the Princess draped over his saddle, covered by his blue cloak. He carefully lifted the rain-soaked hood so her slashed face could be seen.

The three men murmured. Modrun sheathed his sword, dismounted, and walked over to the knight standing beside his grey horse. Both men had their helmet visors down, hiding their identity.

"Who might you be—?" He took a clanking stride closer to the Tirzan knight.

"A friend," came his answer. "No one of importance to you; and no one you want to annoy with your trifling flummery.

Modrun, at a loss for words, lifted his visor and scratched his forehead. "Fancy words for a knight," he remarked. "And though you are beyond the approved boundary lines, it's plain to see you've rescued the princess—"

"— And will bring her safely home," the knight interjected. He took a few steps holding his horse's reigns.

Peredor and Glynne, still mounted, muttered darkly about spies. "Hold up!" Modrun said gruffly. "*We* will take the princess from here. We've tracked her to this spot."

"Good job, Men. Just a bit late," the knight said evenly. "You would have found her, or what was left of her, after she was mauled by yon dragon." He gestured behind him in the gathering twilight, then, paused, seeing their alarm. "Don't trouble yourselves, he's gone, and with a little reminder not to bother the princess again." Eva heard the smile in his voice filtering through his helmet visor. "When I found her, she was quite . . . let's say *displeased*."

"Yes, quite," observed Modrun. "Plain to see." He glanced at the massive tail still moving in the smoke covered field and again at Eva's bloody face. He cleared his throat. "And now to the business at hand. Because you've rescued the princess, we will overlook your trespass and let you live. After we deliver her safely home, news of your deed will be conveyed to King Cedric. You will be rewarded handsomely, no doubt." He stepped forward to lift Eva from the saddle. Raindrops now pelted the group, dribbling and *plinking* on their armor.

"I neither require, nor will I accept a reward from the king." Glancing down, the knight saw Eva's eyelids flutter slightly and knew she was listening. "She's soaked through, and night falls. She must have her wounds seen to quickly and get into warm clothes."

"Yes, right," Modrun intoned. "Glynne, fetch her to her horse."

At this, Eva slid from the saddle of the knight's horse and landed on her feet. "I can fetch myself, thank you." She swayed dizzily and steadied herself on the horse's side. Her head and shoulder felt like they were on fire.

"—A moment, Princess," said the mysterious knight. "You have deep wounds, and I would guess, a fever rising by now." He reached in his saddle-bag and pulled out a muslin pouch filled with dried herbs. "Here, eat, then drink as much water as you can hold. I've rinsed your face and shoulder once."

"Thank you . . . what are these?" she said looking suspiciously at the dried leaves, roots, and twigs.

"Among other things, Fever Few, Ginger and Wolf's Bane. You'll need to get these in you quickly." He opened his water skin and rinsed her cheek and shoulder again, seeing the angry red spread from the claw-marks. Her eyes were dull, glassy. "Here, quickly," he urged.

She took the herbs, began to chew, and made a face. "This is disgusting."

"If you want to live to see the sunrise, Princess, you will do as I say. Chew them well. His claws carry a deadly poison—it brings a slow and painful death. That part isn't told in the legend."

Modrun and Glynne stepped back and exchanged a look. They waited.

The knight held his water skin to her lips. "These *disgusting* herbs have saved my life more than once. Now *drink.*"

She was glad to rinse the bitter taste out of her mouth. She gulped the water down until her sides felt like they might split. She handed him back his water skin and smiled. "Wait. My head stopped pounding!" Her face felt suddenly cooler. She looked at him, ignoring the mud oozing into her shoes. "I can't thank you enough, Sir." She stepped away from the horse and turned to the knight in blue. "This is twice you've saved my life—in one day! What is your name?" She said this addressing the sliver of his face she could see through the helmet visor. "And how did you know I was in trouble?"

"You may call me a friend, Your Highness," he said mounting his horse. "I saw the smoke and came to see what it was about. Glad to help." He reached back and pulled the sky-blue cloak from where it lay on his saddle and handed it to her. "Please do me the honor of accepting this cloak for your trip back to the castle. No need to return it." Once again, she heard the smile in his voice filtering through his helmet.

Modrun muttered, "Your Highness, we have a blanket for you on your own horse's saddle. One in the colors of Dunmoor I might add." Eva turned and glared at him. He fell silent.

Then turning back she said, "I . . . I can't thank you enough, my friend. I hope we meet again in better circumstances."

"In better *or* in worse times, that is my hope as well, Princess." He turned to the trackers. "And now, I bid you farewell. Go in all good speed, in the Way."

"In the Way," they murmured, their horses jostling in the light rain.

He turned his horse back toward the meadow. Eva watched him go, then, called out, "A thousand thanks—and please give my very best regards to your prince!"

"You have my word on it, Your Highness!" His words floated back to her.

The rain began to fall in earnest, quenching the hillside fire. Fat drops and smoke screened his retreating silhouette from her sight. Eva sighed, swung the blue cloak around her shoulders, and fastened it with its golden falcon clasp. She then mounted her horse and turned toward home—and her waiting father. The thought almost quenched her delight at being rescued by the mysterious Tirzan knight. However, the question remained fixed in her mind: *Could that have been Valentino? Were those his lips on mine? And, why didn't he give me a sign?*

The princess touched the gilded ridges of the soaring falcon pin holding the blue cloak around her aching shoulders.

A sign would have been good.

14

Eva and the king's guard clattered across the drawbridge and into the courtyard.

Eva stumbled to her bedroom and splashed warmed water onto her face dripping over her washstand. The water in the basin turned dark pink. *My blood.* She blanched, her head reeling. The effect of the herbs had worn off. Her cheek and shoulder felt stung by a thousand bees. She turned to the looking glass, touched the swollen furrows of her wounds and winced. *I'll go see Archie and Bea.* Their cures were faster and better than the royal physician's bag of painful tricks.

Eva's throat contracted as a wave of nausea rose up. She turned from her marred reflection and retched into her basin, fever blotching her face.

Mattie knocked briefly and bustled into the room. "Your father is wanting to see you, Princess. This will be my last night with you." Eva heard a tremor in her voice. "Let me help you change into something more suitable." As Mattie stepped over to unlace her dress, Eva turned to ask her what was wrong. Her nurse caught sight of Eva's left side and reeled backward. "I...I—" she stammered and fainted on the spot, dropping to the floor like a sack of wheat.

"Poor old thing," Eva murmured. With trembling fingers numb and cold, Eva covered her nurse with a blanket. She unlaced her own dress, peeling it from her shivering body, and wrapped herself in her coverlet. Remembering to retrieve the scale from her pocket, she snipped a patch of cloth from her skirt stained black with Morach's blood, then tied the scale up in it. *There . . . safe 'til later. Should be at least three drops of dragon blood there.* She slipped it under her mattress next to the white stone, finding it curious that the scale was still warm. Seeing Mattie still laid out on the floor, Eva folded the blue cloak carefully and hid it in the bottom drawer of her wardrobe, then pulled on a dry dress.

Archie and Bea probably don't know I'm back. She could still hear Archie's voice in her thoughts, warning her. *Why didn't I listen? Have to get over there. Bea can fix this.* She touched her hot throbbing cheek gingerly. Her left eye was almost swollen shut.

Eva stole down the back stairs, the poison from her wounds now surging through her veins. Fever ravaged her body. By the time she was out the castle doors, she could barely swallow, and her legs weren't working right. *So tired . . . dizzy . . . terrible day.* She gripped the wall. *I can do this . . . have to.* Her thoughts lurched, racing wildly despite the dark sticky fog creeping into her head. She pictured her father finding her dead on the ground during his morning walk. *Would he rush over and hold my lifeless body to his heart? Would he weep for me, his only daughter?* She had no answer. Her eyes, clouded. She wiped tears away fiercely. *Have to just make it to the cottage. Will be alright . . . if I have to crawl.*

Eva finally stumbled, delirious, to the white gate of the cottage. Lit by the moon, Archie paced out on the front walkway. She heard him shout something. *What was it?* Her head felt detached from her body. *Rats, I'm going to—!* Eva slumped into the daisies beside the fence and knew no more.

Sunlight shone warm through her eyelids. *Morning?* She opened one eye. *Where am I?* "Is that bread? *Bea's* bread?" she croaked, through her desert of a throat. Then, remembering, the running, the dragon, the knight, *everything,* her stomach heaved.

How long have I been here? Her head began to clear. *At least I can hold two thoughts together. But, my eye—!* "I can't *see!*" She rasped, panicked. Eva explored her face with her fingertips. Her left eye was held closed by a large bandage that covered the entire side of her face.

Bea came quietly into the room with a tray. Seeing Eva was awake, she sat on the bed beside her, setting tea, toast, and jam on a small table. "So wonderful to hear your voice, little one. We thought we'd lost you for a minute." Bea helped Eva sit up, braced her back with a pillow, and checked the poultices on her shoulder and cheek. "Better, much better," she said softly, peering down her nose through smudged spectacles.

Her voice often reminded Eva of the coo of a dove. She smiled up into Bea's clear blue eyes. "Am I in your bed?"

"That you are, Princess. The best bed in the house." Her eyes crinkled with pleasure.

The only bed in the house, thought Eva. She knew they'd given the other one to Olwen when he moved to the mainland. *I must somehow find a way to thank Archie and Bea; to repay them, somehow.* "One day when I'm queen—" she began, and felt her throat tighten again.

"Shh... Now don't talk. Just drink this. It's good for you." Bea held the cup to Eva's lips and warm bitter-sweet liquid trickled down her throat, relaxing it. Eva swallowed loudly and took a deep breath.

Archie slipped quietly into the room and sat in a chair by the foot of the bed. She looked at their worry-lined faces and knew neither one had slept.

He put his warm, rough hand over hers. "We sent word to the castle of your whereabouts. Everyone was frantic with worry."

"Everyone?"

"Your father," he added. "He was very concerned." He paused. "Something you should know in the days to come, Princess," Archie said gravely. "This is the season of fall harvest. Olwen tells me Morach sweeps over lands plucking up what he wishes and leaving charred villages behind. Especially in Tirzah, farmers have to hide their harvest in the woods or in caves to protect it. They've learned ways to drive the beast away, but so far no one has—" Archie stopped himself.

"—Put an end to him?" She finished for him.

"Yes, that exactly. A prince or princess with a heart of gold." He looked in her face, eyes solemn.

The thought of facing off with this dragon, any dragon, made her head spin. Plus, there was the *'heart of gold'* thing. *So, that takes me off the list.* She leaned back in the pillows, suddenly paler.

"Someday, someone will," she whispered, thinking of Valentino armored on horseback, his knights around him. "I'm sure of it."

"Now Archie," said Bea, raising an eyebrow. "Don't trouble the child. You can see she needs more rest."

Archie smiled his *'yes'*.

"You're so right, as usual, Doctor Beatrix." He stood up with a conspiratorial wink at Eva. "I'll just leave you two and be off to the castle. They'll want to know of your progress." He beamed at them both fondly and turned to leave the room.

"Wait a minute, Archie," Eva said weakly. "I . . . I just wanted to thank you . . . you know for the warning yesterday." Her face prickled. "I was so stupid."

"You're welcome. And I wouldn't say *stupid*, Princess. Headstrong perhaps. Just glad you came back to us in one piece." He patted her covered foot, a smile lifting his crinkled cheeks.

"Yes, we are," Bea said in her no-nonsense voice. "Now, we'll let the child get some sleep, shall we?" She stood up. Archie put on his hat and did a shuffle-y little dance out the door.

Eva decided she didn't mind being called a child by Bea. She snuggled down under the worn patchwork quilt, smiling. Content.

Bea felt Eva's forehead, nodding happily. "The herbs have worked their wonders once again." She arranged the bedside tray neatly. "Now, Princess, I was serious about rest. You *must* have it to heal fully." She patted Eva's hand and tucked the covers under her chin. "Call me if you need anything." She blew a kiss and pulled the door almost shut behind her.

Staring drowsily at the ceiling, Eva's thoughts whirled. However, one thought rose up higher than the others: *The knight called me "princess" before the guards told him who I was. How would he have known—how indeed!* Her eyelids were heavy from the herbal tea and lingering effects of the poison. She yawned and rolled over, promising herself to explore that question . . . later.

Sleep closed her eyes.

Late that afternoon, Eva braided her hair into some semblance of order and stepped into the warm kitchen. Bea and Archie caught her up in a round of hugs, danced her around, and *ooohed* and *ahhed* at her quick recovery. She made her way to the castle on wobbly legs, pockets bulging warm with Bea's crusty, golden biscuits.

Walking down the garden path, dark shadows seemed to snatch at her shoes, but she pushed that aside. Eva tried to imagine what her father would say and how she should answer. *Maybe this will be a good time to say what I saw at the banquet on Fagan's neck. Maybe not.*

She trudged up the wide stone stairs and down the hall. Standing outside the heavy oaken doors of her father's study, she pushed. They opened.

She walked in.

15

Servants found many reasons to walk down the hallway, slowing beside the King's study. Shouts filtered under the door.

"*Care for you?* Don't be ridiculous . . . you are my daughter! How could you say such a thing?"

The King stood looking out the window, hands clasped behind his back. The room was warm from the hearth. For that, Eva was grateful. It would have felt cozy except for one thing; the princess had the distinct feeling she had walked into a trap.

"I'm glad you care, Father," she murmured, feeling her head begin to pound again. She inhaled the familiar smell that had seeped into the fabric of the room: a mixture of polished mahogany, pipe tobacco, and hot wood ash on ancient stones. Leaning forward in the velvet chair Eva held her hands out to warm by the fire; her insides tight.

"And, Archie and Bea are good caretakers, but they do have their limits . . . and, look at your cheek!" He turned and leaned close, examined her cheek, actually seeing her for the first time since she entered the room. She was glad her bandaged shoulder was hidden under her shawl. "Make sure you see the physician in the morning. He can tend to that properly." He settled back in his chair rubbing his eyes with the heel of his hands. "Oh, what *next!*" he muttered.

She touched her cheek with the back of her hand and winced. "I'll get it seen to." She thought better of letting him know how far superior Bea's herbal remedies were.

"Well then, back to what I was saying: You've dishonored and spurned every suitor in the known *world!* I brought them all to the castle for you. None of them would have you now—none except Count Fagan. He still wants to marry you, even after your rudeness over the years." He leaned over the green ottoman. "Your marriage prospects were already slim, and now this!" He pointed to her cheek. "Well, no matter. Count Fagan is not here now; however, he is the *one* you will wed. We have signed a contract, a binding agreement, joining our lands through marriage. The issue is settled. He will make you an excellent husband."

Eva had felt this coming, but hearing it said out loud by her father made the hair on her arms rise and her teeth clench. "Then he must have changed since I last saw him." Her voice sounded brittle, as if any moment it might shatter into a million pieces. To overcome this she spoke faster and louder. "Besides being overly pleased with himself, I, I saw something on his neck . . . *tried* to tell you. I don't think you understan—"

He held up his hand, bristling. "Here's what I *do* understand: no thanks to you, I still have market advantage in the count's province. But, his generosity aside, you have grossly insulted twelve dukes, eight earls, and fourteen princes. This has not helped trade in their provinces and kingdoms." His face flashed red. "I have run out of patience—and money."

His voice echoed from the stone walls. Knowing it was useless to say another word, Eva bit her lip. Clasping her hands in her lap kept them from shaking, but couldn't stop her father's betrayal from twitching down the corners of her mouth and bringing her shoulders up to her ears. She stared at a place on the wall past his head, avoiding his pitiless eyes. *No pity. Not for me.*

He cleared his throat and sighed pointedly. "We have debt—huge devastating debt! The contract is signed. You will now have someone to help you keep your foolishness under control." He stopped himself. His face drooped in weariness. "I'm done. It's settled. You will be married in two weeks time. Leave me." His voice dropped low and he rubbed a jeweled hand over his face. Turning away from her, he looked out the window.

Eva was mute with shock. Tears couldn't touch what had just happened. In that moment, she felt absolutely alone. Leaving the room in a daze, she wandered hollow, aimless in the hallways, her feet ending up in her room.

Lying across her bed, she tried to stop breathing.

What must be done

16

The minstrel's long strides carried him swiftly toward Rabblesdell. Shadows lengthened across the rutted dirt road. He glanced into the woods, shifted his backpack, and quickened his pace. Soon enough, he felt smooth cobblestones beneath his worn leather boots as he entered Rabblesdell, Dunmoor's market town. *Big business*, he thought, seeing merchants hurriedly doing their last deal of the day and closing up shop.

One by one, windows glowed with warm yellow light, defying nightfall. He smelled the aroma of food well cooked, and his empty belly complained loudly. *The Purple Pig . . . got to be somewhere close-by.* He'd heard tales of this tavern, famous for its delicious fare.

Raking a hand through his onyx black, shoulder-length hair, he re-tied it with a strip of deer hide. Settling his tricorn hat on his head, he turned down a side street, his nose directing him. Two blocks down, he saw the sign—PURPLE PIG TAVERN—swinging from a metal rod. The door under it suddenly flung open, and a flood of noise and delicious smells tumbled out, along with a man and woman swaying together, laughing and singing.

Looks like the place. He tightened his leather belt, feeling the comforting bulge of his money pouch tucked inside his brown jerkin. He walked into the boisterous din. The first thing he saw was a roasted suckling pig displayed on a long wooden table. Stuffed with carrots, onions and cornbread dressing, it was surrounded on the platter by potatoes, parsnips, celery, and apples. His mouth watered. Breakfast seemed a year ago.

A very round woman wearing a stained apron handed him a pewter plate. She said: "Help yourself! Pay when you're done." She nodded to the back of the room. Behind a wooden table, a rotund man with a dark, pointy beard and curled mustache caught his gaze. The man nodded. He smiled a humorless smile and narrowed his eyes.

"Is that the owner?" the minstrel asked her.

"What's *that?*" she called out over the noise.

"I said, does that man own the place?"

She nodded, and gave him a pat on his shoulder, gesturing toward the pig on the platter. "Eat!" she yelled cheerily.

He found his place among the merry-makers and piled his plate high. It had been a long day.

He lingered long over the meal, swapping stories with fellow feasters. When he was too full to take another bite, he glanced back to the man at the table, not surprised to find himself being watched.

Threading his way through the crowd, he stood in front of the owner and smiled. "What'd I owe you?"

"That'll be 15 Tika, Stranger."

"Name's Traveler. And, I'll pay the 15 Tika, or I can offer you something else.

"Would it have anything to do with that lute case on your back?"

"That it would, good sir." He smiled, shifting his heavy pack.

"Well then, let's see what you've got," the man said leaning back in his chair. "If I like your music you've got a free dinner and a roof over your head tonight. If not, you pay like the rest of my customers... name's Dimm," he said as an afterthought.

"Agreed," Traveler said, tipping his hat.

The owner watched him move a jumble of chairs aside on a low makeshift platform, set his pack down, and pull his lute from its wooden sheath. The minstrel seemed unaware of anyone in the room as he held the instrument to his ear and plucked the strings. When it was tuned to pitch with his voice he looked up and smiled. Voices in the room hushed to a low murmur, and clatter settled down.

With a quick bow, he said, "Ladies and Gentlemen, I've traveled far and wide, over hill and under hill. And tonight to entertain you gentle-folk, I've songs to sing and tales to tell." He strummed his lute.

A loud voice called out of the dark smoky room, "What's yer name minstrel?"

"Shaddap, ya daft old toad. Let the man play!"

Ignoring this, he said, "I am what many of you are—a pilgrim. I'm called Traveler." He bowed low, strumming his lute again. The room hushed.

He smiled privately, knowing what he was about to sing:

"While walking one day in the wild wood,
I happened across a young maid;
Her dress was all spotted and tattered,
She looked up at me and she said:"

(He paused and smiled broadly, clapping his hands in rhythm, the room erupted in loud clapping, and foot stomping.)

"Please tell them I'll be home in the morning,
You can say I am safe where I stand;
Someone else can slop the hogs,
Boil the clothes and feed the dogs,
Old Bossy can be milked by other hands.
Other hands,
Old Bossy can be milked by other hands . . .

I can't say I'll be back in the morning,
I'll be sleeping 'neath the shining starry sky;
But today I'm gonna spend,
Where the river rolls and wends,
The breeze'll blow me home by and by.
By and by
The breeze'll blow me home by and by . . .

When the old mule begins to grow white feathers,
When the duck leaves the pond to pull the plow.
That is when I will be home,
Then my feet will cease to roam,
Until then my bed will be a pine-y bough.
Pine-y bough,
Until then my bed will be a pine-y bough . . ."

The minstrel flashed a grin at the clapping stomping crowd. Whistling and shouting broke out with cries for more!

The night went on like this only more so, until, one by one, sleepy tavern-goers crept off to their beds.

When the last song was sung and tables cleared, Dimm walked over. "Mighty fine songs," he said, clearing his throat. "Sleepin' rooms is filled minstrel. Take a place by the hearth if you like—not soft, but warm and dry enough—a roof for the night. Reckon it's better'n you're used to."

The minstrel had expected as much. He thanked him and laid out his bedroll in front of the dying fire. When all was quiet, he propped up on one elbow and gazed into the glowing embers.

He would be gone before first light, of that he was sure. Knowing what must be done—and soon—filled his thoughts. *Better get some sleep.*

He called on the favor of the True Voice, rolled over, and slept the sleep of those who journey on foot.

17

The princess slept fitfully that night, waking suddenly before first light of dawn. Thankfully her dragon-fever was gone, but something worse had taken its place. Hopelessness. It had leaked in, spreading like a bitter swamp. No way out. She must marry the count. *Then what? Am I to be the sacrificial offering? And where is my Valentino?* Eva had no answers. But even with all this, a small voice inside said, "Do not give up. Remember your mother's locket."

Eva climbed out of bed, clutching the golden locket around her neck. Standing by the window, she watched the sun rise, then, decided to go see Brookin in the kitchen before her grim Tuesday duties. Picturing Brookin laughing and punching a lump of dough almost made Eva smile while she picked out her dress for the day. Almost. *Maybe we can talk this afternoon,* she thought.

It was only after her thirteenth birthday that Princess Evangeline started dreading Tuesdays. Actually, it was what always *happened* on Tuesdays.

King Cedric thought it wise to groom his daughter to help shoulder the burden of the kingdom, so on Tuesdays, she would sit on her small throne beside his large one and be mute witness to the edicts passed down. At first, she had relished the chance to sit beside her father. But, the dreadful judgements that flew from his mouth—week after week, month after month, year after year, made Eva groan out loud.

The days of sentencing for those unfortunates happened after their imprisonment in the stinking dungeon . . . and only when he saw fit to hear their case. She shuddered, remembering her glimpse through the door.

This weighed heavily on Eva while she dressed and hurried down to the kitchen for some of Brookin's bread and jam. She looked around. "Rhona, where's Brookin?"

"I'm sure *I* don't know Your Highness," Rhona looked at the floor and bowed away from her. *Odd!* Eva thought. *Is she angry?* She puzzled over this while walking down the hall to the throne room.

Another judgement day, no different than the last, she thought. But, she was wrong.

The castle guards escorted two men and a woman at spear-point into the throne room.

From her position on the dais, Eva couldn't see their faces clearly until they came close. The guard growled, "On your knees!" They each dropped to their knees on the polished marble floor. The woman turned and looked up into Eva's eyes; tears streaking through filth on her face. Something about that face . . . *Brookin!* Eva caught her breath and gripped the arms of her throne, white knuckled.

If her father heard her gasp, he disregarded this sign of weakness. Looking the prisoners over, he found nothing of worth. "What do you have to say for yourselves?" He said this only as a matter of form. The King already knew their offenses and his judgement over them.

"Your Majesty," said the first man named Folvick, "we throw ourselves on your kind mercy. Our families and ourselves is wastin' away. Starving we are." Humick, the second man nodded. "My brother and I—"

The King held up his hand, stopping the discourse. "Clearly, you and your brother have been planning this thievery for quite some time. And *you*, kitchen wench," the king glared at Brookin. "Employed under the shelter of my roof and stealing food for rabble from under my very nose. Eight loaves, a ham, and two wheels of my best cheeses—gone! Did you really think no one would notice?"

Brookin knew better than to protest, or even answer. She kept her eyes on the floor, avoiding King Cedric's burning gaze.

"It is one thing to steal, and quite another to steal from the crown," he intoned, as if reading from a book.

Eva saw where this was going and *knew* she had to stop him before he spoke the words. "Father," she said interrupting. "I would ask for leniency in this case." Heat flooded her face. Hoping her father wouldn't notice the sudden color in her cheeks, she arranged her expression expectantly.

The King paused, his scepter in midair. "Why ever for?" he said, annoyed to be stopped mid-judgment.

"The circumstances, I believe, would call for mercy at this time." She sat up straighter. "Grave illness and starving children—"

"Thievery is thievery," he broke in. "And stealing from the crown is a capital offense."

The three prisoners kept their eyes on the floor. She heard Brookin sniff faintly.

He paused, letting the silent space of an eternity slip by, then, turned to the three. "I should take your heads off for this, but considering Princess Edwina's words, I will let you live. However, not without a reminder," he said evenly. "Tomorrow morning before the cock crows, you three will lose your right hands. The royal executioner will take them off as an example to other *would-be* thieves."

The brothers both uttered a cry. Brookin gasped and slumped in a heap to the floor. They knew this was a sentence of slow death. They would be unable to work and be reduced to begging . . . begging in a poverty-stricken kingdom.

"Guards," King Cedric said. The prison guards poked the brothers up from their knees with their spear points. Brookin, in a deep swoon, was dragged by the arms back to her cell behind the brothers.

Princess Eva, feeling her father's heavy scrutiny, watched them disappear into the dark hallway.

No crying. I will do what must be done—before morning! These thoughts were hidden behind her composed, closed face.

"Next!" announced the king. And quietly to his daughter: "Don't even think about it. They are under twenty-four-hour guard."

"What would make you say such a thing, Father. Don't you trust me?" She unconsciously touched her scarred cheek.

The King snorted. "Guards! Next!" he commanded.

The next prisoners were brought in. Morning limped on until lunch.

Eva excused herself after lunch saying: "I need rest to recover from my ordeal. I know you'll understand if I take a nap, Father."

"Yes, rest yourself," came his distracted reply. He was already involved in other matters of court.

Eva went upstairs for a short while, then, when all were busy elsewhere, slipped through the halls and gardens to Archie and Bea's cottage.

Breathlessly, she burst through their door. "I have a plan!" she gasped.

"Child—what is it?" Archie and Bea exclaimed. Bea spilled her cup of tea and hastily blotted it up.

"Brookin . . . and the two men—brothers—have to get them out!" Eva leaned over the table, gasping for breath. "Have to get them to the mainland—before sunrise! Your doves, Archie! Can you send a message? — Get a *rowboat?*"

"Princess, have a seat," he said offering her a chair at the table. "So you have a plan? *You* can release them before—" He pressed his lips together. Brookin was loved by all who knew her, including Archie and Bea. News had spread fast.

"Yes, I'm certain of it," she said. A teacup and plate with cinnamon honey dunkers were placed in front of her. She nodded her thanks to Bea. "So, we need a rowboat left on the shore near the hemlock trees. I've checked; the guards can't see that stretch of beach from their posts. I'll take care of the other details tonight."

Bea poured tea for Eva and exchanged worried glances with Archie.

Eva took a deep breath. "Once they're on the mainland, they can disappear."

Archie looked out the window. The sun was dipping low in the sky. "There's no time to waste." He pushed back from the table. Opening a drawer, he pulled out a strip of paper. Eva watched him write the message.

URGENT — NEED BOAT AND OARS LEFT ON SHORE BEHIND HEMLOCKS ON NORTH SIDE OF ISLAND — BEFORE **9:00** TONIGHT

"I hope you're right, Princess. If they're caught, they'll lose more than their hands." He turned to walk out to the dove lofts, motioning Eva to follow. "And, if *you're* caught—?"

Eva hadn't actually explored those possibilities yet. "I'm not worried about me. Nothing to lose at this point." She closed her eyes, released a trembling sigh and shoved the thought aside.

Walking outside with her, Archie said, "Princess, I . . . that is, Bea and I are here to help."

"It's alright, Archie. There's nothing else to be said or done. And please don't worry." The sound of gentle cooing from the loft was somehow soothing. She watched as Archie gently lifted Celeste and attached the message band to her leg. Speaking softly to his bird to calm her, he and Eva walked to the middle of the garden and released her into the late afternoon sky. She caught an updraft and was lifted high above the castle and over the inlet.

"The wind's with us today," Archie observed. Celeste was soon just a speck in the sky. "Now," he said. "Let's hope Olwen knows two people with boats."

"How will we know?"

"No time to send a reply. So to answer your question, you won't—know. Not until tonight when the four of you go to the water's edge." Archie's face pinched with concern. "The drawbridge will be up. Do we have a back-up plan?" His brow furrowed.

Eva was silent for a long moment. *Hiding? Swimming in the ocean currents?* "No," was all that came to mind. She turned to face him. "Well, thank you, Archie. And if I don't see you again . . . if we get caught, you and Bea don't know anything."

"Just don't get caught."

"That's my plan."

18

That night after Vespers, the princess lay on her bed, waiting. A sleepy hush would soon steal over the castle. Her signal.

She hadn't returned to the hidden bowels of the castle since her discovery four days ago. *Too risky!* Eva felt the scrutiny of many prying eyes. Hushed whispers in the hallway let her know she was being discreetly watched. Glenda, her new lady-in-waiting and Hazel, the chambermaid, had bedrooms on either side of hers. They slept with their doors open. Her father was taking no chances.

Eva explored ways she could possibly escape… *and then what? How would I survive? I'm stuck. The villagers hate me for riding through the kingdom in the golden carriage while they starve. And they despise my father. They would surely turn me in for reward money—and I wouldn't blame them!* The thought was crushing.

She hated being a part of the whole greedy mess. *When Mother was alive, this would never have happened.* Remembering stories of the good Queen Lenore planting orchards and establishing apprentice schools and orphanages made hot shame creep up her neck. *The Good Queen*, she thought bitterly. *And now, my life is over. I'm sold off to a monstrous murderer.*

Eva thought of her reputation. *Maybe Count Fagan will hear how horrible I am and break the marriage contract with Father. I know what they call me.* When spoken to her face, she was Her Highness, Princess Edwina. Whispered behind her back, she was many things and none of them good. *Maybe that's really who I am;* she blinked back sudden tears; *a dreadful crazy lunatic.*

Then there's old Mattie. Eva's mouth quivered down in the dark and she forced her thoughts to what must be done. Before sunrise.

Soon, the quiet she was waiting for filled the castle. Eva opened her door a crack and heard soft snores from the rooms beside hers. She silently closed her door, put on her dressing gown, grabbed a small flask, and lit her candle. The secret panel opened to her touch.

Nothing had changed. Quickly, she descended the dark, dizzying spiral staircase. Her fingers brushed over the rough, damp stone wall, steadying her steps. Finally reaching the bottom, she found the key ring under the cluttered shelf, promising herself to come back one day and sift through the ancient debris.

The dungeon warden had his sleeping quarters outside the heavy prison door, securing the cells against any possible escape—on the opposite side of the dungeon. He was likely asleep, but she couldn't be sure. Taking the small flask of oil from her pocket, she poured some of the golden liquid into the

keyhole and waited. When it had time to do its work, she silently slipped the long rusty key in the now-lubricated slot in the door. There was a small click, and the door opened a bit. She pushed a little more, bracing herself for the stench. Her candle shone through the door crack, cutting a slice of light through the pitch black. She stepped in, covering her mouth with her dressing gown sleeve to keep from retching. Dark shadows loomed and moved around her. Moving past dark, empty cells, she heard quiet weeping at the end closest to the warden's door. "Brookin!" Eva gasped. The weeping stopped.

Stepping up to the thick, wooden door, she lifted her candle to the square barred opening and peered in. A shaft of light fell on Brookin crouched on a filthy stone floor littered with straw. She blinked into the light. "Who is it?" she whispered.

"Shhh . . . It's me." Eva put her face beside the candle. "Getting you out. Need to find the keys!" She looked around the cell doors where she stood.

Nothing. Walking back toward her hidden doorway, she marveled at how it blended into the wood at the far wall of the dungeon. There was no latch on the dungeon side of the door, just a small hidden keyhole. Her candlelight shone on another key ring hanging on a peg. The princess made herself take a slow breath and lifted the keys. She then poured oil into rusty cell keyholes and opened the prison doors.

Tears flowed freely, silently. Fulvick whispered first. "Your Highness, Brookin *said* you'd come. You'd find a way—!"

Eva's voice was barely audible, "No time for that. We've made enough noise to wake the dead. Quick, follow me!"

They each slipped through Eva's door like swift shadows. Then, closing and turning the key in the door, she heard it. The warden's door *skraaanked* open. "What's THIS!!" he shouted, seeing his cells empty of prisoners. He hurled curses at the walls and ran out the open dungeon door shouting, "Guards, guards—it's witchcraft—*WITCHCRAFT I TELL YOU!!!*"

"Quick!" Eva unlocked the door in the castle wall and they stepped into a moonless night. All four gulped the crisp clean breeze like drowning swimmers coming up for air. Hearing shouts, they flattened themselves against the wall. The sentries left their posts and ran toward the commotion, thinking the castle had been invaded. For a brief minute, the fugitives had clear passage to the dense stand of evergreens bordering the inlet.

"This way." Eva double-checked the watchtower. Empty. They sprinted downhill, threaded their way through dark hemlocks, and finally glimpsed a sparkle of water through thick boughs.

Eva heard waves lapping the shore and silently prayed the boat would be there.

Stepping through prickly boughs and onto the rocky beach, everyone saw what they'd banished from their thoughts—a dark empty expanse of shoreline. No boat in sight.

"It's got to be here," Eva panted as panic rose in her throat. "It's *somewhere*," she declared, making her voice sound confident. "*Wait!*" She suddenly remembered. "Over there! Under the hemlock boughs, *hidden*." Eva grabbed Brookin's hand and they all raced to the skiff.

Fulvic got to the boat first. He shoved it off into the water and shouted over the wind, "We owe you our lives, Your Highness, no mistake about that. And don't think we'll forget this kindness." He and his brother bowed low and helped Brookin aboard.

Eva couldn't speak around the lump in her throat. Her eyes stung watching the boat glide into the dark inlet.

"I'll never forget you, Eva," Brookin called out over the waves. "One day . . ." The rest of her words were snatched away by the wind as the tide carried them out.

Eva suddenly became aware of the peril of her own situation. She turned and fled the beach, finding her way back, unseen, to the secret door.

Three minutes later, she stood on the hidden side of her secret panel, hand poised on the wooden button—listening. No voices, not yet. Was someone there, silently waiting for her to show up? She would have to risk it. Waiting another moment, she stepped through, feeling sweat trickle down her back despite the chill in the air.

Her room was as she'd left it with Arlo still curled up on her bed. Voices echoed down the hall, getting closer. Eva clicked the panel closed and slid under her bed covers.

A moment later, there was a knock on her door. Glenda opened it enough to put her head through. "Excuse me Your Highness, I was told to check on your safety." Her voice feigned humility.

"You may enter," Eva said, sitting up and rubbing her eyes. She cuddled Arlo who looked annoyed.

The lady-in-waiting stepped through the doorway, her candle dimly lighting the room. She furtively looked around while picking up a white stocking from the floor. When she was satisfied there were no prisoners hiding, she said: "It seems there's been an escape, Princess. I was told to lock you in until morning—for your own safety." She looked at the floor to hide a smug smile and twiddled the key ring in her hand.

"That's fine, Glenda. No problem." She looked at the young woman, who was obviously enjoying her task. "Just don't forget to *un*lock me so I can go to breakfast. Sleep well." Eva smiled dismissively.

Glenda dropped to a quick curtsy. "Yes, of course, Your Grace. Please forgive the intrusion." She bowed out of the room and shut the door. Eva heard the lock click, snickered to herself, and pulled a twig out of her hair.

Eva closed her eyes. Sleep covered her like a soft blanket, and she dreamed a dream.

In it, she was walking toward Tirzah. Someone was beside her. She turned to see his face and was lifted up outside of the dreamscape, looking down on her own back and on this man. Something poked out of his backpack and a bedroll was tied on top. Looking closer at the backpack, she saw the words stitched in gold:

A. FRIEND

She felt the warmth of these words and smiled in her dream. Then once again she was beside the stranger-friend walking a woodland trail. Suddenly, everything grew dark. A huge bat-like wing swept the countryside away.

Eva awoke. She sat up and looked out the window. The sky was beginning to lighten.

"So, a *friend*," she murmured, and stroked Arlo's neck.

19

That morning in her room before breakfast, Eva wrote something on a small piece of paper and slipped it into her dress. It remained there, over her heart throughout the day. In the afternoon when her schoolwork and duties were finished, she walked down beside the bridge to the water's edge. Standing with inlet waves staining the toes of her blue satin shoes, her thoughts flew back to last night. *Brookin and the brothers? Surely I would have heard if they were captured!* The thought was beyond horrible. She felt the castle sentry's gaze probe the back of her neck and stepped under the shadow of the bridge. *Just for a minute*, she thought. *No one could object.*

Pulling the small paper from her dress front, she whispered its words:

To the True Voice,
Please,
Send your Wind o'er land and sea,
Won't you blow my love to me?
Lest I die.

She then tore the paper into tiny pieces and held them up in her open palm. A light breeze lifted them, fluttered the pieces over the sparkling water, then scattered them on the outgoing tide. She watched the white shreds disappear under the waves and stepped out into the light.

Footsteps crunched on the stone bridge above her. *The sentry?*

"Excuse me, miss," said a deep, sinewy voice. She squinted up into the sky. A tall bearded man was leaning over the side of the bridge silhouetted in the bright sun. He removed his tricorn hat. "I'm a minstrel seeking an audience with King Cedric. At your service. Would you be so kind as to direct me?"

Eva stepped up onto a small boulder and saw something poking out of the stranger's backpack. His brown dusty bedroll was tied on top. Eva's dream flashed in her thoughts.

"Follow me," she said.

Princess Evangeline and the minstrel walked into the castle courtyard through the open iron portcullis, drawing curious stares.

"Would you like something to eat, and a place to wash up?" she asked noticing his bedraggled appearance.

"You are reading my mind, Princess, is it?" From beneath his dark, heavy beard and mustache, Eva heard the warmth of a smile in his voice.

Very odd. This stranger puts me at ease. Careful! She nodded slightly.

A manservant approached them. "Morven," she said. "Would you show Mr.—what did you say your name was?"

"Traveler, just Traveler, Your Highness," he said bowing quickly and tipping his hat.

"Show Mr. Traveler to a place he can refresh himself and have something to eat. Then, he will be joining us in the throne room. Please escort him there as well." She stepped away from the two of them and smiled formally. "I'll let King Cedric know to expect you soon." *This should be interesting,* she thought and walked through the ivy-covered archway into the castle.

A short while later, Traveler and Morven stood at the entrance of the Throne Room, waiting to be announced.

"Traveler, the minstrel, for an audience with the king!" the sentry declared.

"Enter," the King said, intrigued.

Morven bowed out into the hallway. The minstrel, alone now, walked into the room on the red carpet and bowed deeply, removing his tricorn hat.

"What brings you here, Minstrel?" The king demanded.

"I seek a position at court, and not just any court, Your Majesty . . . your particular court," his teeth flashed briefly under his mustache.

The King was flattered, but his face remained stony. "Why should I consider this request?"

The minstrel balanced the corner of his hat on one finger. "Very simple, Your Majesty. The talk in Dunmoor is that you are a man who likes new things." He gave the balanced hat a light tap, twirling it. "I will entertain you and your guests royally. You will all hear stories and songs you've never heard before." With a flick of his wrist, he tossed the spinning hat in the air. It landed solidly on his head with a light thump.

King Cedric smiled, despite himself. "Nicely done, Minstrel. However, in my travels, I hear many things. How can you be sure I've never heard these before?"

"O King, I say this without boasting, only in truth, because they are all recently written and composed by"—he bowed dramatically, sweeping his hat from his head— "yours truly."

The king gazed at him intently. "So be it. Your trial will be tonight at the banquet. If I hear even *one* familiar song, you are banished and forfeit your instrument. Understood?"

The minstrel chuckled to himself. "Yes, Sire. An ancient folk song or tale will not part my lips as long as I entertain you and your royal guests. You have my word."

"Agreed. Dinner is at seven." The king extended his scepter, and the minstrel bowed out of the room.

Eva sat on her small throne, quietly watching. The way this man handled himself before a King he had just met was remarkable, to say the least. And if she was honest with herself, she was a bit envious of his confidence. But, she had questions . . . lots of them. *Something about him feels so familiar.* This was puzzling. She had no rational explanation, so she tried to put it out of her mind.

King Cedric turned to her. "Well Edwina, what do you think?"

Eva met his gaze squarely and forced a smile. "I think it will be amusing enough. Something different for us." She winced at her too-cheerful voice, straightened the folds of her voluminous violet skirt, and wondered again about Traveler. *Peculiar, this minstrel . . .*

She and her father left the throne room through opposite doors. The minstrel was escorted to his room, smiling and humming.

20

This banquet would be a formal function. The princess knew what that meant. *Father and I will have to stand by the table and greet all who enter the Grand Dining Hall.* Eva groaned and closed her eyes, remembering times past standing in receiving lines with feet aching all the way up to her knees. She looked in her armoire at rows of shoes and picked out the silver, square-toed ones. *They may call me scar-face behind my back, but at least my toes won't be pinched, not tonight.*

That night, dressed in a lavender silk gown with white rosebuds, Princess Evangeline peered through the scrolls of the wrought iron balcony railing at the milling crowd below. The Grand Foyer was full of courtiers, lords and ladies, all jostling for position—vying for a place closer to the King, her father.

She chuckled darkly, "Powder your faces and wigs. That changes nothing—you're still savages in silk and satin."

Slowly descended the curving, marble staircase, Eva adjusted her princess-face. Glenda had braided her hair and looped it in front of her ear so her wound was hidden as much as possible, but the scar still hung below it like the jagged end of a branch.

As she stepped down into the hubbub of the crowd waiting to enter the room, she wondered for the thousandth time why every conceivable ancestor's painted face had to line the walls of this part of the castle. Watching her. She imagined her face painted and framed among them. *"The unfortunate Princess Edwina Evangeline"*, it would say. *"She met with a terrible accident and was scarred for life."* Her smile twisted bitterly.

The hallway leading into the Great Room was packed full of courtiers and council members. She would have to walk through them and join her father. Eva cleared her throat. A woman with a tall, jeweled wig turned and smiled, her mouth crowded with yellowish teeth. When she saw Eva's scarred cheek, she quickly stepped to one side and curtsied deeply, smiling slyly to the duke at her elbow after Eva nodded and moved past. Behind her, Eva heard whispering and tittering. *Who cares*, she thought. *I'll be dead soon anyway.*

King Cedric, with his daughter and the Duchess Constanza beside him, finally shook the last hand, having welcomed everyone into the banqueting hall. He then took his place at the center of the long, white, linen-covered table. Eva sat two seats down facing the orchestra balcony. This was her one bright spot for the night. The minstrel. *We'll just see about you, Mister Traveler.*

The King waited a moment then spoke. "Count Fagan is indisposed and won't be joining us tonight. He assures us there is no need for alarm. He expects to be fully recovered shortly, and very well in time for the joyful day." He paused, letting the roomful of people murmur their questions. "Yes—in two weeks time—a wedding held in this very room." He gestured and Eva stood, her lips pressed tight, her face burning. "The bride-to-be and the groom, the honorable Count Fagan, will be joined as man and wife." Murmuring of congratulations, and a smattering of clapping filled the room. It wasn't the response he had hoped for, but would have to do. The King cleared his throat and motioned for Eva to sit back down. "That aside," he announced. "I am pleased to present for your entertainment—our visiting bard, the Traveler."

Polite applause drifted around the room. Traveler stepped through dark, red velvet curtains into the candlelit orchestra balcony. He bowed low. A beam of reflected light from the chandelier high above struck the lute as he pulled it from its case. Something in the way he held his arm reminded Eva of a knight unsheathing his sword. *Seems so different than the dusty beggar at the bridge today. And what a thick beard; but he can't be much older than me.*

"It is my great pleasure to be with you tonight, most esteemed and kindly patrons." He strummed a chord, beamed at the grand room full of royalty; and began—his fingers fairly flying over the strings of his lute. Royal feet tapped tentatively, all but one. Eva sat still, mute, clutching her stomach, remembering her dream.

Well, I'm a roamin' wanderer, a-travelin' around,
Folks who care to lend an ear will hear a happy sound.
I won't be seekin' money while I sing for you tonight;
But if you have an apple pie, please let me have a bite.

Oh, apple pies are wonderful,
Apple pies are grand.
Give me a crusty apple pie,
I'll eat it in my hand.
I'd have them for my breakfast,
I'd munch them for my lunch.
If I had a hundred apple pies
I'd eat them by the bunch.

Once I met a lovely lass, as fair as ever was,
She spurned her suitors roundly, and she said it was because,
They promised her the stars, hunkered down on bended knee;
Then I offered her an apple pie—she said she'd marry me!

Oooh, apple pies are wonderful,
Apple pies are grand.
Give me a crusty apple pie,
I'll eat it in my hand.
I'd have them for my breakfast,
I'd munch them for my lunch.
If I had a hundred apple pies
I'd eat them by the bunch.

By the end of the song, the dignified crowd was singing along. King Cedric, delighted to see his guests enjoying themselves, determined before the night was over: *This minstrel must stay and entertain us for a week, at least!*

Toward the end of the night, the whole roomful of royalty forgot their jewels, their wigs, and their uncomfortable pointy shoes. They laughed and clapped and stomped their feet in time to the jigs and swayed to the love ballads while feasting and sloshing wine onto the white tablecloth. The minstrel chuckled to himself. *I might as well be at the Purple Pig!*

There was at last one song to be sung, and he needed to sing it into a quiet room. The princess must hear every word.

"Ladies, Gentlemen, and most revered royalty . . . I have one last song before I bid you good night. My lute will sing, then I will translate into words, the notes I send to your ears." He began slowly, strumming low and deep; note flowing into note; chords echoing on the stone walls of the Grand Hall. Then, he closed his eyes, his hands seeming to move and sweep over the strings of their own will. The melody quickened in pitch and tempo until finally his voice entered the thrumming harmony of the music:

Warm sun lights the falcon's wings,
(Come glide with me on wind's slipstreams.)
Her time of feathered flight is near,
Soar silver-bright on zephyr dreams.
Flight is near,
Is near,
Near.

The song ended. The room was silent for a moment, then, deafening applause filled every corner. Traveler bowed deeply. Flourishing his hat, he smiled expansively and exited through the curtain.

He would certainly have more than a scrap of floor in front of a hearth this night, of that he was sure. His eyes lit up in anticipation of a warm bath, a clean feather mattress . . . and tomorrow with the princess.

Awake

21

That night on her bed, the princess lay staring at the ceiling. Thoughts too deep for tears swirled inside. It was settled. *Truly.* She would marry Count Fagan, and then what? She sat up in her bed feeling strangely separate from herself, as though a wall had been built, protecting her—the real Evangeline—from what would soon be her life, and death.

The minstrel's song was a wounded bird fluttering against her ribcage:
Her time of feathered flight is near,
Soar silver-bright on zephyr dreams.
Flight is near,
Is near,
Near.'

She bit her lip. *How cruel—to hold out hope of freedom to someone bound without remedy—no feathered flight happening here,* she thought bitterly. *I hate him and his songs. Should have turned him away at the bridge.* Wishing she knew how to use the dragon scale, she rolled over on her pillow, clutched her mother's locket, and squeezed her eyes shut. Willing herself unconscious, she escaped into sleep.

She dreamed that night of a glorious sparkling river.

Standing on the reedy bank, Eva hesitated. Afraid. She longed to jump in, to let the currents carry her. But *where?*

The princess took off her royal shoes, her gown, her jewels, her whale-bone corset and finally, her stockings—like an animal shedding an outgrown skin. Feeling lighter than air, she waded out into the cool, crystal clear currents. There, she was swept along, her face held above the water, hair drifting out in long dark curls on the eddies. Dipping below the shining surface, she caught glimpses of glowing colorful creatures. Somehow, they didn't scare her; in fact, she longed to go below and swim with them. The river, sensing her desire, invited her down. Eva sank gently, until there was only water to breathe. To her delight, she found she could breathe these waters as if they were air. Feeling her fears being drawn out through her fingers and toes, and carried away by the currents, she relaxed. The creatures swam around her, welcoming her to their realm. She looked down, and was surprised to see her body incandescent, lit from within, as if inhabited by a million tiny stars. Looking below, she saw a huge broad fish, the size of a sailing ship. It had stripes that pulsed and glowed, lighting the depths. This behemoth seemed unaware of her presence and swam on,

effortlessly pushing out tidal currents from the powerful swish of its tail. Around her were small fish and other living beings she'd never seen before. Some of these darted playfully between her feet, nibbled at her toes and tugged at her cloud of billowing hair. They glimmered in myriads of colors with spots, stripes, and squiggles flashing, changing from red to purple to green, and to colors Eva had never seen before.

Upon closer inspection, she saw that what she first thought were fish with scales must have indeed been birds with feathers! "What are birds doing down here in the *water*?" she wondered. At this thought, everything around her seemed to shimmer with laughter. She looked down at her own body. It was covered with feathers—*bright blue ones*! She felt a weight on

117

her shoulders and reached up. *Wings!* "Odd—I did think this was water," she murmured. Laughter erupted again, and this time, she joined in the delighted mirth.

Still laughing, she peered through the waters at white clouds beside her. The bird-creatures swirled around her once, twice, then flew out into the rippling colors of the sky.

Eva found she was soaring on windy currents circling an island. Looking closer, she recognized a stand of huge evergreen trees. In the middle of this thicket was a clearing where two children stood—a world unto themselves.

Even though this seemed strangely familiar, she suddenly felt she was intruding, and tipped her wings to fly to the left, but not before she heard the boy say, " . . . our promise should be sealed with a kiss." The girl looked into his face, then up into the sky and smiled at Eva. However, her smile turned to wide-eyed horror as they both turned to see an object hurtling upward. A razor-sharp, black arrow with red bands tore through the sky—aimed at Eva's heart.

The moment was frozen in time.

The dream ended.

Eva awoke to morning light streaming over her windowsill.

She sat up with the boy's promise clinging to her heart.

Valentino, you promised . . . and now it's too late.

That morning after breakfast, lingering in the garden, Eva argued with herself—*No, I'm not hoping the minstrel will show up.* Her questions could be asked later. They could wait. *They would have to.*

Eva heard faint music drifting over the shrubbery. *The minstrel!* Traveler stepped past the tall clipped hedge and saw the princess standing by the pond. He bowed and removed his hat. "Your Highness, what a pleasant surprise."

"Thank you, Mr... ah, Traveler. I trust you slept and breakfasted well?" She smiled her royal inscrutable smile.

"Yes, quite well, thank you. And you?" he inquired politely.

"Yes," she said. "There *was* something I wanted to ask you, if you don't mind."

"And what would that be?"

"So, you're a minstrel?" she asked stiffly, trying not to sound too interested.

"What gave it away?" He laughed easily. "Me? Yes. I travel the lands trading song for food and a roof to sleep under . . . sometimes at the threat of life and limb." The corners of his mouth lifted his mustache, and he waggled his dark eyebrows comically.

Eva almost laughed, but caught herself. She had heard of such people. Despite her natural caution, she was drawn in. "What is a minstrel doing in Dunmoor?" Eva didn't say *of all places*, but wondered how anyone could find profit in such a poverty stricken country. "And Minstrel, why are you walking?"

He shrugged and smiled. "I'm walking because I have no horse with me. And as to why I am here: It has come to my ears, there are some in this castle who could use a bit of song. Am I *right?*" He shifted his lute on his shoulder and raised an eyebrow in her direction.

"Maybe." Eva took a step back. She realized she knew little more about this mysterious minstrel than when they started talking, but felt silly continuing to question him. "Well, have a pleasant stay." She nodded briefly and turned to go.

"Thank you, Princess Evangeline."

What? She whirled around. "Who told you Evangeline was my name?"

"It is my understanding that you are Princess Edwina Evangeline. Please forgive me if I have offended you, Your Highness, but I think Evangeline suits you so much better than Edwina. Yes? Or perhaps I'm *wrong.*"

How annoying! "Yes—I mean *NO!* I meant to say, that is a name only a select few call me." She gathered herself. "I'll thank you to address me as Princess Edwina. Good day to you." Eva rounded on the heel of her blue satin slipper and strode toward the kitchen.

"Forgive me, Princess Edwina. I meant no harm," he called to her retreating back. His eyes smiled. "But, it's no good you know." He spoke just loud enough for her to hear, and waited, softly plucking the strings of his lute.

She stopped walking, hesitated, and turned to face him. "What's no good, Minstrel?" Eva pursed her lips and spoke in her most refined voice.

"I've seen it . . . the look in your eyes. You can't hide it—Your Highness."

"Whatever could you be talking about?" she said, feeling her face flush and a shiver travel up her back.

"It's the hunger—the gnawing desire, way beyond food. A knowing, that you are the only one who can step in. The only one who can do what you are here to do. I'm talking about your destiny—Princess." The minstrel waited, smiled politely, and took a step back. It was a dangerous dance he was doing. Push too hard, too far, and all would be lost.

"Did you eat the stupid berries for breakfast? Because I always avoid those whenever Rhona serves them." Eva glared at him, turned again on her heel, and walked away. *How dare this minstrel intrude into my personal life! Who does he think he is? One more word and I'll have him tossed out!* She exhaled loudly and thought again of Archie's words to her the night before a banquet years ago. *If these two know so much, they need to tell me how I'm supposed to do this—Destiny thing. I'm contracted to marry Fagan! It's settled. The. End. Of. Me.*

She stopped, looked up into the sky and whispered, "Did you hear that? Because, it will take a miracle to get me out of this mess, and last time I checked, that was *Your* department . . . no more ideas here."

By lunchtime, Count Fagan's carriage had arrived. He and his chancellor joined the remaining commonwealth members for a meal in the Grand Hall. Traveler wandered easily around the room strumming his lute, entertaining with poems and songs. Count Fagan, sitting on Eva's left, made his usual variety of snide, insipid conversation. Eva replied courteously, laughing politely at the right places while avoiding eye contact with the minstrel.

But, Traveler's words from the garden still burned like a fire-brand in her soul. *Your Destiny!* She smiled and nodded to Fagan. *No way out for me,* she thought, ignoring tears crowding behind her eyes and laughing again when she thought it was appropriate. The count looked at her quizzically, then at the minstrel. *I wonder what I just laughed at?* She blotted her mouth with her napkin to hide a trembling chin.

When Traveler was finished, the room filled with refined applause. He bowed deeply, walked into the kitchen and joined the staff downstairs at their table for lunch.

The count chuckled derisively and turned to Eva. "So, what do you know about this minstrel—this *Traveler*, is it?" His smile never reached his blood-shot eyes.

"Him, oh nothing really, just that he travels about singing for food and a place to sleep." She shifted uncomfortably in her seat. "Father hired him," she said sidestepping the question. It hung rotting in the air.

"Well, no matter," Fagan sniffed. "Just another peasant trying to get by, I suppose." He looked down at her. "And my sympathy on your,

ah . . . scratches. I hope your shoulder and face are healing well, my Dear." Under his thin oiled mustache he stretched his red lips over large yellowish teeth in an unpleasant smile.

Eva recoiled, then caught herself. "Thank you, Count Fagan," she said, turning up the corners of her lips. "And now, if you'll excuse me, I have things to attend to, so I must be going," she laughed lightly. "School work you know; and then I will need a rest. Still recovering." She stood up to leave.

"Ah yes, I know . . . unfortunate, your ordeal." He stood with her. "And please, call me Fagan. After all, we will be wed in just two short weeks." He smiled again and bowed with his customary flourish.

Why does his bow always seem to mock me? "Won't that be just grand! And you may call me Edwina," she said with as much enthusiasm as she could scrape together. "Glenda and the seamstress are finishing my dress as we speak!" She smiled tightly. "Well, I must be going. Enjoy your afternoon, Fagan." With that she turned and left the room.

Stepping into the hallway, thoughts struck like bolts of lightning. *Wait— how could he possibly know I have a scratch on my shoulder? It's always covered by my dresses. Father doesn't even know about it, only Bea. And Fagan just got here; he and father haven't had time to talk. How could he know about—my 'ordeal', about Morach? Unless . . .* A cold tremor shook her violently. *Unless, truly I was right. I'm not imagining things . . . I'm not a lunatic.* Her knees suddenly buckled. She caught herself against the wall.

"Must . . . talk to Traveler." Her hushed voice trembled under her breath.

22

Eva went up to her schoolroom and pretended to read. Keeping one eye on the gardens from her high window, she turned pages absently. It would be *very* awkward if she were seen waiting for the minstrel in the garden, especially now that Fagan was here.

Glenda walked in and dusted the clean bookshelves. Seeing Eva absorbed in her book, she went on to her other duties.

Just then, a movement caught Eva's eye out the window. Someone she couldn't quite see had walked behind the tall clipped hedge next to the pond. *Traveler!* She quietly shelved her book, stole down the stairs and out the side door. *Please stay there!*

She fairly sprinted around the hedge and into—*Fagan!* Eva thumped soundly into his satin-vested belly and fell back onto the path.

"Ahhh! My Dear! Let me help you up." He extended one stockinged leg and his jeweled fingers toward her. "Where were you going in such a hurry?"

Eva was already up. She brushed herself off and examined a new tear in the elbow of her green silk sleeve. "Me? Oh, I thought I left a book on the bench by the pond. Is it there still? No? Well, Glenda must have brought it in for me. No problem. I hope I didn't hurt you." A bead of sweat trickled down the side of her face, stinging her unhealed scar. She shifted to one foot then the other, aware that her hair was falling loose from its braid. "Well, enjoy the gardens. I'll see you tonight at dinner." Before she turned to go, something caught her eye behind the count. A crossbow and quiver of black, red-banded arrows leaned against the stone bench. Turning, she walked sedately, then, ran through the maze of clipped yew hedges. Breathlessly, she glanced behind. *No one following.* Something flashed hot in her thoughts. *The color bands! The same as the dream arrow—and the one in Ciels' wing!*

Fagan and his chancellor exchanged meaningful glances and looked around. No one near.

"Wonder *who* she was expecting to see," the chancellor smirked.

"Indeed. But, since we don't *have* to wonder . . ." The count straightened the lace on his cuff. "Clearly, a wedding sooner than later will need to happen. I'll see to it tonight," he said, his lip lifting in a sneer.

The chancellor smiled, bowing with hooded eyes half closed and hands clasped at his chest. This posture of mute servitude pleased the count. He knew it. His admiration for the way Fagan could work his will was only matched by his fear of him. He had witnessed terrible punishment meted out to those in the Count's service who crossed him. The chancellor was determined never to be one of those. No matter what he had to do.

Eva swished through a patch of un-mowed grass to the evergreen thicket. Her thicket. Then, finding the path behind overgrown quince bushes, she followed it through giant pines. The pungent smell of this small forest always calmed her somehow. *I wish I could just live here,* she thought. Finally, she entered the clearing and her dream of flying over this secret place bloomed in her thoughts. "He promised," she said aloud to the trees. Then felt foolish; in fact, ridiculous.

The behemoth pine was still standing sentry. She examined the tiny landscape by her foot. "Still here," she said softly. Bending down, she straightened a small stick cottage and replaced its bark roof. The twig orchard had fallen over, but wasn't broken. She righted the tiny trees and put their mossy leaves back in place. *Much better.* She smiled sadly.

A bird's shadow rippled across the clearing. Eva looked up. Caught her breath. *A falcon!* "It's been a long time," she whispered, shading her eyes.

Suddenly, someone cleared his throat behind her. She whirled around. *Traveler!* "What are you doing here? You have no business—!"

He looked stricken and turned to go. "Yes of course; you're right. Please forgive my forwardness, Your Highness. We have plenty of time; we can talk soon." He pushed a branch out of the way and stepped back into the woods.

"No—wait! That is... *please* wait. You wanted to talk?" She stood. He stepped under the branch again and into the clearing.

"How'd you find me?" she asked. "And I didn't even hear you coming. How'd you do that?"

His ears flushed red, and he broke off a twig. "I learned it in the royal guard, from an old scout." He shifted to the other foot. "We have to talk, Princess."

"About?"

He broke the twig in small pieces. "I overheard the count and his chamberlain after lunch in the hallway. I only caught a few words as they passed. But, they're planning *something* . . . I heard your name spoken." He took a deep breath. "I came outside to find you—just in time to see you bounce off the count then disappear down the hedge path."

Eva blushed hotly. "Yes. Please go on."

"Decided to go the long way around and pick up your trail on the other side. I don't think he saw me." He let out a long sigh. "There's something else you must know." He lowered his backpack to the ground.

"There's something I wanted to tell you too," she said. "But first—I'm sorry I was an awful hag this morning."

He smiled ruefully. "Certainly forgiven, Your Highness. I, I . . . this is a hard time." His eyebrows pulled together.

"Hard?" She laughed bitterly. "Hard doesn't touch it. Father's signed a contract binding me to this horrible, horrible—is he even a count! He said something today after lunch. I might absolutely be missing something." She lowered her voice. "He may not even be human. Maybe. Anyway, I plan to find out tonight at dinner, somehow. My own father hardly looks at me anymore, and when he does it's cold and hard. I know he's always blamed me for my mother's death, but this is new." She looked up, catching herself. *I've said too much.* "Sorry. You wanted to say something?" *This is so odd . . . being with him feels so comfortable—too comfortable.* She clasped her hands tightly at her waist.

Traveler dropped his arm to his side. "Princess, I'm so sorry . . ." he began.

"This does seem to be my life," she looked at the ground, not meeting his eyes. "And, and, I've tried to tell myself, you can do this. Kings do this kind of thing all the time to their daughters." Her voice squeezed and trembled. "Thought I could manage it. Thought I could until lunch today, that is. Fagan knows things he shouldn't know. About *me!*" Her chin quaked.

Traveler's words came out in an urgent rush: "Princess, we could go—leave this place!" His voice was low, hoarse. "I, I can help you. I know about so-called marriage contracts—a tradition of grabby kings." He handed her his handkerchief.

"Save your breath. There's no way out for me," she said bitterly, wiping her face. I am the price Father has paid to prosper and keep our kingdom safe. This is a fact." Eva's knuckles clenched white. She swallowed loudly.

"We both know your marriage would be a death sentence. I'm sure you've heard tales about the count's last two wives."

"I had heard that the last one was poisoned, yes," she said woodenly. "I was hoping that's what they were—just tales and gossip for idle tongues. I don't think so now. I'm as good as dead."

He leaned forward. "Fagan will *not* have his way. Not this time! We have two weeks to come up with a plan."

We? She looked into his eyes, hardly believing what she'd heard. "Thanks for the offer, but don't you think I've tried to work that out? Night after night, I've thought of ways to escape this island—*before* the wedding. It always comes down to one thing. How do I live once I've escaped?" She blew her nose. "I *don't,* that's how. The people of Dunmoor hate me. I'm the daughter of King Cedric, in case you haven't noticed. They'd turn me in for a reward and have a good day doing it." She sat down heavily and leaned against her pine tree. The minstrel sat cross-legged on the thick carpet of pine needles and faced her.

"Alright, let's just say you *could* travel safely through Dunmoor; in disguise maybe."

"But, how…"

"For argument's sake, let's say . . . Then what? Where would you want to go?" he asked.

She was silent for a minute then, "If he's still alive, I have a friend in Tirzah who would give me sanctuary—I think he would anyway. Otherwise, I have no place to go." Eva thought of all the years of unanswered letters. Over those years, she had come up with a thousand reasons for Valentino's silence. Then six months ago, she'd stopped writing. Thoughts plagued her: *If he's still alive, what if he's found another? What if he's married? What if I do escape and finally arrive at his castle, and he and his wife invite me to stay with them? Or worse, turn me away?* The thought of this made her stomach clench and quiver. *But I have no other choice . . .* Eva tried on the thought of staying with Valentino and his wife like she would a new dress. It pinched like a corset. Her breath grew shallow and clipped. "If he can't, I don't know. I couldn't stay with anyone in Dunmoor, even in disguise," she said, thinking of Brookin. "If I were found out, they would be put to death immediately, every last one."

Silence hung in the air. "Here's a thought," Traveler said finally. "Maybe your friend could help you find a job. Or I could help you, so you could live by the work of your hands in Tirzah—if your friend can't help, that is."

"How could you help?" Her voice rose doubtful, then curious.

He smiled, seeing her eyes light up. "I'm very well connected in Tirzah, in the castle kitchen especially."

"You would do that? But *why?* You barely know me. No, it's too much." She shook her head, her heart rising to this idea even as her reason rejected it. "I couldn't ask you to do this."

He stood up. "First of all, you didn't ask. And, let's just say I have a soft spot for damsels in distress. I hate injustice and wasted lives. We can leave it at that." He lifted his pack to his shoulder. "So we have less than two weeks to work out our plan."

To work out our plan . . . we have a plan. Eva's heart painfully opened to the wonder of the *possibility* of freedom. *Could this really happen? To me?* "Yes, count me in," she whispered. "I don't know how to thank you, Traveler. I owe you my life!"

"Don't thank me yet. We're not off the island," he said wryly. "And you can call me Trav."

"All right, I'm Eva—Trav." She managed a smile.

"Well, Eva, we have no time to lose." He held out a hand to help her up.

"Thank you, I can manage." She stood and pulled pine needles from her hair, her face solemn. "Let's meet after dinner tonight and decide how we're going to do this?" They both suddenly noticed the clearing was cast in long shadows. "And we shouldn't go back to the castle together." She brushed her dress off.

"Right you are. I'll go first and take the long way," he said. "Where should we meet tonight?"

Eva thought of going out through her secret passageway, then, discarded the idea. *Too risky!* It would only take one careless exit with a servant coming in to check, as they did. That would be it. No more escape route. "Let's meet at the pond by the yew hedge, after dark. That should be safe enough." Eva looked into his face, attempting to read it. "I can hardly believe we just had this conversation." She pinched her arm. "No, not a dream."

"Well, believe it, Princess . . . Eva. We can decide on a plan tonight. See you at dinner—and you can keep the handkerchief."

"Wait! Wait just a minute." Eva palmed her forehead.

He turned to face her.

"How do I know? How *would* I know . . ."

His brow wrinkled. "Oh, yes. Right. That I wouldn't do *worse* to you?"

"I've heard talk . . . terrible things." The princess paled.

"First, I wouldn't. Believe that or not. Second . . ." He unbuckled his sheathed dagger and held it out. "Here. Just in case." Eva took the holstered dagger, frowning at her trembling hand. "I mean, not from me. But, you never know what old Fagan might be planning." He rubbed a hand over his eyes exhaling loudly.

Eva buckled it around her waist and watched the hanging holster slip down in the folds of her skirt. Hidden. Almost. She touched the hilt gingerly and looked up at Travelers solemn face. "So now what?"

The minstrel pressed his lips together. "Let's say, tonight someone makes you feel threatened."

"Alright let's say."

"First of all, speak calmly and try to walk away. But, if they come closer scream 'Stop it!' as loud as possible. Then run to a place with lots of people, like the kitchen."

"Makes sense. But what if I *can't* get away. What *if. . .!*" Terrible scenes flooded her thoughts. She gasped.

"So, calm down. Listen." He stepped back, feeling her panic. "If you're grabbed, first go for the throat fast, with all your strength. Use your elbow or forearm. *Or* if you have your dagger handy, use that. Damage his throat; that's your chance. Run."

Eva pictured Fagan doubled over, gasping for breath and almost laughed. "Well, let's hope I don't have to use these skills, soon." *Or ever.*

"Yes let's. See you tonight." With that, he tipped his hat, pushed back a hemlock bough, and disappeared into the woods.

"A Friend," she whispered. She stared at the minstrel's handkerchief crumpled in her hand. There it was; her future was calling to her in the offer of a stranger. Could this be the friend of her dream? The friend promised by the True Voice? Eva explored this thought.

Am I brave, or desperately, terminally stupid?

23

That night, the King stood at his place at the head of the table. It was too warm for a fire, but he knew he was an imposing figure framed by the massive ornate hearth. "I would like to propose a toast in honor of the soon-to-be-married couple: Count Fagan and my daughter, the Princess Edwina!" He lifted his glass high. The Countess Constanza stood smugly beside him and did the same.

"Here, *here!* Cheers!" Agreement was shouted from nobility around the room.

"May this be a prosperous and fruitful union with great increase for all concerned—in every possible way!" The king drained his glass, beamed broadly, and looked around the room. "Since you all have been invited, I will expect to see your faces in two weeks for the blessed event!"

Murmurs of "Yes, delighted!" and "Of course!" floated among the nobles amid polite applause.

Then silence.

"And, *I* would like to propose a little change in schedule," said Count Fagan, chuckling, his glass still raised. His brittle laughter crackled in Eva's ears.

"Say on, Fagan." The King was already flushed and merry with wine.

"Since the princess is ready in every way for our marriage, including her dress," he said arching one side of his eyebrow and stroking his oily mustache, "why should we delay any longer? The priest is here, and we have these honorable witnesses *and* plenty of food." He smiled winningly. "If we marry tomorrow, it will be much *less* expensive and spare these good people traveling back here in two weeks. *And*," he added. "there is no reason we shouldn't have the lavish banquet you had planned; don't you agree?" He reached over and took Eva's hand in a show of affection. She smiled weakly, cringing, sickened at his touch.

King Cedric didn't look at his daughter. He considered the expense and his increasing load of debt, and said, "You make a good point, Count. Yes, that's a grand idea! We'll plan it for tomorrow before the sun sets. I'll let Rhona know." Then turning to the room at large he asked, "What say you, noble friends? Will you join us tomorrow for the joyful event? A wedding and banquet for the illustrious Count and my daughter, Princess Edwina Evangeline!"

"Here's to the bride and groom to be!" they all shouted, "Huzzah!" and, "A thousand blessings on your union!" A great clamor of laughter, cheering, and pinging of silverware on goblets followed.

Eva knew she was expected to join in the uproar. She managed to stretch her lips in a smile, but words stuck in her throat.

"How about you, Daughter. This must make you happy. No more waiting, rehearsing and planning, right?" Suddenly, all eyes were on her. Eva felt the heavy scrutiny of her father like a black raven beating its wings against her face.

Eva stifled a laugh, knowing that she was in danger of becoming hysterical if she once started. "Looks like it's all settled then," she said lightly, feeling her mouth go dry. "Hooray!" She added and smiled widely to hide her quivering lips.

Tomorrow night by this time, I'll be married to this—monster! Her mind blanked briefly with a white wordless terror. She felt the floor shift sideways. The plan, her plan, had been thwarted, ruined. Or had it? She managed another watery smile and gripped the mahogany arms of her chair to steady herself. No one seemed to notice.

Traveler's and Eva's eyes met in the air. She was strengthened somehow and sat up straighter. Forcing a laugh, she flung her arm out to join in the revelry. At that very moment, the wine steward reached over to fill Count Fagan's goblet. Their two arms connected, knocking over the gilded candlestick and spilling most of a decanter of mint liqueur onto the Count's sleeve—which immediately burst into flames, struck by the burning candle.

Eva gasped and threw her glass of water onto the flames. The count snatched off his blazing jacket and yanked his soaking wet sleeve up to his elbow. But, only for a moment. That brief fragment of time was enough for her to see: *Scales!* His wet arm was covered with them—skin colored, but the scaly pattern was unmistakable. She looked away, not wanting him to suspect that she saw . . . she *knew* . . . now, without a shadow of a doubt. Then she laughed loudly, boisterously like one of the simple courtiers that decorated the room. As far as she could tell, no one else had seen. She looked at the laughing faces. No, she was the only one.

The disgruntled count was brought a fresh jacket, and the evening rolled on.

Steaming platters of venison garnished with onions, parsnips, beets, potatoes, and parsley were brought in and placed at the head of each linen-covered table. Servers carved the meat at the table and arranged plates with vegetables and sauce. Quickly, the guests were served and glasses refilled. Eva's plate was conspicuously absent of meat, having made arrangements with Rhona earlier in the day. In place of the venison was a poached egg. In recent weeks, she had found herself gagging on meat; imagining the death of the animal that she ate—and her own.

Fagan said nothing. The possibility of being discovered had silenced him briefly. He wanted attention to go elsewhere.

Traveler perched on a stool in the center of the room and waited for the King's command. Having only caught a glimpse of the candlestick incident, he steeled himself. *Something* monumental had just happened. Eva's face gave no clue.

The King waved his hand. "Play on, Minstrel. We are waiting."

At this, the musician smiled and bowed, then opened the lute case. The polished wood reflected warmly into the room. The minstrel turned the tuning pegs, plucked the strings—then blithely spoke a poem:

"While wearing out boot-leather, walking the road,
I caught a rare glimpse of the whing-dangle toad.
This is only a grin, not the song that I bring;
The Tale of Two Turtledoves, for you, I'll now sing."

Strumming the strings gently, he hummed the beginning of the ballad:

"Deep in fragrant forest flew
Two young doves with eyes of blue..."

The song flowed through the heat of Eva's mind. *Two young doves . . .* her thoughts rushed past like the tide. Finally, she knew what must be done. Tonight.

Traveler played on. The royal party-goers fell into the rhythm and melody of his songs until there were smiles and foot tapping all around. King Cedric looked from face to face and was delighted. This was *his* victory. He decided then, that the minstrel should be appointed a place at court, no question about it. He would command him to sing at the wedding tomorrow as well. In his mind, it was settled.

The count, however, was not delighted. Far from it. He had intercepted two quick glances between Eva and the minstrel. Those were enough to confirm his suspicions. He knew what he must do. Tonight. He calmed himself with the knowledge of his former dealings with the king. His lips stretched in a smile of genuine relish at the thought of his power over the situation.

The night was far spent. The council members, one by one, paid their respects to the King, the princess, and the groom-to-be. This done, they left the Grand Hall for their rooms, heavy with food and drink.

"Now, if you will both excuse me," the King said, "I must take care of a certain matter. I'll see you in the study, shortly." He nodded to Fagan who smiled knowingly. Then to his daughter, he said, "Thank you for another *peaceful* meal. I will see you tomorrow at the wedding. It will be my delight to walk you down the aisle to be the bride of our most notable and esteemed friend. He nodded to them both and left the room, Countess Constanza at his elbow.

Eva felt her stomach heave. Her face drained of color. She wanted to slam her fist on the starched white tablecloth, and then into Fagan's snide smirking mouth. The princess closed her eyes and leaned back in her chair.

"My Dear," murmured the count. "You look tired. Maybe an early bedtime will help that." His voice was sweet, like perfume masking a rotten stench.

"Forgive me, Count Fagan—"

"Why would I need to forgive you? I've suffered no harm from you, have I?" he probed.

"No, that is to say . . . goodnight, Fagan. I trust you will sleep well also." She meant every word.

With that he stood and bowed with a flourish. "And, as always, I remain your humble servant," he intoned. She ducked under his extended arm, thinking: *You mean serpent don't you?*

Glad for an excuse to flee the room, she excused herself. With another quick glance at Traveler, she made herself walk, not run, to the arched doorway and turn down the dimly lit hall. However, instead of going up the stairs at the end of the hall to her bedroom, she turned left down a little-used corridor that led to the chapel.

24

The last two servers left the room. Traveler and Fagan eyed each other warily, now alone.

The count spoke first. "You did an admirable job tonight, my boy. Yes, very admirable indeed, considering . . ." He started walking toward the hallway.

Traveler whistled lightly through his teeth as he packed his lute in its case. He seemed not to have heard. Slinging the case over his shoulder, he walked toward the tall arched doorway where the count stood. He said lightly, "Considering . . .? Oh—and, I'm not your *boy*, so you can drop that." He smiled with his mouth only.

Fagan chuckled; his words had hit their mark. "*Considering*—you can sing, but you are certainly not a minstrel, *my boy*. Exactly *who* might you be?" He didn't wait for an answer. "Well, no matter, by tomorrow night, the princess will be mine and far beyond any of your little plans—And yes, I've seen how you look at her." His eyes glittered maliciously. "So now, you must just put her out of your mind, *my boy*. She. Is. *Mine*." He smirked. "I was prepared for a battle of wits, but it seems you are unarmed." He stepped casually into the hallway and tossed a purple grape up to catch it in his mouth. He missed.

Traveler stepped in front of him, and leaned in. "I know what you are up to," he said through clenched teeth, though he had only guessed at the evil behind the words overheard in the hall. The count was the taller man, but the force of Traveler's words made him stagger back.

"You do not! That is to say—" The count saw controlled fury in the minstrel's eyes and paused. "Oh, the little *pretend* minstrel is angry, is he? Is he threatening me?" With a sneer of contempt, Fagan's left hand slid toward his waistband, touching a dagger. He knew a few never-fail nasty tricks, and he planned to use them. *All* of them.

"I never threaten." Traveler shoved his anger down, knowing better than to allow it to cloud his senses. Fagan feinted with his right hand. Like lightening, the minstrel knocked the hand away and pulled Fagan's knife from its sheath, throwing it down to clatter on the floor. To Fagan's dismay, the minstrel skillfully parried each calculated move. The count sweated and strained under his satin jacket.

"I know who you are, *Minstrel*—" He lunged forward grappling with the smaller man for a controlling hold. He reached into his jacket. "This is a fight you cannot win," he panted.

Traveler broke free. "*No?*"

The next thing the count knew, he was pinned by his neck against the wall—his arms flailing the minstrel's shoulders.

Traveler's voice was dangerously quiet. "So it's *Count* Fagan is it? May I call you Fagan?" The count nodded frantically. "I have some news for you, *Fagan*. If you attempt this farce of a marriage—you'll curse the day you were born. You will *pay*—with—your wretched life—*understand!*" He leaned in closer, ignoring the stench of the Count's sulfurous breath. "Consider that a promise . . . And I always keep my promises."

Fagan attempted to pry the minstrel's forearm from his neck unsuccessfully and managed to squeak out, "Right . . . you win. I yield."

Traveler released Fagan's neck. The count collapsed to his knees on the stone floor, coughing and wheezing. He crouched there clutching his throat until his breaths came easily.

Leaning back in a chair against the wall, the minstrel waited in watchful silence. The count furtively glanced in his direction, his lips pressed into a smile, calculating.

Traveler spoke, "Let me know when you're ready to listen, sly whisperer; cowardly poisoner of kings and women."

Fagan coughed. "Speak away," he hissed, still on the floor. "I'm all ears."

Traveler bent over until he was eye level with the count. "I know what happened to your last wife. I can guess at your disgusting plans for the princess. Need I say more?"

Fagan's eyes flitted nervously up and down the hallway. Seeing no one, he shook his head, "No. Not another word need be said." The count unbuttoned his dinner jacket, straightened it, and casually reached inside.

"And—if you want to keep that hand, hold your dagger with two fingers . . . Now, drop it to the floor," Traveler said, teeth clenched. "Go ahead. Give me a reason to—"

The dagger clattered to the floor.

Traveler yanked Fagan up from his knees by his jacket lapels and shoved him into the chair he just vacated. "So let's end this, shall we?"

"A capital idea," the count said snidely, then seeing the dangerous glint in the minstrel's eye; "As you say."

"You call off the wedding. At dawn tomorrow, you leave. Go back to your castle or whatever rock you live under. I won't kill you now. But, the next time we meet is *your* misfortune. Your sorry hide will be mine—*Agreed?*"

"Yes, certainly." The count winced, managed a weak smile and held out his hand. "A gentleman's agreement."

Traveler laughed shortly. "Was that a *joke?* Your pledge and two tika would buy me a slice of shepherd's pie at the Purple Pig."

Fagan adopted a wounded expression. "Surely you don't think I would lie about so grave a matter."

"What I think doesn't matter. Know this—I'll hold you to your promise however I need to." The minstrel glared. "Sleep well." He reached down, put the count's dagger in his waistband behind his own, then picked up the other one. Raising a warning eyebrow in Fagan's direction, he shouldered his lute and strode down the dark hallway.

Traveler did not put an end to Fagan's life that night. If he'd known what Eva saw at dinner, he would have. But, he'd only guessed, and guessing was not enough to put a man to death. Not in his mind.

When the echo of the minstrel's footfalls had faded to nothing, the count slicked his hair back and muttered, "Fool. We'll see whose hide will be whose."

He stood and straightened the lace on his cuffs. "You have no idea who you are dealing with. The world is crawling with such as you." With that, he sniffed derisively. "*You* sleep well tonight, *Minstrel*. It will be your last." He rubbed his neck, stood painfully and limped toward King Cedric's study.

25

Eva entered the small candle-lit chapel, walked across the round domed apse and down the aisle of the empty room. Coming up to the crucifix at the altar, she bowed and crossed herself. The memory of her encounter with the True Voice flooded over her like a tidal wave. It seemed like a lifetime ago and like yesterday all at once. "I haven't forgotten," she whispered. A whisper deep inside said, "Nor have I."

Turning left, she opened the door leading down a flight of stairs to the crypt of the House of Dunmoor, where her mother's body lay entombed. Eva had come here in times past when she missed her mother so desperately; she had to do something. Somehow being close to her body helped a little. She opened the iron door and entered the crypt. Three candles always burning in the underground room lit the shadowy way to her tomb. Eva sat on the floor and leaned against the smooth marble. "I'm leaving for a while, Mother. You understand. But, I'll be back one day—" She paused, hoping she hadn't just lied, "—to restore Dunmoor as we dreamed it, as we would see it. You and I." Eva closed her eyes, reached back and placed her palms on the cold marble, sighed and left the crypt.

A full moon and fireflies lit the balmy September night. Eva ran down the garden path to Archie and Bea's cottage, one last time.

After spilling her story and plans, she and Archie released the messenger dove. Eva watched Celeste, the night flier, catch the wind and soar over the castle, silhouetted black inside the moonlight.

"So you trust this man, this minstrel," Archie said walking back to the apple tree lofts. It wasn't a question but seemed to need an answer.

"With my life." She heard her voice waver. "So it would seem." The soft sleepy *coo-ing* of doves barely touched the thoughts scorching her mind.

Archie didn't reply but nodded in silent agreement.

They walked wordlessly back into the cottage and steaming cups of tea. Bea awaited them, her face pinched with worry.

The thought of leaving Archie and Bea—of not being able to sit in the world of their warm cozy kitchen again, made a sob catch in her throat. They held each other wordlessly, tightly, then, it was time. Bea reached into her cabinet and pulled out a small pouch, which she pressed into Eva's palm.

"Keep this. You remember how I used these herbs to draw the poison from your wounds? You'll know what to do. If the time should come." She wiped her eyes with her apron. "May the True Voice be your way. His Angels go before you," Bea said softly, looking into her face. "Until we have tea again . . ."

"And may He guard and keep you," Archie added solemnly. "We'll see you back here in the kitchen." His voice faltered. "Don't break our hearts."

Eva looked up, memorizing their faces. *Will I ever see you again?*

26

*E*va ran down the dark garden path to the meeting place. Feeling the comforting weight of her dagger, now around her waist, she smiled grimly.

She stumbled and caught herself on a tree branch. The bench behind the hedge was empty! "Where *is* he?" she caught her breath, realizing again, she barely knew this person.

Sitting, waiting, gripping the seat, her heart pounded high in her throat. This minstrel had given her a choice; held the door open for her escape . . . and then what? He'd given her his dagger. *Still,* could he be trusted? "Stupid question. I have no other choice." The words clawed her throat. *If Celeste doesn't make it to Olwen's, could I swim to the mainland? Doubtful. The tide would pull me out to sea and I'd be fish food.* Eva closed her eyes and willed her thoughts to stop spinning. *Find a good thought,* she told herself. She pictured Arlo, where she had left him at Archie and Bea's . . . curled up on a scrap of blanket under their warm stove.

Eva fidgeted with the folds of her skirt. Then suddenly, silently, the minstrel stepped around the hedge and sat beside her.

She caught her breath. "Where have you been?" she whispered fiercely. "I thought you weren't—"

"—*Coming?*" he finished for her. "Here's something you can know about me, Princess. Unless death prevents me, I keep my promises."

Eva considered this bold statement and knew his was a story she must know.

"Who *are* you," she demanded, feeling a prickle of fear in the back of her neck.

He looked in her eyes solemnly. "You're wanting answers, but time has run out . . . Will you trust me?"

She looked up at the moon. "Why me? What did I do to deserve this?"

"That question, I never find helpful in situations like these. No good answers. Try a different question?" he suggested.

"Such as?"

"Like, who holds the key to my future?

"Well—?"

"Surely you're not waiting for *me* to reveal the plan." His laughed shortly and raked a hand through his hair. "You *know* this. Your destiny has chosen you—choose it back, or not—it's up to you."

"I don't exactly know what the *Plan* is. I just know what it's not . . . and I know what I want." She wiped her eyes on her blue silk sleeve.

"Good enough for me," he nodded. "Alright, I can get us to Tirzah. How do we get off this island? Tonight."

"So look." Eva picked up a stick and drew a map to their meeting place in the dirt, grateful for the light of the moon. "That's it. Got it?" she asked and rubbed it out with the toe of her shoe. "Should be a boat hidden in the hemlocks."

"Right. I'll meet you there," he said, shrugging on his backpack. "This I know: when dawn breaks, if we're still on this island—we're both as good as dead. You're going back into the castle. Remember what I told you."

"Go for the neck. Got it," she said, touching her dagger's hilt in the folds of her skirt.

"So, you now have a dagger. Ever used one?"

"Maybe you could share a few tips." She looked dubious.

"Ah, tips . . . Always stay on this end," He pointed to the hilt and raised a wry eyebrow.

Eva pressed her lips together. "I *do* know that much."

He gave her a half-smile. "It does have an advantage over a sword in certain situations.

"And those would be—?"

"You can conceal it, un-sheath it in a flash, and pierce your attacker before he knows what's happening."

"Hmm . . . Can't picture myself *piercing*." She bit her lip.

He paused. "Probably use it as a last resort. A poorly handled dagger is a weapon used against you."

"Right. I've never actually, you know . . ."

"*Used* one before?" He prompted.

"No, *touched*. Was going to say touched or *pierced*." Eva felt her face warm.

"Yes, well, not a problem. Desperate times call for desperate measures, Princess. We'll soon see what you *can* do." He looked at the moon, now high in the sky. "But, our time is short. We're set, *right?*"

She nodded.

"I'll be waiting. It's full moon. Be careful."

"Yes, and I owe you—" she didn't finish.

"—Please, don't mention it. I couldn't live with myself, knowing I let you marry that foul dirt bag. What kind of life would that be?"

"A short one," she said simply. "Glenda will be checking my room. It's past my bedtime." Eva clutched her shawl. "Hope the dove made it." The whisper barely left her mouth.

Trudging toward the castle, her skin prickled. Glancing up at the study window, she saw a movement by the curtain, felt a probing stare. *Look well, Fagan.* Eva almost laughed. Tomorrow she'd be gone.

Running up the stone stairs and into the castle, she appeared to be swallowed whole by the dark, yawing mouth of the door.

Traveler whistled and walked casually toward his room; every muscle strung tighter than his lute strings.

The moon shone brightly in the study window.

The King sank down in the chair beside the hearth, his face a mask of weariness. Fagan stood gazing out the window overlooking the garden, the curtain shadow falling across his face. When he turned away from the window, his mouth was twisted into a snarl.

"Ah . . . there they are, meeting by the pond again. How cozy." The count strode over and stood by the hearth. He faced the king. Composed. "What do you know about this minstrel? Where—?" He was interrupted by a knock on the door.

"Yes, enter." King Cedric waved the royal steward in, motioning for the server to put the tray with two wine glasses on the table by the window. The royal taster was right behind him. With a deep bow to the king, he turned, poured a small amount of the purple liquid into his glass and drank it. He stood for a few moments at attention beside the table. When it was clear he suffered no ill effects from the drink, he nodded, obviously relieved. "Safe, your Majesty." They both bowed out of the room and closed the massive study doors.

"Very prudent to take precaution. There is much mischief afoot these days. You never know." Fagan smiled, walking over to the table. The king started to rise from his chair. "No please . . . allow *me*." He poured a generous amount in each goblet, and with a swift almost imperceptible motion, emptied the contents of a small vial from his sleeve into King Cedric's glass. The white powder fizzed momentarily and dissolved into the liquid.

"As I was saying." The count bowed, handing the King his goblet. "Where is this minstrel from and why has he befriended your daughter?

"When I questioned him, all he said was he had wandered here and there letting his music earn his keep." The king paused and took a deep drink. "He did name Tirzah as one of the places he had sojourned . . ." His words trailed off. The count watched him as an owl stalks a mouse.

"Tirzah, you say!" The count stood and paced the carpet. "I suspected as much. He's a spy of course," he said matter-of-factly sipping his glass, noting with satisfaction the King's eyes beginning to glaze. "Being *perceptive*, I'm sure you must have seen it."

"Well yes—yes of course. That would make perfect sense. We don't know what his Tirzan ties are. For all we know, he's in the service of King Justin. He *would* stoop to something like this . . . hiring a traveling minstrel to spy on me . . . *if* he is a minstrel." The King's head began to droop as his drugged mind came further under the influence of Count Fagan. As usual.

"Yes, a despicable move on the part of King Justin—our sworn enemy!" The count cleared his throat. "It would be my observation that a wise king, such as yourself, would not entertain such riff-raff. This minstrel should be questioned and lose his head over this matter. First thing in the morning."

"Right you are," King Cedric's voice was flat. Toneless. "He will be brought before me for questioning first thing in the morning. If I am not satisfied with his answers, he will be taken immediately to the tower and be-headed." He paused. "I will not tolerate this, this . . ." he paused, searching for words.

"Espionage! A spy within your very castle walls!" The count finished for him. "A brilliant and decisive move on your part, Your Majesty, I must say." He leaned over the King and spoke deliberately in his ear. "You are respected by your people for this reason. You *will* find the minstrel guilty of espionage and execute him quickly."

"Yes. Quickly," the king parroted. "This is why I command respect..."

"And after the trial in the morning, no more delay. My marriage to your daughter *will* take place tomorrow." He stroked the curl of his mustache and tugged on the lace at his neck.

"No more delay," the King said. "The joyful event tomorrow before night-fall." His head fell over against the side wing of the chair. Eyes closed, he snored softly.

Fagan grimaced and strode over to the window just in time to see Eva enter the castle and Traveler wander toward his room. He smirked. "Fools."

The count turned to look at the king drowsing peacefully in his chair. "I am *surrounded* by fools, it would seem." Eva's reluctance to marry him only nagged for a moment. He thought of his previous wives, and his lips lifted in a cruel smile.

Count Fagan left the room, satisfied, leaving the King to doze in a drugged stupor.

27

Once again, Eva lay on her bed waiting for the quiet she knew must come before she could even think about leaving. She pinched herself to stay awake. The thought of waking up to morning in her window sent a trill of horror through her. That would be it. *No more chances.*

Soon Glenda knocked and poked her head around the door. "G'night Your Highness. Sweet dreams," she said blandly.

"And to you as well, Glenda," the princess yawned and stretched convincingly.

Glenda pulled the door shut, and Eva heard the key turn in the lock. She almost laughed out loud but swallowed it instead. *Can't make anyone wonder why the princess is amused about being locked in her own room,* she chuckled inwardly.

Waiting until shadows finally stopped moving across the strip of pale light under her door, she slipped out from under her coverlet, fully dressed. Reaching under her mattress, she retrieved the wrapped dragon scale. "One day I'll learn how to use this thing. Strange it's still warm," she mused then put it out of her mind.

Eva put it and the white stone in her travel bag along with the blue cloak from the mysterious knight. Six gold coins in a drawstring purse went in the bag as well. It was far too risky to try to sneak down to the kitchen and back. Food was the last thing on her mind anyway.

"Well, you're as ready as you'll ever be," she whispered to the dark room and touched her gold locket. She struck her flint onto the tinder in the fireplace. The spark blazed up long enough to light her candle. Stomping smoldering sticks out, she pressed the carved rosette, and stepped through the open panel . . . lighting the dark.

Moving once more through the castle's musty hidden passages, her feet flew down the winding stairs. Ignoring rustlings just outside her candle's light, Eva fit the trembling key into the lock, and shoved the weight of her shoulder against the low door. Slowly, it creaked open. The princess stepped over the crumbling threshold and into the night. The air, damp and thick with salt spray, clung to her skin. She shivered despite the warm breeze. Staying close to the castle, she edged toward the stand of hemlocks standing guard over her path to freedom.

Finally reaching the back corner, Eva heard voices high above in the watchtower. She slipped back into the moon-shadow, pressing her body against the rough castle wall. Words drifted down to her.

"How goes it, Sentry?" It was the captain's voice.

"It goes middling well, sir. As well as it should be," came Modrun's rumbling voice.

"Just middling?"

"Yes sir. Referring to the fog-bank rolling in from yon ocean. Always a concern, Sir," he said gravely. "Should be here shortly."

"Hmm . . . yes. Carry on."

"Yes, Sir," came the solemn reply. Eva heard Modrun click his heels and his boots scrape as he turned to walk his watch.

Fog! Was that a good thing—or a disaster?

When the sound of his footfalls could no longer be heard, Eva bunched her skirt into a knot and ran as fast as she could toward the hemlocks. Pushing through the prickly boughs, she found her way once again to the beach, thinking of Brookin. The waves lapped the shoreline. Eva stayed close to the sheltering edge of trees, moving quickly toward the overhanging hemlock bough—the meeting place. She strained to see. Where was the boat? And Traveler? Where was *he*? She thought of the angry starving villagers. *Would Olwen truly help me—King Cedric's daughter?* She twisted her fingers together, panicked.

Mud sucked at her shoes at the water's edge. Without warning, Traveler stepped out from the hemlocks, a silent shadow. He signaled wordlessly to Eva, pulling their little skiff up onto the shore. Tucking her bundle of belongings under the seat, she helped him push the bow into the waves. "We're in luck. Tide's going out," he whispered.

Eva nodded, climbed in, and they slipped through gravelly mud—slicing a dark path through shining moonlit waters. Overhead, a velvet night glittered with a million stars. The turret guard sounded off—"One o'clock, and all is well!"

"*Is* it?" she said under her breath, pushing down the fear threatening to choke her. Looking over her shoulder, the great gray Castle of Dunmoor, now a dark silhouette, loomed over the inlet. Over her.

Will I ever see you again? Eva thought of her father and wondered what he would do. *Probably send out the guard to fetch me. Then, he'll marry the rich Duchess despite her stinking perfume. And Archie and Bea . . . The gardens would fall into a sorry state without them. They'll be well cared for. Father will see to it.*

She listened to the measured swish of Traveler's oars carrying her away. *My friend?*

"Fog coming up the inlet." Traveler whistled softly through his teeth and nodded toward a wall of gray mist. It scudded toward them on the water, engulfing the mainland. The minstrel pulled hard to steer the boat in the right direction. Moonlight made the front wall of the fog bank luminous, but behind it, no stars could be seen—and worse—no village lights would be guiding them to land.

"Maybe we can make it to shore before . . ."

"Right." Traveler said, his voice low.

"Olwen's supposed to be meeting us with a lantern," she whispered hoarseley.

"Actually, I doubt we will see him. Fog's closing in fast. But, that's good. We won't be seen." Even as he spoke, the mist slid across the moonlit waves, swallowing them in a chilling dark shroud. He whistled again. Something *whooshed* directly over their boat. Ahead of them a shrill whistling cry sounded.

"You hear that?" she whispered, leaning closer. "Maybe you should stop whistling."

Traveler chuckled softly. "Did you know falcons can find their way in the dark, and in the fog . . . and in the dark fog?"

"So, that was a *falcon?*"

"Handy to have one around sometimes." She heard the relief in his voice. "He's headed to shore, same as us. We'll just follow his whistle," he said turning around to smile at her reassuringly. "You cold?"

"No, I sometimes just do this." She shivered, clutching her knees.

"Here, wrap this around you," he said handing her a brown cloak. "I'm sweaty. Don't need it."

"Thanks." Eva wrapped herself in its woolen warmth. She hugged her knees more tightly under her chin, hardly believing this was her life: escaping in a borrowed boat with someone she hardly knew, swallowed in ocean fog, at the mercy of a falcon's whistle.

She smiled ruefully. *But it could be worse.*

28

The sun's rays crested Dunmoor's mountains as Glenda's shrieks pierced the castle air.

"The *princess* . . . she's *GONE!* Oh, Heaven help us—*KIDNAPPERS!*" Soon, the whole castle was in an uproar. *The princess had been taken!*

Word quickly reached King Cedric, who ordered the castle searched, and in particular, her bedroom. This sort of scandal would look bad. *Very* bad. Count Fagan and the gathered royalty were expecting a wedding that afternoon. No time to lose! Servants and courtiers alike swarmed the castle, poking into every nook and cranny. No clues were found, except one. A page asked why there was ash from a small fire in her hearth. Nobody knew what to make of it, so it was dismissed. Meanwhile, the enraged king ripped and snorted through the castle, his bellowing echoed in the hallways. The mounted royal guard rode pounding across the drawbridge; the King's orders still ringing in their ears.

Quickly, it was discovered that the minstrel was gone as well. A heavy eye of suspicion landed squarely on him as the kidnapper.

In the kitchen, this new delicious gossip flew in the air through clouds of pastry flour like so much mincedmeat.

"I never did trust him, always so cheerful, and him with his songs."

"—And that backpack o' his! *What* might'a been stowed in there, *eh?*"

"Trying to get in our good graces . . . And for what—so he could nip away with the princess."

"No doubt he'll be sendin' the King a ransom note for—who knows how much?"

"Him and his smiles and songs." Rhona said, looking at the floor and clucking her tongue.

"A real flibbertigibbet, he was," the butcher agreed.

"When the Kings men find him, he'll get what's comin' to him sure; no questions asked."

"Don't expect we'll see him again—alive."

Rhona turned her back to the gossip. "Alright, you twattlin' whiffle-waffles, get back to work. We have a castle full o' people to feed!" She stirred the spiced apple filling and murmured, "Him with his smiles . . . Swift travels . . . the both of you." Tears blurred her vision and splashed onto her piecrust.

Olwen paced anxiously on the bank of the inlet. Uncovering his lantern, its light was absorbed like a sponge by brooding fog. "Not that it'll do much good in this pea-chowder of a night . . . a blessing and a curse."

Something flew over his head. "Hmm," he muttered. "Mighty late for *seagulls.*"

After minutes that stretched into eternity, he heard the faint swish of oars. Running toward the sound, he met Eva and Traveler as the bow of their skiff scraped the shore. "The Way be praised!" he whispered. "It's *Olwen.* Come with me." With surprising strength for so thin a man, Olwen grabbed the mooring line and dragged the boat well up on shore. Eva saw his muscles strain like taught ropes under his weather-worn skin. He stowed the oars in it, motioning silently for them to follow.

Walking dark alleyways through the village, they arrived at a small, neat cottage on the outskirts. A soft glow from the window welcomed them. Olwen opened the door and ushered them into a room smelling of tea and vegetable broth. His wife walked over from the hearth, wiping her hands on her apron, beaming. "Here safe and sound!" She nodded to Traveler and curtsied deeply to Eva.

"Princess Edwina Evangeline, Traveler, this is my wife Peggy . . . my Peg." Olwen grinned, giving her an affectionate pinch on her cheek, rosy from cooking by the fire. She giggled and slapped him playfully on the shoulder, causing more strands of curly brown hair to fly loose from the braided bun on her neck.

"So pleased to meet you, both of you—yes, so very happy," Eva and Traveler both said at once, hardly believing they were there. Their travel bags rested on the wood-plank floor and they shook hands happily with Olwen and Peggy.

"And you can just call me Eva," said the princess.

"Oh, thank you, Your Highness," said Peggy and curtsied again.

"And please, let the curtsies go away." Eva smiled and took her hand, giving it a friendly squeeze.

"Thank you . . . Eva. Please, do have a seat," she said shyly gesturing to a rough oaken table resting on a green braided rug. The table was fitted with plank seats made from the same wood.

Olwen solemnly turned to Eva. "The message Celeste brought said you'd be needing some travel clothes. We don't have much, Your Highn . . . Eva. These pants and shirt from my younger brother are all I have to offer. Oh, and I have this scarf and hat." He placed the bundle on the table and shifted uncomfortably to his other foot. "Hope they'll do. At least they're clean." He raised his dark eyebrows. One corner of his mouth turned up under his mustache. "And here, these boots are from Brookin. She sent them over when we told her you were coming."

Eva was delighted. "Well, of course they'll do! They're a wonderful, perfect disguise! I can't thank you enough." She smiled brightly at both of them, knowing this tattered bundle of clothes cost them dearly. *They were likely saving these for their son*, she thought. *And now I'll have them.* She was sad and overwhelmed with their generosity. Eva thought of the coins in her purse. "Please tell Brookin thank you from me too. Tell her I miss her."

"She would have come herself, but knowing the guards would be out looking for you, she stayed away, hidden, that is," Olwen said solemnly. "She sends love. We're all grateful for what you did . . . wantin' to help how we can."

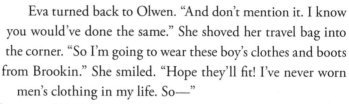

Eva turned back to Olwen. "And don't mention it. I know you would've done the same." She shoved her travel bag into the corner. "So I'm going to wear these boy's clothes and boots from Brookin." She smiled. "Hope they'll fit! I've never worn men's clothing in my life. So—"

"This'll be another first. A night full of firsts for you!" Traveler announced gleefully.

Laughter filled the room.

Suddenly Eva felt light, as though an iron lid had been lifted from her head.

"It's a perfect disguise. You'll look like my young cousin," Traveler grinned. "Go ahead. Try 'em on!"

Eva went back to the bedroom, changed into her "cousin" clothes and came out carrying her blue silk dress with tiny white rosebuds that had always reminded her of stars.

Traveler whistled low. "They fit, but we've gotta do something about that hair. One look in the village and they'll nick you right quick."

"I can braid it and wrap it around the top of my head," she offered.

"And under the scarf and hat…" Olwen muttered, stroking his beard thoughtfully.

"No one will ever guess!" Eva said, getting excited about the prospect of traveling as a boy.

"Maybe," Traveler mused.

"But what about this?" She held out her dress and heard Peggy catch her breath.

"What about it." the minstrel said.

"I can't very well carry it in my bag. Too *bulky*. And if it's found here—" She drew her finger across her neck, thinking of the sword that would part them from their heads for helping the *kidnapped* princess.

"Right. That would never do." Olwen cleared his throat nervously.

"True," said traveler, matter-of-factly. "And now that you mention it, I'm glad you didn't fall overboard. That dress would've dragged you to the bottom of the inlet . . . and me, when I jumped in and tried to drag you back up."

Eva shuddered and looked at her dress, her favorite dress. She shrugged. "You know, so far I've been a princess every moment of my life and look where it's gotten me."

"Another truth." Traveler nodded, then glanced pointedly at the fire in the hearth.

Peggy stepped closer. "Wait. Just let me touch it before you, *you know.*" She couldn't say the words. Stroking the rich blue silk, her fingers slid over white embroidered rosebuds. Holding the material to her cheek briefly, she opened her mouth, closed it, and exhaled. Peggy handed the dress back to Eva. "There now," she said with a crooked smile. "All done. Just wanted to . . ." she didn't finish. Eva saw a tear slide quietly down her cheek. The princess gently received the dress, vowing in her heart: *If I live; one day Peggy will be dressed in the finest silks. I will make it happen. The end.*

Silently, she tossed her dress onto the hearth fire. It crackled and blazed. The room grew quiet. Eva sighed and thought of her life at the castle and the *Promise* made in the garden. *His* promise.

Flames licked the blue fabric, turning it to black ash. Sparks flew up the chimney, whirling into the night sky. Eva's castle life whirled up with them, now a distant dream.

Traveler reached in the fireplace, grabbed a charred stick, and stuck it in the bucket of water beside the hearth stool. It sizzled and steamed. When it cooled, he said, "To make the disguise complete, we should darken your eyebrows . . . *Alright with you?*"

Eva sat on the stool and submitted to Traveler's artistry on her brows. He worked intently, then paused. "What should your name to be?"

"Not sure." *Another decision!* "Maybe Archie . . . no, no *Aric!*"

"A stalwart strong name as ever was," Olwen commented, his arms folded across his ragged brown jacket. "It suits you, Princess—that is—Aric!"

"Aric it is then," the minstrel agreed.

Eva grinned and tried out her 'Aric' voice: "Why, thank you kindly," she said, pitching her voice as low as she could.

Olwen chuckled. "Good. But remember, you're a *boy* not a man . . . *you* know."

Eva snickered and blushed. They all laughed, filling the little cottage with good cheer.

So there it was, that simple: new name, new clothes—new life. Something nagged at the back of her mind. "We can't sleep here," she said to Traveler. "The guards." She stopped herself.

"No one saw you leave, right?" asked Peggy and lifted little Gwenneth to her hip.

"I don't think so; it got pretty foggy," Eva said.

"Good." beamed Peggy. "You'll have time then for a wee morsel of food."

They finished their tea and broth, swapped stories and enjoyed each other roundly. Traveler looked out the window. He jumped up from the table. "It's almost dawn. We have to *go!*" Eva leapt up horrified. With hasty goodbyes their travel bags were shouldered.

Eva reached in her purse and pulled out two gold coins. Thrusting them in Olwens hand, she said, "This isn't enough to properly thank you for all you've done. Know that you both have my eternal gratitude. And please, this one's for Brookin."

Olwen looked in his palm and inhaled sharply. "Princess, each one of these is a year's wages. How can I thank you?"

"You already have. Both of you," she said, her voice small. Peggy squeezed her hand; placing a small wrapped parcel in it and said softly, "Travel in the Way."

The fog had lifted. The sky was indeed lighter.

"Come on, *Cuz,*" said the Minstrel. "Let's go."

29

The pre-dawn sky gave just enough light to see a weedy path winding its way out of Cedricsburg and into the open countryside. They sprinted through barren fields and pasture, their speed fueled by need to travel unseen, to disappear. By breakfast time they neared the foothills of the Trion Mountains.

Eva caught her breath and cringed remembering her clash with Morach and pondered the mysterious knight once again. Her stomach gurgled. "Hungry?" she said, pulling Peggy's parcel out of her bag.

"I could eat." Traveler glanced behind them. "But, let's wait. I thought I heard horses a few minutes ago. Maybe."

They left the narrow path, entering what was left of Dunmoor's ancient forests. Slipping under the fragrant shade of the evergreen canopy, Eva sighed. "I do love the smell of hemlocks."

"One of my favorites," he tossed the words over his shoulder and headed uphill.

They found a spot at the mouth of a small cave in the hillside. Eva spread out the contents of the cloth on the thick evergreen carpet. Wolfishly, they ate the cornmeal journey-cakes and half an apple each. *Fresh fruit*, thought Eva, *very costly in Dunmoor*.

"I don't *ever* remember being this hungry before," Eva said, wiping the crumbs from her mouth. "Or being this sore." She rubbed her feet.

"No doubt," Traveler said cheerily. "But, it won't be the last time. We'll live off the land a bit on our way." He munched the last of his corn-cake thoughtfully. "I think you might enjoy learning how to survive without food from a kitchen."

Now, I'll know how the starving people of Dunmoor feel. "Great!" she said making her mouth smile.

Finding a stream, they refilled their water skins. Watching them swell as they filled, Eva felt weariness settle in her bones.

The minstrel looked up. "We'll stay off the roads. Let's rest now and walk again this afternoon."

The cave hidden behind a bank of evergreen trees seemed safe. Eva unrolled her blanket on the lumpy rock floor, her travel bag placed between her and the minstrel's bedroll. The princess somehow arranged her body between the rocky bumps. Sleep wouldn't come. She sat up, frowned and rubbed her itchy eyes.

Traveler sat at the mouth of the cave, his back to her, watching.

She sat beside him. "Hey, how about I keep watch first. I can't sleep anyway. Maybe no one is searching up this far yet anyway."

"You serious?" He gave her a half-smile.

"I'm always serious. You know that." She smirked and looked into his tired, dirt-smudged face.

He caught her gaze. And to her surprise, agreed, "Well, for just a few minutes. Wake me if you see or hear anything. I mean *anything.*"

"Got it."

He went back into the cave, stretched out on his bedroll. Exhaustion did its work. After a few minutes Eva heard his breathing deepen and turned to see his arm flop to his side. Asleep.

The Princess edged closer to the mouth of the cave and stared out into afternoon. She thought about dragon-men, demons and angels, a world hidden in plain sight from the one she knew . . . or thought she knew. Last of all, she thought of the Voice from so long ago. *Are you still with me, like you said?*

An owl hooted. Her head jerked up. Had she fallen asleep? There it was. *Men's voices!* She gasped. Her hand felt for the clammy floor of the cave. Fully awake now, she crawled back and shook Traveler's shoulder. "Hey!" Her whisper echoed in the dark.

He sprang to his feet, sleep-tousled and wildly alert. Silently he slipped his dagger from its sheath.

She spoke low. "It got late . . . *People!*" She peered out the entrance into dusky twilight.

Traveler didn't answer. He rubbed one eye with the heel of his hand and held his finger to his lips. "Stay here," he mouthed. Bending one of the thick evergreen boughs veiling their cave, he peered over it, slowly letting it return to its place. Without a word, they noiselessly carried their bags deeper into the blackness.

Remembering stories of cave creatures, Eva felt sweat trickle down her back in the chill breath of the mountain. Something dripped on her head, sending a shiver through her. With her shoulder pressed against the damp, slick wall behind the minstrel, she quieted her breathing and listened. Waited.

The sound of grunting and hacking through forest bramble echoed in the cave. A man's raspy voice muttered: "Someone's been here and gone. Footprints. No sign o' campfire." Eva felt Traveler tense.

The other man's voice was high and thin. "It's time we wuz headed back too, Pard. Look—see, sun's long since down. The lizard—he'll be out. Afore we make it home, sure." His words rose. Shrill.

"Shaddap," came the low reply. "He smells fear? Get a-hold a yourself." Eva heard the other man cough. *Or was that a whimper?* "Wait here. I'm lightin' the candle. Checkin' out yon cave.

"Wait, what? You're leaving me here alone? Madness—it's *madness* I tell you. The lizard—he's *out* now. I don't fancy being—" his voice rose to a wail then choked off.

There were sounds of a scuffle, panting, a howl of pain, and a loud *whump*. Eva imagined the nervous man thrown by the one he called Pard.

A scream of terror echoed in the cave. "It's him, *HIIIM! Aiieeeee—*" Muffled curses tore through underbrush, as the two men tumbled down the hill hidden under the forest canopy. Enraged *shrieeeks* from the dragon blasted the darkened sky, ripped through the forest, and filled their cave. *Earsplitting!* Eva clamped her fists over her ears and squeezed her eyes shut, willed herself to think of anything else.

Anything but *Morach*.

The screams faded in the distance. Eva looked up to see Traveler silhouetted darkly in the mouth of the cave, his sword drawn. Ready. She stood beside him quietly. "Nice sword," she finally spoke.

"Thanks," he whispered. "Those two have big mouths. We'll stay under cover of the trees. Put as much distance as possible between us and this place—starting now." He shouldered his rucksack and sheathed his sword at his belt. Eva saved her sword questions for later.

They swept the area free of footprints, and scattered leaves over their site. They journeyed through the woods, guided by the stars, and the next day kept the morning sun to their right. By the next afternoon, Eva could hardly put one foot in front of the other. Traveler, seeing she was at the end of her strength, found a place to make camp just inside a high hillside thicket. A silvery moon rose in the sky.

Pulling off her boots, she rubbed her feet.

Traveler scanned the horizon. "Later tonight, we push on."

Eva groaned inwardly.

They munched on wild blueberries with bits of corn cake, and fell into a dreamless sleep.

Waking in starlight, they were up; headed north.

Drinking moonlit waters

30

Eva and the minstrel traveled for seven days, making camp in the morning and sleeping hidden in the daylight hours. At night, they moved like silent shadows, over fields, through forests, drinking moonlit waters from nameless streams.

Finally entering the northern region of Dunmoor, they walked in the light of day.

After sunset they made camp on a hillside, shivering in a sharp breeze that bit through their clothes.

"When wolves and worse come looking for us tonight, they'd be hard pressed to find us in here," Traveler placed his bedroll on the ground in a stand of gnarled walnut trees. He scanned the sky as usual.

"Doubtful *anything* could find us, here in the back of beyond." Eva said half to herself. A brook cut a swath through the small clearing. She longed to dip her feet in it but, instead, put her bag down and set about their daily task—gathering wood for the fire and food for their bellies.

Just at sunset they dined on walnut, crawfish, and mushroom soup; and afterward, drank a pungent tea Traveler brewed from pine needles and sassafras roots he'd dug.

Eva sat cross-legged by the tiny fire, savoring her tea and their view of the misty hollow. She stole a glance at the minstrel's face, remarking to herself again, how odd it was that she should feel so at ease with this man she hardly knew. *Well, he did risk his life for me. That counts for something . . . and there was the dream.* Looking away, she drained her tea in one gulp.

"Ready for some knife skills?" Traveler asked, munching a walnut.

He reached over and pulled a sheathed dagger from his bag. "Got yours?"

Eva touched the buckled leather around her waist and faced the minstrel across the low fire. "Alright now what?" she heard a tremor of excitement in her voice.

Traveler pulled his dagger from its sheath and stood, knees bent, swaying slightly from side to side. "Now, you . . ." he nodded her way.

She grabbed the hilt of her knife and pulled. *Hard.* It landed at his feet. "Probably not the best way to win. However, you *will confuse* your opponent." He handed it back, a smile slowly spreading across his face.

He's laughing at me! She shoved the blade back in its leather holder. "Again," he said and solemnly took his position across the fire.

The next try, she was able to hold the dagger securely and find the swaying "ready" position. She paused, seeing herself fighting off a band of bounty hunters—her whirling kicks smashing swords from their hands. They would try to capture her but were no match for her skill and speed. She would disappear like a shadow into the forest and leave them scratching their heads in a cloud of dust. *Probably.* She smirked, imagining their furious bewilderment.

"You *here?*" Traveler waved his hand in front of her face.

"*Me*—of course! Ready when you are!"

"Alright, then—*defense* moves." The minstrel first played her part. She attacked him and was blocked at every move, ending up each time with her dagger taken and her arm pinned behind her back. Then it was her turn. "Now, don't let me win!" she panted, gathering her wits for his attack. *How annoying! He's not even out of breath.*

"Don't worry—I *won't!*" He flashed her a half smile and looked up in the treetops, giving her a moment. She quietly slipped her dagger from its sheath. "No," he said. "You don't expect this, remember." Her knife went back in its leather holder. The minstrel walked toward her, looking into the darkened woods, whistling through his teeth. Then, quicker than two blinks of an eye—her dagger was in his hand and her arm pinned behind her back.

"This is just not fair!" she wailed. "I'm *never going to learn!!*"

He released her and looked in her eyes. "Now, I want you to notice every move I make," he said gravely, steeling himself against how close he was to the princess and the faint scent of lavender wafting from her unbound hair. She saw him hesitate, take a small step closer, inhale deeply and step back. Twirling his dagger deftly along his fingers, he slid it into his belt sheath without glancing down. Raking a hand through his dark hair, he turned to her, face flushed.

"Noticing," Eva murmured and caught her breath. *Is he about to kiss me?*

"What?" He shook his head. "Oh, *yes*, yes . . . you'll get this. You have to. But maybe not all of it tonight," he said a bit too brightly. "Now, watch." He began to go through his moves very slowly, pointing out every hold, every position of release and defense. He showed her how to use small movements to block and to use the force and weight of her entire body behind her thrusts. They did this over and over, until Eva was able to counter his holds and set herself free without losing her dagger. She stepped back panting and plopped down beside the fire. "Amazing," she mused. "I can actually do this. You didn't go easy on me—*right?*"

The minstrel sat quietly beside the princess, took a long drink from his water skin and laughed shortly. "I'm giving you as much advantage as possible, for later. Highway-men and bounty hunters won't go easy on you either—should you happen across any, that is," he added hastily, seeing fear spring into her eyes.

The mist had thickened and crept toward them, unnoticed. They saw no sunset that night, just a slowly deepening darkness. Eva felt swallowed up in it. The forest suddenly grew silent.

Traveler leaped to his feet and shoved dirt onto their fire. It sputtered and died. They were plunged into complete blackness. Breezes rustled the treetops and the fog thinned, pale patches of moonlight shone through the canopy.

Eva hugged her knees, making herself as small as possible. Waiting, for *what?*

The minstrel wordlessly pointed to the sky beyond the trees. The moon hid behind a cloud, glowing its edges. She heard the drone of something immense in the air high above them, wheeling on the wind. A dark shape sailed across the open night sky, blotting out stars as it flew; something long with enormous wings.

"I *know* that shape, *it's*—" she whispered under her breath. Talons of fear gripped her shoulders. Eva edged closer to Traveler, then put her hand in her pocket. The scale was still there. She fingered it, feeling it grow suddenly hot. She jerked her hand out of her pocket, turning the lining inside out, and spilling the *suddenly glowing* scale onto the dirt between them. She shoved a mound of dirt over it. Traveler stared at her. Incredulous. They turned to watch the dragon swing and circle over them once, twice, three times. He dipped, then, sailed away, growing smaller in the sky. Breathless, they watched his dark form disappear behind the foothills.

"Anything else you want to tell me?" he whispered fiercely. "Like, why would you have *that?*"

Eva winced, her face hot. She bit her lip and released it from its capture, groping for the right words. She explained how she'd found the page in her father's book of spells. "This particular one needed a dragon scale," she said, "and later this very scale fell into my possession! It seemed like fate or something. I mean, how often does someone run across—a dragon's scale?" She smiled weakly her brow wrinkling. They pulled the dirt off the scale, now a harmless gray thing. She held it out in her hand. "See, nothing to be afraid of." Indeed, the scale lay innocently in her palm.

"Another thing they didn't teach you back at the castle," Traveler said, his voice thick, accusing. "If you hadn't buried it, we'd be *his* right now. *Like* calls to *like*—surely you know that."

Eva had, of course, guessed that but was so intent on using the scale to make her plans happen, she had pushed this to the back of her mind. "I'll be more careful. I'll bury it every night when we make camp. But I have to find out how to use it; please understand. There are things that must be done—things I could never accomplish by myself, don't you see? *Very* Important Things!" Her voice rose, eyes imploring. "I'm sorry I didn't tell you before."

"Forgiven," he said quietly. "Guess we both have things to tell when the time is right." He shifted uncomfortably. "So, he didn't find us. A dirt covering must mask the signal, and we know he's not out before sundown."

"Right. So I can handle this," she smiled winningly. "It's not very big, or heavy." She mounded more dirt over it.

"One night, someone has to put an end to him, or you'll *never* have peace—dirt or no dirt. Scale or no scale, you'll always be looking over your shoulder, wondering. You can talk to Zephira the Seer. She'll have some answers." That said, Traveler turned and pulled his short sword from its scabbard in his ragged rucksack. The moon slipped out from behind low clouds. The sword gleamed softly in its light. The ruby glinted in its hilt.

"That is no minstrel sword," she whispered. "I've seen that hilt before; gold with the falcon emblem of Tirzah worked into it. Anything *you* want to tell *me?* Like—where did you get that weapon?"

"I served the King of Tirzah for years and fought beside his knights in the borderlands and abroad. It was said our swords were sharp enough to part a man from his thoughts."

"So, Archie was right," she whispered. "There *is* more to you than meets the eye. What else should I know about you? And how old are you, by the way?"

He scanned the night sky and shifted uncomfortably. "Oh, not too very much to know." He glanced briefly at her moonlit face. "And I'm seventeen. Well, enough about me. How about you? What was the childhood of a princess like?"

"No, not until you tell me more . . . I'm waiting."

"Ok, I promise I will, but another time." He poked the embers with a charred stick. "The trees have ears, as they say."

Speaking in whispers seemed like a good idea. Even as they spoke Eva realized her teeth were starting to chatter. She pulled her blue cloak tighter around her. Traveler handed her his wool blanket.

"Here, use this."

"No, I'm fine," she said hugging her knees tighter.

"Stop being *noble*. Take it . . . I have my cloak." He leaned over and tossed the blanket around her shoulders. "You won't get much sleep, shivering like that. You'll need all the rest you can get for tomorrow."

"It's not the cold, it's..." her words trailed off.

"I know what it is, Princess. We all deal with it—or we don't." An owl hooted nearby.

"I can't imagine actually falling asleep in all this noise." She rubbed her eyes.

He smiled. "When the sounds stop, that's when I pay attention. When Morach flew over, it got real quiet, *right?*"

"Got it." Crickets, frogs and katydids thrummed away happily again. She yawned. "Maybe I *will* try to sleep."

"Good idea." He stretched and lay back on his bedroll.

Eva curled up on her blanket beside the coals of their campfire and tried to quiet her mind. She stared up at stars twinkling through the leafy canopy and sighed deeply. *These stars are so bright, I can almost smell them.* She closed her eyes; visions of Archie's garden bloomed in her mind. Her head jerked up. *Did I fall asleep?*

She edged closer to the dozing stranger, her mysterious friend.

"Trav, you awake?" she said, under her breath.

"No."

"I heard you breathing, over there..." She whispered and wished she hadn't.

He rolled over to face her. "Wasn't asleep. Thinking about tomorrow. *You?*"

"Thinking about stuff..."

"Stuff?"

"So, when you were very young and just learning your songs, did people ever teach them to you wrong?" she asked.

"Sure. Lots." He rubbed his eye with the back on his hand.

"But you figured it out, right? Now you make your way in the world with songs so wonderful that even kings ask you to stay longer."

"That has happened, yes. *And . . .?*"

"Well, that's what my life has been like, until we left Dunmoor . . . *off-key, wrong,*" she sat up. "Father made my choices for me." She squinted her eyes. "I did say 'no' whenever I could get away with it though," she muttered.

"Word *had* gotten around about all the suitors you turned down before Fagan. Is that why you told them all '*no*'—to prove you could do it?" He propped up on an elbow.

Eva gazed at the moon behind his head. "That was different," she said quietly. "I was waiting on *someone.* We'd made promises . . ." She felt her insides squeeze and immediately regretted the words. "He could be dead. I, I just don't know."

"Who is this liar—this wretch?" Traveler frowned. Something flickered in his eyes she couldn't quite catch.

"No—don't say that. Something terrible must have happened to keep him away." She poked the faintly glowing embers between them with a stick. They sputtered and flamed briefly. "Anyway, my point was—my life at the castle was the only song I knew . . . until now."

The silence that fell between them filled with forest sounds.

Traveler closed his eyes, and just when she thought he might have gone back to sleep he smiled. "Tomorrow, it's Miracle Mountains, so get some sleep, Princess." He sat up on his bedroll, looking out over the meadow. "Think I'll be up for a few minutes."

Eva sat up, wanting to keep watch with him. She no longer jumped at forest sounds, but found them comforting, much like the presence of this minstrel. Out of the corner of her eye, she again secretly studied his profile in the moonlight. His hair, black as onyx, lay on his shoulders unbound. The dark eyebrows and heavy beard were inscrutable, but his high cheekbones seemed oddly familiar. One thing that did bother her was: she could only see a small part of his lower lip. His mustache had grown thick and long covering most of his mouth, and he seemed fine with that. *Strange.*

Finally, at the end of her thoughts, her eyes closed. It seemed only moments later Traveler was shaking her shoulder. It was morning.

Price must be paid

31

Count Fagan had returned swiftly to Ravenia upon learning of Eva's escape with the minstrel. He now paced the floor in front of the window overlooking the twisted road through the forest leading up to his castle bridge. He saw what he was waiting for and strode into the Great Hall.

Presently, a small ragged man with a pointed rodent-like face entered the room with his hat in his hand. He was brown and dusty like the ground he traveled.

"G'day, your Grace," he said, bowing deeply. Looking out of the corner of his eye he could see the look of satisfaction on the count's face. Give what was expected. That was his motto. That was how he got on in this life. However, Jack had already decided: this was going to be his last job for the count. He didn't have the stomach for the things required to get his money. Not anymore. *I'll be paid handsomely enough to live the rest of my days when I deliver the*—.

The Count broke into his thoughts. "So, out with it! *What?*" he snarled.

The wirey little man leaned away from the count and spat on a white square of marble on the floor. Disgust washed over Fagan's face, but he shoved it aside to hear what he was waiting for.

"Yes, your Honor. I have brung news of their whereabouts."

"Well, speak, Man! *Where* are they?" Count Fagan's eyes flamed. Enraged, he gripped the arms of his chair, not striking his spy down into the small brown puddle on his polished floor. He *must* have this information.

"Beggin' your pardon, your Eminence. They was past th' Trion Mountains, headed north t'ward Tirzah when last they's seen."

"Well, what are you waiting for, *Fool!* Bring them to me!" He towered over the cringing man. "Now, *GO!*" he shouted, flinging his arm in the direction of the castle entrance. "And don't come back without them."

The count waited until his spy was out of earshot and summoned four men. "Follow him," was all he said.

Jack would have to travel through Fagan's land, this he knew—and hated. But to get the reward money *and* save his life, this price must be paid.

His wagon creaked, complaining loudly as he hoisted himself onto the wooden bench seat. Whistling his ancient horse into action, they rumbled on. Jack's shoulders sagged under a dark, heavy sky-shroud. *Hangin' on me, as it does*, he shrugged. *No use trying to shake it off. Not 'till I'm out of this cursed place anyway*. It was beyond him why anyone would want to live there.

The answer to this lay buried deep in decades past.

The old ones remembered the days before Fagan came into power—before the color seemed to drain from the land and sky. Afterward, they had spoken out for freedom, but that was long ago. Sadly, each one had died a mysterious death or disappeared without a trace. Now, only those who knew how to keep quiet and mind their own business remained.

The people of Ravenia staggered, every day, under the heavy burden of taxation and usury. Yet they somehow found a way to live in uneasy peace. Morach didn't grab children from their villages, burn their crops, or pluck sheep from their herds. Not usually. He chose other lands. They told each other they were very fortunate indeed to live in a country *mostly* free from those problems. At least, that's what they said.

Truth be told, the entire countryside was veiled in a dark, palpable, shadow of evil. This shadow could be felt by most, not seen. However, some children born into this perverse time could see the heavy shroud with their natural eyes. They said it looked like a huge black wing. The old ones knew the truth of this. These children were truly seeing the evil overshadowing their country.

And black birds that drove the songbirds from their land still skulked about. They lurked in shadows, spying for the count; reporting any hint of insurrection.

The parents were sternly admonished to silence their children who *saw*. These few little ones were quickly hushed and punished for their foolish imagination. *No one must speak ill of the count!* At bedtime, a proverb was repeated over sleepy children:

"Keep it un-said, or wake up dead."

Soon, the children believed what they saw *was* foolishness, and they no longer saw the dark wings—or the claws.

Life went on.

Count Fagan's castle staff, his underlings, had learned how to navigate the violent storms of his temper. There was a lot of bowing, and, "Yes, as you wish, your Eminence!" and, "They are most certainly wrong, and you are *right*, your Grace!" They learned to turn a blind eye to the dark dealings of the count; they must, *if* they wanted to stay on his payroll, keep the lash from their back . . . and stay alive.

As a boy, Fagan had learned to hide from his own father's rage and the brutal beatings that left him bruised and broken in body and spirit. His mother became a shadowy figure, crushed, fading daily from his life until one day she was gone. He realized then, he was truly alone.

Seeking refuge in dark places, the boy made vows and alliances with the shadow creatures promising him revenge . . . and exacting a terrible price from his soul.

Years later, as an iron-fisted ruler, he made his final covenant with darkness.

At night when sounds too hideous to tell came from the turret of the highest tower, the women hid under their bed covers and plugged their ears with cotton wool. The count's men could be seen clattering down the stone stairway to the wine cellar. There, they would try to drown their guilt and fears in flagons of the red drink. It might have worked, but for one stubborn thing: they *knew.*

They discovered no amount of wine could make them *un-know.*

So, after twilight, before anyone needed to plug their ears or drink themselves into oblivion, before the terrible sounds from the turret echoed through the castle, he would send his staff to their rooms, then wait for silence to fill the stone halls. Thinking himself hidden then, and his nighttime movements undiscovered by his staff; he would begin his ascent up the steep turret stairwell. Always cautious, always careful that no one would see. No one must follow him. No one must know about the liquids in the vial and the power they held over his life.

Unlocking and re-locking the stairway door behind him, Count Fagan, Dragon-Lord, would slip through deep candle-lit shadows to his turret, spiraling upward like a shapeless horror in a nightmare.

Angel Falls

32

Eva and the minstrel scoured the area in the light of dawn for walnuts. Hunger scrabbled at their insides.

"I can't walk far without something in my stomach," Eva muttered to Traveler's back and then wished she could suck the words back in her mouth. "But, I'm sure I can find more walnuts," she said, making her voice sound chipper. As she stood, a thought rose darkly: *This is what it feels like to starve to death. Most Likely.*

"Not to worry, Princess," Traveler said. "I have a packet of rabbit jerky and dried thyme in my bag. Saving them for just such an occasion." She saw a flash of teeth under his mustache.

"Oh!" Eva pulled a twig from her hair. "I was just thinking, 'what I wouldn't give for some rabbit jerky stew'." She squinted one eye. "Not even joking!"

He smiled broadly and pulled the leaf-wrapped packet from his bag.

Soon, the rabbit-walnut stew simmered over the fire. After finishing, Eva tipped her bowl to get the last drop. "When I come into my throne, we'll have this stew at least once a month. I'll make sure you're invited."

Traveler snorted, shot her a grin; they swept their camp and were gone.

Skirting fields, they headed north, always north toward Tirzah. For lunch, it was walnuts again. That afternoon, ignoring their complaining stomachs, they fell into an easy walking silence on a rutted dirt road.

Eva finally spoke: "I've wanted to tell you something." She kicked a rock into the woods.

"What's that?" Traveler said, scanning the trees to the left.

"I really like your songs and poems . . . I mean, *really*," she shot him a quick look.

"You do? That's . . . um, nice." He raised his eyebrows and looked sideways at her. One side of his mustache twitched up.

"You're welcome," Eva warmed to her subject. "I write too," she said almost inaudibly, immediately wishing she hadn't. *Maybe he didn't hear that last part!*

"Really! What do you write?" He turned to her, genuinely interested.

"What do *I* write?" *Think Eva.* "Well, when I was writing, I would often be inspired by sitting in the garden. Not while I was doing the *actual* writing, of course; a person has to have quiet and solitude to be able to think. And, you know Archie works around the garden a lot." She took a deep breath. "Not that he wouldn't have encouraged me in my writing—He certainly would have!"

"Yes, certainly!" Traveler agreed, smiling at her, bemused, intrigued.

"But actually, it would go like this," she pressed on. "While I was sitting there, I might need to go to the kitchen and get Arlo a saucer of milk, that would make me want a slice of Brookin's delicious bread with jam, which would mean cleaning the drips and crumbs off my dress afterward—and there I would be, cleaning and walking around—but *thinking* for most of the afternoon." She looked at him, squinted, and turned up the corners of her mouth, cat-like. "What I'm saying is: most of my writing ideas *did* happen in the garden."

"Oh?" Traveler said, fighting back a grin.

"Well, a couple did at least." She rolled her eyes skyward. "To be honest, just one idea came while I was there, but I kept going back in case it might, you know, work again . . . But it didn't. And, now, it doesn't matter." Eva hoped this might throw him off wanting to actually *hear* something she'd written.

The minstrel beamed in her direction. "So let's hear it."

"Hear what?" She shaded her eyes and peered up into the treetops. "Oh, look—is that a woodpecker?"

"So . . . a song or a poem?" He prompted.

"Oh, that—no actually, mine stink next to yours. I'd rather not." She stopped and looked again at the trees.

"I'd really like to hear it. But, maybe you can't remember it. That's fine. No problem." He stood beside her and studied the trees with her, humming lightly.

"Well, *certainly* I can remember it! The song has just four lines." She put her hands on her hips and gave him a watery smile. "But, first I have to say this: I do most of my writing in my diary, now hidden in the secret passageway behind my bedroom hearth . . . or what *used* to be my bedroom." She paused, pulling two gold chains up from her ragged shirt. On one hung her locket. The other held two keys. "These are the only keys." She chewed the inside of her cheek and scrunched up her eyes at the minstrel's face. " –To the trunk and diary that is."

"Stalling again?" He smiled and whistled through his teeth.

Eva sighed. "Alright, but don't forget, you did ask. Here it is." She cleared her throat dramatically.

"I like potatoes,
You like 'em too.
Let's add some butter,
And eat a few."

"That's it. The end." She walked on. "I wrote it for Brookin. We both laughed our heads off. Then we ate the buttered spuds." She tossed these words back over her shoulder.

He came up beside her. "Ahh, that's *great!*" His stomach growled. "I wish I *had* some of those buttery spuds—right about *now.*"

She arched an eyebrow his way.

"No, really—I like it!" He flung out an arm. "In fact, I was just wondering how you would feel about me singing it at the Purple Pig tomorrow. I won't name you as the composer though, you being in hiding and all. So, how about I just say this song was written by my good friend—*Spud?*"

"Spud! *Well*—" She stopped in the road. "That's *Princess* Spud to you, Mister!" Eva grinned, a giggle fluttering in her chest.

A dust cloud floated past them.

Without warning, Traveler grabbed Eva's arm and hauled her into the woods.

Eva suddenly found herself propelled through the air, stumbling, tripping through underbrush after the minstrel. Stunned, she gasped and cried out. Immediately, his hand clamped over her mouth, his arm clutched her waist, and pulled her down behind a great oak. Her mind screamed silently at him. *Please don't hurt me . . . I trusted you! I'll give you money . . . lots of it . . . I'll find a way!* Her eyes stung. *Betrayed. Again! Some things never change!*

Crouched next to her, panting, Traveler looked into her panicked eyes. Silently, solemnly he nodded toward the road and turned her face toward it.

Men's voices drifted toward them.

Traveler inclined his head toward the sound and released her, motioning to be quiet. She saw them then. About 30 paces away, four men on horseback rounded a bend in the road with an extra horse in tow. She heard the clink and jangle of horse tack and caught her breath as they trotted through a sunny patch. The front rider wore a long black riding coat that flapped back against his horse's flank like a loose sail.

Eva's heart pounded. She felt the heat and tension of Traveler beside her. They sat, not moving a muscle. The riders moved out of earshot. Eva leaned away, shaken, trembling.

"You alright?" Traveler's voice was low and tight. He smiled apologetically.

"Warning me *before* your cave-man act would have been good. But, thanks—again. That was too close." She made herself smile back. "Saved my skin."

"I saw the look in your eyes. You *didn't* think I—? *Did* you?" He shook his head and frowned at the ground.

"What? That you were *attacking* me?" No point lying. "The thought did cross my mind." Her eyes darted to his and away. She clenched her fist and bit her thumbnail.

Travelers eye's flashed, angry that she could believe this of him; then softened, realizing the truth: she'd known him less than two weeks. "You can trust me," he said quietly. "I hope to prove that to you before too long."

Eight breaths passed through an eternity of silence. The minstrel spoke again, this time more softly. "You need never be afraid of me. Ever."

"—I'm *not* afraid," she said, too quickly and loudly, then, exhaled. "I do trust you, obviously, because here we are . . . Let's just go, *can* we?"

Walking through the woods, Traveler showed Eva how to place her feet. They moved swiftly, silently, not crunching a leaf or snapping a twig.

"We'll make camp tonight in Miracle Mountain valley," he said, stopping by a stream to fill his skin-flask. "We're almost there."

Eva and Traveler poured water down their parched throats and slogged up the skinny mountain trail, stopping often for Eva to rest her blistered feet.

When they reached what Eva thought had to be the top, he slashed through some brambles with his sword and nodded toward a vast green valley. "I never get tired of this sight. No place like it." On a nearby ridge, decorated by purple lupines and white daisies, wild goats munched. Swallows swooping in the updrafts disappeared into low hanging clouds, then, re-appeared elsewhere.

Eva whispered, "So beautiful, I think my eyes might melt."

"Angel Falls." Traveler nodded across the valley to cliffs decorated by a white plume of waterfall cascading into a river. "Tonight's camp. We'll make our own trail for a bit." He raised an eyebrow in her direction. "You ready?"

They hiked and hacked their way downhill. Eva limped painfully through the luxuriant valley. They made camp by the waterfall just as daylight was fading.

Eva plunged her feet in the crystal clear water, feeling its cold delicious sting up to her knees. Almost sobbing with relief, she flung her arms wide. "Beautiful—MAJESTIC! But, about this name: *Miracle Mountains*. I mean; I connect the word *Miracle* with things I can't understand, like being raised from the dead . . . angels showing up. You know—things *beyond—Miracles!*"

"Right," he said, picking up some shiny rocks on the riverbank. "But, names come from somewhere. Something must have happened that made the name stick." He rinsed a handful of rocks and held them up to glint in the dimming light. "Rose quartz," he mused.

The minstrel placed the shiny stones in a patch of light in the stream, then, lay down propped on an elbow and watched the water. "Shhh . . . I'm fishing. Have you never fished before? *Shocking*." He whispered, then flashed her a grin, his hand poised over the stones.

Eva walked over and peered past his shoulder. "Maybe they're taking a nap?"

The rocks sparkled under the rush of water. "You just wait. It's shiny things. Fish like 'em." He nodded toward the water. Eva sat silent beside him.

In a minute, a handful of small silver fish shimmied over to the shiny rocks. Traveler's hand was motionless. A larger fish swam over. Like lightening—his hand flashed into the water and the big fish flopped onto the bank. "Hello dinner," his face flushed with pleasure. "—And that's how it's done." His mustache lifted with his grin. "It's a *trout,* Eva! You ever seen a mountain trout?"

"Whaaat!" Eva's mouth flew open. "How did you do that? Did your father teach you?"

"I learned it watching bears in the river." He scooped his hand. "But, my father did teach me a lot about the forest. For one thing, if you have to eat an animal to survive, make it a quick and merciful death." He pulled out his dagger and with a swift motion, cut the trout's head off. Eva looked away. Then, realizing she was going to eat this fish, Eva watched him prepare it. She looked in Travelers face and smiled. "Yum," she said without enthusiasm.

He laughed out loud. "You'll get used to it, Princess." He laid the motionless fish on a log. "We only take what we need to survive. Never for sport." He frowned briefly. "And, back to my father. He has a home in Tirzah. I'll take you to see him sometime if you'd like."

"I would love that." Eva wondered what kind of wild mountain man his father might be.

That night, after the most delicious meal Eva could ever remember eating, she and the minstrel sat around the campfire covered by the cool mist from the waterfall. The spongy air frizzed Eva's hair and made her clothes stick to her like a second wrinkley skin. She tucked a lock of hair behind her ear and gazed up past the cliff. *The stars seem to be dropping down, resting here,* she thought, watching them glimmer. A halfmoon glowed delicately above the misty bowl of mountains surrounding the valley. "I can almost taste the moonbeams," she whispered.

"I know what you mean," he agreed. "The sky does seem closer somehow." He sighed happily and leaned back on his elbows. "This should be the last night camping. Tomorrow night, we'll have a roof over our heads—in Tirzah." He frowned, at what lay in their path.

"I wonder if there have ever been any, you know, unwelcome *visitors* here," she said in a small voice.

"No reason for Morach to come here unless he suddenly develops an appetite for wild mountain goat," he said dryly, then frowned again. "I didn't see any signs—no scorched land. But then, there's no one here to tell us, is there?"

"Not unless these are talking goats." She rubbed her eyes sleepily, wanting to change the subject. "Hey, I've never asked anyone this . . ."

"What?" he asked, looking at the night sky.

"I was just thinking—did you ever wish your good dreams could just soak into your pillow; then, the next night you could put your head right where you left off?"

He laughed and shook his head. "And what about the bad ones?"

"Well, you *could* shake your pillow outside the window, and they'd fall out . . . You know, like pebbles from a shoe." She yawned and divided her hair to braid it for the night. "If you *had* a window, that is."

"That thought has never crossed my mind. But if anyone could do it, I'd bet on you." He gave her a sleepy smile, tossed a rock out from under his bedroll and stretched his back.

"Thanks." She smiled, wrapping a leather tie on the end of her braid. "And one more question."

"And that would be?"

"When you came to the castle, did you *really* come to win a place at court, or was there something else?"

"A bit of both, really."

"Are you lying or telling me the truth?"

"A bit of both, really."

Eva heard the smile in his voice. "Aaahh . . . *fine*. Which bit is *what?*"

"That's would be hard to say at this point. Could we talk about that more in a few days? I promise I'll tell you anything you want to know soon."

"Alright. Holding you to that promise." She sighed. "One more question then."

"Listening."

"Were you afraid when you stood in front of my father that first day?"

"Me? Surely you *jest!*"

"So—the truth?"

"Yes."

Eva chuckled, then they laughed easily. The sound settled on the two pilgrims like joyful dew. "Thought so." She smiled sleepily.

He tucked his folded jacket under his head. "Sweet dreams, Princess." He covered his eyes with his forearm and sighed.

"You too." Eva was weary from travel, but sleep evaded her. An unease about tomorrow crept in, filling her mind. *Was it those riders? Was this about being near Tirzah?* Sorting through her thoughts and finding no answers, she yawned, finally drowsy. "I'll think about that tomorrow," she murmured. Rolling over, the princess wrapped up in her blue cloak and slept.

The two vagabonds were up at dawn's first light, the thought of Tirzan soil nudging them from their sleep. The sun's rays crested the mountains, turning the night's misty haze to rose, then fiery gold. Wandering through the waking valley, they found the narrow goat-trail through the mountains and headed toward Rabblesdell.

A nameless wariness still clutched Eva's shoulders.

33

After walking all morning, the minstrel looked over at her, "Well, *Aric* we're getting close." He took a deep breath through his nose. "Ah *yes*, the sweet perfume of tavern-food."

Eva sniffed the wind. Her eyes brightened. "Yes—what *is* that? I can hardly wait!" She walked faster. "Let's see, first I'll have some shepherd's pie, then a mountain trout in a lake of butter, then a big slice of apple pie with cheese on top."

Traveler laughed. "Then I'll get a cart and roll you on down the road. Seriously, Princess, we have to stay sharp. Your disguise works. But I'm sure the riders and others are there, waiting for us to show up.

"True," she muttered. "Guessing Father *did* put a bounty on my head?"

He laughed sharply. "Do you have to *guess?* No matter; there's the village."

About a mile down, the rutted dirt became cobblestone paving. Houses with brown brick chimneys squatted on the roadside ahead with their brown tiled rooflines. Eva was somehow unsettled by their brown sameness.

Traveler stopped and looked her over from the top of her hat to the soles of her ragged dusty boots. "I guess you'll do," he muttered. "Your eyebrows— dark enough, scar's hidden, hair's under the hat. Hold on." He reached down beside the road and scooped up some dirt. "Hold still—just a *minute,*" he said as she shied away. "You don't want to be recognized do you?"

"Honestly," Eva said, letting him rub dirt on her cheeks. "If my own mother was alive, I doubt she'd know me—there, that's *enough,*" she sputtered and pulled away. Rubbing her cheeks with her sleeve she tucked a strand of hair up in the blue plaid scarf under her hat.

Traveler surveyed the results. "Good," he said gravely. As they continued walking, he pulled out an eye-patch and slipped it over his head, settling it on his left eye. "A little extra precaution," he said. "You'll have to stay on my left and be my sight there."

"Can do." Eva felt the weight of what they were walking into settle on her shoulders. Then, the aroma of well-cooked food shoved it out of her mind.

"Do you remember what I told you about being Aric in public?" Traveler quizzed her, the corner of his mouth quirking up.

"Yesss . . ." Eva hissed, rolling her eyes. "Alright, for the tenth time," she said and cleared her throat. "My Oaf Lessons:

Number one: When eating, always grip my spoon with my fist.

Number two: Always suck soup loudly from the spoon while leaning over the bowl, then pick up the bowl and drink the last half making sure to dribble some down my chin.

Number three: Never use a napkin. Use the back of my hand or sleeve only.

Four: Always reach across the table for anything I want . . . Only not something on someone's plate, unless I want my hand stabbed with a fork.

Five: Make sure I have food *in* my mouth before talking and laughing.

There, I think that about covers it," she said blithely, raised her charcoaled eyebrows and bared her teeth that now shone brightly in her dirt-dark face.

Traveler grinned. "Aric seems to have it down—all but one thing."

"And that would be—?"

"Number six—Be sure to belch with enough force during a meal, so people nearby wonder if you might have done yourself harm. But you haven't, of course. You've simply mastered a skill," he chuckled gleefully, imagining Princess Evangeline releasing such a sound.

"I know you can't wait to hear me do that, but I just can't . . . not that *loud* anyway," she said flatly.

"Oh, it's easy. You just have to swallow air. When you get enough in your stomach—out it comes!" He stopped in the road and began swallowing huge gulps of air. Then his eyes crinkled up at the corners. "Simply tighten your stomach like so . . . and *viola!*"

"Consider me enlightened." Eva smirked, picturing Mrs. Fledge instructing her on the *"Elusive Skill of Boisterous Belching."* Mid-smirk, a sound emerged from Traveler's open mouth. First, a deep and throaty bass note vibrated the air, changing in pitch and timbre to a tone that made her ears ring. Ending with five staccato notes—it echoed throughout the forest, resonating among the trees. Birds grew silent. The woods quieted as if listening. A dog howled in the distance.

Eva stared at him, mouth open. Wordless.

"Pretty amazing, *right?"* he said, pleased with the effect.

"That wasn't the word that came to mind, but definitely something I can check off my "Hear-sounds-that-frighten-birds-and-cause-dogs-to-howl list." She tilted her head to the side. "So . . . you're pretty *full* o' yourself aren't you?"

He smiled broadly. *"Was*—was full o' myself."

She narrowed her eyes. "Thanks; thank you so very much—for the lesson! However, I can safely say that Eva *and* Aric will never master that skill. I've spent my whole life holding back such things, so I don't think I actually *could* now, even if I wanted to. Which I *don't!"* They continued walking toward the village and lunch.

Traveler beamed. "Sure you can." He said, encouraging. "Anybody can. Give it a try—come *on.*"

"I guess I won't hear the end of it 'til I do." She stopped walking and started gulping air. Her stomach grew tight under her shirt. She opened her mouth to say, 'See, I can't do it,'—and it happened. A deep, froggy sound flew out of her mouth, making her laugh mid-belch—much to Traveler's delight.

"Ah haaa—*see!"* He slapped his thigh. "I *knew* you could!"

Eva fanned her hot face with her hat and clamped it back on her head. "Well, that's it then. I'm as ready as I'll ever be." She pictured herself belching with the roomful of the men at the tavern and bit her lip. *What would Valentino think if he knew?*

Eva and Traveler strolled into bustling Rabblesdell.

She looked over and met his gaze. "What is it?"

"Just relax," his jaw muscle tensed. "We're just two cousins, stopping in for a bite of lunch."

"Yes . . . *so?*" She prompted.

He exhaled and a flicker of a smile caught up his mustache. "Just watch your step and try not to . . . *you* know."

"Trip and fall on my face?"

"Well, maybe." He rubbed his palms on his pants. "Or act like a princess."

"Don't worry about me. I got high marks in *Belching Oaf.*" She lifted her chin and walked on.

The two *cousins* calmed their faces to fit the bland crowds, matching their pace.

34

Traveler and *Aric* stepped into the noisy din of the Purple Pig Tavern. Traveler muttered under his breath, "Looks like the same people are here from the last time I set foot in this place." The only exception was a round table by the wall opposite the door. From this vantage point, the three men hunkered there saw every person who came or went from the tavern.

Traveler and *Aric* felt the heavy scrutiny of those three pairs of eyes. As they walked past these men to a small table in the back corner, Eva heard loud cursing. But what made her flush with alarm was hearing her name, *Princess Edwina*, from the man with orangey hair on the right. She walked on as if she hadn't heard. *Were those the riders? Where was the man with the long, black coat?*

They settled in their chairs at the dark corner table and waited for the server. "Look," Traveler elbowed her, "only two men at the table now." Eva wondered what that meant. Had one of them gone for weapons for other members of . . . the *gang?* She denied a shiver that tried to rattle her spine and the impulse to run out of the place. Like some dark bird of prey, her foreboding hovered. She glanced at Traveler.

"Should we go?" she mouthed under the clatter in the room.

"Maybe . . . let's wait just a minute though." He pretended to yawn.

Eva looked out of the corner of her eye, through the hazy smoke-filled place, at the remaining two men at the table. The older one sat hunched over as if hiding something. His grizzled gray beard stuck out, laying helter-skelter over his ragged brown shirt. His bushy gray eyebrows shadowed a pair of baggy eyes. *Like hairy awnings over two dark doors*, Eva thought. As she watched him talk to the younger man at his elbow, those eyebrows would leap and knot themselves together on his wrinkled forehead. However, Eva thought the most noticeable thing about the old man's face was how it seemed to be pulled forward into a point. "Like a rodent's face," she whispered to herself.

The younger man was lean and hard, except for his hair. Eva watched, quickly glancing away if their eyes met, she saw the orange-haired man lift his grey tweed hat. His hair immediately sprang up like some wild thing on his head. Aware of this phenomenon, he quickly clamped the hat back down, capturing the hair. Mostly. Brownish-red stubble traveled like an un-tended crop over his large Adam's apple. Fascinated, she watched it bob up and down when he threw back his head and emptied his flagon of ale. Draining the container dry, he slammed it on the table, wiped the foam from his mouth with the back of his red-spotted hand, and let out a belch that momentarily overshadowed the noisy din in the room.

"Stop staring." Traveler mouthed.

"Right . . . *Sorry*," she said, dragging her eyes away.

"Looks like they have a new server since I was here last," he said nodding to the black-haired young woman with thick bangs over her eyebrows. Her rouged cheeks shone like red apples. She came over to their table smiling. "G'mornin'. What can I get for you folks today," she asked brightly.

Traveler nodded to the young woman. "G'day to you, Miss."

That smile—that face, thought Eva. *I've seen this girl before. But how? Where?*

"Aric, what'll you have?" he nudged Eva.

"Oh! Yes. I'll have the shepherd's pie," she said pitching her voice low.

"Would you like bread with that, young Sir?" the server asked.

Bread! That's it— "Brookin!" Eva leaned closer and whispered hoarsely. "Is it really you?" She kept herself from leaping up from her chair.

The young woman's face turned as white as her blouse, and she gripped the table. "You must have me confused with someone else, sir." Her trembling hand was quickly shoved in her apron pocket.

"Aric, what are you *doing*?" Traveler said through gritted teeth, forcing a smile.

Eva ignored him. "Look—Brookin—it's me, Eva!" She turned slightly and pulled the edge of her scarf back quickly, showing the scar in front of her left ear.

Brookin touched trembling fingers to her lips and murmured: "The True Voice preserve us. So it is." A smile spread over her face. "It's really you. I never thought I'd see you again—not on this green earth." Her eyes brimmed.

They all felt the curious probe of eyes in the room. Brookin glanced to her left and took a step back from the table. "—And shepherd's pie for you as well, Sir?" She turned to Traveler and smiled thinly, all business once again.

"Yes, thanks. Same for me. And two lemonades," he said.

"I'll put your order in. Your pies should be right out. I'll bring your drinks." She nodded and turned, walked to a small square table in the other corner, then disappeared through the kitchen doors.

Traveler lifted an eyebrow in Eva's direction. "Anything you want to tell me?"

"I'll tell you later," she promised. "Too hard in all this noise. Plus, those two at the round table are making me nervous . . . *really* nervous."

And, with good reason. The two men were openly staring at them now. The orange-haired one fingered his dagger on the table. They kept glancing at the door, as if waiting for the third man to walk back in.

"I wonder what happens when their friend comes back?" Eva forced a nonchalant smile.

"Was just thinking the same." He fidgeted with the hilt of his dagger. "Remember what we practiced . . . with the daggers?"

Eva's throat tightened. "Ye—Yes." Looking straight ahead, her hand went down to the leather sheath on her belt. *So this is it.* Her senses on high alert, she tensed for a slashing horror ripped from one of her nightmares.

At that moment, Brookin stepped up to their table with their drinks and food, her forehead creased with worry. She looked at Eva. "Did you notice the men at the table over there?" Brookin leaned her head toward the small square table in the back of the room.

Eva saw two bearded men eating but didn't recognize them. One of them caught her glance and nodded slightly.

"It's the brothers . . . Fulvic and Humic," said Brookin. "They told me the King's guard and others are lying in wait on all roads into Tirzah. They know once you set foot on Tirzan soil, you're safe. Should be, anyway."

"Bounty hunters watching the roads," Eva whispered. "Thought so."

"Yes," Brookin said grimly. "A hefty prize for bringing you both in. Roused most men in the kingdom out of their beds—wantin' that money, they are. Out scourin' the countryside for signs of *you*."

Eva thought about how careful Traveler had been about covering their campsites, walking in the woods as much as possible . . . even in disguise. Not much trouble, until now.

"I've brought some oiled parchment for the both of you, pies and corn cakes for the road. Wrap your food and leave this place, at once, if you value your lives."

"Those men at the round table—I doubt they'll let us just waltz right out the door," Traveler said ruefully, his hand on his dagger.

"They won't be letting you out without searching you, for sure. They suspect all strangers in town. You're no exception."

"A *back* door?" Eva glanced around the room.

"Yes, around the corner—a hallway with a locked door—opens to an alleyway. I know where the key is." Brookin smiled into her eyes, both remembering promises and the night Eva unlocked the door to her own freedom. "Reckon it's my turn." Her eyes shone.

"Any ideas on how we get out unnoticed?" Traveler said leaning back, casually dropping his wrapped pie into his bag.

"The brothers said they'd do it—grab the attention of the room. When they do, that's your cue. I'll be waiting by the door."

Eva wrapped her pie and tucked it in her bag. Suddenly, the brother named Fulvic started gagging and pointing to his throat. He fell on the floor, convulsing, arms and legs flailing wildly. His brother leapt up on a chair and shouted for help. Brookin disappeared into the pushing crowd, shouting for help at the top of her lungs.

Eva and Traveler's eyes met. "Time to disappear," she whispered.

"Yup." He shouldered his bag and glanced at the (now-vacant) round table by the door.

The tavern was soon in clamor and confusion. Eva and the minstrel jostled and threaded their way through the crowd and slipped unnoticed into the candle-lit hallway. Brookin stood by the open door, key ring in hand. She held Eva's dirty face in her hands for just a moment. Tears finally spilled from their eyes. "Prayers for you both . . ." Brookin whispered. "Here." She handed them each an apple from her apron pockets. "Remember, stay off the roads. There's a trail leading north—"

"Many thanks," Traveler broke in, hearing the room start to quiet. "We owe you our lives."

Brookin just shook her head. "Go *now!* Fast and far from here." They were out the door and the lock clicked behind them.

They strode silently behind dingy brown buildings; by the filth in street gutters, rats slinking around corners, by the children playing in cobbled streets, north. Always north.

Just as they neared the outskirts of Rabblesdell, a loud commotion erupted in the streets. Men's voices shouted: "*They're HERE!* THE KIDNAPPER—THE PRINCESS!! *BLOCK ALL ROADS—!*" The whole town flew into an uproar. Dogs barked. Babies wailed. The town's people pushed and clawed each other, trying to be first to each alley, every dark doorway, anywhere someone might be hiding. Every mother's son *knew* he would surely be the one to find them, get the reward money, and live a life of ease for years.

Meanwhile, Eva and the minstrel sprinted north through the woods.

High on a green hill, twenty miles north of Rabblesdell as the falcon flies, an old woman sat sipping a cup of tea on her tiny porch, in front of her tiny white cottage. Without warning, an un-ease, then a tremor went through her slender body, disturbing her thoughts. Then she knew.

Zephira looked up. "Help them, please," she whispered.

3 5

ow much further?" Eva wanted to know.

"On foot—a good half a day, if the weather holds. No catching a ride, not 'til we're on Tirzan soil."

"Right." She tucked a slipped braid up under her kerchief.

"There's another thing," he said stopping to sharpen his knife on a stone.

"Tell me."

The dagger went back in its sheath. "Did you see the bounty edict tacked to that post in the town square—the one Brookin was talking about? They didn't recognize you, but I'm on it too." He smiled acridly.

"Didn't see it." Her mouth curled bitterly. "Father's slipped his moorings."

"Anyway, I'm sure Fagan put him up to it." He gave her a wink. "Don't worry, I know a few tricks."

"I'll just bet you do," she said. "But, no reason *you* should be on the wanted poster."

"I am a kidnapper, didn't you *know?*" He snorted.

"You mean —"

"Yes, I'm wanted dead or alive—and if Fagan has his way . . ."

Eva was horrified. "What have I dragged you into? What can I even say?" She steadied herself on a tree.

"First of all, you *didn't* drag me in—and don't worry." He emptied a pebble from his boot. "Like I said, I know some stuff . . . and we need to get going."

The two hiked uphill, following a stream. Finally cresting the top of a rocky outcropping they scanned the path ahead. The trees grew sparse. A stone's throw from the bottom of the hill the stream disappeared into a green morass that spread east and west.

"Vapid Swamp." Traveler answered her unspoken question. To the east it dwindled and was flanked by a well-traveled road. Beyond it lay the green borderlands of Tirzah. Her heart thundered in her chest. *So a bog in the way?* The stink of dead rotting trees and who-knows-what else wafted up the hill. She shuddered. *Probably a path around it. Most likely.*

"I think we can make it through to Tirzah before dark." She heard the forced cheeriness in his voice. Then he asked: "So, what's the difference between a river and a swamp?"

"Is this *really* the time to torment me with riddles?" she muttered, then, caught her breath. "Wait. What did you just say? *Through* the swamp?" She ran to catch up. "Not me—not *this girl!* I don't go through swamps with snakes and spiders and—?" Immediately she imagined creeping things trying to climb under her pants, into her boots, and drop down her shirt.

"It's that or risk Fagan's men on the road—as you know." He pulled his skin-flask from his belt. "We should get some water." He walked down to the stream, whistling through his teeth. "Sleeping under a roof tonight!" His words drifted back to her. "Good news, *right?*"

Eva stood fixed on the path, her legs refusing to walk toward this place that must be a particular kind of hell. She saw two choices, neither of them good. But, imagining beyond Vapid Swamp, she pictured a safe, cozy cottage with a bed . . . and herself in it. That was good. *Very good.*

"All right. Let's go," she sighed.

Traveler sent her a sideways glance as they dipped their water-skins into the stream. "Don't worry; it'll be fine. We'll get through this. Then it's *Tirzah!* Just stay close."

"Close—*Close?*" She laughed acidly. "I'll *try* not to wander off into the stinking swamp—and be swallowed by quicksand." *Or worse!*

The minstrel gave her a quick smile. "You've done harder things, Princess. You can do this."

Walking toward the swamp, she tried to picture herself held securely, wrapped once again, in the starry, blue-blanketed arms.

As they neared the entrance Eva asked, more lightly than she felt, "*Oh*—so, the difference between a river and a swamp? Or was that some kind of trick question?" She stopped to tuck her pants down into her ankle boots. Her stomach convulsed at the sour reek of rotting things.

He sent her a wink and threw her an extra bandana for her neck. "This should help keep bugs off," he said. "And we're in luck—look!" He stripped some leaves from a bush beside the path. "Here, crush these myrtle leaves and rub the juice on your skin."

She smeared on the pungent green sap.

"Bugs hate this stuff." He smirked grimly.

"And I know why," she tied the cloth around her neck and tried to breathe through her mouth. "Well, I'm waiting. So—*what?*" she pursed her lips.

"What?—Oh, *banks.*"

Eva sighed. "Must you—?" She tightened her bootlaces.

He ignored this. "Actually, *lack* of banks. Get it?"

"Sooo, *riverbanks?*" she gave an airy wave. "Yes, of course I *get* it. The water spreads out, gets shallow, loses direction."

"As it is with rivers, so with life," Traveler said lifting an eyebrow. "A little gem from my father. Yours at no extra cost." His smile unfurled across his face.

"One day, I'll have to meet this father of yours," she murmured.

Traveler smiled at a private thought. "I'll see what I can do to make that happen."

The minstrel looked up. Fluffy white clouds drifting across the sky were now dark. They scudded rapidly from east to west, disappearing behind Tirzah's border mountains. A cool breeze raised bumps on their arms. His jaw muscles clenched. "Let's go."

Eva kicked a rock and frowned. "So, back to swamp creatures. What did your father say about avoiding these so-called blood-suckers if someone *must* walk through a swamp?"

"Nothing. Just stay on the path."

"Well, thank you. Thanks so much." Eva muttered, not realizing she was gnawing on her lower lip. *Are you going to let some stinking goo get in your way? Pull yourself together!*

He held a branch back for her to enter the steamy green shade. "Coming?"

"So, we know our way?" she ducked under and her ears filled with the drone of insects—clouding the ground, the air, and high in the mossy tree canopy. The trail immediately narrowed to a soggy path, no wider than a deer.

"I've been this way before. It's not too bad; in fact, it can be interesting . . . in a swampy kind of way," he said lightly.

"I'm sure," she said under her breath. "Let's get moving. Let's be done with this place," she hitched up the waist of her pants and pulled her hat down tighter on her head.

"Right," he said, holding out his hand.

She wordlessly took it, then whispered hoarsely: "I wonder if anyone ever tried coming through here and didn't—you know, make it." Her voice trailed off and blended with a buzzy cloud of tiny gnats drifting across their path.

"I've heard tales," the minstrel said and quickly regretted it. He changed the subject: "Hard to believe it's still daytime in here, isn't it?"

"It's dark alright." She moved closer trying to sound casual. "What if we find it—you know, the body?"

"*What* body?"

"You know, *the* body! The one who didn't make it."

"Oh, that one." He turned slightly on the path and laughed lightly. "I'm sure we won't come across any *body*. Don't worry. I know the way. Been here before."

"I'm not worrying!" Her voice rose.

"Yes, I can tell . . . you're crushing my fingers," he said in a loud whisper. "We have to keep it down—don't want to wake anything up from its afternoon nap. Things in here are surly on a *good* day; if they're sleep deprived—well—" He didn't finish.

Eva let go of his hand, feeling her face flush. "Yes. Right. I'm fine," she whispered. They walked silently for a while through ever-present clouds of frantic insects. None of them landed on her or Traveler. "Guessing the stinky leaf juice works." She muttered. The acrid odor reminded her how hungry she was. Her stomach growled.

"There's a swamp-apple tree in here somewhere," he said under his breath. "I think it's the right season."

"Good, because I don't know what happened to lunch."

Eva and Traveler step carefully on the narrow, oozing trail snaking through dark sulfurous waters and rotten logs. "Dreadful," she whispered, then, bit her lip, resolving to keep those thoughts to herself.

Something black and long slithered off the trail in front of them and disappeared into the water with a quick swish. Eva stifled a scream. The surface swirled violently. Something huge moved in the depths.

"*Wha*—?" She gasped. Traveler sent a warning glance over his shoulder. She nodded silently. They walked on.

To her left was another dark shape at the bottom of the shallow lagoon. A chill gripped her spine. She shivered, despite the steamy atmosphere. *Keep your eyes on the path!* A pair of bubbles floated to the surface where she thought the nose might be. Eva quickened her pace and caught up with Traveler.

"Nothing to concern yourself with." He spoke low, tense. "Just keep close. We'll talk about it later."

"Nothing here *I'll* want to talk about later," she muttered through clenched teeth.

36

Yes, Your Majesty, how may I serve you?" The wine steward bowed before King Cedric and his chancellor, having been summoned to the study.

"A bottle of our best red wine, steward. And, it is to be opened in our presence." The king waved him off. Then with a grave look to the chancellor: "Can't be too careful these days. Much mischief afoot . . . *too* much." He passed a hand over his eyes, assumed a royal expression and stiffened his back.

The chancellor nodded agreeably. "Quite so. And how are things going with, *ah* . . . the unfortunate incident concerning your daughter." If Cedric had looked in his eyes he would have seen a gleam of morbid curiosity. But, the King was staring out the window.

He expected these annoying questions and had answers prepared. "Everything's fine. Progress is being made. The reports are good, all things considered." But, his face belied his words. His eyes that had been dark, decisive grey slits, hard and narrow, were now wide in dismay, drooping at the corners; the sagging bags below them swollen. Even his skin had become sallow, yellowish and slack, a testament to how he spent most nights—in utter turmoil.

After walking wordlessly all afternoon, Eva and the minstrel were both famished. However, the thought of not getting through before dark and spending the night in the swamp put a fire under their feet. *If it's this dreadful in the daytime, night must be—* She shuddered, overcome by a sudden longing for Bea's warm, bright kitchen.

"I think that's the swamp-apple tree up ahead," Traveler whispered. "It's got *fruit!*"

Eva tried to contain herself. "Alright, we'll be quick!" she chirped.

They carefully squeezed through some scrubby bushes with thorns the size of daggers. On the other side was the apple tree. A branch hung over the trail, bent with small red fruits.

"Good. We'll hurry . . . Come stand under here." She picked up the apples as he shook them off the branch, filling his bag.

"Oh, I can hardly wait!" Her mouth watered.

"Me, too. When we get out of here, we'll wash them in the stream and feast. Trust me, you don't want this mud in your mouth. You alright waiting?

"Sure, not a problem," she lied.

Eva watched the last of the muddy apples disappear into his knapsack, hardly noticing the ever-present swarms of bugs. *I could starve before we get out of this stinking place.* She kept that thought to herself as well.

As the minstrel continued their muddy trek, she saw two small apples left on the branch just out of reach. *But maybe if I stand just on the edge here, and hold onto the branch,* she thought, *I can get these for us before they fall in the mud . . . then we won't have to wait!* Eva's shrunken stomach complained loudly.

She steeled her nerves, put the toe of her boot, *just the toe,* in the shallow stagnant water, stirring up stench and a frantic cloud of tiny black bugs. With her other foot on the path's edge she ignored the bugs and reached up to grab the branch.

Not hearing her footsteps, Traveler turned around. "Eva *DON'T—!*"

The bank under her foot sagged, plunging her boot into putrid mud—then deeper and deeper into the dark cold liquid . . . too thick to be water, too thin to be mud. The swamp swallowed her knee. Brownish bubbles rose in the disturbed water along with black pieces of—*what!* She yanked her boot.

It was sucked deeper as though an invisible hand was dragging her down, down into the black slime. And the bubbling creature—*where was it?* Her head prickled, unbelieving.

Something wriggled down in her boot, then something else. Her foot was trapped, laced in, wedged in her boot with mud. She screamed then, hearing her voice swallowed up in hanging moss. A huge grey bird exploded into flight, trailing long legs behind it. Eva hardly saw it.

In a flash, Traveler was on his knees, plunging his arms down into the black muck. Grabbing the top of her boot, he pulled, sweat rolling down his face and dripping off the end of his nose. Finally, the mud released her leg with a loud, angry sucking sound.

Eva was free.

They both lay panting on the trail. Eva found her voice and was about to thank him when she felt an odd sensation on her leg. She pulled her pants up past her knee and saw—*what?*

Black shiny things about the size of the end of her finger dotted her muddy leg. She started to flick one off. Traveler glanced over and shouted, "—*NO!* Not like that! *Wait!*" He rolled over to his knees and pulled out his dagger. "Take off your boot!" he barked.

"What *are* these disgusting things?" she gasped, tugging at the soggy laces.

"I'll tell you, but cover your mouth first." He leaned closer and split open the end of her pants leg.

"What—my *mouth?* And what are you doing with that *dagger?*" Her eyes widened, terrified.

"Just do it. You're not going to like this . . . You *can't scream again.* Draws too much attention." He rocked back on his haunches and waited.

"Alright. I can handle it. Just tell me," her hand muffled her words.

"Those are leeches." He paused, waiting for the scream.

This news caught Eva sideways. She'd heard tales of blood-sucking leeches before, but never seen one. And now, there they were attached—lots of them, wriggling on her leg from her knee down into her boot. Her insides twisted and heaved; the minstrel's voice was muffled and distant. *"Eva? Eva!!"* Treetops cart-wheeled over her . . . The world went black.

The sound of rushing water woke Evangeline, then the sensation of her left leg being very cold, and very wet. A memory nudged but evaded her like the wind when she tried to recall it. "What *happened?* Where!" she croaked in a hoarse, stunned whisper; her throat a desert. Her eyes peeled open to see Traveler's face looking into hers, wide-eyed.

"I wondered when you'd come around," he said and grabbed her water flask.

"What . . .? Wait, I remember now!" She sat up, making her head spin. Looking down at the cold leg, she saw it covered by currents in the stream—and by angry red welts. She shot a questioning look at the minstrel.

"These particular leeches have a nasty bite," he explained. "They have to be detached carefully with something sharp, like a knife blade. Otherwise, their mouth stays attached. Poisons your bloodstream."

Eva shuddered.

He lifted the water flask to her lips. "And, now your leg should be clean from their nastiness. Hopefully, you'll be able to make it the rest of the way to the cottage. About two hour's walk, if I remember right."

Eva looked behind her. The mossy treetops were just visible beyond the meadow knoll where they sat. She shuddered again, "So you carried me all this way? *Traveler?*"

"You're not exactly what I'd call a heavyweight," he said and sent her a smirk.

The princess glanced at her arms and legs, now just skin, muscle, and bone. "Guess you're right." She smiled wanly and stood; cautiously putting weight on her cold, wet leg. Suddenly, she remembered the herbs Bea had given her, and dug down in her bag, pulling out the little pouch. "This should help," she muttered and pulled on her clean soggy sock. Traveler watched with interest as she packed it with herbs from her pouch. The wet sock held them tightly to her leg.

"Well, somebody's full of surprises!" he observed cheerily, and rocked back on his heels.

"Bea's parting gift," she said and looked up. "Well, that should do it." She tested her weight again on the leech-bitten leg. The herbs were working. There was only a dull ache where fiery pain had been.

Lacing up her boot tops, the thought of sleeping under a roof made her fingers fly. "Alright—I'm ready! *You?*" she said, sounding much brighter than she felt. She picked up her bag, slung it onto her shoulder, and winced in pain.

"Well, I was just thinking I needed another bag to balance my other shoulder. Feeling a bit one-sided," he said nodding toward her bag. "May I?"

"Very kind of you. But I guess I've been enough trouble for one day." She managed a smile. "Anyway, I'm sure I can handle it. No problem." She straightened her back and squinted.

"Yes, I can see that." He lifted a wry eyebrow her way and held out his hand. "Now, how 'bout it?"

Eva realized the ache in her shoulder from her bag's weight would only get worse and slow them down. Embarrassed, she lifted the strap and laid it across his palm. He hoisted it easily onto his shoulder.

"Not to worry, *Spud.* One day you'll be giving me a hand," he said over his shoulder. "We're off then!"

Eva turned that possibility over in her mind and trudged on.

The rest of the afternoon was spent slipping silently through the woods, with the thought spurring them on: *If we can just make it to the cottage.*

Finally, hacking through vine-covered bushes and branches, they emerged into a clearing. Eva tried to ignore her complaining feet, now blistered from wet boots. She suppressed a groan, and saw what looked to be a narrow path leading up into a wooded hillside.

"Almost there," he said, answering her unspoken question. "You gonna make it?" He looked down at her boots.

"Lead on," she said grimly, holding her hand out for her travel-bag. He handed it over. Lifting her bag back onto her shoulder, she pasted on a smile.

Traveler looked sideways at her. "Seriously, let me carry that. You need a break. No arguments, young lady," he said in mock sternness, and started to lift her strap from her shoulder.

"No, Trav. I've got this . . . Do *not* make me fight you. I'm in no mood." She pressed her lips into a grim line and nodded toward the path. "Let's go."

"Have it your way, Princess," he shrugged.

Walking up a winding path into the forest, they stopped in front of a huge hollow tree grown into the side of the mountain. Its gnarled roots splayed out in all directions like long knotted fingers grasping the earth. "And, here we are. Trail's end," Traveler tossed the words over his shoulder. Then motioning to her, he bent low and walked into the dark cleft of the tree trunk, disappearing pack and all.

Eva gasped. A hundred thoughts raced through her mind as she watched his leg swallowed by shadows. *What is this place?* "Trav?" She called into the hollow trunk and heard what sounded like his muffled voice. Then nothing. Eva held her stomach, feeling it tighten under her shirt. "Nothing else for it," she whispered fiercely, and stepped in.

Pausing to let her eyes adjust, she moved cautiously. Traveler's voice came from deep in the tunnel. "Eva . . . you *coming?*"

37

The smell of damp, rotted leaves and wood filled the still air inside the enormous tree. Peering into the dark, she saw a light bobbing ahead, coming closer! "That *you*—?"

"Eva! Where *are* you?" The minstrel held a small flaming branch; the tiny torch burned a hole in the darkness lighting the side of his face. She unclenched her jaw.

"I'm *here!*" she shouted and rushed forward only to have her head jerked back by one of the roots dangling from the dark earthen ceiling. Eva ducked lower, moving carefully. "Nice place you got here," she muttered.

"Well, it's not much, but I like to call it home," he said lightly, his voice thudding dully on the dirt walls. "Relax, Princess. We are now officially in Tirzah—*Ta-daaaah?* So, what'd you think?"

Eva heard his smile. "Could use curtains, but *nice . . . really!*" Even underground, she felt the atmosphere shift. It had become *Tirzan*, lighter somehow.

"Wait just a couple of minutes. You'll see."

The passageway twisted and turned through the hillside, opening into a sun-dappled clearing canopied by massive, ancient pine trees. Nestled between two giant trunks was a tiny, thatch-roofed cottage; whitewashed, *like Archie and Bea's!*

The two pilgrims shared a smile; then, the minstrel shouted over his shoulder— *"RACE YOU, SPUD! Last one cooks dinner!"*

They bounded through tall grass, leaping onto a path overgrown with feathery ferns and bracken. He heard her panting and stopped, pretending to be winded. She ran past him and turned, laughing. "Come on, *Pokey!* I'll help you cook— *maybe!*"

"Right—thought you might." His grin turned into a chuckle. By the time they reached the cottage, the two pilgrims had melted in tired-to-the-bone laughter.

Reaching down beside the front doorstep, he pulled out a long brass key. He turned it in the lock, and with a loud rusty *screee*, the door swung open.

The chilly air in the cottage rolled out the door past them, smelling of cut wood, hay, and damp earth. Standing in front of the small stone fireplace, the hair on Eva's arms prickled pleasantly. She sighed and felt the corners of her mouth lift.

"Let's have a fire," Traveler muttered, and shoved the logs in the hearth with his boot. He lit the tinder, then the candle on the rough wooden table in the middle of the room.

Eva pulled up two crosscut sections of a tree trunk that served as seats by the little hearth. She perched on one, letting her soggy boots dry in the warmth and looked around the tiny dwelling. Several small paintings of flowers hung on the walls. Short white curtains with blue rosebuds hung on either side of two small square windows. These opened the whitewashed walls on either side of the thick oak-plank door. Late afternoon light filtered in. Directly across from the door against the wall, was a low rectangular enclosure filled with fresh hay. "So, do you know the owner of this cottage?" she asked. "I mean, what if they should come back, and here we would be? Awkward.*"*

"My father still owns this place. He and my mother liked to come here to get away—and things, before she died four years ago." His gaze flickered toward Eva, then, he turned and pulled a black iron pot on its hanging rod away from the heat of the hearth flames.

"I'm so sorry, Trav. Do you want to talk about it?" she asked softly.

He looked long at Eva and exhaled. "My father hasn't been back since then, but I come here sometimes. I like it. It's quiet. Peaceful, like her." He paused, letting a meadowlark's song sweeten the silence in the room. "I think, while loved ones are here, we love them the best we can, so no regrets."

Eva stared into the fire. "Archie and Bea are the closest thing to parents I know. Always felt safe around them." A shadow crossed her face. "That'll have to do for now." Her voice quieted.

Traveler gave her a half smile and lugged the iron pot to the open doorway. "You want to clean this pot while I scare us up some dinner?"

"Did you just say—'clean the pot?'" She put a hand over her heart and rolled her eyes. "I think you must have me confused with someone else. I have no idea how to clean that pot. *Shocked?*"

"Not a bit," he said evenly. "Exactly what *did* they teach you back at the castle?" Traveler carried the black cauldron onto the path and rubbed it vigorously inside with sand and straw, then rinsed it with water from the stream beside the cottage. Tipping the muddy water out, he brought it back to the fireplace and hung it.

"Well alright. Now I know. My turn next time," she said cheerfully. "To answer your question, I was taught a few useful things at the castle. The other things were beyond annoying!" Eva snorted. "Like walking with a board strapped to my back and a cup of tea on my head—for noble posture." Her voice rose. "I was managed and trained—groomed to within an inch of my life! And for *what?*" She palmed her forehead. "I was a . . . a prized horse auctioned off to the highest bidder." Taking a deep breath, she stopped herself, sat by the fire, and held out her hands out to warm. Her mouth turned up wryly. "What was the question again?"

"Consider this your night off, Princess," he said smiling with his mouth only. "Actually, two different questions: Who is Princess Evangeline *really?* What does she want?"

Eva laughed shortly. "What do I want? You mean for dinner?" She said and poked the fire with a stick. Sparks jumped.

"Right. Yes, that's exactly what I meant." A muscle flickered in his cheek. He looked into the fire and whistled through his teeth.

"Sorry. Not meaning to be lumpish. I know what you're asking, but for the life of me, I hardly know anymore." A not-uncomfortable silence filled the little cottage.

Eva and Traveler sat quietly by the fire, watching dusk fall outside the open door. The comfort of roof, walls and hearth settled into their bones.

Eva closed her eyes briefly. *So, who am I—a motherless child? King Cedric's lunatic, runaway daughter? A forgotten friend?* She settled her chin in her hand. Waited. A pinecone crackled in the fire. Then, a thought bloomed: *These things happened to me. They are not me.* She turned and met Traveler's gaze. "I'll let you know when I know. That's it for now." A smile touched her eyes.

38

Eva and Traveler carried buckets by the door to the stream, through a wild tumble of garden beside the pathway. The ground beneath her bare feet was a soft mossy carpet of green with tiny yellow flowers. She pressed her toes into its cool sponginess, leaving little indentions. The air was sweet and heavy with the forest fragrance, the silence broken only by birdsong and water splashing over smooth rocks.

How easy it is to be with this minstrel, she thought. *No entertaining. No protocol.*

A cool breeze filtered through the forest and fluttered their tattered clothing. She hugged her blue cloak around her shoulders.

Traveler finally spoke. "Storm's coming." He peered up through the branches. "A little warm broth would do us good tonight," he said scooping up a bucketful of water. A school of tiny fish flashed through sunlight and skittered away.

"How do you know?"

"Smelling rain. Take a deep breath. Smell it?"

Eva closed her eyes and inhaled deeply. "It smells like cold sky, like clouds."

"Like rain," he nodded.

Eva opened her eyes and smiled. "Exactly like it." She rolled up her pants legs and waded into the stream. The delicious coldness bathed her aching feet and legs. "I'll just be here a while." She sat on a rock midstream. "So back to broth?" Her stomach gurgled.

"Never fear." He gave her a meaningful look. "Watch this." Traveler walked over to a log and broke off some hand-sized fungus that looked like ruffly orange shelves. He held one out for her to see. "Behold—dinner!" He announced.

She looked doubtful. "Yes, and . . . we should *eat* this?"

He laughed. "Definitely. Some villagers call this *Chicken of the Woods.*" He dropped it in the pouch slung over his shoulder. "This is a safe one. Now these," he said poking a group of mushrooms with neat white caps.

"A bit more dinner-ish," she grinned archly.

"These would be your last meal. Called *Death Angel* by local folk."

She curled her lip. "So, let me get this straight. No eating the *Death Angel*—no matter how fresh."

He scrunched his face. "Yup. All the time." Then squatting on his heels, he peered into the water and muttered: "There really *are* fish in this stream. You just have to know where to look, that's all."

That night they dined on leek and fish broth, thickened with Tapioca root and chopped *Chicken of the Woods.* Afterward, Eva and the minstrel sat staring into the hearth fire trying not to accidentally touch. The twilight moon cast soft light through the oiled parchment windows. She'd slept beside him many nights under the stars, but somehow, in this little cottage it was different. *Very* different.

Eva sipped her cup of tea. "I can't remember a meal ever tasting this good at the castle," she said lightly. "Wherever did you learn how to cook like this?"

"Oh, you know, here and there." Raking a shock of hair back from his face and scratching his beard, he yawned. "Well, *I* could sleep."

Eva was beyond exhausted. "For a week, at least."

Traveler stood and stretched. "I'll be in the cottage right behind this one. It's in shouting distance, so if there's any trouble—" He walked to the door and sent her a sleepy smile. "Well, g'night, Princess."

"Alright, g'night, and—for all you've done."

"Consider me thanked." He swept his hat off his head in a deep flourished bow. "Bar the door behind me."

"Don't worry. I will."

Eva spread her blue cloak over the hay held inside the bed-sized rectangle of wooden planks. It was clean and smelled like old Destry's stall. A little shiver traveled through her, and a strange sorrow rose from her heart to her throat. *Don't be ridiculous. You've escaped. You're finally safe. You're in Tirzah. Now what?*

She pulled the cloak around her and thought again of the mysterious knight. Traveler's unanswered questions rose again in her mind. *What does it even mean? Who am I, truly?* A wave of weariness washed over her. She closed her eyes and curled up in the hay.

The moon touched the western mountains and wind began to moan. It wailed through the valley, tearing leaves and branches from treetops, sending them flying like so many flocks of birds. Outside the cottage, it howled around the corners threatening to tear off the thatched roof. Eva sat up, panicked. *Where am I?* The thin windows rattled, and the door thudded against the bar. At once, everything came rushing back—the escape, the journey, the swamp—*Traveler!*

Someone banged on the door. Eva jumped out of bed, her cloak clutched around her and wrenched the heavy bar up from its iron holder. The wind's force hammered the door open, knocked her onto the floor. Traveler blew violently into the room and sprawled across her legs. Scrambling up, they leaned hard into the onslaught of the wind, and put their shoulders against the door.

"*Holding* it. Drop the bar!" he shouted over the shrieking gale.

Eva swung the heavy wooden beam, and it *thunked* into its metal clamps. Somewhere outside, a treetop snapped and crashed to the ground. They backed away from the door and locked eyes, panting. Rain pelted the cottage, thudding on the rush-thatched roof.

Eva pictured the roof blowing off bit-by-bit and looking up, soaked, through rafters into the night sky. As if reading her thoughts, Traveler said; "This place has been here for at least sixty years. I don't think a little storm is going to take it down now." He walked over and tossed another log on the sputtering embers. Sparks rose and flashed up the chimney.

Eva realized her nails were digging into her palms. She unclenched her fists. "Thanks for coming. I was having strange dreams anyway."

He shrugged. "Thought you might like a little company." He poked the fire with a stick, and a knot popped, sending a spark out onto the stone floor. They both watched it fade and die.

"Got any more stew, or did you finish it up?"

"Not likely!" she shot him a look. "There was enough to feed the entire royal guard."

He swung the iron pot over on its metal hinge, lifted the lid, and smiled. "Join me?"

Sitting at the rough wooden table, finishing off another round of dinner with the storm raging outside made them both giddy with safety and comfort.

"I don't think I can sleep," she said laughing.

"Me either." Traveler grabbed an extra blanket from a shelf, stretched out in front of the fire, rolled up his cloak for a pillow. He sighed contentedly. "All we need now is a good story. Got one?"

The cottage was toasty warm near the fireplace. Eva, wrapped in her cloak, pulled a chair over and managed to curl up in it. "Not me . . . *you*, Mr. minstrel?"

He gazed into the fire for a long moment and looked somberly at Eva. "As a matter of fact, I have one saved up for just such an occasion." He closed his eyes.

"A story told on stormy night,

While sitting by a fire bright . . ."

His voice dropped low, quoting a snatch of an old Tirzan poem.

Eva hugged her knees under her chin and listened to the eerie keening of the wind around the cottage. Another spark popped out of the fire and landed on Traveler's boot. He shook it off and flashed a grin. "Ready?"

She nodded, tucking her hands under her cloak. "Yes, please."

Traveler sat up, stared into the fire, and began:

"This is the story of a woman once called Trudy.

For many years, she lived with her husband in a fishing village by the sea. They enjoyed a happy life together, though childless.

Her husband had been fond of saying, 'My Trudy, am I not better to you than a dozen daughters and sons?' And although this was true, she did love the smiling faces of the village children and wanted a houseful of her own.

As a fisherman, Trudy's husband had earned them a decent living, but now he was eight years in his grave. She continued to take in washing and mending as always; and they had scraped aside a bit of money for the future. She hoped that would be enough to live on.

One winter morning, she pulled her money pouch from under her mattress and discovered she had only three brass dalmas to her name. Hard work and meager food had only delayed the inevitable.

'Alas,' she said. 'My days of washing and mending have come to an end. These old bones creak and pop, and my stiff fingers can no longer guide the needle through cloth. I've grown old and weak. My money and my days are finished.'

With that she put the three coins in her skirt pocket, her basket over her arm, and set off for the market square. Hobbling down the dirt road, she thought to herself, *I've had a good life. If this is my time to leave this earth, so be it. I'll buy a measure of cornmeal and a small fish . . . I'll cook my last meal.*

And that is what she did. Or so she thought.

That very night a north wind began to blow and with it came lashing, freezing rain.

The old woman cleaned up her supper dishes, put her tiny cottage in order, and settled in her rocking chair by the fireplace. Her stomach was full, her feet warmed by the fire, and her favorite shawl wrapped her thin shoulders. She thought of happy days with her husband and the rosy-cheeked children of the village. Trudy felt warm inside and out. What rose up from her heart, some would call a poem, others, a prayer.

'For all the days of sunshine bright,
For beauty in the starry night,
I thank you.
For loving husband, children sweet,
Their smiles have made my life complete;
I thank y—'

Suddenly, the wind howled down Trudy's chimney, scattering ashes into the room. Quickly, she swept these back into the fireplace. A loud thud shook her door—*something* slid down it.

"What on *Earth?*" She whispered, in case the *something* was dangerous. Then she tiptoed to the door, hesitating a minute with her ear pressed to the wood. Hearing only silence, she lifted the bar and opened the door just a crack. Seeing nothing but stormy darkness, she opened it further and peered into the night. Still nothing.

She decided leaving the door open on such a night was foolish and started to push it shut. However, a small movement caught her eye on the stone step. Bending over, she saw a brown soggy lump, about the size of a loaf of bread.

Not knowing what to make of it but seeing it was a creature in trouble, she hobbled to her larder. Pulling out an empty cornmeal sack, she wrapped the creature up, brought it inside and set it down, with some effort, to warm by the fire. Sitting back in her chair, she studied it.

At first, the creature was motionless. The wet fur (or were they feathers?) was plastered to its body. The eyes remained tightly shut. Trudy rocked, hummed softly, and watched for signs of life.

Her patience was soon rewarded.

Water puddled onto the sack. Something that resembled a beak appeared; mostly hidden by what she thought must be (Aha!) feathers. The bird began trembling violently. She took her shawl from her shoulders and laid it over what she now saw were the tops of wings.

She said aloud: 'Ah, you poor dear. You must be half drowned, frozen, and famished besides.' With that she went back to her larder and fetched the small piece of fish she'd saved for her breakfast. Placing it before him, she sat back, waited and watched.

His eyes flew open! He looked from her to the fish and ate it, every last bit.

Trudy was speechless. The brilliant, amber eyes of a golden eagle gazed through her eyes into the very depths of her being. Then he spoke, and it was her turn to tremble.

'Good woman,' he said in his reedy bird voice, 'you have shown uncommon kindness to a wretched creature, with no thought of repayment for yourself. Your heart of generosity and compassion is rare indeed.'

The eagle stopped talking then and began to set his feathers straight, pulling each one through his beak. Trudy still had no words that seemed to fit the occasion. She thought: *Close your mouth, Trudy. Something wonderful is afoot here.*

The eagle finished his task and she saw what a truly handsome bird he was. His feathers, no longer a sodden brown, gleamed like dark spun gold in the firelight.

She finally found her voice. 'I believe you are the most beautiful bird I've ever seen.' Her gray eyes shone with pleasure for having rescued such a noble creature.

'Many thanks to you, fair one. However, in times to come, you will see things more wonderful than this.' The eagle stretched his wings and hopped up on a chair nearby. 'And because you have a heart of gold, I have two gifts for you,' he continued.

Trudy straightened herself as best she could in her chair.

'Trudy, henceforth your name shall be Trueheart. You may keep this to yourself or share it with a trusted friend.' He gave her a meaningful look. 'Just be wise about whom you tell. Jealousy is a thief and a murderer.'

Trueheart could think of many she loved, but none she could trust. 'Thank you,' she said with a quick nod. 'This will remain between us.'

'It is my honor and pleasure,' he said. 'The next gift is *provision*.' He glanced around the tiny bare cottage. 'Trueheart, kindly put your market basket in your lap.'

She quickly took her empty basket down from its hook, wondering what might happen next.

'Now, what do you desire?' He waited.

She had to stop and consider . . . *My own desires?* Those had not been thought of in a long time. Then her eyes lit up. She had it!

'I should like some tea and a slice of strawberry cake, please—and a bit of honey for the tea, Sir,' she said with a twinkle, feeling very bold indeed. She had almost called him *Your Majesty* because of his regal presence, but felt silly saying it out loud to a bird. '—And something for yourself?' she asked.

The eagle chuckled. 'Thank you for asking, but I'm full from the fish you shared. I also have food to eat that you haven't tasted yet.'

Trueheart wondered where he kept this food, but thought better of asking. She just smiled and nodded.

'Now, you might want to look in your basket,' he suggested.

She felt the basket suddenly grow heavy in her lap and looked down. In it sat a small sky-blue teapot, a plate with a generous slice of strawberry cake—and a jar of honey!

'Oh...*OH!*' she gasped, hardly believing her eyes. She rubbed them and looked again. Everything was still there!

The eagle laughed with delight. 'Taste them; they're real. And I think you will find all of it delicious. They do good work where I come from.'

Trueheart could no longer contain herself. 'If I may be so bold, where *do* you come from? Certainly not from around here?'

Traveler paused, frowning.

39

Eva waited, then prompted, "Yes, *aaand* . . . the eagle is from *where?*" She shifted impatiently. "And why does this eagle *talk?*"

"Oh, sorry. I just had a thought." He closed his eyes and kicked off his right boot.

"Alright, this is not good. You were in the middle of a story. Can you *finish* it? Please?" Her voice rose. She shrugged and made herself lean back in the chair.

He gazed at her with an expression she couldn't read. "This story just reminds me of something—talk heard around a campfire."

"Well, since it can't wait, go ahead . . . listening." She pressed her lips into sort of a smile.

"A prince once told me of a girl, a young princess, who possessed such a heart—a true heart. In fact, her heart overflowed with such compassion that she brought healing to a wounded creature . . . a bird, I believe it was." Traveler's words slipped through Eva's ears into a deep place.

The princess caught her breath. "This prince—did he say anything else about, this girl—the princess?"

Traveler gazed into the fire. "Let's see if I can remember."

Eva was silent for a moment, then, "*Please*, you must remember." She heard her voice pleading.

"Ah, yes . . . it's all coming back to me now." One corner of his mouth twitched under his mustache.

"Well?"

"Well, why are you so keen to know?" He sat up and faced her.

"*ACH!*" She made a noise in the back of her throat and slapped her forehead. "You are so *mean!*" She stopped herself, closed her eyes, and sighed through her nose.

He raised an eyebrow and smiled. "The prince said he had yet to meet her equal in all his travels—among all his simpering royal acquaintances. Oh yes . . . he also told us, her cheeks blushed pink like a rose whenever she laughed or was embarrassed." He kicked off his other boot. "There—happy?"

"Wait. He had yet to—?" She covered her hot cheeks with her hands, her eyes glistening.

"That's what Prince Valentino said, sitting by a campfire on border patrol a year ago."

Valentino! She gasped. "So, this was the *Tirzan* border patrol you mentioned a few days ago?"

"I believe it was."

Eva's heart raced, her thoughts colliding. *Valentino was alive a year ago. He hadn't married—a year ago.*

Traveler cleared his throat. "Eva, we have to talk," he said, breaking into her thoughts.

She looked up and met his solemn stare. *Was that a tear on his eyelash?* "Traveler? *Trav*, what is it?"

Just then a violent gust of wind blew down the chimney, scattering live coals across the floor and onto his blanket. They jumped up and swept ash and coals back into the fire. The wind then whistled around the cottage, rattling windows and *whanging* the door against the bar. Then it stopped as quickly as it had started.

He brushed off his still smoldering blanket. "So back to the story." He looked up and smiled at her. "I'm tired. *You* finish it? We'll talk another time."

"Surely you jest."

"Who me? I never jest." He lay back on his rolled-up jacket, his arms folded behind his head.

Eva stepped into the glow of firelight. "Maybe I just *will*." She dragged her chair closer to the hearth and leaned forward, stretching out her hands in its warmth. After a quiet minute gazing into the flames she said, "Alright. Got it."

"Listening." He closed his eyes.

"The eagle answered her question. 'You *will* know about this land one day, but not today. Neither can I tell you my true name because there is no word for it here on earth. However, you may call me Valor. That will do,' he said cheerfully.

Trueheart considered this, then, set out her delightful delicacies on her rough wooden table. She smiled, thinking what a wondrous night this had turned out to be. Looking again at the eagle, she wondered if her eyes were deceiving her. *He looks much larger than he did earlier. And his voice sounds deeper,* she thought.

But no, it wasn't her eyes; *truly*, the bird was now *much* larger than a loaf of bread and seemed to radiate light. He sat taller than the back of her chair!

'Sir—Valor,' she began. 'I don't have enough words to thank you.'

'You just have.' She heard a smile in his voice. 'You now have two gifts: To know your true name and provision to live truly in the generous overflow of your heart. You are the gatekeeper of these gifts. Use them well.'

'Yes, yes I *will*.' Trueheart noticed the storm had stopped beating on her cottage. She looked again at Valor. He was now as tall as her hearth mantle and radiated golden splendor.

'I am sure you will.' Once again there was a pleasant sound in his voice that soothed her old soul. 'I must take my leave now, Trueheart. But, know this. I will return to you. I must return. I hold you in my heart.'

'But, I'm just getting to know you,' she pleaded. 'It's dark outside. Won't you just rest here tonight before you go?' Tears stung her eyes at the thought of his leaving.

'Come close,' he said, and stretched out one immense golden wing.

She stepped under the shadow of the wing and immediately felt a river of comfort flow through her.

'Keep this with you,' he said, plucking a shining feather from his breast. 'When you feel sad or alone, place it over your heart.'

Wordlessly, she received the feather and placed it in her pocket.

He hugged her quickly to himself, hopped down from the chair, and walked to the front of the cottage. Longing too deep for words held her tongue as she opened the door. With a warm glance into her eyes, he lifted his shining wings and soared onto the night.

A tear slipped down her cheek. She tucked the golden feather into her dress over her heart, and there it remained.

In the months and years to come, Trueheart learned to use her gifts well. And as time slipped by, she noticed she seemed to be getting *younger*, not older! She stood taller, her back was no longer bowed, and her fingers became nimble once again.

One spring while planting tulip bulbs in her garden, her thoughts turned to the wonderful basket and its provision for her and the people of her village. There were now wells, orchards, and plenty of seed for planting time. But, her favorite things were the children's schools, libraries, and homes for orphans. In these places, children were raised and taught with a wise and loving hand. Money from the basket had also made handsome, sturdy homes and beautiful gardens for many—including a garden for herself!

Trueheart didn't need thanks or attention, so she found a way to give secretly. She liked her little cottage and continued to dwell there, living her quiet life. *Because*, she thought, *what if I move away and Valor doesn't know where to find me?* This fear, as we all know, is utterly false. Valor can find anyone anywhere.

Soon, word spread among the orphans that she was their benefactor, and they began to visit her. They would sit and talk with her beside her fire and have tea and cake—usually strawberry—and always honey for the tea.

Through the years, she watched the children grow up and learn their trades. One by one, they left the village to go out into the world, each with their own adventure ahead of them. It was a day she knew must come, so she always sent them off with a fond farewell and blessing. But in her cottage, she shed many a private tear.

Trueheart found, as time went by, she was alone more and more with her memories. The golden feather stayed tucked inside her dress over her heart at all times.

I should not be sad, she thought. *My work here is done. The years have been good to me.*

One evening, she was knitting and rocking by the fireplace; crickets chirruped in time to her memories. Trueheart was content.

There was a knock at the door.

'Who could that be?' she whispered to herself. Visitors came seldom and never at night.

She went to the door and listened. 'Who is it?'

'An old friend,' came the reply.

With a rush of excitement, she flung the door open.

There on her stone step stood a handsome prince, radiant in golden splendor. His brilliant wild eyes looked into hers, seeing into the very depths of her being.

'Valor,' she whispered. 'You've come.'

Eva, felt her throat tighten. "Alright. The End."

No answer. Traveler's hat was pushed over his eyes. From under it came the sound of quiet snoring. "Fine, Mister. Sleep on. You need it." She yawned and swept stray coals back into the dying fire, then felt her way in the darkness outside the circle of firelight to her waiting straw bed. Wrapping herself in the blue cloak once again, she lay down, grateful for shelter from the storm. *Wonder what he wanted to talk about . . .* The thought drifted away unfinished. Sinking into the soft straw, a wave of fatigue settled over her, and she dove deep into a dream.

The minstrel rolled to his side and gazed solemnly in her direction.

40

That night, King Cedric sat up in his canopied feather bed, fretful. Sleep had vanished with the moon behind the Western mountains. He slid down to the carpeted floor and with velvet-slippered feet, walked over to his window. Across the inlet, Cedricsburg lay sleeping.

Standing, staring, the King's hands gripped one another behind his back, clenching, unclenching. Peering out over the darkened countryside, it struck him that he seemed to be searching for something. Certainly not Edwina, she was long gone by now.

But what? That was a question he had no answer for.

A tiny light glimmered in Cedricsburg, then disappeared. *Someone else having a sleepless night, no doubt.* Somehow, the thought of someone (a man?) staring out the window of his little hovel fighting terrible thoughts was darkly comforting. Feeling better, he climbed back up into his royal bed and pulled the brocade covers up to his chin. Rolling over, he plunged down into the abyss of his sleep.

At dawn, Eva awoke to fresh stillness drifting through every crack of the cottage. A solitary nightingale's song echoed through the forest, the miracle of it seeping deep into her. Drowsing in that delicious place between waking and dreaming, she saw herself playing in the castle gardens—the sun bright on Valentino's dark hair. She watched this girl. Loved the girl she once was—but that wasn't her. Not anymore.

Her insides hummed with joy. *It's this place, I feel safe here . . . no, it's more*, she decided. A deep sound flowed like musical water within her. *I know that sound.*

Pale morning light pierced the King's room in a slanting thrust. Rolling to the bedside, he sat breathing like a man would before a deep dive. His neck prickled with creeping dread. He glanced at his looking glass and laughed, a short, bitter bark. On the surface, his life was a well-manned sailing ship; but he felt rudderless. And he knew this: in the depths something evil waited—biding its time.

"Oh, why did Lenore have to die?" His rusty voice was barely audible. *If she were still here, she would know what to do. None of this would be happening. If only . . .* He rubbed a hand across his face. *Get hold of yourself. You are King—the ruling Monarch!*

He stood decisively and strode to the bright window and took a deep breath. Exhaled forcefully. Without warning, a large black bird dashed against the panes, pummeled the glass with its wings and beak.

Then it was gone.

King Cedric reeled backward, lurching against his red velvet chair; and sprawled onto his silk Timbrake carpet. His heart seized then beat wildly. Clutching his chest he gasped, "It's a *sign*—a harbinger. My *death*." Curled on the floor, he held his head in misery. Three sobs wracked his body—sounds that belonged on a dark and desolate road, not echoing in a castle from its monarch.

"WHAT HAVE I *DONE*? My *daughter . . .*"

Traveler lifted up on one elbow from his place by the hearth, stretched, and began lacing up his boots.

"G'morning," she yawned, sitting up, rubbing her eyes.

"Morning, Princess," he said, standing and shifting his knapsack onto his shoulder. "Well, morning for me. You can go back to sleep if you like." He started toward the door.

Without saying a word, she shoved her foot in her boot and began to lace it on. "Wait . . ." she said.

"Not this time." He gave her a somber, sleepy look and tied his hair back.

She stopped lacing. "Where are you going?"

"Not too far. Paying my friend at the castle a visit. You still want to work in the kitchen?" His voice sounded oddly distant.

"Well, that was the plan, *right*." Eva bit her lip, her brow wrinkled.

"I think you'll like it. *Really*." He stood in the open doorway, silhouetted in the morning light.

"Trusting you on that one." She laughed shortly.

"I'll order you a dress. What's your favorite color?"

"Blue, like the sky," she said softly, smiling back into his face—or what she could see of it.

"And tomorrow we go to Fernhill to buy some cornmeal and beans from the mercantile. It's just this side of the Tirzan border. Should be safe."

"Let's hope," she agreed. "And what about that seer you mentioned?" Eva raked the hair and straw out of her face, remembering her dragon scale buried beside the step.

"Well, she lives up the mountain, just beyond Fernhill." He leaned on the doorpost. "You can pay her a visit tomorrow, if you like," he said with a yawn. "So, I'll be back before dinner. And tonight I have a surprise for you."

"What?" She brightened.

"A *surprise*." He smiled mysteriously.

"I *know*, because my life's been pretty boring lately."

"Only compared to some." his eyebrows waggled, wrinkling his forehead comically.

Eva snickered.

Traveler belted his dagger on. "While you're here, maybe you could make some of your famous broth, *eh?*" Eva snorted. "It'll sure go down easy, when I get back. Need to keep body and soul together, *right?*" He flipped his hat in the air and caught it on his head. "And I don't mean to scare you, but stay close—bounty hunters've been known to stray—need I say more?" She caught his forced lightness. "You'll be safe here. No one else knows about this place, not yet anyway."

Eva considered her blistered feet and a shoeless day of not walking for miles. "Alright, you talked me into it. I'll be fine, Trav." She paused, nodding in his direction. "*You* be careful."

"That's my plan." He flashed her a grin and was gone.

Picking her way barefooted down to the stream, Eva knelt, bathing her arms and face in wonderfully chilly water. Her gaze traveled down her lean hard arms to fingers that seemed like they belonged to someone else. Instead of a small writing callus on one finger from her pen, they were tough, scarred, browned by the sun . . . her nails broken and bitten short. *Definitely not the hands of a princess.* The thought jibed. Eva smiled. *Another piece of my clever disguise.*

Back inside the cottage she barred the door. It still smelled like dinner. She warmed her hands on the hearth stones and watched a field mouse scurry across the floor, his cheeks packed with seeds.

A falcon sounded off, his clear whistling cry echoed in a distant part of the waking woods. Up the hill, she guessed. Eva practiced making the shrill sound. "This would be a good secret signal, not that we'd ever need it," she mused. *I'll have to show Trav tonight.* She smiled at the thought of teaching this minstrel something—in fact, anything.

Then, lost in thought, she imagined going with Traveler to the castle kitchen and meeting the staff. Becoming one of them. The princess smiled at the thought. Somehow it wasn't unpleasant.

Then her mind instantly filled with scenes of meeting Valentino: *He'd come to the kitchen unsuspecting and our eyes would meet. He'd fling back his cloak and we would embrace—or maybe, I'd be turning a corner with a tray full of food, there he would be in the hallway. I would drop the tray and we would embrace. Of course we'd embrace! Surely he would still be waiting. We made a vow—didn't we?* Her thoughts flashed through years of waiting, of no letters—of her reputation as a crazy, spiteful *lunatic!* Surely he'd know she couldn't *possibly* be *that!* "He *knows* me!" She whispered fiercely into the cottage air.

A darker scene crept into her thoughts: *Maybe he and his wife would come to the kitchen together (the hag), and he would see me and realize what a terrible mistake he'd made with this other woman. A tear would fall from his eye and splash onto his scarlet jacket, but it would be too late! TOO LATE! He would be honor bound to remain married—to this interloper! This horrible woman who bewitched him—HOW COULD SHE!*

Suddenly, the princess was back in the little cottage, her breaths coming in quick snatches. She stood frowning open-mouthed into the dying embers. *No good.* With great effort, she heaved these thoughts out of her mind, braided her hair back, stepped out the cottage door and down to the woods by the stream.

That afternoon, Traveler strode up to the cottage, whistling through his teeth. Eva threw the door open and a delicious aroma floated out from the hearth.

He tossed his hat onto the peg by the door. "Smells like dinner!"

Eva flashed a grin, "Good Sir, we have trout stew with leeks, *or leeks* with trout stew . . . What'll you have?"

"I'll have the stew, thank you," he said sending her a solemn nod and a wink.

"Excellent choice, Sir. You won't regret it," she said and placed a steaming bowl full on the table in front of him.

After exclaiming over dinner and finishing every last drop in his bowl, Traveler rubbed his stomach contentedly, *ahhh-ed*, and said, "Before it gets too late, there's something I want to show you." He walked to the door, a smile lifting his mustache. "It's the *surprise.* Come on, put down the bowls. I'll wash up later. You've got to see this."

Not needing to be told twice to let him wash the bowls, Eva followed him outside. They circled behind the cottage, stepping over rotting tree limbs. Traveler stopped, squatted on his heels, and studied the fungus on the fallen branches. "Ah *HA!*" he announced and cupped his hands over a cluster of brown ruffled fungi, shading them further in the twilight.

"Ah *ha?*" She echoed.

He laughed triumphantly and nodded toward his hands. "Behold—*Foxfire!*" A smile spread across his face.

Eva got on her knees and peered into the darkness under his hands. Small bluish-green lights glowed brightly. Astonished, she sat back, eyes wide. "Fox-*what?* I've never seen—"

Without waiting for her to finish, he said, "Watch this!" With that, he broke the cluster of fungi off of its branch. Night was falling fast and as they picked their way down the little hill to the stream, the foxfire glowed brighter. He splashed water on his face, then rubbed the fungi on it, making his cheeks glow ghostly green. He chuckled darkly and growled. Eva gasped and jumped back despite herself.

"*Stop*, you idiot!" she slapped his arm, sister-like, embarrassed by the quiver in her voice.

"Hey—it's just me!" He rubbed some of the glow off, making his face look even stranger in the gathering dark. "Here, you try it," he held out a piece of the fungi.

"Me?" she said with a quick laugh. "No, I've sworn off foxfire-skin-rubbing, for tonight anyway." She gathered some glowing clusters and stood, not wanting to admit how jumpy his ghoulish face was making her. "Well—going inside now. Coming?"

He splashed the glow off his face. "Go ahead. Admit it. That scared you, didn't it?" He snickered and followed her up the hill.

"I admit *nothing*," she threw back over her shoulder, making her legs *not* run toward the friendly light in the cottage windows.

"Oh—*NO!*" Traveler shouted and threw his handful of glowing foxfire past her.

Eva gasped and broke into a full gallop up the hill; then stopped herself in the light of the window and turned to face him, arms folded, fighting back a smile. "Alright for you, funny man. That's it."

"The dreaded stink-eye." He passed by her, the corner of his mouth quirking with amusement and playfully bumped her shoulder with his. Standing beside the open door, he flourished a deep bow in her direction.

She entered the warm light of the cottage. "Don't you ever get tired?"

"*Me?*" He stepped into the room. "Do you want to make tea?"

"Do I *look* like I want to make tea?" She squinted one eye.

"So, that would be '*yes*'. . . be right back."

He grabbed a basket and stepped out into the night.

The minstrel stepped back through the door, his basket full of the brown ruffly fungus. Striding around the room, he tossed clusters of the foxfire into dark corners of the cottage.

"Night lights! Or, no . . . cottage *stars,*" Eva beamed, delighted.

Traveler chuckled and handed her the basket. "Here, do with the rest of these what you will." He put another log on the fire and settled down on a stool. "Today went well. At the castle, I mean." He sent her an encouraging smile.

"*Great!* When do I start?" She felt her stomach tighten.

"They'll be expecting you in a couple of days." He poked the fire. Sparks flew up. "Don't worry. I think you'll like it. Some good people work there." Eva heard a catch in his voice and tried to read his face, unsuccessfully.

"Anything *else?*" She asked.

"Just, tomorrow we go to Fernhill. You can visit the Seer, if you like."

"And you're getting food?"

"Right. We should be back before dinner." He cleared his throat. "We'll still have to be careful. You'll still need to be . . ." He pointed in the direction of her face. "*You* know."

"When do we leave?" She would have to dig up her dragon scale in the dark, but no matter.

"Day-break sounds good to me. How 'bout you?" He shouldered his pack.

The thought of touching the scale suddenly made her nauseous. *Don't be silly. This is what you've been waiting for. Snap out of it!*

Traveler's question hung in the air.

"Anything you want to share?" He asked lightly, walking toward the door.

"No, just thoughts . . . gone now." She smiled and waved her hand blithely. "Everything's fine. Just fine."

But it wasn't.

41

Eva lay awake in the half-light of pre-dawn. She turned over in her straw bed, wrestling her nimble thoughts down. How had it happened? When she wasn't noticing, somehow she'd grown extremely *fond* of this stranger. *That's it,* she thought, *fondness for someone who helped me escape. But that's all it is. Yes.* She sat up. Someone was whistling outside the cottage. *Trav!*

"Mornin' Princess," he spoke brightly, as she opened the door.

Eva rubbed her eyes. "So *cheerful* this time of the almost-morning." She opened the door wider. "Do come in." She stepped back and waved him in.

After a mouthful of breakfast, they drained the last of their tea and were out the cottage door. Eva ignored her complaining stomach and feet, giddy with thoughts of the day ahead. *Finally the answer to her questions!*

Soon, the sun crested the mountains, filtering pools of light through the trees.

"So the other night, you know, the story-storm night . . ." Eva said, squinting up at him.

Yes, I remember." He nodded slightly, his lips pressed together.

"Well, you wanted to talk about something? Do you still?"

"No, that was nothing. I forgot even what it was." He kicked a rock off the road.

"Really? Because it seemed important." She hesitated and lowered her voice. "I thought I saw a tear in your eye?" Eva panted, trying to keep up with his fast pace.

"A tear?" He laughed shortly. "No. And if there was one, it was probably ashes. Ashes in my eye . . . does it every time." He stretched his legs, striding faster still, not meeting her gaze.

Alright mister Traveler minstrel, she thought. *You sure could use some lying lessons.* "I'm convinced," was all she said, running to catch up. However, the unanswered question hung between them, prickling the air. "Would you *mind—?*"

"Oh, sorry," he slowed down, then spoke; "I'm going to ask you to do a hard thing."

"Wonderful, because I haven't had to do anything hard lately . . . definitely needing a challenge," she said catching up to his stride.

"A bit different." He stepped in front of her and walked backwards, matching her steps. "I *will* tell you what that was about. I promise. Can't tell you now though. Not yet. Would you trust me . . . just a few more days?"

They both stopped in the middle of the dusty road and finally looked into each other's eyes.

"And if I say *no?*"

"Then I tell you—take you to safety, we say our farewells. The end." He shrugged sadly.

Eva crossed her arms over her chest. "Well, I say" She exhaled forcefully. "yes. Yes I will trust you again. I'll trust you a million times and then more." She shook her head. The truth rose up and she caught her breath. "How could I *not!* After all, you're the reason I'm even standing here on this road and not married to—" She couldn't say it.

The minstrel laughed and yanked her hat down over her eyes. "Couldn't let *that* happen—*Spud!*"

"Fine, *Traveler,* if that *is* your name, which I doubt." she said, knocking his hat off onto the road.

Then, they had to scuffle and shove each other a bit before they could walk on, somewhat civilized.

"Alright for you, *Mister,*" Eva announced, lifting her chin, eyebrows raised. "Funny man." Eva stood tall, erect, every inch a princess, and glided regally down the rutted dirt road in her ragged Aric clothes.

The minstrel smirked. "Careful, *Aric.* Someone might recognize you."

A pair of eyes belonging to one, Rufus Bodewyn, watched the whole scuffling exchange with great interest from his shadowed spot behind a maple tree. He kept a gray tweed cap pulled down low over his greasy orange hair, which poked out from under it.

You can never be too careful in the spy business, he liked to say with his cronies after throwing down a few pints at the Pig. Now, he kept himself perfectly still, blending in with the browns and grays of his surroundings.

Holding tight to the tree trunk with square nail-chewed fingers, he carefully controlled his breathing, making it noiseless. It was one more thing he prided himself on. *Float like a bat, sting like a bee.* He chuckled silently. *I reckon those swells who been t' school couldn't come up with a sayin' no better'n that.*

When Eva and Traveler were a safe distance down the road, he yawned, scratched his red spotted arms, and took off in an easy wolfish lope through the woods. He would get to Fernhill about half an hour before they did and give this juicy morsel of news to old Jack. He and Jack went way back.

And they had a deal.

As they drew near to the little hamlet of Fernhill, a nobleman trotting by on his horse shot them a glare and grimaced. "Peasants!—*Out!* Out of my *way!*"

Traveler stepped to one side, swept his hat from his head, and bowed low. Then, he and Eva exchanged glances, slapped each other's shoulders and howled with laughter. The nobleman chose not to get involved with these two who were clearly lunatics, likely dangerous. He spurred his horse and disappeared around the bend in the road.

Still bent over catching their breath, they heard another sound. A wagon clattered up behind them full of pots and pans. They stepped off the road, but the driver reined up his horse.

"G'mornin' to you'uns. Name's Jack Rabbitt. Jackson Q. Rabbitt, at your service." A snaggle-toothed, Jack-o-lantern smile creased the old man's cheeks. His grey beard and mustache looked recently trimmed and stood out in stark contrast to his dusty, ragged clothes.

"And to you, Mr. Rabbitt," Traveler replied, tipping his hat.

"Well-a-day. . . looks like you're a headin' towards Fernhill. So that's lucky. Ol' Jack can give you'uns a lift in me wagon as far as I go." He looked expectantly at Traveler.

"Now, that *is* a fine offer, but not this time," he said. "We find walking very invigorating. Don't we Aric?"

Eva stared openly at the minstrel. Her feet already ached from the morning's walk. The thought of a ride was beyond wonderful. After all, they were in *Tirzah*, not Dunmoor. "But, maybe we could." she said in her Aric voice.

"No, remember we were going to go see our friend just outside of town— *remember?*" Traveler raised an eyebrow and gave her a warning glance. The minstrel had misgivings about this tinker and was sorting through them. Jack's all-too-friendly offer rankled. Something stunk. And it wasn't just his clothes.

Eva fell in with the story. "Oh, yes. Our *friend!*"

"Right—*Jem!* Good ol' Jem." The minstrel nodded.

Standing in the road talking, the pain in Eva's feet had traveled up past her knees. The thought of Jack's wagon grew ever more inviting. "Could we not go see old Jem another time?" she offered, shifting to her other foot.

"You heard the lad," Jack jumped in. "The boy could use some rest—plain as day." He ran a hand through his matted gray hair, settled his hat back on his head, and waited.

Traveler's eyes rested briefly on her feet and he sighed, "Alright." His hand strayed to the hilt of his dagger.

"Well, that'll be fine as frog hair. You two jes' jump on up here and let old Clovis carry us all a-ways down yon road." He patted the rough wooden bench beside him and wheezed out another guffaw.

"We *were* planning to be home before dinner, *right?*" Eva offered, her voice small. She felt Traveler tense beside her.

"True." The minstrel shrugged. "My thanks to you, Jack!" With that, they stepped up into the wagon. Traveler sat on the bench beside this man who appeared to be a tinker. Clovis flicked his brown ears and rolled his eyes, at this new burden.

"*Git* up!" Jack shook the reins, and the horse plodded forward; resentfully it seemed to Eva.

Jack wanted to talk, so Eva and Traveler were spared the task of making conversation.

"I been pretty much a rambler, a rumbler . . . blowin' like a tumble-weed all my life . . . this town, that village. Jes' doin' one thing and another—keep'n body and soul together, as they say." He shot a glance their way. "Course my favorite thing is palaverin' with me mates down at the Pig. And that do take some money." His voice lowered to a mutter.

"The *Pig?*" Traveler sat back, letting the words sink in. Eva saw his jaw flex.

"You know, the tavern in Rabblesdell—the *Purple* Pig Tavern." Jack turned, squinting briefly at them. Eva flinched, feeling the weight of his scrutiny.

Like a thunder-clap, who Jack *was* struck both Eva and the minstrel. Eva leaned slowly forward, peering around at their driver, then, leaned back, hidden by her friend's shoulder. Traveler stared at the road ahead. There it was, as plain as the nose on Jack's rodent-like face—*Mr. Rabbitt was a bounty hunter from the round table in the Rabblesdell tavern.* His neatly cropped beard and trimmed eyebrows had thrown them off. But, he was here. Now. And *way* too close.

"Ah, yes," Traveler said evenly. "I *have* heard of it, like most folks in this part of the world, I would guess." His voice was calm and casual. The only thing showing his alarm were the tips of his ears. Eva saw them flush red.

She and the minstrel fell silent once again.

They rounded a bend in the road, and Jack remarked: "No, it would never do to be caught out on the road at night these times."

"Have there been a lot of robberies?" Traveler asked, knowing full well what he meant.

Jack snorted, "robberies, my eye —I wish that's all 't were."

"*Oh?*" Traveler remarked, sending Eva a quick look.

"It's—" Jack leaned toward them and whispered dramatically, "It's Morach, the lizard . . . the night-flier!" He shook the reigns again, muttering something under his breath.

Eva shrank behind the minstrel's shoulder.

Jack was just getting warmed up. "He's been spotted near a month now most nights, flyin' over farmlands and those mountains there." He nodded behind them. "So far only sheep and cattle been snatched. But us'uns who seen the beast—flyin' back and forth, back and forth in the sky of a night—we think he's a-*lookin'* for somethin'." He paused for effect. "Or *someone*."

Eva caught her breath, not daring to look at the minstrel.

This train of thought rendered them all wordless for a minute. Then Jack whistled sharply and shook the reigns again, urging old Clovis to greater speed.

"We all hope he finds what he's a-lookin' for and moves on to greener pastures," Jack said in a low, confidential voice.

Eva's face paled. She clasped her hands in her lap, twisting her fingers together.

"Or maybe someone should put an end to him," Traveler said casually.

"Now that *would* be the trick wouldn't it," Jack laughed mirthlessly. "People've tried, died, and become dragon-fodder for longer'n *I* can remember, and that's a fact . . . a true fact."

"So I've heard," Traveler mused.

Jack stroked his beard. "Course, there *is* talk about *'two with hearts of gold'* puttin' an end to him. But then, they'd have to be a prince and princess, right? So we're all done for—that's what I'm sayin'."

The sun rose to the top of the sky, its heat pounding them, shimmering the air. Eva's stomach quivered. She could almost believe she'd stepped into one of her nightmares.

"People *do* get strange ideas," Jack said, after a long pause.

Rather than explore that line of thought, Traveler said cheerfully, "Well, this is where we get off. Thanks so much for the ride, Jack. Maybe we'll see you in Fernhill sometime." He swung his knapsack over his shoulder, and Jack reigned up Clovis.

"Yes, thank you, Jack. Nice chatting with you." Eva smiled her Aric smile and hopped down with Traveler.

"Well, it was a fine way to spend the mornin'," he remarked, glancing toward the western sky. "You helped old Jack pass the time and I'm beholdin' to you . . . and hold up there," Jack called after them. "In case you don't make it home and need a place to stay the night, you'll see the Pumpkinvine Inn up the road. But, I'd sooner sleep in the woods." He paused.

"Thanks," Traveler said and turned again to go.

"—Because, if you *was* planning to stay there, I'm here to tell ya, those beds've got bugs the size of me big toe. They's hungry too." He grimaced.

"Well, thank you, Jack. We'll just be going now." The minstrel nodded and turned again.

"In fact, I wouldn't even sit on one of those beds without wearing a suit of armor, I wouldn't. And I left me spare suit home today." Jack announced and doubled over in wheezy laughter until Eva feared he might fall over on his head.

She gritted her teeth and tried to push the thought of toe-sized bed bugs—and Jack's big toe—out of her mind.

"Appreciate the warning, Jack." The minstrel took another step backward and tipped his hat. "Travel in the Way"

Jack waved and clattered on down the dusty road.

"Let's go—*Aric*." Traveler muttered through clenched teeth and shifted his bag on his shoulder. They sprinted then, forsaking the road, and plunged into the cool green forest.

Jack squinted briefly behind him and marked their forest entry in his mind.

42

Sitting hidden on a log in the woods, a stone's throw from the main road, Eva and the minstrel munched wild berries. He looked into her eyes and saw questions and fears, huddled in a corner like so many blackbirds. "I know you want answers," he said.

Eva turned away. *Of course I do. Who wouldn't?* She cleared her throat and said, "Yes. Lots."

"Old Zephira lives just a short walk up the mountain that way." He pointed north of Fernhill.

"But what could I bring to her? My promise as a princess is all I've got. That'll have to do." Eva knew she *should* present the Seer with a gift. But, she had to find out how to work the spell. Her future was calling. "And, who is this Zephira, anyway? Was she raised by witches?"

Traveler peered through the trees up the road. "Nobody knows who her people are or where she's from. The story goes: one day about fifty years ago, someone from Fernhill saw smoke coming from the abandoned cottage on the hillside north of town. When they went to see about it, there she was . . . sitting on a chair outside the door, drinking a cup of tea. She seemed friendly enough. And since no one else wanted the rundown cottage, they let her stay."

"So that was fifty years ago. She must have been young."

"They say she was white haired even then. No one knows how she's even still alive."

"So does she use a crystal ball or a gazing pool—or maybe read palms?"

"Not a fortuneteller, a witch or a mage. None of those." He paused briefly. "No use trying to explain. You'll see." He buckled his bag. "Well, that's it then. I'll walk with you there, make sure you're safe, and get in and out of Fernhill as fast as possible with our provisions. Wait for me up there. Sound good?"

Eva knew she had to go alone. "No, you go on into town. We can meet back here at the log when we're both done. If I wait for you up there we won't be home 'till after dark." She rested her hand casually on her dagger. "Don't worry about me. I'll be fine. And, I'll make it quick—as quick as possible anyway," she said brushing brown leaves off her pants. "I won't be stupid. Again." she paused glancing at the ground, then at the sky, anywhere but in the minstrel's eyes.

He gave her a half smile and shrugged.

"I messed up. Wanting a ride with Jack, I mean." She clenched her jaw. Suddenly, everything she'd done seemed wrong. "I, I should have *known* better."

"Known *what?* That Fagan has stooges in unlikely places. Anyway, Jack somehow had us pegged. He wasn't surprised to find us on the road." He stopped and looked in her eyes. "We both should have known. Let's just face it and know what we know." He squinted up the road toward a green spot on the hillside. "Strange," he mused.

"What?"

"The area around the Seer's cottage. It's green, no fall colors like the rest of the mountain," he pointed out.

"Yes." *No time to figure this one out.* "So that's where she lives?" Eva fingered the scale in her pocket.

"Sure is." He stood and a shaft of light crossed his face.

Eva tried to smile, but didn't quite make it. "I'm off then, Trav. See you back here this afternoon?"

"That's the plan." He picked up his knapsack and gave her hand a quick squeeze. "Don't forget what you know about your dagger. Journey in the Way."

Eva gave him a tight smile, feeling her chin tremble. She suddenly wanted to throw her arms around her friend, but pushed down the urge. She stepped out onto the road instead. *Time to figure that out later.*

Traveler waited a few minutes before he left their meeting place.

Stepping onto the dusty road, he looked toward the Seer's mountain. Eva had disappeared around a little copse of birch trees. *She'll be there soon. Best get going.*

Looking toward Fernhill, the minstrel's stomach clutched with caution. Eva should be safe on the Seer's mountain. *This must be about something else.*

At that moment, the minstrel broke his number one rule: Heed the Voice. It usually came from somewhere deep in his gut, not shouting, but as sure and reliable as the rising sun. However, the gnawing hunger in his belly shoved this Voice aside. He left the safety of their woody clearing and headed for town, tightening the belt to keep coins from jingling in the purse inside his jacket.

Entering Fernhill from the east, he strode past some small, whitewashed cottages on the outskirts of the village. Then, coming into the merchant section of town, he passed booth after booth with colorful cloth awnings and flags fluttering overhead. "That's right, it's Saturday, Market Day," he muttered.

He'd almost walked past them into the main part of town when he heard what he thought was a voice (or was it a rusty hinge?) calling out to him. "Hey . . . *Hey*, Sonny!" Beside the last booth on his left, a toothless old woman sat on a barrel. She swung her legs in rhythm to the raucus market music and leaned back against the wall. Her mouth puckered and tucked back behind her gums. Her gaze was riveted on Traveler as she pointed a crooked, claw-like finger at him.

"Good day to you, Grandmother," he said turning aside. "Did you call me?"

"That I did, Sonny. And it's good for you that I did. I see *Destiny* on you. Something important you must do—and I like your looks." She grinned, a pink gummy grin.

Traveler smiled back. "I'm looking for the Dry Goods store. But, how can I help you, old one?"

"Help me?" She rasped out. "There's nothing *I* need, 'ceptn maybe some teeth. You got any t' spare?" This set her off again into chortling cackles and snorts.

Traveler was about to bid her 'good day' when she stopped laughing abruptly and fixed her eyes on him. "Not so fast, Sonny. I kin tell you how to find the store. I'll tell you somethin' else too, though, because I like your eyes, and you've been kind to an old woman." She paused to make sure he was listening. He was. "The dry goods store you're seekin' is across from the tavern. Fagan's men is there now . . . comin' and goin' day and night they are. That bunch'd just as soon cut out your gizzard as look at you."

So, that's what I was feeling. "Thank you, good mother. Let me give you something for your kindness." He reached in his coin purse and pulled out three Tika.

"Keep your money, Lad. You'll be a needin' it soon enough." Her face contracted into a hundred wrinkles of concern. "You have somethin' to do, somethin' that's goin' to change this world we live in . . . take care. Remember, every choice *counts*, even the small ones."

Then, she smiled her pink grin and waved him cheerily on his way, as if they had just been chatting about the weather.

43

A dark haired man dressed in black weather-stained leathers left his cronies at the Dewdrop, Fernstone's Tavern. Sunlight glinted through his sparse scraggly beard revealing a face strewn with pockmarks and scars. Crossing the cobbled street that ran through the town, he tied his long riding jacket closed. Weapons concealed, he entered the store, eyes darting around the room. On one wall, shelves from the wooden floor to the low plastered ceiling were filled with jars of preserved fruits, sausages of all shapes and sizes, bags of grains, salt, cocoa, and spices. On the opposite wall, bolts of fabric and ribbons lined up in a rainbow of colors. A mother and daughter were bent over them whispering intently.

But, he hadn't come to buy. He was looking for someone.

Spyder, for that was his name, approached the pudgy clerk behind the counter. "Could we have a short *private* word?" He nodded toward the back of the store, his voice gravelly and smoky.

"Not now, Sir," the clerk replied crisply. "As you can see, I have customers." He gestured toward the two picking out ribbons.

"It'll just take a minute, Mate. Then I'll be on me way. Y'see I'm looking for someone." He pulled the folded bounty paper out of his pocket and showed him the sketched face of the princess. "You seen anyone lookin' like this? She's got a scar in front of her left ear, right about here." He stroked a filthy sausage finger in front of his sunburned ear.

The shopkeeper frowned. "See here—I *did clearly* say I could not have this conversation during store hours. And, no, I haven't seen anyone resembling this girl—*mate.*" A bead of sweat trickled down the clerk's shiny bald forehead. He wiped it away with a handkerchief and tugged at his white collar.

Spyder leaned over the counter. "I think you *do* know. I think you're *lyin'* to me. I can smell a liar a mile away." He fisted the clerk's apron and twisted it, jerked him close—face to face. Breath to reeking breath.

The shopkeeper pulled his dagger from it's sheath. "And I think you're drunk. It's not even noon. Shame on *you.*" He lifted his blade to Spyder's neck.

"Aww, what would make you say such a mean thing?" Spyder slipped his own dagger out from his jacket.

"You stink of beer, plain and simple. Now get out." The clerk put the point of his knife under Spyder's stubbly chin. His voice was dangerously low. "—And I mean *now.*"

The bell above the door jingled. A man walked in. Spyder backed up, released the red-faced clerk, and put his dagger away, suddenly aware of all eyes in the room on him.

"No need to get all riled up. Just having a little palaver wit' ya." He took another step toward the door, shrugged his shoulders, and straightened his jacket. "Well, if you do hear of the girl's whereabouts, you know where to find me. Me and me mates'll be at yon tavern. We're all very concerned for her safety."

The shopkeeper snorted.

Spyder swung around toward the door. A hand clapped him on the shoulder. He spun around, his dagger out.

"The princess with the bounty? I know where she is. I'll take you there." Traveler stood eye to eye with Spyder, captain of Fagan's henchmen. "I need a man with a horse. You need the girl. We both have needs. We split the reward."

"Lead on, Mate," Spyder said with a humorless smile.

Eva trudged on, a war raging inside. "I have to do this . . . have to find out how to use this scale, cast this spell . . . future depends on it," she muttered, turning right onto the skinny, winding trail. She paused and peered upward through nearly leafless trees to what *should be* green beyond them, but wasn't. It was white. A snowflake landed on her nose. *Very odd,* she thought. *But maybe that's just the way it is with Seers.* Eva pushed her fears aside and continued upward, wishing again she had something to give this woman.

After almost an hour of winding upward through the trees, light snow became a howling blizzard. Eva clutched her thin coat around her and pushed upward. *Too late to turn back!* "What is *going on?* Somebody Help! *HELP ME!*" She screamed into winds that swept her words away. Numb, now beyond shivering, she pushed one foot ahead of the other until she couldn't make her legs move. Darkness engulfed her. She fell into a drift of snow and lay there.

Immediately (was this a frozen dream or was she *dead?*) a warm hand gripped her arm and lifted her. Eva opened her ice crusted eyes and saw, for an instant, the face of a beautiful woman. She blinked and the face was a grandmother swathed in scarves and blankets with boots up to her knees. Tears froze on the princess's eyelashes.

The woman peeled two of the blankets from her shoulders, wrapped Eva up and held her. Then with surprising strength, the old woman propelled them forward a short distance, pushing through a blast of frozen whiteness as one might step through a curtain—into the edge of what appeared to be an apple orchard carpeted in buttercups and daisies. Every branch hung low with the weight of its fruit and fragrant white blossoms. Eva looked around, hardly believing her eyes. But here she was, alive . . . and warm! *Extremely odd!* She brushed snowflakes off her jacket and looked around.

A movement caught her eye. Just to her left under an apple tree was a woman (*her woman?*) bent with age, with her back to the princess. Ignoring Eva, she hummed a tune, lifted her cane and began *whacking* the lowest branch. A few apples fell into a brown cape spread on the ground.

Eva wondered, *is this the seer or her housekeeper?* She cleared her throat and coughed a little. The woman paid no attention and continued her fruit gathering, although lifting the cane seemed hard for her. "Must be *deaf,*" Eva muttered to herself and walked toward her. *At least this woman might help me find her.*

Eva walked around in front of the woman and smiled. She would have dropped to a quick curtsy, but remembered she was still in her boy-clothes. She and the woman shook hands.

"Very pleased to meet you," Eva said, using her Aric voice. "Was it you? Did you just save my life? And may I help you?" She looked into the ancient face, her silvery hair gathered at the nape of her neck in a scraggly bun. The old woman smiled then—her eyes, blue-grey like a twilight sky, disappeared in the warm brown folds and wrinkles around them.

"So many questions," she laughed softly and stepped back from the tree, then said; "If you have time to help, *Sonny*. Looks like you're going somewhere." When this old woman spoke, Eva felt—rather than heard—*Spring. Another odd thing*, she thought, *but not unpleasant . . . not at all.*

"Well, yes. I'm going to visit the Seer, but I have time. Would you know? Is she home?" Eva looked into the woman's face; then without waiting for an answer, she scrambled up the tree and shook the low branches, sending an avalanche of apples onto the ground. "How's that?" she shouted down.

"That should do nicely, Dearie," she called up to Eva. "And you must be talking about Zephira. She lives up yonder." She pointed her cane toward a small white cottage just beyond the orchard. "Should be home directly." With that she chuckled and rolled fallen fruit into a pile.

Eva slid to the ground and joined the woman, tossing apples onto her cape. When they finished, Eva bent over to tie the corners together and looked up. "Carry this for you?"

The woman smiled her thanks. They walked through the orchard toward the neat cottage tucked into the hillside. Eva looked up to see a mama goat and her kid munching thick grass on the sod roof.

"So you live with the Seer?" Eva asked, seeing where they were going.

"You might say that," the old woman's eyes crinkled up at the corners. "But, we haven't introduced ourselves, have we?" She turned to face the princess.

"Yes, how rude of me," murmured Eva. "I'm—" she stopped, and looked down at her Aric clothes, trying to work out an explanation.

"Yes, I know who you are, Princess." The old woman stood straighter. "And, I know Zephira, the Seer—I *am* her. But, maybe you already guessed that."

The thought *did* cross my mind," Eva said, shifting the bundled cape-full of fruit to her other shoulder.

"And, here, let me carry that," Zephira said, standing to her full height and easily lifting the heavy bundle from Eva's shoulder to her own. "Thanks for the help, Princess. Some have been in such a hurry to see Zephira they've missed her," she said with a wry smile. "Missed her entirely."

"Well, I heard she was extremely old and . . . " Eva bit her lip, and blushed.

Zephira chortled richly, enjoying the joke. "Yes, I do get that a lot, usually from the townsfolk," she said and nodded toward Fernhill. "Not to worry though; weak or strong, I'm still Zephira." They walked up to the low cottage door painted the color of the red roses beside her walkway. "And to answer your other question; yes that *was* me in the snow. Something or *someone* didn't want you coming to see me . . . but here you are." Zephira turned the brass rose-shaped knob, and they walked in.

Eva had felt the truth of those words while slogging through the freakish snowstorm. She nodded silently, grimly, and looked around the room; eyes exploring shelves full of books and cabinets holding white gleaming dishes—and what else? The cottage was small, tidy, and smelled like Bea's kitchen. She closed her eyes, inhaled deeply, and felt herself relax.

Zephira put the apples beside the door. "Now, let's have a cup of tea, and you can tell me what it is you wish from the *Great and Powerful Seer*." She chuckled archly, and set the kettle to boil over the fire.

Eva leaned back in her chair and looked around the room again. "So, I don't see a crystal ball or a gazing pool anywhere. Are they in the back?"

Zephira shook her head, the smile in her eyes faded. "Oh, no, no, Dearie . . . never touch that stuff. Muddy the waters, they do." She glanced in Eva's direction.

Eva was curious. "What *do* you use?"

"Use?" She looked directly in Eva's eyes for the first time. "I don't *use* anything. I listen . . . when the True Voice speaks, I hear. When He shows me things, I see—then I *do*."

Still, the princess wanted to know more. "But how?"

"Sometimes, I hear His Voice deep in my thoughts, sometimes in dreams, many ways. There's no mistaking Him, though. He is like a high mountain stream . . . clear and pure." She smiled happily. "I think you know what I'm talking about, or am I wrong?"

"You're right," Eva said, then decided to talk later about her own experiences. Right now the most pressing questions burned in her thoughts—how to tell this Seer about her dragon scale, her dreams—and how to cast the spell to make them happen.

The Seer smiled softly. "Everyone comes into this world with gifts. Some are obvious, others tucked away, ready to be opened when the need arises. Our gifts connect us to the path of our dreams—our destiny."

"*Gifts?* So more than one?" Eva asked.

Zephira's mouth was composed, but she couldn't keep the smile from twinkling her eyes. "Truth be told, most do, but usually, you'll find one gift overshadows the rest. This one leads to the high road—the dream that once looked impossible. Then, what seemed *impossible* is possible."

The high road, Eva thought, feeling the scale grow warm in her pocket.

The Seer noticed a shadow passing over Eva's face. "Just because this dream, your destiny, has chosen you, doesn't mean you're bound to choose it back," she said with a nod.

With a potholder, Zephira picked up the hot kettle hanging over the fire. Eva noticed an unusual number of colors dancing around in the flames and

made a mental note to ask about those later. Right now, she just felt like listening—soaking up whatever it was in this atmosphere, this place. The longer
she sat there, the more she felt her thoughts lift and soar. And it wasn't just
her thoughts, even her body felt lighter. Her shoulders no longer ached from
the leather straps of her bag. The blisters on her feet had stopped stinging. *If
I stayed here much longer,* she thought, *I might . . .*

The scale grew hotter. *Strange. Is it moving?*

"Tea, Dear?" Zephira stood with the kettle poised in the air. If the woman
knew what was going on, she showed no sign.

"Yes, please," Eva said, watching the rich amber liquid fill her cup. She
breathed in its warm sweetness and smiled, deciding to ask the Seer about the
scale and spell after her tea.

"I love that smell, too," Zephira's eyes sparkled. "You'll find this tea
strengthening for your journey . . . a longer one than you first thought, I'll
warrant." She pushed the honey jar closer to Eva. "But you have some important
questions; that's why you're here. And unless I'm very wrong, I'd say you carry
with you a particularly heavy burden . . . yes, *very* heavy indeed," she mused
thoughtfully, gazing out the window. When she spoke next, her words were
edged with sadness. "In fact, something that promises success, but would lure
you from your true path." The Seer's brow furrowed momentarily.

This time, Eva definitely felt the scale move, as though it flinched at Zephira's
words. It wriggled out of its bloody wrapping cloth, and down into the lowest
corner of her pants pocket! *Trying to hide!?!* Her leg was suddenly scorched.

Eva leapt from her chair and jerked the pocket inside out; sending the
steaming scale scuttling across the table, along with its wrapping. Eva's face
flushed bright red. Pressing her lips together, she covered them with her fingertips and glanced quickly toward the Seer. She watched in horror as the
grey-green *thing* on the table *somehow* vibrated toward her teacup. She slumped
down heavily in her chair and stared at the floor, her cheeks hot. She'd wanted
to present her questions later, revealed sensibly in good order. Not like *this.*

Zephira leaned across the table and gazed into Eva's eyes. She nodded
toward the scale. "No need for embarrassment, child," she said with solemn
tenderness. "Many have made the same mistake. Some realize it in time,
others—" The weight of this thought stopped her words.

Eva blinked rapidly and looked again at the table. The scale inched away from Zephira. Wordlessly, they watched it shimmy to Eva's side of the table, teeter on the edge, then, drop into her pocket. Once again, her leg felt its heat. The scale squirmed next to her skin. Her stomach clenched and heaved. It was crystal clear: *I won't use this thing to get what I want—it plans to use me!*

The air around the scale felt suddenly slippery, pulsing and pulling on her. Even now in the presence of the Seer, she felt its desire to draw her in further, to consume her in its will. Then she knew. The power and desire held in the scale and blood was the very pull she'd felt from Fagan and Morach himself—desiring her life. She heard a high wheedling voice arguing in her ears: *You need us . . . no other way will you work your will in this world. You will miss your destiny without our power. Don't be a FOOL!*

"No!" Eva shouted, leaping up from her chair. "You *LIE!*"

Zephira had been quietly looking into the flames. Now she spoke: "Yes, your heart instructs you rightly, child. You're wise to listen."

The scale seemed to writhe in agony in her pocket. Silently, Eva fought it—agonized with it. "What must I *do?*" Eva wailed and felt her mind being dragged downward.

"Do?—What do you *want* to do?" Zephira's voice echoed in her ears.

Eva closed her eyes for a moment. Then she heard it . . . something deeper—a powerful flow underneath the clutch of the scale's niggling pull. A secret underground river surged inside. The familiar music resonated, not pulling, not pushing; but quietly, joyfully, calling to her; the music of spring, of Love itself . . . of the *True Voice!*

Eva gasped. "I have to be rid of this thing," she said thickly. "Too long—I've kept it far too long!" A dew of sweat rolled down her face, washing jagged stripes through the dirt on her cheeks. She pulled off her hat and scarf, letting her unbound hair tumble over her shoulders.

Zephira stood beside her. "It must be destroyed in the Fire of the True Voice, by the will of the one who held it as a treasure. You've probably noticed this fire looks a bit unusual?" she said nodding toward her hearth.

Eva *had* noticed. The flames were now higher, brighter, as if anticipating. All the colors of the rainbow, and some colors she had no name for, danced among them. Her eyes were fixed on the Seer. "I'm ready," she said, pushed her hand into her pocket and grabbed the scale. Throbbing, pulsing, it clung to her palm, burning, biting deeply into it. Eva screamed, ripped it off along with her scorched skin, and threw it with all her strength into the waiting flames. Teeth clenched against the pain, she flung in its bloody wrapping cloth and the page from the book of spells.

Zephira placed her hand upon the princess's shoulder, and Eva felt the fiery throb in her palm begin to ebb away. They shared a long knowing glance, then stared silently into the heart of the fire.

The scale turned red, then black, sizzling and popping. It squealed, the sound rising higher and higher, then thinner, fading to nothing. A smell of sulphur drifted into the room and was carried up the chimney along with the black ashes of what once was.

Zephira smiled sadly and sighed. "May I?" she asked and placed her palm under Eva's hand, no longer painful, but showing a circle of raw bloody skin.

Eva grimaced. "Yes please," she whispered. *I would trust you with my life.*

The Seer brushed her cool fingers over Eva's palm, closed her eyes briefly, and whispered, "Thank you." When she removed them, new pink skin had replaced the dark, angry burn. A light breeze circled inside the little cottage, ruffling their clothing and hair.

Eva glanced around the room; everything looked brighter—fresher some-how. She gazed at Zephira's face as if seeing it for the first time. It now looked ageless, radiant, *other-worldly.* Eva smiled into the Seer's eyes. "How can I ever thank you?" She sat down, realizing she was exhausted.

"Thank me?" Zephira said, chuckling softly. "You just have. Now, with two good hands and a clear heart, you'll continue your journey. And, if I might say, your pilgrimage is not just about you . . . *or* finding your beloved. The fate of kingdoms rests on your shoulders, but not yours alone. Someone else with a heart of gold . . ." She lifted the tea kettle, "More tea? And, I'm thinking some soup might be in good order." Eva started to help her. "No, you just rest, Dear," Zephira said. "There will be plenty of time for you to *do*—"

Eva nodded mutely, delighted at the thought of Zephira's soup, and rest-ing in this place. She could feel clouds inside her blowing away, her thoughts clearing like an ever-widening summer sky. "I can hardly believe how much lighter I feel," she whispered.

Zephira beamed and ladled soup into bowls, then grew somber with the weightiness of what she was about to say. "I have a question for you," she said. "Do you believe because you have first seen? Or do you see because you first believed?"

"Not following you."

"For good or for ill, what you believe about yourself—about your future will direct your steps. But, you know something of that, don't you. That's why you left. That's why you destroyed the scale, the thing that was prodding you away from the truth of your life.

"What could my future possibly hold now," Eva murmured doubtfully. "I'll be fine kitchen help, I'm sure."

"Will you now? If that *was* your path, it would be a fine one. But, there's something else. Something you've known since you were a wee girl in your nurse's arms . . . since you built and tended the first little stick village among the pines in your secret place. You were meant for more."

Eva felt this mighty truth rise in her, but had no words. Not yet.

She silently received her warm steaming soup and smiled into Zephira's eyes.

After their soup, the Seer sliced two hefty slabs of apple cake and set them on the table. She laughed, seeing Eva's eyes grow big, then settled down in her chair. "Don't wait for me. Go ahead . . . dig in!"

Eva chortled and plunged her fork into spicy, sweet lusciousness.

After a moment, the Seer spoke softly: "I knew your mother . . . a beautiful woman, inside and out."

This made Eva's throat suddenly feel thick. "I . . . I didn't know that. I wonder why no one ever told me about you," she stammered, searching the Seer's face.

"We were good friends, she and I." Zephira's eyes sparkled faintly at a distant memory. "Your mother was hardly more than a girl when she came to the castle as his queen. We met many times over the years, more often as her time grew near to bring *you* into the world," she said smiling into Eva's eyes.

Eva put her fork down. "Please, tell me about my mother. I want . . . I *need* to know everything. Everything you know. What was she like with you? What did her voice sound like?" Eva stopped herself and folded her hands on the table. Waiting.

Zephira leaned back in her chair and closed her eyes. "Her voice was soft and musical, much like yours; that's an easy one." She opened her eyes and leaned forward intently. "She and I met on many occasions. Lenora would always come in a cloak and hood, riding in a plain carriage and, later, on horseback alone. These times always seemed arranged by the True Voice Himself. Divine appointments, if you will." She pushed her uneaten cake out of the way and folded her arms on the table. "We'd sit right here by the fire, talking . . . and listening. Yes we did."

"So, you said *listening*. Did she *know* stuff, you know, like you do?" Eva leaned forward.

Zephira smiled. "There's something you should know about her; she was a gifted Seer in her own right. We both received assurance two months before your birth—you were one who could bring freedom to our world. We both saw you being strengthened and helped. Later you would have the choice to join strengths with another, and battle extreme evil. *Or* you could take another path."

"My mother saw this." The thought settled over Eva like a warm blanket.

"She became more and more troubled as the time of your birth approached. Count Fagan had wormed his way into your father's confidence. Some suspected witchcraft."

Eva took a deep breath. "Well, *was* it . . . witchcraft, I mean?"

"Truth be told, it was witchcraft *and* a powerful drug the count had used to secure the affections of his many wives. May their souls rest in peace."

"I *knew* it must be something like that; thought so anyway," Eva covered her eyes with her hand and leaned her elbow on the table. "Go on. Don't stop—please." Zephira reached over and lightly squeezed Eva's other hand. The princess looked up and saw deep concern etched into her face. She felt a great friendship growing for this woman she'd just met, as if they had known each other always. She managed a slight smile. "I'll be alright, really. I just need to hear this."

The Seer spoke: "Being warned in a dream of the Count's plan to kill you both, she surrounded herself with her ladies-in-waiting at all times, even to the point of having her chamber-maid sleep in her bedroom and a guard posted outside her door at night. I begged her to come here and stay with me, but she felt her place was at the castle. However, on the day of your birth, she sent a message to me on the leg of a dove . . . a troubling word saying 'come quickly.' I left immediately but, sadly, arrived too late. I was barred from the birthing room and never saw her again—alive. Only Rhona was willing to tell me what happened." She pressed her napkin to her eyes for a long moment, then, continued, a tremor in her voice.

"The day before your birth, her old chambermaid fell sick and was replaced by a woman, named Isola, recently hired into the castle household. She was full of smiles and very attentive, so when Lenore began to feel her pains and was brought into the birthing room, Isola stayed beside her, holding her hand. On a table by the bed was a drink that quelled the pain during childbirth. This drink that was supposed to bring relief, instead, brought *death* to your mother—and was meant to be the end of *you* as well."

The princess squeezed her eyes shut and captured her trembling lower lip with her teeth. Her hands clenched into fists.

Zephira's eyes blazed. "When no one was looking, Isola had slipped poison into the cup from a vial hidden in her sleeve." The seer closed her eyes briefly. "You see, the count had been warned by a wizard named Zimrod of the probability of your gifts. The wizard and count, both, had guessed at your destiny. I suspect it was Zimrod that sent the snowstorm your way."

Tears hung on the ends of Eva's lashes and trembled. She flicked them away. "Wait—*Zimrod?* I thought he was just a legend! He was *real?*"

"Was and is . . . Legends *do* come from somewhere, Dear. Not always true on every point, but true enough to heed."

"Got it. Go ahead," Eva murmured.

"So where was I; oh yes . . . the count." She absently sipped her empty cup, then got up and poured herself and Eva some fresh tea. "Fagan, knowing the power of your *and* your mother's gifts, paid Isola a large sum of money to kill you both. That was his plan, to rid the countryside of any that could put his wretched life to an end."

She stirred a generous dollop of honey into her steaming cup and inclined her head toward Eva. "Because your mother waited until right before your birth to drink the draught, you survived. Later, after discovering the poison in the cup, many said your life being spared was a miracle. There was enough poison in the liquid to kill a horse." Zephira paused and took a long sip of tea. "That morning, Isola disappeared from the castle grounds and was never seen or heard from again."

Trembling, Eva wrapped her arms tightly around her knees, tucking them under her chin. She rested her forehead on her knees. "Keep going. I'm listening," she said, her voice muffled.

"Are you sure? Because this will keep. I can save the rest for later," Zephira said softly.

"*No*, I mean I need to hear it, all of it—*please*." She lifted her head and gave the Seer a weak nod.

The Seer's eyes were liquid with compassion, but behind them was steely resolve: a profound understanding that the princess must take this truth deep into her heart. She would need it in the days to come.

"After the poisoning was discovered," Zephira began, "Fagan realized it was too risky to try to kill you outright. Instead, he chose to poison your father's heart against you . . . and your own soul with the gall of bitterness. He knew this anger you would likely carry against your father would accomplish his purpose in your life—your heart of gold would become brass with bitterness. You would then be unable to step into your destiny when the time came."

Eva felt this truth lodge in her chest like a stone. Her head fell forward onto her knees. No tears came, just the sure knowledge that she could do nothing about this. *How can I forgive someone who has sold me to get riches for his treasury? Someone who has never had time for me—drugged or not? This is a question with only one answer: I can't and I won't.*

The princess sat wordlessly thinking of her lonely years at the mercy of her father's whims and wishes. She lifted her head. "Well, I don't wish he was dead, does that count?"

A minute passed in silence, then Zephira spoke. "That *is* a start. This is nothing that can be rushed, My Dear. Just remember, forgiveness doesn't mean what someone did was right; it just means the prison door of hatred swings open for you. It's no longer your job to make sure he is punished. Someone greater than you will handle him rightly. Walk free and live your life."

Eva lifted her head and looked into the fire. "Maybe I will forgive him—one day. But *not* today."

"It's always best to take time in these matters. Trust your heart to speak truly." She reached over and gave Eva's hand a little squeeze.

The princess stared silently out the window, remembering the words spoken to her in her bedroom, that night after vespers so long ago. " . . . *I'm there with you, for all time . . . a promise.*" She felt the starry arms around her once again and closed her eyes.

They sat quietly then, listening to the fire pop and crackle in the hearth.

Then Zephira spoke: "Princess, your hour is upon you *and* your friend. You must be feeling this in your bones. That's why you came."

Eva gasped. She felt the weight of the Seer's words. She opened her eyes, almost surprised to see she was still in the homely cottage. "It's true," she whispered.

45

Which way, mate?" Spyder wanted to know. They stepped onto the cobblestones outside the store. A sudden gust of wind swept their jackets to one side, making them squint and grab their hats. "Name's Spyder . . . yours?" He cocked a dark eyebrow and jerked his chin toward Traveler.

"Call me Bard, and we'll leave it at that."

"Whatever you say, *Bard*. So which way's the princess?" Spyder stopped and sent him a piercing stare.

"Down Fernhill Road a-ways." Traveler gestured away from the Seer's cottage. "You got a horse?"

"Yeah . . . horse's in the livery. Wait by the Dewdrop. I'll come 'round with him." With that, he turned on his heel and walked off, the wind flapping his long coat like a loose sail.

Traveler headed toward the tavern. *A nasty piece of work, that one.* He thought of the old woman's warning. Spyder must be handled carefully, of that he was sure . . . *One of Fagan's, I'd lay money on it. I'll take him through the woods, lose him—then a quick knock on the head. By the time he comes to and finds his way back to town, we'll be long gone.* He smiled to himself, thinking of dinner with Eva in front of the fireplace. *We'll take the long way. Wouldn't do to be found on the road.*

Leaning under the red-striped awning outside the tavern door, he cast a quick glance up the road toward Zephira's cottage. Nothing. *Just give me a little while.* He sent a loud thought in her direction.

After waiting a few minutes more, he wondered if the bounty hunter had decided to strike out on his own—*in the wrong direction.* He smiled ruefully.

Traveler pushed off the wall to go get the supplies then head over to their meeting log in the woods. *Tomorrow night,* he thought happily. *All will be told then. Her questions will be answered.*

He walked past the tavern corner and heard a cough by his left ear. He turned—too late. Someone dropped a noose around his neck, twisted it; a lightning strike. Practiced hands wrenched his arms behind his back, pushing him to his knees in pain. A filthy wad of cloth was shoved into his mouth and tied in with a gag, a burlap bag jerked over his head, and a sickening blow delivered to the back of his head—all was black.

Spyder sniggered, "Where's yer lute, Bard—or should I say *Minstrel?*" He hoisted him over the horse's saddle like a sack of turnips. "C'mon, boys." He and the rest of Fagan's henchmen mounted their horses and headed toward Ravenia and two thousand gold pieces. The bounty hunter reached down from his saddle, grabbed the reigns of Traveler's horse and handed them off to Madowg. This man, scarred from his left eyebrow to his stubbly right cheek, usually brought up the rear. The black patch over his eye succeeded in making him look formidable, but, it simply meant he was blind on his left side.

Spyder spurred his horse to a trot, taking his place at the front of the group. "Stay together and keep your eyes peeled for the princess-wench, mates." He turned in his saddle. "Tonight's camp, Mount Crowley; Fagan tomorrow." The wind shook branches overhead, and leaves rained down. "Unless we hole up in a cave. We'll see."

46

You've done well," the seer said softly. "You are now free from the dark destroyer. But, make no mistake, he *will* try to lure you again through desire and emotion. But, you know his voice now—and you know the *True* Voice." Zephira gathered up their empty plates. "The power of the false voice is his lie. Don't believe him, it's that simple."

Eva sat silent. Thinking.

"Be on your guard," Zephira continued, "You *do* have a friend. However, evil will seek to use you, then destroy both you and your friend."

"Why would they want to kill Traveler? He's just a *minstrel.*"

Zephira's eyes crinkled and shone once again. "This *minstrel* is much more than he seems. *They* know this, and I think you've guessed as much."

"So who is he?" Eva wanted to know, thinking again of the knight.

"That's something you will discover for yourself as you step into your own truth. You are no pawn, nobody's tool," she said. "But, you know that too, don't you?"

"I do."

Zephira stood and smiled, gesturing toward the apples by the door. "These are juicy and delicious. How about some for your bag?"

"Juicy and delicious?" Eva echoed absently, wanting to cry and laugh at the same time. She sat trembling, perched on the edge of her chair, thinking she might fly apart at any moment.

Then feeling an urgent tug to leave, she stood and walked with Zephira to the door, packing four apples in her bag, enough for herself and Traveler.

"Choose your destiny—or *not*," the Seer said, handing the princess her hat, "without looking back over your shoulder, wondering. It's the covenant way." She grew suddenly somber. "Today, you will encounter difficulties. *Tomorrow*—danger beyond what you ever imagined you could face."

"But, wait! What will happen? Surely you can tell me—!" Eva stepped back, feeling panic rise, hot in her chest.

"That curtain is closed to me, Dear One. And you've been wondering about the tears. Know this; the True Voice will show you—be sure to pay attention." She paused and said, "Oh yes, don't leave without this. Keep it close." She pulled a small brown drawstring bag from a drawer under the cake platter. "This has dried yarrow, to staunch blood flow, and anti-venom herbs to combat poison . . . Archie and Bea know all about this, as you well know. These saved your life once."

Princess Evangeline and Zephira said their farewells, embracing at the cottage door. Eva walked a few steps down the path, turned to wave, and saw Zephira silhouetted in the afternoon sun.

For a moment, instead of the ancient Seer, Eva saw a beautiful young woman in the very spring of her strength and splendor. Her lovely head was crowned with brilliant white hair cascading over her shoulders, then, rippling over her long gown like a waterfall. *Miracle Falls*, Eva thought. The golden gown under the flow of hair shimmered with a light that seemed to come from the very fabric itself.

Eva blinked and rubbed her eyes. Once again, the old seer stood before her, smiling, her face falling into familiar soft wrinkles. They waved goodbye again, and the princess turned toward Fernhill, feeling as though the weight of the world had rolled off her shoulders.

For the first time since she was very young, Eva felt like singing and skipping. And so, she skipped through melting snowdrifts, and down the hillside toward their meeting place.

Rounding a bend in the road, four men on horseback with a loaded fifth horse approached her, filling the narrow passage through the woods. Eva jumped to the side, letting them go by.

"Give way, there's a smart lad." The rider in the rear growled at her, giving the reins of the loaded horse behind him a tug. It trotted a little faster, kicking up clods of dirt as it passed. She stepped back farther into the woods, her scarf and hat tight on her head.

"A good day to you, Sirs," she said pitching her voice as low as possible. This greeting was ignored.

As the horse loaded with a strangely shaped burlap bag passed by, a low moan came from the bag. Eva stifled a gasp. *I know that voice!*

They had just rounded the bend, and something occurred to the lead horseman. He shouted back over his shoulder, "Madowg, did you see a scar by the ear of that boy you was flappin' your jaw at?"

"Naw, Mate. You know I can't see off me left side."

Spyder snarled a curse. He jerked his horse's head around, galloping past his posse, back to the spot where Eva had stood.

There was no sign of anyone having been there, not even a broken twig.

She had disappeared deep into the woods.

She silenced panic

47

Eva slipped through the low bushes on the edge of the woods and ran as traveler had taught her, landing her feet where no leaf or twig would be disturbed. Finally, seeing a thicket, she entered it, falling to the ground under an alder tree, as one might drop into the ocean from a cliff. Currents of misery carried her.

Everyone I've ever loved has been ripped from me . . . and now you, my truest friend. Gone! Thought talons tore at her. She held her face, absolutely and utterly—alone. *What if this is it? What if this is all my failure-of-a-life amounts to? I'm nobody's anything. Not Dunmoor's Queen. Not Valentino's bride.* She saw the life that should have been hers slipping away from her like inlet waves through her fingers; sparkling as they went. *I'm not even Traveler's . . . friend.* Eva caught her breath. A thought lifted. Bright. "—But maybe." she said under her breath.

She suddenly realized her throat was as dry as dirt. Lifting her water skin to her mouth, a thin stream dribbled onto her parched tongue. It would have to do.

She heard something. Silence. The forest had gone completely quiet. Eva stilled herself, remembering. Listening. Had someone followed her? A breeze slipped through the woods, ruffling dry leaves. *There, I heard it! Did something just exhale?* Someone was in the woods. Close. There was no more sound, just the thrumming of her nerves. Panic rose in her throat. She pushed it down, and with it, the urge to run like a deer, blindly, wildly. Instead, she closed her eyes, took a deep, silent breath. Waited.

The princess was squeezed back into the brambles, ignoring the thorns piercing her shoulders, her head. Barely breathing, she crouched, her hand on her dagger. Was that a flash of orange she saw through the leaves. Eva thought of the man at the Purple Pig and held her breath. She thought bitterly of the starry arms that had held her—the Voice that had spoken. *Where are you now?* Even her time with the Seer felt cloaked. A *dream.*

A twig snapped further away. Whoever or whatever it *was* had moved past. *Moved on!* She blinked, hardly believing.

A voice spoke in her thoughts; deep, quiet. A plan bloomed and buzzed. She sat up, eyes wide, her hair a jumble of twigs and leaves. The plan coursed and flashed through her body, her arms, and finally—settled in her head.

She stood to her feet, thoughts swimming. Bracing herself against the tree, she stepped over a rotted trunk, searching the ground. Finding some small brown shelves of fungus on branches behind the alder, she cupped her hands over the cluster, casting it in deep shade. Inside the cave of her hands, tiny bluish-green lights glimmered! "Behold—Foxfire!" she whispered, eyes shining.

With her bag full of the brown glowing fungus, she steeled herself and ran. Sprinting west toward Fagan's castle, Eva ran until she could no longer feel her legs; then, she ran some more. Finally, with her chest burning and heaving, she stopped, doubled-over in the woods beside a dirt road. She had to find those men. Had to find Traveler before they made it to Ravenia. *Somehow.*

Then, she heard it; the unmistakable sound of someone whistling through his teeth! *Traveler?*

Eva thrashed through the thorny bushes beside the road, shouting. "You *goose*! Where'd you *go?* I thought you were—!"

Been a-lookin' for you

48

"Well-a-day, fancy finding you out here, so far from home—Your *Highness*."
Jack Rabbitt jumped from his wagon and in a flash, stood beside Eva.
"And, to answer your question; I been a-lookin' for *you!*"

"Your Highness? Why do you call me that?" she said pitching her voice
low. The princess edged away toward the woods. *He's old. I can make it away.*

He wheezed out a laugh, and rasped, "First things first." With a sudden flick
of his wrist, he jerked a rope from his waist, slinging it around her, cinching
her arms to her side. Then relieving her of her dagger, he pulled her hands to
her back, binding her wrists with the tail end of the rope. Jack dragged her,
struggling and screaming, to his wagon. He hoisted her up onto the seat beside
him and bound her feet at the ankles.

When Eva realized she and Jack were alone in a desolate land, she stopped
screaming.

"More like it," Jack muttered. "*Get* up, Clovis!" He clucked his tongue,
sending his horse forward.

"Would you be so good as to untie my wrists," the princess asked curtly.
She studied his scruffy whiskered profile.

"And why would I do a thing like *that?*" He squinted in her direction.

These ropes are cutting into my skin—and yes, I *am* Princess Evangeline,
heir to the throne of Dunmoor." *There, I've said it.*

265

"So, Miss Heir-To-The-Throne, I'll make you privy to a fact of life: there's a double bounty on your head. And, ol' Jack's not in the habit of turnin' up his nose at such. In fact, if I did, I would be neglectin' my sworn duty."

"Double—?"

"You're *wanted*, by a king *and* a count. Kinda makes you feel special, don't it? And ol' Jack's gotta keep some grub in the larder . . . feedin' the inner man, as they say." He shook the reins. Clovis sputtered and trotted faster. "So, here's the long and short of it: the count wants you for his wife; won't take *no* for an answer. He and yon King, yer *Pa*, set a hefty sum on your head. So get ready to be the new Missus Fagan," the gnarly man barked out a harsh laugh.

"I'd sooner throw myself off a cliff," she said dully.

Jack Rabbit made no comment. He'd made it a personal policy never to get involved with his hostages. It made doing the deed and collecting the money much too hard, too complicated. He'd already felt his chest start to tighten. Again. He wheezed and spit something off the side of the wagon. Eva looked away, then, made herself look back at Jack's face.

"But, I can't die, don't you see!" Her voice rose. Desperate. "There is something I must do for the kingdom—for the people of Dunmoor! And I am the only one who can do it, the only one I know of anyway." Her voice trailed off. "Please." Eva hung her head, eyes stinging. Her pulse raced, thinking of Traveler—in the hands of murderers. *And it's my fault.*

"Thinkin' about your boyfriend?" Jack's words prodded her.

"He's not my boyfriend, and yes, I was. The only reason he's captured is because he tried to help me," she muttered bitterly. "Everyone who's ever cared about me has been taken from me, my whole life—starting with my mother, the day I was born—and now this kind-hearted minstrel, my true friend," she added, then immediately regretted it.

"Aww, so touching—Shaddap!" Jack spat out the words. However, if Eva had glanced at his face she would have seen moisture collecting in the corners of his eyes and the grizzled whiskers on his chin twitching and quivering.

They rode in tense silence for several minutes. Rolling past a grove of alder trees, Eva saw the mountains of Ravenia in the distance. On top of the highest peak, she could just make out the dark spires of Fagan's castle.

Then she spoke, "You remind me a little of someone I had to leave behind. Archie is about your age. He was like a father to me. I miss him," she said quietly and glanced over.

No response.

Eva remembered her travel bag, thrown in the back of the wagon. "I have money. It's yours. Just let me go." She leaned forward. "You can leave the country if you like. Start fresh somewhere else. Or if you stay, if I come into my place as Queen, I'll grant you a full pardon. You will live as a *free* citizen of Dunmoor!" Her words came out in a rush, intent, hopeful.

Jack had been sitting silently, letting old Clovis plod on, closer and closer to the Ravenian border—and his reward at the castle—which would mean another meeting with the count. He shuddered involuntarily, remembering the burning hatred he'd seen in Fagan's eyes at their last meeting. He'd played the part of an ignorant lackey as always, but knew with certainty the count would just as soon cut him up and feed him to the wolves . . . *Or that dragon of his,* thought Jack. His head began to throb. He pulled off his hat and fanned his face. But here was another offer, made by the princess herself. Another way to live for a while longer—a long while . . . *if* she was telling the truth.

He reigned up his horse and reached back to grab Eva's bag. "A lotta *if'n.* How much you got here?"

"Enough for you to live for years. Probably." Eva's eyes brightened. "On my word as Princess and rightful future Queen of Dunmoor, I shall hold you blameless."

He grabbed her chin with his crusty hand and looked her squarely in the eyes. "Alright. We got ourselves a deal." He pulled her dagger out of his belt, cut the rope from her hands and ankles. Her bindings fell around her feet. He studied her warily.

"You don't have to worry, you're a free man," she declared. "I've given you my word." She reached down in her bag past the foxfire and pulled out a drawstring bag of coins. "Here," she said. "It's yours, all of it."

He poured out the contents of the bag in his palm, whistled low and thumbed through the coins. "This is enough to take me through a couple o' years, easy—or out of the country if you should get—"

"—Killed," she finished for him. "Yes, I know."

49

So, which way, Your Highness?" the bounty hunter squinted in her direction.
"Which way?" Eva echoed, thinking about what had just happened.

"Sure. You just tell ol' Jack where you're headed. Me and ol' Clovis here, we'll carry you a far piece in the right direction." He stared at her expectantly. "So, back to Tirzah?"

Back to Tirzah? Back to my Valentino! Back to my future as Princess and one day Queen of a nation. "Give me a minute," Eva murmured. She bent over, cradling her forehead in the palm of her hand.

Or is it . . . on to where I was going? The scene of the four men on horseback, the fifth horse loaded with a long burlap bag, rose in her thoughts. *It was Traveler's voice coming from that bag. I'm sure of it. How could I let him suffer—what horrible tortures—at their hands, and Fagan's.* The thought was too terrible to explore.

"I must!" she announced and sat up suddenly.

"And just what, *must* you do?" Jack sat back and scratched his shiny bald forehead.

"I have to... have to help my friend, the minstrel. They have him. *Fagan's* men. At least, they did when I saw them last . . . just outside Fernhill. Can you help me? Do you know where they are? Where they'll camp tonight? Can you take me there—*now?*" The words tumbled out.

In Eva's mind, there was no time to lose. She had the plan from the alder thicket. She had the foxfire in her bag. Now, what she needed was *valor!* "If you are bound to do something and lack courage, just do it scared. The courage will show up at the right time." Eva realized she had just said Traveler's words to her out loud and felt her cheeks burn.

Jack looked off in the distance. "You've been kind to me. And as much as ol' Jack'd like to help you out, you need to know, those men is called Fagan's *cut-throats* for a reason. Yer as smart as fresh paint, Princess, but one skinny girl ain't no match fer them four hooligans . . . not *any* day of the week."

"Thank you, Jack, but you just let that be *my* worry. I have to do this." She sent him a steely smile. After a minute she said quietly: "I sure would appreciate your help getting there."

Sunset was fading to dusk when Jack's wagon rolled to a stop at the base of Mt. Crowley.

"Not seein' any campfire smoke. Yer in luck." He pointed up through bare-branched trees to a group of large boulders halfway up the hill. "That's where they's gonna camp tonight; I'd lay money on it." He shot her a questioning glance. "You sure you want to go through with this?"

"No question about it." Eva gave him a quick smile, showing more confidence than she felt, and picked up her bag. "And once again, thank you." She laughed ruefully. "Funny, how things work out, right?" She shook his hand and stepped from the wagon.

"You don't hear me laughin', do ya?" Jack leaned over the other side of the wagon and spat. Then, he pushed back his hat and looked her in the eye. "O-right. I've one more thing fer ya. Maybe it'll help—maybe not."

Eva was anxious to find a hiding place up on the hill, but put that aside and turned to meet Jack's stare. "And, what would that be, Jack." She pulled nervously at a hangnail.

"You likely don't know this, bein' a princess an' all, but folk who grow up in Ravenia live in mortal fear of *faerie beasts.* And you might a' guessed; Spyder and all his men was born and raised there. Cut their teeth on stories o' these creatures spiritin' folks away—never to be seen or heard from again." Jack made a sweeping gesture with his hand.

Eva's eyes lit up, then her eyebrows knotted together briefly. "And what exactly would a *faerie beast* be?"

Jack leaned over and rasped out a whisper, "You know, spirits, demons, and the like— ghosts!" He shifted his shoulders and his eyes darted up the hill. "Ol' Jack likes a warm hearth and a roof over his head of a night, he does." He took up the reigns and tipped his hat in her direction. "Well, it's our partin' of ways, as they say. All the best to you, Princess."

"And to you, Jack. Travel in The Way."

Jack made no comment, but nodded and shook the reigns. The wagon rumbled down the road and disappeared around a stand of birch trees.

With no one in sight, she trudged up the hill, hoping Jack was right.

Eva settled herself behind a massive boulder directly above the campsite. Well hidden, she sat and sorted through her bag, pulling out every shred of foxfire she could find. Then, smiling to herself, she thought of Jack's story about faerie beasts and the superstitious Ravenians. She wondered if Traveler knew this about his captors. *In all his wanderings, likely, but, maybe not,* she mused. Taking off her jacket, she rolled it, put it under her head, and leaned her back against the smooth warm surface of the boulder. Traveler would need to be a part of this plan. She was sure of it. *But how do I let him know?*

In her mind, the princess mapped out every scenario she could think of— but one. She hadn't figured exhaustion and hunger into her careful planning. Resting her head against the giant stone, Eva ate another apple. Her blinks became slower and longer, until finally her eyes closed.

Images of ghosts, screeching black birds, and men on horseback swirled together in her head. Then, like a dark veil, the wing of Morach eclipsed it all.

50

ight settled on the mountains, a dark brooding bird.

Men's voices woke Eva. She popped out of her sleep as if cresting the surface from a deep dive. Fortunately, she had the presence of mind not to move or make a sound. She listened.

The sound of a crackling campfire caught her attention. And, there it was, the aroma of something cooking. Was it bacon and cornmeal? *It was.* She was sure of it.

At the very moment her stomach growled, one of the men said: "No need to feed this 'un. He'll be Fagan fodder tomorrow—let the Count feed him."

"Right!" said another. "*Feed* him to that dragon of his, likely, eh, Mate?" This was clearly hilarious.

Eva heard them cackling and thumping each other, and the dull *whump* of someone's boot kicking a body. She couldn't stand it. She had to know. The princess inched her face over, until one eye could see beyond her stone and into the camp. She quickly moved back into the night-shadow behind the boulder, her heart pounding in her ears.

Traveler lay, bound hand and foot, on the ground, his back to her. Across the campfire, the four henchmen sat in a semi-circle, guffawing at the minstrel's pain. Eva marveled that her friend had not even cried out. Fury made helpless tears sting her eyes and her insides burn.

Spyder stepped over, kicked Traveler in the ribs again, then jerked him up by the arm to a sitting position. "D'you think it's nap-time? Think again, Bard!" He backhanded him across the face, sending him sprawling to the ground once again. "I said, sit!" he bellowed and jerked the minstrel up again, basking in the shouts and laughter of the other three.

"Hey, Boss. It's dinner," Madawg announced. "You might want to save your strength for tomorrow." He ventured with a crooked smile.

Spyder crossed the clearing in three strides, grabbed Madawg by his coat lapels, and shoved him away from the food he'd just prepared. "So, you gonna tell me what to do? Maybe you'd like to be boss! Or maybe we should truss you up like the minstrel here, and deliver you as a *bonus* to the Count himself. I hear that dragon of his stays hungry!" Their leader relished his power and rolled the words on his tongue, savoring their raw strength. He barked out a short mirthless laugh and shoved Madawg one more time for good measure.

Spyder took advantage of the cowed silence of the group to serve himself a tremendous helping of bacon-cornmeal mush. "Well, I can't eat *all* this. Who's gonna help me?" he said, suddenly jovial. He sat, and the three men split the little that was left. Laughing nervously, they all sat in a semi-circle once again—acting as though nothing had happened.

The night wore on.

The bounty hunters, drowsy with dinner, found themselves a place to hunker down by the fire. One by one, they nodded off.

The wind picked up, gathering storm clouds. The shrouded moon, cast the hillside in darkness for stretches of time. *But, not long enough or dark enough. Not yet*, she decided.

Eva was faced with a dilemma. She needed to let Traveler know she was here—somehow—without alerting the other men. And, though the fire had died down a bit, it was still way too bright for her foxfire to glow. It must be dark. Very dark. Suddenly, Eva felt foolish. *What was I thinking?* She berated herself. *How can I do this?*

She bit her thumbnail and waited . . . for *something*. What, she wasn't sure. Back in the alder thicket how certain she'd been. Her plan couldn't miss, she'd thought. But now . . .

The wind savaged the tops of trees around them. They creaked and groaned. Without warning, a triple-strike of lightening flashed the clouds, turning the countryside to day for a brief moment. An ear-splitting boom of thunder followed, raising the hair on the back of her neck. More thunder rolled, crackling across the sky. The men muttered and shifted, huddled closer to the dwindling flames of the campfire.

Suddenly, Eva realized this was what she was waiting for. A storm! It was time. She prayed her friend would remember, wet her lips, and whistle-called her signal—the falcon's cry. Would Traveler hear it over the howling wind? No sign. The princess tried again. Leaning close to the edge of the boulder, she gave the whistling cry as loud as she dared. Then, she waited again. Listening.

"Did you hear that?" Traveler shouted to the men crouched under their oiled-cloth ponchos. "The call of the falcon. This time of night it happens for one reason, and one reason only!

"So, yer gonna talk now—shut yer *face*, Minstrel!" Madawg shouted.

"Let him finish," Spyder bellowed. "Well—*finish*, Vermin!"

The minstrel ignored the insult and shouted, "It's a herald. The falcon announces the supernatural. Things coming. I thought *you'd* know this, of all people. Something's coming. No place to hide. *Get ready!!*"

"Alright, *that's it*—SHADDAP or I stuff your *mouth!*"

The minstrel fell silent, knowing his words had hit their mark. The men muttered and inched closer, fear binding them with invisible ropes.

Eva heard their campfire smolder and hiss as raindrops pelted it. Her soggy clothes clung to her like a cold skin. What was left of the campfire dwindled on the muddy ground, barely glowing. Then, the wind quieted. *Alright! It's now or never.* She stood.

Smearing her wet face *again* with the glowing fungus, she picked up branches and propped her jacket over her head; it became a circular hood filled with glowing foxfire.

Hoping her disguise would work, she prayed they would see her as a floating, glowing head in absolute darkness. Eva swallowed air. She gulped mouthfuls, until she thought her stomach would split. Finally, she stepped out from behind the boulder, behind Traveler. At least that's where she remembered he was. Swaying eerily behind the dead campfire, she uncovered her green, ghoulish face. She began.

Pitching her voice as low as possible, she released a belch in long, deeply vibrating syllables, moving her lips. The bounty hunters leapt to their feet and clung together as one man. The sound increased in pitch and volume, surrounding them. They each knew—they *knew*. This disembodied, glowing, *creature* brought a loud, certain, yet unknowable judgment against them. Their dark deeds were discovered. Their time was up. It had come to spirit them away.

Bound at the ankles and wrists, Traveler toppled to the ground and wriggled away from the *apparition,* wailing and quaking.

Madawg pulled out his dagger, thrust it in front of him, his hand trembling.

Panicked, Spyder screamed, "*Idiot!* You can't fight a *faerie* beast with a knife!! Put it away! You want it to go *worse* for us? I know their *ways!*" The knife was slapped back in its sheath. "We mean you no harm!" Spyder cried out toward the floating phantom. The men backed slowly into the dark forest.

The short one said, "What about the minstrel . . . our *reward?*"

"What *about* him." muttered Spyder. "Let the beast take *him!*"

In a flash, the princess uttered a deafening, unearthly *shriek.* That was it.

"*Yiiiieeee!!*" The cut-throats screamed and ran into the pitch-black.

Briefly, Eva listened to them falling, cursing, slamming into trees, and getting slapped with wet branches. From the noise, she could tell they were downhill, almost to the road. She shrieked again, three short blasts, sending them faster and farther.

Quiet settled around Eva and the minstrel, except for five spooked horses, jostling and whinnying in the woods.

Storm clouds raced across the sky. The full moon suddenly shone between them, giving Eva and her minstrel a minute's purchase of light.

"That went well," Traveler said from the ground.

"I thought so." Eva pulled the branches out of her jacket and cut his ropes. "You alright?"

"Been better. No complaints though." he stood rubbing his wrists. "How can I thank—"

"After all you've done for me? Don't even—" She sheathed her knife, her teeth shining in the moonlit clearing. Touching the swollen bruise under his left eye, she frowned. He winced. It would have to wait.

Feeling their way through dripping trees, they unbuckled the saddles and halters from the first three horses. The leather trappings slid off and were tossed into the woods.

"Come on!" she said breathlessly mounting one of the saddled horses. "In a minute, they'll figure out what just happened. Let's *go.*"

"Right," agreed the minstrel, swinging himself onto the other horse with a quiver of arrows and longbow in the saddle pouch. "I'll have to send Spyder a thank-you note for this," he muttered.

Their horses found their way through the woods and out onto the road.

"Miracle Valley's our best bet for tonight. Rain's clearing." he said squinting at clouds scudding to the north. A full moon lit the puddles in the road. "I think I can get us through the valley passage," he said, turning in the saddle to face her.

"I'm with you," she said looking over her shoulder.

Expecting Fagan's men at any moment, they urged their horses into a gallop.

51

Their horses thundered across fields and through sleeping villages. Thin rain pelted Eva's face like clusters of watery needles. Her breath tore down her throat in gasps. She realized she was praying in rhythm to her horse's hoofbeats; each word snatched from her lips and flung into the dark.

Leaning onto their horse's necks, the two dark riders hurtled down the road, all pounding hooves and driving speed.

She couldn't shake the feeling of being watched as they neared the narrow passageway into the Valley. She stole glances over her shoulder as the world flashed past in blacks and greys. A dark movement between the clouds caught her eye. In a moment it was gone. Did she *imagine* it?

Dismounting, they led the horses under the tree canopy and found the narrow valley trail. Eva told Traveler what she'd just seen in the sky.

He walked quietly for a moment. "So, Morach sees where we're headed. I knew it would come to this. It had to," Traveler said matter-of-factly. "I have to face him. And I know where it needs to happen."

"I'll *help* you!" Eva whispered urgently.

"You have already helped me," he turned solemnly to look at her face, half hidden in moon shadows. "One day this epic story—our escape from Fagan's band of hooligans—your rescue, using only foxfire, and a *particular* skill," he smiled sadly. "This will be told around campfires. What you've done—our friendship—is *legendary!*" his voice darkened. "And *someone* has to be alive to tell it." He pushed a branch aside.

"But *wait*. No! I have to, to help you fight. Don't you *see?* It's why we're here, why we're together," She panted, running up beside him, her words tumbling out. "I know the legend. You're not a prince. And, I'm not a princess—not anymore—but if you die," her voice caught. "I couldn't bear it." Her chest ached with the thought.

He turned to her, his face shadowed. "Princess—*no*." She heard his voice, deep, resolved. Final.

Reaching the end of the passageway, they stood looking across the valley. Angel Falls shimmered faintly in the distance.

The minstrel faced her. "I'll kill Morach and meet you back here under the trees," he paused gravely, "and I am so serious about you not coming with me." His eyes searched her's. "You *know* I mean it. If anything happened to you, because—"

"Oh, *Trav*—*!*" Sobbing, Eva clutched him and buried her face in his shoulder.

Traveler's arm encircled her waist, swift and strong. He pressed her body to his, released a loud sigh and stepped back. Holding her shoulders at arm's length, his fierce gaze settled on her face. He opened his mouth to say something, then, closed it.

"*Go* in the Way." she whispered, quaking.

The minstrel mounted his horse and, with one final glance at Eva, sprang from their cover of trees at a full gallop. The next instant, Eva leapt onto her horse's back and raced toward Traveler's dark silhouette.

52

By the time the two reached Angel Falls, the rain had stopped. Traveler saw her and shouted, "*GO—GET TO SAFETY!!*" He braced the longbow against his instep, bending it and pulling the looped sinew string onto the bow's grooved tip.

They heard it then. The howling *shriek* of the beast, meant to paralyze his victims with fear. He tore through the clouds.

"*YOU*—the horses—to the *woods*—*NOW!!*" The minstrel grabbed the sword and shield from the saddle of his horse, slung the bow and quiver of arrows over his shoulder, and ran toward the cliff.

Eva grabbed the horses' reins and ran with them to the woods. Throwing her bag down beside an enormous oak, she released the horses among the trees. Trembling, she turned to see the dragon descend, slowly circling the air above Traveler, biding his time.

Eva's eyes traveled up, above where Traveler waited, *ready*. There, crowding the edge of the cliff, clustered *boulders*. On the ground behind her friend were smashed boulders. Tons of them.

That's it!

Screened by the tree line, she made her way, unseen, to what *could* be a pathway to the cliff's edge. Scrambling, sliding over loose rubble, Eva made her way upward. Almost to the top, the narrow passage was so steep, she had to crawl to keep from sliding back down.

Traveler didn't have long to wait.

The beast, seeing his opportunity, landed and filled his lungs. An *enormous* breath. No need to involve himself in a skirmish, he would scorch the minstrel to ash in his boots.

Knowing the ways of dragons, Traveler darted behind the waterfall into a shallow cave. Pressing himself into a crevice, he covered the entrance with the shield—then braced himself.

The next instant, black smoke swirled around the cliffs, blotting out the moon. Wind snatched Eva's clothes, flapping them around her frail body. Desperate, she pressed against the rocks. Her fingernails torn and ragged, filled with dirt. Still, she forced them into cracks and fissures—any handhold she could find. *Have to get up! Help Trav*—"Please keep him alive!" Her voice pleaded, lost in the roaring furnace of Morach's fiery breath.

In her haste, Eva shoved her foot clumsily into a crevice, knocking loose a clod of rubble. It tumbled downward, landing on the dragon's shortened tail.

Holding her breath, she flattened her body against the cliffside, willing herself invisible. *Ahhh—Just a few more feet.*

The creature looked up. The minstrel was an inconvenience. An *annoyance.* He saw what he was after. Princess Evangeline—clinging exposed on the rocky cliffside.

Almost lazily, he unfolded the thick membranes of his wings, unfurling them to the wind. His searing glare pierced her. Paralyzed her, but only for an instant.

She watched Traveler run from the scorched cave in the cliff-side, loosing volleys of arrows against the belly of the beast. Striking his neck, his head; their points found no entry between the thick scales.

Morach pummeled the air with his wings, lifting his armored bulk into the air. He stretched his neck upward toward the prize—*his* prize. He was close now, so close his sulphur-breath blew her hair back in a blast of hot, putrid air. Eva shrank into the cliff, willing her agonized fingers to hold on. Then, she heard his voice. Deep. Rumbling. "I've *come* for you. It is pointless to resist."

Trembling, the princess screamed, "I'm not *GOING!*"

53

In years to come, what happened next was told and re-told until the story spread throughout the known world.

The monster, seeing she was within reach, spread his wings wider and opened his talons to pluck her from the rock where she clung. *"Finally,* he exulted deep in his throat, *I win."*

With her free foot, she frantically kicked the black claws.

At that moment, the minstrel loosed his final arrow. It sped powerfully, directly and deeply in the open maw of the dragon's mouth.

Morach, instead of snatching the princess with his claw, used it to paw his open mouth, now drooling green acid saliva down the side of the rocky cliff. But, the arrow stayed lodged firmly inside, infuriating him with pain.

Flying higher, he saw Traveler on the ground, waving his sword in one hand and his shield with the other—openly taunting him: "Come and get me, you vile sack of scales and skin!" he shouted. "What's the matter, *short-tail?* Used up all your fire?" Then, the minstrel started shouting his Apple Pie song at the top of his lungs while running away from the cliff where Eva hung motionless.

It only took her a moment to figure out what Trav was doing. She'd seen birds in the garden do this to distract barn cats from their nest of hatchlings. *Always, the bird would fly away at the last possible moment—fly Traveler! Run! Hide!*

Morach gathered himself and began his descent, bearing down on the minstrel in a screaming dive. The wind keened over the thick taught sails of his wings. She saw him tuck them closer, tipping his body, banking his dive. The minstrel spun wildly, facing the dragon, his sword and shield high.

After what seemed like an eternity, the beast unfurled his wings, slowed himself, and dropped down, claws extended.

Eva craned her neck to see beyond the enormous wings. "*NOOOO!*" she screamed, her voice clogged and broke. She watched, horrified, feeling no pain in her bloody fingers.

Wind rushed down the cliffside, catching the dragon under his wings as though they were autumn leaves. He was dragged up—swiftly and surely, away from his prey. The creature bellowed in rage as the strong gust suspended him helplessly in midair, then calmed to a breeze. No longer held aloft, Morach tumbled head over tail . . . down. His head, then his body, slammed against the rocky ground, sending quaking ripples throughout the valley and up the cliff into Eva's fingers.

The minstrel raced to the beast to cut off his head. Morach gathered his legs under him and sprang over his attacker, landing at the foot of the cliff where Eva clung.

Once again, the beast looked up at the *Princess*.

Eva knew what she *must* do.

She pushed her burning, quaking arms and legs to

climb to the top of the cliff. Peering down from her foothold, she saw thumbnail sized horses. Her thoughts spun dizzily. She imagined herself falling head-long—plunging into the mouth of Morach. Her body shook; her fingers slipped, losing their grip. Despair and fear perched on her thin shoulders.

So this is it, the end . . . Eva imagined the faces of Archie and Bea and longed to hug them just once more. She wished for the soft purring comfort of Arlo. She wished for Valentino to take her hand and pull her up over the cliff ledge. But, none of them were here. Not one.

It was up to her.

Then, the face of her father loomed large in her mind. She squeezed her eyes shut. "Yes," she gasped. "Even *you* . . . I even love you, my poisoned fool of a father. I *forgive you!*"

Her head cleared. Strength and heat surged inside, flowing into her fingers, her legs.

Eva forced her eyes upward. *Don't look down,* she thought fiercely. *See yourself on top! You're up on the cliff! You're by the boulders! Now move!!* She forced her fingers into the next rocky handhold, the next crevice, then the next. Her boots followed. Finally, her fingers grasped the cliff-ledge. She hooked a leg over the top and was up and over, sobbing with relief. How she did it, she couldn't say. But there she was. *No time to waste!*

Eva knuckled the dirt and tears from her eyes, rolled to her feet, and sprinted to the group of boulders crowding the cliff-ledge.

She peered over the edge.

Morach scaled the cliff below, wings folded tightly against his body. He strained against the rushing wind—eyes blazing, talons scrabbling for footholds. "You are *mine!*" The voice burned. Malevolent. She shrank back, but only for a second.

If the legend was right, and she hoped it was, Morach had used up his fire. But, how much longer would he be in his dragon form? No time to wonder. She heard his claws crunching into crevices, closer. The stench of his breath fouled the air around her.

Willing herself not to vomit, Eva leaned all her power against the boulder directly above his head. She pushed. It didn't budge. She pushed again, wailing in desperation—nothing. Squatting down, peering under the boulder, she saw tiny pebbles wedged between it and the rocky shelf. She franticly kicked them over the cliff.

Eva lunged against the giant stone and began rocking back and forth, back and forth. The boulder rocked a little, then a little more . . . then it wobbled.

She gave one last push with everything she had, and the huge stone pitched over the edge of the precipice.

Plunging downward, it *found* its mark!

Stunned by the blow, Morach reeled backward, ripping huge chunks of rock from the cliffside. Shrieking his rage to the heavens, he plummeted down, down, flailing wildly. Crashing, thundering to the rocks below, his head was pinned down by the boulder.

The beast thrashed blindly, trying to shift the boulder and shred the minstrel he knew must be close. Indeed, Traveler was close. *Very* close.

As the dragon fell, Traveler slid down from his climb up the cliff. Running to a place just outside the reach of Morach's razor claws, he waited, crouched. Sword ready. But, *when* to dash in and part the beast's head from his body? *That* was the tricky part.

The scaly legs slowed and were still. *Finally.*

Then what shouldn't have happened—did happen. The dragon was inching his armored head out from under the boulder. In a few moments, he would be *free* again.

Seeing this, Traveler vaulted over rocks, running in for the kill. His sword found its mark under the scaly jaw. He thrust it in. Instantly, thick black fluid spewed from the wound, covering him from head to boots. The creature's legs thrashed in a wild frenzy; slashing the air, gouging deep furrows in the ground.

Traveler sprang over a crushing claw. And, out of the corner of his eye, he saw the dragon lash out again. Before he could leap, razor claws raked his chest, shredding it. Catapulted through the air, he slamming into the side of the cliff.

The minstrel lay there for a minute, stunned. Still dazed, he crawled out of range, his sword still lodged in the neck of the beast. Traveler dragged himself across the stream, and fell to the ground.

54

Eva saw everything. As soon as the dragon fell, she was on her way down, half-falling, half-sliding to the ground; not knowing what she would do, only knowing she *must* be with her friend.

Eva leapt over boulders to where Traveler lay still on the scorched dirt. She pulled the blood-soaked shreds of his shirt from his chest, exposing a ripped, red, expanse of skin. Sobbing, she ran to the stream and filled her hat with cool water, a small parcel slipped from her right pocket. Caught by the stream's dark currents, it bobbed on the surface for a moment and sank below.

Across the stream, Morach lay quiet, black blood pooling under his head. Eva saw Traveler's sword in the beast's neck and shuddered.

The princess ran back to her friend. She poured water slowly over his wounds. Blood and something that looked like black tar flowed from his chest to the ground. Momentarily, white ribs gleamed through mangled flesh. He moaned. Eva clenched her teeth. *What can I do!*

His face contorted in agony.

"Come *back* to me, Trav. You can't go, please, *please*— she pleaded, feeling him slip away.

Beautiful, dark eyes, barely visible through his swollen face, opened upward then turned from the starry sky to her face. Resting on it, they glazed and closed. The poison was working its will in his blood.

Up until that moment, the princess had been able to steel herself against the horror. Now she knelt on the muddy ground holding her face in her hands, rocking back and forth. Feeling his searing pain in her own body, she sobbed.

He gasped, fighting for breath, "Thought I had time . . . more time . . . need to tell you—" The words escaped in a ghost of a whisper.

"Shh, don't . . . just rest." She laid a finger softly over his cracked lips. In the moonlight Eva saw a thread of pulse ebbing in his throat.

Then she remembered—the pouch of herbs! The princess plunged her hand franticly into her right pocket, then into the left one. *Nothing!* Jamming her knuckles into her mouth, she shoved panic away—keeping her thoughts from vaporizing. She leaned over again and peered into his face, now beaded with pearls of sweat.

"True Voice," she whispered under her breath, "you said you'd never leave. Where *are* you now? *Help. We need help!*" Eva leaned over and put her cheek close to the minstrel's mouth. He was still breathing.

Casting a wary eye toward the lifeless carcass of Morach, Eva thought of dragging Traveler closer to the woods and shelter. Then, realizing she couldn't lift him over the boulders, she leapt up and ran into the woods to get her bag. *At least I can keep him warm*, she thought. *And keep the animals away tonight!* She touched the hilt of her dagger.

Finding her bag where she'd left it by the oak, she heard a noise. Looking up, she caught her breath; the horses were still there, quietly cropping grass and leaves. She saw their reins tangled in some low branches, holding them fast. One of them whinnied in greeting.

Eva ran over and patted them both on their withers. "Thanks. I'll be needing you," she whispered breathlessly. Then, grabbing her bag, she ran back to her friend.

Climbing over the boulder into the blackened clearing, her eyes fell on the minstrel's torn body. He lay where she'd left him—absolutely motionless.

Her insides crushed, Eva threw down her bag. Falling on her knees beside him, she gripped his shoulders and placed her cheek close to his open mouth. No breath. Trembling, she placed a hand on his neck. No pulse moved his cooling skin.

Eva shuddered. The weight of knowing gripped her. "My truest friend," she whispered. "You could have left me. But, *now* . . ." Eva gasped for air as though she were drowning, threw herself over his lifeless body, and wailed from the depths of her soul. Her voice echoed against cliffs and mountains—filling Miracle Valley with unspeakable sorrow and horror.

55

Much later, the moon shone softly on Eva and her minstrel. The princess lay beside him on the cold, bloody ground, the blue cloak covering them. Exhaustion dulled the throbbing pain in her hands and feet. She stared briefly into the stars. Her eyelids fluttered and closed.

Eva slept. Then, she dreamed.

In her dream, she and the minstrel were leaving the castle island. As they stepped into the little boat on the shore of Tidal Inlet, she watched the fog bank roll across the waters toward them. This time, Eva felt no dread.

Somehow, she knew the oars would be of no use on this trip, so she left them on the beach.

Sitting in the boat, rocked by the gentle lap of waves, Eva and her minstrel were carried out into deep waters. The fog found them, surrounding their boat in a soft, white, mist smelling of cinnamon and roses. Eva lay back in the boat and noticed her friend had done the same. He rested his head on his folded cloak in the boat's bow. "Good," she said. "You need to rest."

Startled, Eva suddenly realized waves no longer slapped against the wooden hull. They were being lifted up out of the water. She sat up to see their boat break through the white mist. It rose up into a brilliant blue sky—alive with singing birds and bright winged beings flickering in and out of her sight.

Eva poked Traveler's foot. "Wake up! You can't miss this!" she said in a loud whisper. The minstrel lay motionless and pale. *How can you possibly sleep?* She wondered.

A yellow bird perched on the side of the boat nearest Eva. He lifted his head and sang, his tiny throat trilling each note. When he was finished, Eva said, "That was very pretty. Thank you! Why does everyone sing up here?"

The bird chirped, hopped on one foot then the other and flew back to the flock.

Eva felt the boat sway and looked to her left. A winged *being* sat on the other side of the little rowboat. When she looked at this bright creature, it stopped flickering. A shimmering rainbow outlined its human-like form, but Eva couldn't tell if it was a man or woman. She laughed inwardly. *It's a heavenly being, so maybe neither.*

Then the being spoke, its voice sounding like a thousand silvery bells. "My name is Lasriel. I bring a *gift* from the One." It's light pulsed brighter.

Eva raised her hand in greeting. "Many thanks to you, Lasriel, and to the One," she murmured, not knowing what else to say. She nudged her friend again. He gave no sign of feeling or hearing anything.

Lasriel shifted its wings, causing rainbows to flow from them like ripples in a pond. He spoke, "Before I place this gift where it belongs, I'll answer the question you asked the bird: When the One brought us forth before the dawn of time, we sang our joy to Him in a grand chorus, and we've not stopped singing to this very day."

Eva felt Lasriel's bright gaze upon her as she sat cross-legged in the bottom of the boat, imagining the dawn of time. She leaned her head to one side. "This *One*..." she asked, knowing the answer, "what is His name?"

"Do you not know?" The being was surprised, his brilliant eyes, bluer than blue, fixed hers with a quizzical stare. "In your world, He is known by several names: The True Voice, the Truth, the Way. You know of Him already, Princess Evangeline."

Eva paused, "Yes, I do know Him—a little. And, I *do* believe what He told me is true. Despite . . . everything." Instantly, Lasriel shone so brightly that Eva had to shield her eyes with her arm. When she looked again, he was gone.

Swiftly, the boat rose above the flying singers and rested in a field of stars. *I've been here before,* she thought of the starry arms that night so long ago. Smiling, she leaned over the side to touch a glimmering orb. The boat tipped, and she sat back quickly, her heart racing.

Eva peered once again into Traveler's pale, lifeless face. "Come back . . . *please,*" she whispered then closed her eyes. "Let *this* be my gift. My gift from the One: please, bring my friend back to life."

Eva opened her eyes. Traveler's foot twitched. As she watched, color flushed his cheeks, spreading to his face and neck. Then, he sneezed twice, sat up, and looked around. "How long have I been asleep? Did I miss anything?" he asked, smiling broadly.

"*What!* Traveler—you're back! You're *alive!!*" she shouted. Then she laughed, "No, you didn't miss anything, "she giggled. "Well, you did actually. I'll tell you about it later!"

"How'd we get up here?" He rubbed his eyes and yawned.

"Look, I'll show you." Eva grabbed his hand, pulling him over to see the vast singing flock far below. The little boat tipped once again. Eva lurched backward, trying to balance it, but only managed to tip it in the other direction. She felt herself slipping out and windmilled her arms wildly, trying to grab something, but it was no good. She was falling.

Traveler grabbed for her hand; their palms slapped together. His grip held her fast while she dangled down among the stars.

She raised her eyes to his face. A gasp squeezed through her throat. Traveler was no longer *in* the boat. He hung from it, clutching the empty oarlock on the side. Eva screamed and kicked, trying to somehow throw her leg back into the boat. She only succeeded in loosening the minstrel's grip and making her sweaty fingers slip inch by inch from his hand.

She hung very still. And waited.

She didn't wait long. Eva silently watched her friend's face. He gave her a half-smile and did something that turned her dream into a nightmare: he let go of the oarlock. They hurtled down, falling as a golden comet would— streaking through the night sky—still holding hands.

Plunging through the flying singers, through the white mist, they hit the ground with a bone-jarring thud.

Eva felt Traveler's hands shaking her shoulders.

"Wake up, Spud!" he shouted. "It's morning!

She heard him laughing. *Laughing?* Eyes still shut, she shook her head, unbelieving. "No, Trav. Stop it. We fell, hit . . . going to die. I just want you to know—" she mumbled.

Then, suddenly feeling the rough ground under her back, Eva's eyes flew open.

Songbirds returned

56

That very morning, the people of Ravenia awoke to bright sunlight streaming in their cottage windows and the sound of songbirds.

Men and women, boys and girls, rose from their beds, wondering. They wandered out into cobblestone streets, pathways and neighborhoods, hardly daring to believe what their eyes were seeing and their ears hearing. "We must *all* be dreaming, but what a wonderful dream!" they muttered in a daze, blinking in the brilliant sunlight and bumping into one another.

But they weren't dreaming. Morach's death had lifted the shroud of darkness from their land. The count's black, needle-taloned birds felt the atmosphere shift and the darkness lift. Immediately they flew away, fast and far. There were other dragon-men to serve and feast on the spoils of their greed . . . and they would find them.

The songbirds, having long ago been driven from their country, also sensed the change in the air. Before the sun had touched the mountaintops, they had spread their wings to let the wind carry them back to Ravenia, their homeland. This very morning, they sang for joy among a people now free!

It was a new day.

Eva and Traveler quickly mounted the horses and headed back to Tirzah before the sun had climbed too far in the sky. Riding through the narrow, wooded passageway out of Miracle Valley, Eva finally said what was burning in her mind:

"So, last night, I thought you were—you know—dead."

"Well, maybe I *was*—you know—*dead*." He gave her a bemused smile. "That's what I've been thinking about. At first, it was dark, and I couldn't move or open my eyes. Then, I had this amazing dream," he said softly, and ducked under a low tree branch.

"You dreamed?"

"Well, I'm not even sure if it *was* a dream. But it had to be—I *think*. Maybe," he muttered, half to himself. "I got in a boat with you then lay back and fell asleep. I smelled cinnamon and roses and heard lots of singing. Then, I heard you talking to someone whose voice sounded like bells. After that, the True Voice spoke my name." He took a deep breath. "Then all I heard was His voice. We talked for a long time, then He said I was still needed on Earth, if I was willing."

Eva caught her breath, hardly believing her ears. "And *were* you?"

The minstrel raised an eyebrow. "Well, here I am."

"Yes. Here you are . . . Anything else?" Eva asked, after riding in silence for a few minutes, sorting through her thoughts.

"That's about it. I woke up in the boa—"

"Yes, you did," Eva broke in. "You sat up in the boat—"

"And, after I did, you pulled me over to see something, and tipped the boat, and fell out. Then I caught your hand—*Whew!*" Traveler whistled through his teeth.

"And then you let go of the boat, and we fell!"

"After I let go, I woke up on the ground beside you—"

"And you shook me by the shoulders to wake me." Eva was stunned by what she was hearing. But, the fact remained she *was* hearing it. It was true. "Trav—we were both in the same dream—if it *was* a dream! How does that even *happen?*"

"You're asking me?" The minstrel chuckled and turned in his saddle and sent her a puzzled smile.

The forest of Miracle Valley resounded with their laughter.

57

On horseback, they made much better time than on foot and were back at the little cottage before dark.

Eva noticed that Traveler was beginning to droop in the saddle as they neared their mountain. So, after they fed and watered the horses, she took him by the hand and led him into the cottage. "You rest," she said nodding to the straw bed. "I'll make dinner."

"Eva," he protested. "I'm not that tired. I can at least get some water in the pot."

The princess stood with fists on her hips and fixed him with a stern look. "Alright, Mister, I'll hear no more about it. *Rest!*" she commanded. Then she gave him a half-smile with an arched eyebrow. "You're not scared of my cooking, are you?"

"*Me?* Noooo . . . not me. Never." The minstrel climbed into the soft hay, cradled his hands under his head, and smiled broadly.

They dined on trout stew with mushrooms and wild onions and talked far into the night, reliving the adventures of the last few days. When the moon was high in the sky, Eva said, "Trav, you take the straw bed. I mean it." She noticed his face was no longer swollen, but despite his miracle, the deep red gashes on his chest were still closing and healing.

Since she wouldn't hear of anything else; Traveler said, "Alright, just for tonight, then." Eva grabbed the blanket and curled up in front of the embers in the fireplace.

That night, they slept like two stones.

At dawn, Eva woke to faint sunlight through the window. She rolled over silently, not wanting to wake Traveler. His snores drifted from the straw bed.

They'd eaten all the stew for dinner last night. Eva had scrubbed the pot and refilled it with fresh water. All she had to do this morning was put a little salt and two scoops of oats in it. Doing that, she swung it around over the fire to boil. *Breakfast coming right up*, she thought gleefully.

She glanced over at her sleeping friend once more and thought about her plans for the day. She knew he'd want to come with her to protect her, but she couldn't let him. He needed to rest and heal. The real reason came up in her thoughts, making her blush. Eva pictured herself, Traveler, and Prince Valentino in the same room. *So awkward.*

Her thoughts swirled. Traveler. Her minstrel. Her true friend. She knew they had deep feelings for one another. *How could two people face death together and save each other's lives—and not at least care about each other? Very dear friends,* she told herself. Then whispered under her breath, "But, much *more* than friends." Her hands covered her hot cheeks.

The truth was, Eva loved Traveler with all the depth, admiration, and fullness that one could have for a friend—and not cross an invisible line she'd drawn. She would *not* step into the kind of love she had for only one person. *Valentino.* But with each passing day, that line became a bit more blurry, and Eva found herself bumping up against it, without warning, more and more. She was determined, but it grew harder every day; some days close to impossible. Like today.

She buttoned her ragged jacket up to her neck against the morning chill and pressed her lips together decidedly. *After all,* she chided herself, *you are betrothed to Valentino. Maybe.* She frowned momentarily. *Well, I'll be at the castle all day. I'll find out the truth before I come back here tonight.* She began lacing up her boot.

Traveler raised up on one elbow, and sat up, straw sticking out of his hair and beard in all directions. "G'morning," he yawned and rubbed his eyes.

"Morning, Trav," she said brightly, then stood and lifted her travel-bag to her shoulder. "Well, morning for me. You should go back to sleep and get more rest. There's porridge for your breakfast in the pot," she said nodding toward the fireplace. She started walking toward the door. "I'll be back tonight with some food for us." Eva giggled a little at the straw in his hair, thinking he looked a bit like a scarecrow, then blushed, imagining what she must have looked like when she'd slept there.

Without a word, he shoved his foot in his boot and began to lace it on. "Wait—" he said.

"Not this time, Trav," she said solemnly.

"Where are you going?" He stopped lacing and gave her a sleepy smile. "Oh, I know."

"Right. I'm going to the castle kitchen, like we talked about," she said, shifting her bag on her shoulder. "I would wait, but the money's gone, and all we have here are oats and salt—and of course, what's outside. You'll be strong again soon," she smiled back. "Let me do this for you, Trav. You've done so much—" Her throat squeezed the rest of her words. She threw her long dark braid over her shoulder and stepped toward the door once again.

"I guess it's decided then," he said and leaned back in the straw. "You got your dagger?"

"Right here," she said patting her belt. "Not that I'll need it now."

They smiled in each other's eyes at the relief of this truth: Morach was dead, and his henchmen would no longer be out to take their lives.

"Take it easy, Trav. I'll be back with something delicious for us tonight. A surprise," she said, trying to sound confident. Eva smiled in his direction, waved goodbye and shut the door behind her.

And with some answers for me, she thought and tied her bag to the saddle of the roan horse grazing by the stream. "Your mane almost matches my hair," she said in a quiet voice. "You got a name? No? —How about Foxfire? That suits you, I think." He flicked his ears. Eva lifted herself up into the saddle, and they were off to the Castle of Tirzah.

58

That morning, Eva rode over the moat bridge into the courtyard of the castle. Foxfire was taken to the livery stable, and she was shown to the kitchen.

Walking into the bustling room brought back memories of the kitchen of Dunmoor and of Brookin. She pushed these thoughts out of her mind, determined to make herself useful, earn some money, and bring back some left-over food for Traveler's dinner that night.

The head cook walked over to Eva, her round face beaming. "So you made it! We've been waiting for you. Could *use* an extra set of hands around here."

The princess looked around at the scurrying kitchen help and agreed. "As you know, those clothes will never do," she said nodding toward Eva's dirty pants and jacket. "Your friend, the minstrel, bought you a dress to change into when he came by three days ago. (*Has it only been three days?*) He thought you might find it more suitable," she bubbled on. "Oh, and he said you would *not* be wanting, *or needing*, a corset. So, here you are," she said lightly, handing Eva a neatly folded blue bundle, with a pair of low-heeled sky-blue slippers on top. "You can change in the back room. There's a basin for washing up in there as well." She winked and pointed to a room down the hall.

Eva went into the candlelit room, set her bundle on a table in the corner and looked around. Everything was neat and clean, and most surprising of all for a kitchen washroom, was a large, gold-framed mirror hanging on the wall in front of her. She looked at herself and cringed. Despite her efforts of washing her arms and face in the cottage stream before she left, she was a dirty, ragged mess. "Pitiful," she sighed, and tossed her crumpled hat in the corner. Unbraiding her hair, she let it fall over her shoulders. "I'm surprised they even let me in the kitchen. Traveler must be *very* good friends with this cook," she muttered, making a face at the girl in the mirror. Eva pulled dried mud and leaves out of her hair. *I guess it would be a bit much to ask for a warm bath*, she thought.

Quickly, she shucked her clothes, piling them in a heap in the corner. Grabbing the washcloth folded neatly beside the pitcher and bowl, she poured warm water into the bowl and went to work on herself until her skin glowed pink. Finally satisfied, she pulled on the white pantaloons, unfolded the blue part of the bundle—and caught her breath! This was no scullery maid's work dress! She slipped the sky-blue frock over her head and shoulders. The gathered skirt slid down over her hips, with lace at the hem brushing her ankles. Tears gathered in her eyes. *I never thought . . .* Eva reached into her pants pocket and pulled out a carved white stone, slipping it into her dress pocket. Then, she clasped her mother's golden locket around her neck. Her eyes glistened at the sight of it gleaming at the base of her throat.

Eva buttoned up the front of her dress and slipped on the shoes. These are a perfect fit too," she whispered to herself, hardly believing what she was seeing. "And, if I didn't know better, I'd say these were *dancing* slippers! But, why would Traveler order me dancing slippers to wear for kitchen duties?" Eva flexed her toes in the soft, glove-like leather and whispered, "So impractical, but *absolutely* wonderful." Her face lit up and she twirled in front of the mirror watching the skirt bloom out.

Quickly running her fingers through her hair, she braided it again in a long plait over her shoulder and folded her ragged brown clothing into a small bundle in the corner.

When she came out of the changing room, a girl about her age smiled and introduced herself as Lily and beckoned Eva to follow her. They first went to the hen house and gathered eggs through clever trap doors located below each nest.

After the egg basket was full, Lily took her to what she called the boose: a part of the barn where the cows came in for milking. She stepped into a stall and showed Eva how to squeeze and aim the teats into the milk pail. "If you'd like, you can finish the job with Gertie while I go mix up grain mash for the old girl's lunch," Lily said.

The thought of milking a cow delighted Eva. She mused to herself how the prospect of milking such a large cow would have frightened her not too long ago—in her other life. "I would like that a lot," Eva said softly, not wanting to spook old Gertie and make her kick over the pail. Lily grinned and turned down the hay-strewn corridor, disappearing around a stall.

Eva stepped back into the stall where Gertie waited, watching her with patient soft-brown eyes. The princess stroked her back gently, feeling the slight, pleasant prickle of her short brown fur. She settled herself on the stool. Leaning her head on Gertie's warm solid flank, she breathed in her pungent smell and sighed contentedly. Then, pressing and pulling the teats, she brought warm streams of milk into her bucket, adding its sweet scent to the aroma in the barn. "How much life I've missed . . . living as a princess," she whispered to Gertie's twitching ear.

That afternoon, Eva was informed by the head cook that she would need to stay late. It seemed the prince had just returned and requested a special celebration held for his beloved. It was to be held this very night.

Eva was stunned. *After all these years, all I've been through . . . I'm too late,* her thoughts spun dizzily. *I've missed it.* She felt herself tipping and sliding toward the edge of her world. The princess steadied herself, leaning on the wall. She wanted to run back to the cottage, to have dinner with her minstrel—to tell stories by the fire. But, something held her there at the castle. "I have to see him," she whispered to herself, *"and* his bride-to-be."

She stood straight then, steeling herself against burning misery, and went on with her kitchen duties.

That night, satisfied with her arrangement of the last platter of pastries, Eva wiped her hands on her stained apron, carefully lifted the tray by its silver handles, and handed it off to the server waiting outside the kitchen door. "There," she said to herself, "I'm done . . . for a while anyway." It had been a busy day. She looked around for any food scraps she could take back to Traveler. She found broken biscuits and scraps of meat and vegetables. All these she wrapped in oiled parchment, tucking them down in her apron pockets. *I'll make him a nice soup with these in the morning.* The thought made her smile as she washed up from the day's chores, taking special care with her new shoes.

She had planned on going up to the ballroom *after* the festivities to catch a glimpse. But, try as she would, Eva could not make her feet stay in the kitchen. They insisted on taking her up the dark winding servant's staircase to sear her eyes with the celebration above . . . or truthfully, with the sight of Valentino and his beloved.

The sound of violins, lutes, singing, dancing, laughing couples and the aroma of excellent food well prepared, engulfed her before she ever set foot on the top stair. She was overwhelmed with it—all of it. Memories of other banquets buzzed in her head.

Eva reached the top and was dazzled by the light, her vision obscured for a moment while her eyes adjusted to the brilliant grandeur. There she stood, heartsick, half hidden in the dark doorway, twisting her fingers together in an unlit corner of the ballroom. This allowed her a vantage point—to see without being seen. Or, that's what she thought.

The princess leaned against the stone wall watching the procession of swirling elegance, wounding herself with thoughts of how much Valentino must love this woman, to arrange such a magnificent feast for her. Tears stung her eyes, blurring her vision, so when someone approached her out of the crowd, she didn't see him until it was too late—too late to disappear down the stairs. Too late to blend in with the other servants in the kitchen.

Valentino, in a deep scarlet waistcoat, stepped in front of Evangeline, swept her a low bow, and asked: "May I have this dance?" Beaming, he held out his gloved hand to receive hers.

Eva stood stunned as a deer in torchlight. It was *him*—her Valentino—his face smooth, cleanly shaven, his dark eyes shining with delight at the sight of her. Could this be? As if in a dream, she placed her hand in his and was drawn up and out of her dark hiding place.

Because their voices were overshadowed by the music, he gestured for her to take off her soiled apron. When she did, her food scraps fell out of the pockets—the beginnings of tomorrow's soup at the cottage! Horrified, Eva jumped away with such force that she slipped, falling backward onto the polished marble floor. The music stopped. The dancers stopped, and the princess cringed, mortified under stares from everyone in the room. She scrambled quickly to her knees and tried to clean up her mess—evidence of her awkwardness—mute witness to the fact of her being out of place, out of line, out of time, and wrong . . . *she* was just wrong, wrong. Wrong. *Again.*

Brilliant lights overwhelmed Eva's bleary eyes. All details around her were obscured. She felt the floor with trembling fingers, and began shoving scraps and crumbs back into her pockets.

The prince lifted his hand, waving for the musicians to continue playing and the dancers to resume dancing. He then knelt on the floor beside her. "Here, let me," he murmured and gathered the remaining scraps, putting them out of sight in his waistcoat pocket. However, his words were lost to the princess in the rising music and voices in the room.

Still trembling, heart pounding in her ears, Eva pushed herself up from the floor and ran away from the prince, from humiliation. She dashed to the safety of the dark stairwell—determined to keep running until she was back in the cottage with Traveler—her true friend. Eva imagined Valentino's future bride (the hag) watching from the crowd, laughing at her behind a fluttering fan. *Laugh well*, she thought. *You'll never see me again!* Her mind raced ahead. The scraps weren't important. She would catch a fish in the morning; she would find some good mushrooms . . . make a fine broth. All of these thoughts tore through her mind while stumbling to the stairwell.

Something about Valentino's eyes leapt in the back of her mind, but there was no time to explore that now. "I have to get out of here!" She shouted, gasping great gulps of air.

Eva's feet fairly flew down the narrow stairs until she rounded the second turn and was plunged into absolute darkness. *Someone must have shut the kitchen door*, she thought, panicked at the thought of picking her way down the black, steep stairwell. Feeling for each step with her toe on the narrow tread, she steadied herself on the rough stone wall, not risking a fall headlong into blackness.

Rounding another bend, she heard steps on the treads above her, then a voice.

Traveler's voice?

How could that be? She stopped and listened in the quiet; held her breath for a long moment. Yes, those were footfalls, but the *voice—?"*

"Wait!" the words echoed down to her. "I'm coming . . . Don't go—*Please!*"

"Trav, what are *you doing* here?" she whispered fiercely into the darkness.

"I'll show you . . . Just *please* trust me one more time. Here's my hand. I'll explain everything," he said low, his words now only a few steps above her. "Eva—*Spud.*" She heard the smile in his voice.

Pressed against the wall, the princess hesitated a heartbeat more, then feeling his hand brush hers, her arm prickled up to the top of her head. "Yes," she whispered. Releasing the wall, she placed her small hand in his familiar grip and followed him upward. Finally rounding the last turn, they stepped again into the light of a thousand candles. Blinking against the brightness, Eva shaded her eyes with her other hand, not believing what she was seeing, and blinked again. *Hard.*

There, smiling his lopsided grin, was Prince Valentino—and Princess Evangeline was *holding his hand!*

59

va gasped. "You—it's *you!*" She wanted to grab him, to punch his shoulder, to kiss him—to shout like the lunatic they said she was. But instead, she gaped.

The prince touched her hand and stepped closer. "And, it's *you,*" he said softly, looking into her eyes. Then, beaming into her face, he led her out onto the balcony overlooking the moonlit gardens. She walked beside him unbelieving, as if in a dream. They stood at the balustrade and Eva glanced down. His fingers were knotted together. *He's afraid,* she suddenly realized.

Eva's face flushed crimson. She rounded on him, eyes blazing. "One word would have *done* it. Would that have been so *hard?* Isn't that what *friends* do . . . tell each other the *truth?*" Her words tumbled out. "So why did you—*you*—?" Eva's question was so enormous, she couldn't find the end of it.

"Why did I disguise myself as a minstrel?"

Eva stepped back into the shadows. "*Yes!* And why didn't you tell me?" Her words leaked through gritted teeth.

"I told Father I had to bring you here to safety, because . . . *you* know." Eva nodded and folded her arms over her chest. "He made me swear an oath: to travel with you disguised as a commoner and not reveal myself. This was his way to prove you were still as wonderful as I told him you were. Not—" he stopped, winced.

Eva smirked darkly. "Don't worry. I know all about the gossip." She looked down at her feet. "But wait. You told him I was *wonderful?*" she whispered, savoring his words.

"Of course." He gazed intently into her face and sighed. "I wanted to tell you—all of it—in fact I almost told you twice, but the vow made on my honor as Prince . . . it held me back. It was the only way I could even have a *chance* to marry—"

"—So, when did you start to tell me?" she broke in.

"What? Oh, in the cottage, that night of the storm."

"You said *twice?*"

"Yes, and the night I left you at the edge of the woods to fight Morach. I wanted to tell you—everything. But, I would've betrayed my promise and been unable to marry you . . . if I lived, *which I did.*" A quick smile flickered across his face. "Obviously."

Eva took a step closer. "Yes. I'm listening." She sighed. "And your *timely* little visit to the castle?"

"When I heard you were pledged to Fagan, I . . . I couldn't let that happen. Coming to your castle in disguise was the only chance I had to help you escape, and still *keep my head*—so to speak." He cleared his throat. "And, that day . . . on the mountain with Morach. The knight, that was me."

"Thought so." The corners of her mouth turned up.

"I couldn't show myself or Cedric's guards would've—*you* know."

"Taken you captive?"

"They would've tried to. I didn't want to *ah*—*you* know."

"Have to hurt them?"

"Or kill . . . kill them. That wasn't why I was there. I told you I'd come for you, *remember?*"

She tipped her head to the side and frowned slightly. "But, wait, what about your future bride . . . the one this banquet is for? Where is *she?*" Eva's gaze flicked out to the night gardens below their balcony.

"Oh, *her*," he said solemnly, and stepped around to face the Princess. "I'm *looking* at her . . . if she'll still have me, that is."

"Looking at her?" Eva echoed. Her words floated in the cool night air.

"Don't you see?" Valentino said, his eyes crinkling at the corners. "There *is* no other. There never *has* been. This celebration is for you . . . all of it. *Yours.*" He gestured toward the lavish banquet.

"It is?" Eva inhaled quickly, the truth rising inside her.

"Believe me. *Please.* It has *always*, only and ever been you." He caught her other hand. "Everything I've done has been for you. I love you like the blood and bones of my own body."

They were silent then, searching each other's faces for a timeless breathing space.

Eva leaned on the balustrade, her thoughts whirling and colliding. She closed her eyes for a moment. *So, the two I love best are one and the same.* She looked into his eyes and stepped closer. He pulled her to himself then, fiercely. Eva wrapped her arms around him and squeezed—with all her strength. Her cheek mashed against the front of his jacket, his breath warm in her hair. His heart thudded in rhythm with hers. *This is so, so right.*

The rest of her questions could wait.

"You're the bravest, the, the—" Her words seemed too small. She stopped and exhaled.

The Prince stepped back, reached inside his waistcoat, pulled out a tiny golden thimble and held it in his palm. The Princess wordlessly reached in her dress pocket, and revealed a small, inscribed white rock. EVA+VAL. Valentino placed the thimble beside the white stone in her palm and cupped her small, rough hand between his two scarred and calloused ones, as one might hold a dove.

Years of waiting fell away from them like an ill-fitting garment.

Eva couldn't take her eyes from his eyes, his smile, so long hidden. His face, handsome, no, *beautiful*—so beautiful—made something deep inside her ache with the wonder of it. The waiting was over.

Is it possible to fall even deeper in love? To be so full . . . Eva felt as though she had been kissed awake from a dream; her senses thrummed with joy. She swayed forward, dizzy.

Valentino's dark eyes glistened. "My love for you, brave one . . . deeper and higher than—" He stopped, caught up in the moonlight shimmering silver in her hair. "Will you be my bride, my queen? Will you live out your days by my side—as I live by yours?" He swallowed loudly. "This I vow to you; I will cherish you in faithfulness to my very last breath on this earth."

Tears coursed, unashamed, down Eva's face and onto her sky-blue dress. "I love . . . love you, more than my own life. So, yes, *yes*, a thousand times . . . yes, as long as I live. *Yes!*"

They leaned together, her tears darkening his scarlet jacket. He lifted her chin to his and they kissed; their love sealed, their two hearts, one.

There are places on this earth where streams join and flow making mighty rushing rivers. Eva and Val trembled in the power of their new river. It's currents mingled and sparkled with their laughter and tears.

Epilogue

Princess Evangeline and Prince Valentino were married in the castle gardens of Tirzah amid much celebration, laughter, tears, music, throwing of flowers, eating of cake, and dancing until the break of dawn.

That next morning, the bride and groom went out from the presence of their fathers, radiant in royal apparel of flowing white linen woven with threads of fine gold. Their clothing shone and glistened in the sun, but seemed drab beside the love shining in the eyes of the prince and princess . . . two with hearts of gold.

King Cedric was deeply grieved in his own heart.

When Eva and Val returned to Dunmoor after the wedding, he looked for his daughter in the garden the next morning.

"Ah. There you are," he said, finding her by the roses.

"Good morning, Father." Eva looked into his face and smiled wanly.

"So good to . . ." the King began and glanced quickly in her eyes. "When I thought I'd lost you—lost my daughter, I, I . . ." He exhaled loudly. "I cursed myself for the fool I was. You endured things no daughter should ever have to go through. Can you ever find it in your heart to forgive me?" His words rasped and he looked down at the path. "*Somehow?* One day?"

"I already have," she said quietly.

"You . . . you have? You *did?*" A strangled sound came from his throat and he covered his eyes with his hand. Eva saw his beard sparkle with tears.

She touched his shoulder. "You're forgiven, Father."

He inhaled and clasped her hand, looking into her face. "Saying 'thank you' hardly touches . . . I will find a way to, to—" He straightened up to his full kingly height. "But look here; see what you've done? You've saved the lot of us . . . saved us *all!*" His voice was thick with emotion. "*Well* done, Brave One!"

"But not *me*, Father. Not only *just* me. *Valentino*—" She stopped, sat on the stone bench, and her father sat beside her. Then, from beginning to end, she told him the story.

King Cedric, broken and sick in body and soul, humbled himself before the people of his kingdom he'd brought to ruin. He stepped down from his position as king, abdicating the crown of the House of Dunmoor to his daughter with Valentino as her co-ruler. This was gladly received and letters were sent throughout both kingdoms with the announcement. The citizens of Dunmoor and Tirzah, both young and old, turned out in huge, happy crowds for the coronation.

On the morning of the ceremony, Eva and Val stood side by side on the high terrace overlooking Tidal inlet, its waters shimmering under a vast, blue spotless sky. Gentle ocean breezes played among the crowd, and swirled around the Prince and Princess, billowing her dress and his cape.

Incandescently happy, they exchanged a long gaze, then smiled out at the sea of faces. When the oil was placed upon her forehead and the crown upon her head, a shout rose up from the people. This shout was said to echo in Miracle Mountain valley (where the bones of Morach lie to this day).

The two kingdoms were united as one, and Eva lived to see both her and her mother's dreams fulfilled in the land. The newly united kingdom was named Ruah, which means wind or breath in an ancient tongue. The people and their lands soon began to flourish and prosper.

The citizens soon became known as the happiest people on Earth. They were so full of joy, in fact, that they had to invent new holidays. A favorite one, Sweet Surprise Days, found the people happily feasting on pies, tarts, cakes, custards, and éclairs. In the giving and sharing of sweet surprises, grudges and feuds were wiped out of the kingdom of Ruah!

And from this time of gladness, a saying was born; *maybe* you've heard it:
"*If I was any happier, I'd need to be two people.*"
The reply would be: "*And which two people would they be?*"
The speaker would then say: "*Why the King and Queen, of course!*"

Eva and Val ruled the new kingdom of Ruah in truth and wisdom, using the sale of golden articles from their treasure rooms to build schools, libraries, and plant orchards. They also made sure all the young people had opportunity to apprentice to masters according to their life's goals and dreams.

Archie was knighted, *Sir Archibald, Master of Doves and Gardens*. He and Bea were then offered a home befitting such a title, which they graciously declined—as Eva suspected they would. Too many memories lived in their little cottage for them to leave it, and of course, there *were* the doves—and Arlo the cat, who could be found luxuriating by their stove most days. Truly, a grander house seemed a trifling reason to move.

Olwen and his family were offered a position at court and a home on the castle grounds, which they graciously accepted. Peggy was given a silk dress for every day of the week; however, over time she found her royal frocks a bit confining and was usually seen wearing her homespun skirts and blouses.

Brookin was given a new title and position in the castle kitchen: *Mistress of the Mysterious Ways of Bread*. Many younger girls apprenticed to her in the years to come, so her skills and knowledge were passed down and spread throughout the kingdom—to the delight of many.

Jack Rabbitt, having no family and still owing much money, gathered his meager belongings and fled to the coast, *despite* his royal pardon. There, he booked passage on a sailing ship headed for Bana, a remote island in the southern seas. He found work there as a foreman at a pineapple plantation. His whereabouts after this remain unknown. Eva always hoped she would see him again. Val, not so much.

In the midst of all this, *and* the pressing business of the kingdom; Eva and Val made sure to carve out time to be together. Sometimes, they could be seen riding over the arched bridge to the mainland. Many guessed they had a picnic in their horse's saddlebags because they were never hungry when they returned. Their destination was a mystery to all; all but a certain falcon. Ciel often followed them, flying to a small cottage in the Tirzan hill country. On a good day, a juicy mountain trout would be left for her outside the front door.

Inside, the King and Queen would sit by the tiny, warm hearth, having a bowl of broth, telling love's stories.

Acknowledgements

Writing your first novel is somewhat like sailing out to sea for the first time, exciting and breathtaking—also terrifying. Peering out over a vast ocean of words, you wonder if you'll ever reach shore. My undying gratitude to everyone who believed I could. You were the wind in my sails. And here we are.

To you, my readers and cheerleaders go a million thanks: Christy, Jill, Capa, Eliana, Laura Lee, Amy & Addyson, Mary Ellen & Clare, Sarah & Kay Dee, Sharon, Greta, Anna, and so many others . . . and to my mother who read to me. You made sure we always had books and art supplies, even when money was scarce.

I especially want to thank Katie Isabella. Without your advice, long ago, there would have been no dragon; and to Christopher, who told me when my writing stunk and pointed me in the right direction. A gold star goes to my family for their patience.

A special thank you to the team at Trimble Hollow Press. Doug and Terri McKittrick, you are both amazing and wonderful!

And to my beloved King, the inspiration and *raison d' être* for this story, I am more grateful than I can say.

About the Author

Born and raised in Florida, I have loved writing and drawing since I first held a crayon and drew on the living room wall. My parents quickly realized I would need large paper and supervision.

I grew up, married my college sweetheart, and moved to Atlanta.

There, I worked as an artist/illustrator, with my work published and bought by private and corporate collectors. Even though I had two wonderful children and success as an artist, somehow I knew there was more I was meant to do . . . I became an Art Teacher! Watching students blossom and grow in their creativity for the next 20 years was wonderful.

Near the end of my years teaching middle and high school students, I began to feel the tug of the written page. It started one day after inviting several art students over to my studio to paint. As we talked, a story began to form that I knew must be told. I needed to write it – but wait, I was an art teacher not a writer. So, I held the story in my heart for years. Then, one day I knew I was ready. I plunged into the river of creating new worlds. Writing and illustrating stories for YA readers has become my new place of bliss.

* * *

I live in the north Georgia woods with my husband and abounding wildlife.

Wonders
Connecting Points

1. What was your favorite part of the book? Was there a part of the story that made you feel angry . . . or feel sad?

2. You are a castle kitchen servant and your good friend, Brookin, has been given a terrible unjust sentence by the king? What would you do?

3. Did this story remind you of any other book?

4. Did you identify with a particular character?

5. What songs come to mind when you think of this story?

6. What were some important themes or ideas in the story? Talk about which ones you think are most important, and why.

7. What could we learn from Eva about fear?

8. What gave her courage or boldness to do hard/fearful things when she was living in the castle?

9. Was it a good idea for Eva to trust a stranger in her escape from the castle? Why?

10. What gave her bravery to do things that could cost her life, near the end of her journey to Tirzah? Talk about how these two motivations are different?

11. How did Eva's time spent with Zephira change her?

12. Would you say Val was a 'promise keeper'? What would that tell you about his character? How did this affect the outcome of the story?

13. If you were Val, would you have kept your secret or told Eva before the banquet? Why?

14. When do we first begin to see a heart change in Jack? What provokes this?

15. Have there been times when compassion for others caused you to change your mind, or keep going?

16. If you were Eva, how would you have reacted when you discovered who Val was at the top of the stairwell in the ballroom?

17. How would events have been different if Eva had not forgiven her father? When was she finally able to do this? Did her forgiveness mean what he did was ok?

18. When we forgive someone, who benefits?

19. What part did the 'True Voice' play in the story? How was Eva's life changed through their encounters?

20. Could you have done what Eva did? Why or why not?

21. Is there a place in the book you'd like to visit?

You can contact G. Claire on Instagram: @gclaire333

CPSIA information can be obtained
at www.ICGtesting.com
Printed in the USA
JSHW021418300421
14155JS00001B/2